Kate went into the house and climbed the central, curving staircase. But she didn't see Sarah in the hall or on the stairs. She peered down the main upstairs hallway. The door to Sarah's suite was closed.

"Sarah?"

For some odd reason she sensed her friend was up here.

Kate turned the big brass doorknob to the sitting room where she and her hostess had spent some "grand" hours, as Sarah put it. She clicked on the light.

All was in order and the scent of the late roses curled around her in their usual welcoming way. But some strange, acrid scent hung heavily in the air, too.

She went in, glanced around, and saw something spilled on the carpet near the Shaker blanket box. But the crystal vase on it was not tipped or broken. She put her hand in the water on the coral-colored rug and saw that it was blood. Horrified, she wiped her hand on the gown.

"Sarah!"

Kate ran into the adjoining bedroom, which looked undisturbed, each piece of furniture, each bouquet untouched. Then she noted the bathroom door was closed.

She knocked on the door. "Sarah, are you in there? Are you all right?"

No reply.

KAREN HARPER

SHAKER RUN

MIRA®

MIRA

ISBN 0-7394-1558-1

SHAKER RUN

Printed In U.S.A.

This book is dedicated to all the hardworking volunteers,
docents and guides who keep
America's many historical villages alive.

Especially to Ellen Maurer,
administrator of the Milan, Ohio, Historical Museum,
as well as to Lois Wolf and the staff there.

1

O Rose, thou art sick.
The invisible worm
That flies in the night,
In the howling storm,

Has found out thy bed
Of crimson Joy,
And his dark secret love
Does thy life destroy.

—William Blake
"The Sick Rose"

Toledo, Ohio
Saturday, September 25, 1999

The mansion and grounds of Groveland were awash
with lights, roses and people, most of them in appropriate attire of tuxedos and evening gowns, though
Sarah had seen some of the younger set in outrageous
jeweled jeans. But then, from a generation that
thought tattoos, branding and body piercing were perfectly *de rigueur,* what was one to expect? At least
they had all come with generous donations for the
Shelter for Abused Women, which would profit from
this charity event.

People seemed to be everywhere, even about the

house, though that was a risk the seventy-five-year-old Sarah Denbigh was willing to take to help a good cause. Her husband Palmer might be turning over in his grave, but she really couldn't abide police officers or security people lurking about—though an off-duty officer did control the traffic out on River Road. At least it was a great help to have Kate about, not only to keep the massive rose beds in late bloom, but to help tonight. Sarah had given up asking her own two children to set foot here, since they were furious she insisted on supporting so many charities with "their" money. The "Denbigh heritage," as Palmer, Jr. so snidely put it.

"Oh, Kate, there you are!" Sarah called to her rosarian, who had become her dear friend too. A tall, willowy blond with a darling page-boy haircut that softened a classic face of wide-set, smoky blue eyes, elegant nose, and full mouth, Kate was the very best "refugee" Sarah had ever taken in. Imagine her being held responsible for something her husband had done. He'd absconded with a fortune and had left Kate to shoulder the blame. It had shaken Kate deeply but hadn't broken her, Sarah thought with deep pride and affection.

The thirty-six-year-old woman looked stunning in the only dressy gown she hadn't sold to consignment shops, one in simple black satin with a deep square neckline and long sleeves, though she refused to wear the pearls Sarah had offered to lend her tonight. Despite Kate's dire financial straits, Sarah knew her friend detested anything that smacked of charity. A modest person, perhaps Kate would never grasp the priceless gift of companionship she had given an old woman deeply disappointed in her own daughter.

"The silent auction for the bouquets and rose bushes seems to be going well," Kate reported, out of breath as if she'd just taken a run through the acres of gardens.

Until two years ago, Katherine Browne Marburn and her husband Mike had been very much on the social scene here in Toledo—flashy, new fish in the small, old pond, in which the Denbighs and others had swum circumspectly for years. Michael Marburn, with his business acumen and Irish good looks, had been a prominent broker and investor of other people's money. A widower with one daughter, Mike had brought his second wife, Kate, into his burgeoning business as a sort of silent partner, mostly because she was hardly silent. Kate had many prominent contacts from her small business designing flower gardens.

Kate and Mike's companies merged like a David and Goliath into the now-infamous Marburn Securities, though Kate, who knew next to nothing about brokerage or investments, spent most of her time mothering her stepdaughter Erin, breeding roses and entertaining for Mike. Until everything exploded in her face.

Before Mike could be arrested for illegally selling millions of dollars in promissory notes to investors, he was evidently tipped off. About to be charged with fraud, by federal prosecutors and the Securities and Exchange Commission, for what amounted to swindling, he disappeared with millions of dollars, leaving his wife to take the brunt of public outrage. He'd also left a suicide note, but a body was never found, and Kate had testified she could not believe Mike would kill himself. After a year, she'd divorced him *in absentia* for desertion.

"I'd love for Erin to see the way we've decorated tonight," Kate was saying. Erin was a freshman at Ohio University in the southern part of the state; she'd only been gone a little over a month, and both Kate and Sarah missed her greatly. "You realize," Kate continued, "not only the rose swags and arrangements, but the Shaker rocker and set of oval boxes are drawing fabulous bids."

"Mmm, well, you know what authentic Shaker furniture and memorabilia are going for these days," Sarah said, patting Kate's arm. "Fortunately, Palmer and I got into collecting before prices went sky-high. We started about the same time the Rockefellers collected Shaker, but long before several other wealthy Americans began buying up a lot of it, cornering the market so items are getting to be like rare gems— Oh, dear, what's going on over there?"

Kate spun around to glance in the same direction. "It looks as if someone's fallen or jumped in the fountain with the floating petals," she observed. Her eyes were much sharper than Sarah's, even with these new glasses.

"Probably someone," Kate went on, "with so much champagne in him he thought he could walk on water. I'll see to it and call Security if I need to."

"That's all right, dear. I know you don't like to get in the midst of brouhahas anymore, or rely on the police, so—"

"No, Sarah, it's all right," Kate insisted, and hurried toward the melee, rolling up her long sleeves as she went, as if she were going to spray some sort of garden pest.

Kate had become what Sarah's own daughter Varina refused to be. Varina as ringleader with her younger brother Palmer in tow thought the Denbigh fortune should be their due before they'd done one thing to earn it, or before Sarah was cold in the grave. And that is why she'd changed her will to make Kate an heir, along with the charities close to Sarah's heart—not that she'd cut her own children off.

Sarah shook her head as she recalled a painful, unfortunate accident last month, but it had taught her a lesson, too. She'd been clipping long-stemmed tea roses for one of her bouquets and trying to talk to her daughter on the cell phone at the same time. Juggling things, she'd pressed the phone between her neck and shoulder.

"Varina, I know you and Brad lead busy lives," Sarah had said, "but I would so like for you to come meet these people at dinner here tomorrow. And since you asked, yes, I suppose a lot of the conversation will be about Shaker antiques but—ah-ah!"

Sarah dropped her armful of roses and stared aghast at the deep slice she'd made on her own left index finger. It didn't look bad at first, but as the pain increased, crimson blood filled, then spilled from, the long cut.

"Mother? What now?" Varina had asked over the phone Sarah still had propped to her ear. With her uncut hand, Sarah grabbed the receiver.

"I—I've cut myself with the rose shears. Deeply."

"Ugh, I hate blood. For heaven's sake, tell the staff

to call your doctor or maybe 911. Or have that assistant of yours, Saint Kate of the Catastrophe, get help. I can't believe you cut yourself after years of doing that, especially after you fell and hit your head a while back. You've got to be careful—with yourself—and others,'' she scolded ominously, though Sarah was no longer listening to a word she said.

Kate must have seen what happened from across the gardens, for she came running. She gasped at the blood and immediately wrapped Sarah's finger in her own shirttail.

''Getting an ER squad can take a while out here, and they'd only make you go in for stitches,'' Kate said. Her eyes filled with tears but her voice was steady. With one hand she put pressure on the base of the cut finger and elevated Sarah's arm until it yanked the shirt up. ''I can drive you right to the hospital, Sarah. Let me cut off this part of my shirt. Or is someone on the line bringing help already?'' she added as she pried the phone from Sarah's grip.

''No,'' Sarah had said calmly, despite her growing pain and panic at the throbbing, slippery finger. ''No one who wants to help.''

''Let me know if you feel faint or dizzy,'' Kate said, cutting the bottom of her shirt away with the offending shears, then hustling Sarah off, even as her maid and the gardener came running to see what was wrong.

''I'm fine. Just fine with Kate here,'' Sarah called to them in a quavering voice.

It was only later that Sarah realized Varina had heard all that over the phone. Blood may be thicker than water, but a friend can be better than a daughter,

Sarah had told herself then. Kate's just being here was hands-on healing. And Sarah knew she'd done the same for Kate when she had been cut to the core by Mike's desertion and betrayal, and everyone's baying for her blood.

Sarah shook her head to snap her attention back to the party. Kate had the contretemps at the fountain under control, but Sarah noted that the lights were on in her bedroom suite overlooking this patio and the sweep of gardens at the back of the house. That shouldn't be. People going upstairs to the powder room might think they could go in the bedroom, too. Or maybe someone had wandered in already. Besides, she had to visit the powder room herself, so she'd just pop up and be sure her private suite remained just that.

Chatting with a few others, shaking several hands along the way, Sarah slipped out of the crowd, went in the kitchen door and then up the servants' back stairs. Along the second-story hall, hung with her husband's old English hunt lithographs, Sarah hurried toward her rooms. Her eyes caught her full-length reflection in the long mirror at the end of the corridor.

It always shocked her to see that she had aged so much. How foolish to still expect that lithe, blond debutante she'd been when Palmer first came calling, instead of this delicate, silver-haired doyenne with a beginning widow's hump her doctor insisted on calling osteoporosis. These days that woman in the mirror was truly happier in the company of her heirloom flowers and antique Shaker furniture than with parties and people, just like dear Kate.

The door to her room was closed, so perhaps she'd

been wrong about someone being up here. Or else they'd gone and had closed it on their way out.

Before Sarah entered her sitting room, she pictured it abloom with flowered wallpaper to echo the bounteous bouquets of fragrance and extravagant color. Two of her larger pieces of vintage Shaker furniture sat there, a double work desk and a sturdy pine-and-fruitwood blanket box she used as an end table next to the sofa. Also, before the large windows, sat two rockers. Kate loved the simple sturdiness of the Shaker style—something Varina always called primitive and plain.

Traversing the soft hall carpet, Sarah swept open the door to her sitting room and gasped. Two strangers, dressed in baggy dark coveralls and with baseball caps pulled low, were busy packing into wooden wine crates two of her smallest but most unique Shaker pieces: a child's rocker and a washstand. No, maybe they were unpacking them.

For one stunning moment, they all froze and stared agape at one another.

Muted orchestra music wafted in, merging with the distant buzz of people's voices. "Whatever do you think you're doing?" Sarah got out.

"Grab her," one barked.

A woman?

Sarah tried to run. Flicking the light switch off to plunge them into darkness, she got as far as the hall, when one of them grabbed her arm and yanked her back. Her glasses flew off and she spun into the dark sitting room. She fell and hit her head hard on something. She touched her hand to her head and felt warm, thick wetness—her blood?

No...no, she must have simply cut her finger on the rose shears again or taken another tumble on the flagstones of the garden walk. That was it, because the sun came back out now. That music must be from Kate's favorite classical radio station she listened to as she tended the roses, the wet under her head a puddle from the early morning sprinklers. Kate was calling something to her about her roses.... Kate was saying she would take care of her cut finger, her head. Sarah could hear the bees buzzing again and smell the petals of every single, stunning bloom....

But as Kate tried to help her up, a cloud cloaked the sun, and everything went oh so dark and cold.

As soon as Kate got the fountain fiasco under control, she slipped away behind the fragrant boxwood hedges into the first tier of antique roses. Her huge cuttings for this party and the early chilly temperatures were bringing the roses to an end for this year. These Apothecaries and Gallicas were far beyond their brilliant, once-a-year June bloom, but the spills and sprays of their graceful, leggy stems pleased her as no fountain ever could. Even the new strain of Blood Thorn she'd bred from Bourbons and Chinas in the next tier of bushes couldn't hold a candle to these heirlooms with their iron constitutions—just like Sarah's, she mused.

Kate glanced back at the house and watched the lights in Sarah's suite go off, then back on again. Sarah must have gone upstairs after they'd spoken, though it was nearly time for the announcement of the silent auction winners. Sarah had promised to read the names and would no doubt give a little speech about each Shaker item.

Kate hoped Sarah kept her promise not to call on her to present the rose prizes. She preferred to stay behind the scenes right now. She'd been badly burned at center stage, though she'd be damned if she was going to skulk around as if she were guilty of anything. If it weren't for Erin—and if she knew where to look—Kate would have found and forced Mike to return, not to her but to stand trial. That, at least, would be worth the glare of the limelight again.

With another glance through the gardens, Kate skirted the party and headed toward the mansion. Sarah had insisted Kate and Erin live in the guesthouse by the pool after Kate had declared bankruptcy. They'd had to move and auction off most of their goods to cover their lawyer Mason James's fees, but his help had been worth it.

He had established in court that however much Kate *should* have known about Mike's fraud and embezzlement, she hadn't. Of course, Mason had to make her look like the town idiot to keep her from having to assume all Mike's massive debts or serve prison time—but then she *had* been the town idiot. She had totally trusted and loved Mike Marburn and had paid a huge price in reputation, sanity and circumstances. But never again…with a man. Never.

Kate went into the house, quiet by contrast with the noise outside, and climbed the central, curving staircase. It rose from the marble-tiled floor, but the wonder of the Denbigh mansion was its tall glass windows, which seemed to suck in sun or stars. Versailles on the Maumee, Sarah jokingly called the place, built in the 1930s with the Denbigh fortune made from industrial glass in the city once called the Glass Capital of the World.

But Kate didn't see Sarah in the hall or on the stairs. She'd better go look for her outside. Sometimes the unpretentious woman used the back servants' stairs. Strangely, the house now felt deserted, however alive it had seemed before. Kate peered down the main upstairs hallway. The door to Sarah's suite was closed.

"Sarah?"

For some odd reason, she sensed her friend was up here. Sarah had become somewhat accident-prone lately. She'd cut herself not long ago, and had fallen last month on the stone walk in the farthest garden, bruised both arms, and seemed a bit unsteady on her feet at times. What if she'd fallen again?

"Sarah?"

Kate turned the big brass doorknob to the sitting room where she and her hostess had spent some "grand" hours, as Sarah put it. Sarah had been her angel sent from God when things looked the blackest. After she'd hired Kate and Kate and Erin had moved into the pool house, Sarah had invited the younger women to tea, and the three of them had picnicked on the grounds. And then there were the times she'd invited them to candlelit, dress-up dinners in the mansion.

Erin had rolled her eyes and sulked at first, saying it was all so out-of-it to do those things at her age, but eventually she'd come to love the old woman, too. Somehow Sarah's fussing had helped Kate pull Erin from the depression that lingered after her father had left. These last weeks Erin had been at college and Kate had missed her so, with the result that Kate and Sarah had become even closer.

Kate clicked on the light. All was in order, and the scent of the late roses curled around her in their usual welcoming way. But some strange, acrid scent hung heavily in the air, too.

She went in, glanced around, and saw something spilled on the carpet near the Shaker blanket box. But the crystal vase on it was not tipped or broken. She put her hand in the water on the coral-colored rug and saw that it was blood. Horrified, she wiped her hand on her gown.

"Sarah!"

Kate ran into the adjoining bedroom, which looked undisturbed, each piece of furniture, each bouquet untouched. Then she noted the bathroom door was closed. Sarah was in there and just hadn't heard her calling, that's all. But the blood...

She knocked on the door. "Sarah, are you in there? Are you all right?"

No reply. Slowly, as Kate opened the door, she saw the room was black. Its soft mauve and ecrus muted to grays in the dim echo of light from the bedroom. Her shadow leaped across the tiled floor and darted up the wall; her hand trembled as she reached to flick on the light switch.

Sarah was sprawled facedown on the floor by the commode, her white head in a halo of crimson blood.

"Sarah! Sarah, it's Kate!" She fell to her knees beside her friend and fumbled for a neck pulse.

Nothing. Had she slipped and hit her head while coming to use the toilet? Or had she fallen in the other room, then come to wash the blood away but fainted here?

"Oh, God, oh, God, please help Sarah!" she cried as she ran for the phone in the bedroom and dialed 911. It was a frenzied call that would be played repeatedly on newscasts and reported word for word in the papers.

2

The fairest things have fleetest end,
Their scent survives their close;
But the rose's scent is bitterness
To him that loved the rose.

—Francis Thompson
"Daisy"

"**Y**ou just went out in the gardens by yourself," the detective repeated patiently, "and then took the long way around back into the house through the side door which you seldom use?"

Weren't there at least three questions in that question? Kate agonized. Exhausted and drained—stunned—she sat in the Denbigh library in a fog of grief. She knew she should call her lawyer, but she wasn't accused of anything, and most certainly was not guilty of harming the most generous, wonderful woman she had ever known.

The most wonderful, that is, since her mother had died so early Kate could barely recall her. Sometimes she wasn't sure if she was really remembering or just calling to mind the few photos of her.

Right now the forensic team was taking photographs of every inch of this house. It was the return of a nightmare she had thought she'd escaped, only worse. Mike's body had never been found, and she and Erin had first grieved, then harbored hope, then bitter resentment, that he might yet be alive. But she could still hear Erin's inconsolable wails, feel her shaking body as Kate tried to comfort her on the girl's bed, after the police had confiscated the suicide note and most of Mike's things.

"They can't take his goodbye note, too—like his computer and his other stuff," Erin had choked out, gasping for breath, racked with hysteria, her red-blond hair matted to her face with tears. When Kate tried to hug her, the girl held to her pillow instead, so Kate rubbed her trembling back.

"Erin, sweetheart, I can't believe he'd—he'd hurt himself."

"They took his things, but they can't take him away!" she screamed. "Mom, he can't be dead!" She tried to shrug off Kate's persistent touch, but Kate had held her tighter, frantic with her own fear at the enormity of it all, until Erin's sobbing stopped and she clung to Kate, too.

But now there was no one to hold on to, and Sarah's body lay upstairs. Worse, it had been there for hours until the so-called rescue squad finally took it to the morgue in a dark green, zippered plastic bag.

Police and a forensic team in white coats still swarmed the house. Crime-scene tape wrapped the grounds, though Detective Rudzinski and his older, brusque partner, Lieutenant Tina Martin, both told Kate that no one was being charged with anything. Seeing a bloodstain on her gown, they'd asked her to hand it over, and she now wore one of the maid's extra dresses. The forensic team had taken scrapings from under her fingernails because she'd touched the blood on the floor. But then the detectives also took fingerprints and the names and phone numbers of all two hundred guests, before releasing them in the wee hours. The silent auction remained silent, though the memory of Erin's voice kept screaming in Kate's head to rival Stan Rudzinski's questions.

"Go ahead," Lieutenant Martin prompted Kate with a decisive nod of her head. "You saw the blood by the end table..."

Tina Martin seldom spoke, and seemed to be overseeing everything as well as questioning Kate. The prematurely silver-haired, no-nonsense woman popped in and out, either to observe Kate or to advise the apparently wet-behind-the-ears Rudzinski. He was a few years younger than Kate, blond with a buzz cut and a military bearing. But Tina Martin's taut, leathery skin—too much summer sun or a tanning booth— made her look old enough to be the man's mother. Besides, Lieutenant Martin was built like Ms. Universe, and by contrast Rudzinski seemed the ninety-pound weakling.

"It's an authentic Shaker blanket chest," Kate corrected him automatically, but she couldn't focus and her voice didn't sound like her own. She felt dazed, as she often had after hours of questioning by the federal prosecutors over Mike's financial scam.

"Right, but you said there was much more blood where you found the body in the bathroom, is that right, Ms. Marburn?"

"You saw her there, too, so what do you think? That's what I said when you asked me that the last two times, Detective. Look, I want to be a good eyewitness, but I'm exhausted. Can't we go over this again tomorrow?"

"The guest house is being searched right now, too," he admitted, as Lieutenant Martin left the room again.

"Without a warrant?" she challenged, sitting up straighter.

"It's being searched as part of the estate, not as your domicile, Ms. Marburn, so just sit tight and you can go soon. Once they case the place, you can sleep there tonight, though the heirs are so distressed I think you'd better figure on finding another place soon."

"Oh, yes, they'll come swooping in now," Kate muttered, "but they've hardly been speaking to her for months."

"Is that right? Bad blood—pardon the wording—between them?"

Blessedly, a police officer poked his head in from the hall. "Guest house is clear, Zink—Detective," he said and closed the door behind him.

"I was a patrolman until recently," the young man said, almost to himself. "You heard him, Ms. Marburn—let me walk you over, as you were always free to go. Your guest house is ready."

The way he said that reminded Kate of the O.J. Simpson case, in which that hanger-on, Kato Kaylin, had been in residence in a guest house on the grounds during a double murder. But these detectives hadn't said Sarah had been murdered. And Kate was no hanger-on.

"I insisted Sarah deduct rent from my salary," she told Rudzinski, as they went out across the back patio and started through the rose gardens. "I'm an employee, even if I'm living in the guest house."

"And a friend, as you said. You know, I understand the deceased's daughter didn't put it so—so nicely or objectively.''

Kate's stomach lurched. Something was being said just under the surface that threatened her. She'd gravely misjudged Mike and paid the price, but surely no one would never suspect her of harming Sarah. But if Varina was turning really vicious...yes, she could imagine that. Kate would have been furious with anyone who alienated *her* mother's affections. But then, Varina had done that on her own. Kate jerked when the detective spoke again.

''There'll be officers on the grounds tonight, ma'am. And when they've released the site tomorrow, I'd like to take you back to the scene to have you tell me if anything looks amiss. That all right?''

''I'd do anything to help, of course,'' she said, as he hesitated at the door of the guest house. She shuddered to think of that group of white-coated forensic people going through her personal effects. It was just like the time their very lives were violated when the police had searched for proof that Mike—and his wife—were in collusion in the Marburn Securities scandal.

''Ma'am—Ms. Marburn, I know all this is double hard on you, considering what you went through before and all.''

Kate could only nod. She felt she was swimming in a sea of exhaustion and disbelief. And she was beginning to be swept under by the familiar, cold riptide of terror.

The phone's shrill ring pulled Kate from the dark depths. Why was she on the sofa instead of in bed? She fought her way up from sodden sleep. Often she had insomnia, so at least she'd been sleeping soundly for once, but—

The slant of morning light blinded her. Then she remembered.

Sarah was dead. Kate had lost Sarah—and the disaster of her marriage made her doubly fearful of being implicated and blamed.

But she was not going to be a victim here. Never again.

The phone continued to ring. If this call was from someone wanting a statement, she'd slam the receiver down and take the phone off the hook. But she had to call her lawyer—maybe he'd heard and was phoning her. She swung her feet to the floor, astounded at the instant slam of a headache behind her left eye. She picked the receiver up gingerly, as if it would bite.

"Hello."

"It's Erin."

Kate squeezed her eyes tight shut as her stepdaughter's face flashed into her mind. Huge green eyes with pale lashes she mascaraed dark blue, freckles she tried to cover, a pert-nosed face framed by shoulder-length pale strawberry-blond hair that she insisted on calling "Irish red" because that had pleased her dad.

"But it's—oh, it's eight on a Sunday morning, sweetheart," Kate managed with a glance at the clock. "Is anything wrong?"

"Why didn't you call me last night? A newspaper reporter did and asked all kinds of questions about us and Mrs. Denbigh. He said she's dead and you found her."

Kate hunched over her knees, her forehead resting on her free hand. For one moment she thought she would be violently ill. She'd only had about two hours sleep, though for her that was a normal stretch.

"Kate, are you still there?"

"Yes, sweetheart, I'm here. I'm sorry—so sorry if you've been pulled into—another tragedy."

Now nearly nineteen and a freshman in college, Erin had been eight when her own mother died. That loss had been one of the things that had initially made them close, for Kate and Erin had each survived the same loss early in life. As Erin's stepmother since the girl was nine, Kate had worked hard at building their relationship. So hard, she realized in retrospect, that she had overdone time with Erin, trying to make up for Mike who was obsessed with his investment firm. When Mike disappeared, he'd left a love letter to them, though it was part suicide note. Unfortunately, his departure and its aftermath had not kept her and Erin as close as Kate had hoped. Just the opposite.

"Now I'm *really* an orphan!" Erin had wailed when they had first found the note from Mike. They had just walked into the house from shopping for things for Erin when they found the note that had begun the nightmare. That day, Erin had actually locked herself in her bedroom and had refused to be comforted or counseled. And more often than not these past two years without her father, Erin had called her "Kate" instead of "Mom."

"They aren't going to blame you, are they?" Erin was asking now. "I mean, some of this reporter's questions sounded really kind of, well, suspicious."

"Of course they're not going to blame me, but since I'm the one who found her..."

"I'll bet that witch Varina had a hissy fit because you were with Sarah at the end."

"Erin, you're not to speak disparagingly of Sarah's children."

"Meaning adults can do no wrong? But Dad left and you didn't know what was going on or how to help or keep him..."

Erin began to cry. There was so sound, but Kate knew. Her stomach cramped at the accusation, both spoken and implied.

"Sweetheart, listen, don't mix this up with what happened to us. Everything will be all right. But just to be sure we're not bothered by reporters any more, I'm going to call Mason James to—"

"Not a lawyer again. Not all that."

"You're upset, Erin, and I understand. I am, too, believe me. Sarah was more than a friend, maybe like the mother or grandmother we never knew."

"A fairy godmother," Erin whispered, and sniffed hard.

"The point is, I don't want you to worry about things here. I'll be down to see you as soon as I can get away. I might have to change my phone number again, move too, but I'll let you know. Is everything all right there? You're not homesick?"

"My roommate Amy is, but by comparison I got over that years ago after—"

"After your mother died, I know. I *do* know."

Audible sobbing now. Kate's eyes burned with tears, and she gripped the receiver to try to seize control. She had hoped and prayed that when Erin went away to college they could both start over, looking forward to their reunions and maybe living together again someday.

"Sweetheart, if you can, concentrate on things there. I'll call you every day—and see you soon.

Maybe you can help Amy feel better, take her somewhere or have a good talk with her. Don't let her be
alone.''

"Yeah, I hear you." Another big sniff. "Reach out
and touch someone and that will help you, too. It used
to be your motto. Then you do the same, okay? Promise.''

"Yes, I promise.''

"But if we—you—have to move out of Groveland,
where's our home now, Mom?''

Above all else, that last word so swamped the remnants of Kate's control that she couldn't even answer.

The gong of the doorbell only made Jack bury his
head deeper in the covers. Then he squinted...what
time was it? Dawn had not yet lit the eastern sky, he
noted as he glared at the digital bedside clock. Six-
twenty a.m. Now who in hell needed an antique furniture builder at this time of the morning? And on a
Sunday—not that he wasn't going to put in a full
day's work.

He stumbled to his feet on the cold, bare wood
floor and didn't even bother looking for his shoes or
socks. He liked to live a spartan existence—deserved
to. Still groggy, he lurched out of his bedroom and
across the hall into the front room he used as his
office. It looked out over the old turnpike road that
ran toward the Shaker village about half a mile away.
He lived alone in this place, but once so many had
lived here together.

He remembered he still had his screens in the windows. He hadn't taken the time to put in the storms
yet or even to clean out his frost-blasted garden. He

hated to do household things. He unlocked and heaved up the sill.

"What is it?" he called out into the gray autumn mist.

"It's Josh Harvey and my dad, Mr. Kilcourse," a young boy's voice called up. "I'm just helping him 'cause it's Sunday and this is a real special 'livery letter. We got it for you here, and you got to sign for it."

Jack leaned closer to the screen to see the squat, white mail van pulled up close to the house. It annoyed him that Frank Harvey often let his kid do his work, official government work. It annoyed him how the boy hung on to his father's every word, adored him. Damn, maybe it was his own harsh, bitter self that annoyed him.

"Be right down," he called.

He pulled on jeans and a sweatshirt. Downstairs, he snapped on the porch light before he unlocked one of the two front doors. The boy did not hold the letter or the clipboard, but stood there all bright-faced and important-looking when Frank handed them over. The pain of that simple scene sliced Jack so deeply that he could have shoved them both off the porch.

He scribbled his name and managed to make some sort of small talk.

"See you later, Mr. Kilcourse! Have a nice day of rest—that's what my Mom calls it. She said we should've waited 'til it got light!" the kid called back as they started away. Mild-mannered Frank just patted the kid's head and smiled, either sheepishly or proudly, and turned away, too. The boy practically skipped along next to his dad before they got into the little truck, beeped the horn and drove away. Its headlights slashed across Jack's face and startled him. Then the western darkness swallowed them. He stood staring blankly down the road, until he realized he was shaking from the predawn chill.

He went in, slammed the front door, clicked on the hall light and ripped open the registered letter. It was from the Toledo, Ohio police department. He was used to getting orders and requests from all over—but the police? He skimmed it for the signature: a homicide detective named Stanley Rudzinski. Never heard of him.

*Since you are the closest expert in assessing the authenticity of Shaker furniture, and we have an emergency where we need your help…*the letter began.

Jack sat down on the lowest step and let the letter drop to the floor between his knees. That's about all he was an expert in. *We have an emergency.* Yeah, that was a good one. But anything to fill his hours, to have different, solid things to do to keep his own emergency away.

3

Money, which represents the prose of life, and which is hardly spoken of in parlors without an apology, is, in its effects and laws, as beautiful as roses.

—Ralph Waldo Emerson
Nominalist and Realist

"Since you discovered the deceased in the bathroom, can you suggest any way she could have fallen to get blood here?" Rudzinski asked Kate, pointing at the missing square of carpet labeled "4." "Then," he went on when she didn't answer immediately, "there's nothing but tiny drops until she made it into the bathroom, where she bled significantly again."

Kate glanced at where he pointed. In daylight, she could see a line of speckles—numbers "5" through "12" laid out on the carpet in Sarah's suite. "I didn't see those last night," she said, trying not to sound defensive.

"You were in a hurry. So what if you didn't see a few drops?"

Though he seemed to be on her side, Kate's wariness level skyrocketed. He kept watching her face for a reaction to each thing he said. She wished Mason

James would get here, even though she had absolutely nothing to hide.

"For one thing," she replied, "those other drops might have led me to find her faster, to get help sooner."

Detective Rudzinski—Zink, Kate kept hearing the officers call him—seemed much more nervous as he took her back to the place of Sarah's death late the next afternoon. He looked like some retro preppie college kid with loafers and a V-neck sleeveless sweater over his button-down shirt. A college kid...damn, she had to get her mind off Erin. And though she was still slogging through exhaustion, she had to concentrate on everything this man was saying.

In Sarah's suite they stood on a plastic runner that was there to keep everyone's feet off the carpet. The plastic ran from the hall door to the blanket chest, then into the bedroom and to the distant bathroom door. The piece of coral carpet with the bloodstain had been completely cut out, and the floor was flagged with little signs in a scrawl Kate could not read from this distance, though the numbers on each paper stood out.

Her insides lurched. She supposed this had to be treated as a crime scene. But surely no one would have murdered Sarah.

"You said last night that you 'sensed' she was up here, though you heard and saw nothing out of order except the light going off and then back on," Rudzinski pursued. "You often have these feelings? Is it ESP or something like that?"

Suddenly everything he said sounded accusatory, though Kate told herself she was just overly sensitive after all she'd been through. She noted Rudzinski had a habit of never taking notes, unlike the government and financial investigators she'd spent hours with over Mike's case. She was tempted to ask him if he had a photographic memory, but she said only, "You know what they say about women's intuition. And I've called my lawyer. He'll be back in town tomorrow and said not to answer any untoward questions."

"Untoward, that's me," Rudzinski said, stretching to his full five feet six inches. She noticed his slacks and shirt looked wrinkled, as if he'd slept in them or been up all night. Yes, that was what he'd worn yesterday, at least she thought so. Adrenaline coursed through her, but she still couldn't clear her head. "Look, Ms. Marburn, I'm just trying to find out how the woman you call your mentor, and say you cared deeply for, died, because it's real hard for me—and others—to figure how it could've been an accident."

Her heart began to beat faster, harder. "I'm surprised, too, but she did take a tumble last month."

"So the maid and her doctor told us, and the coroner mentioned previous external bruising on her arms. It's lucky you were there to find her then, too. So maybe she just tumbled into the chest there," he said, turning and pointing again, "then managed to stop the bleeding on her head except for a few drops, long enough to stagger into the bathroom where she fell again." As he spoke, he paced the walkway to the bathroom, then came back. "But we found her with nothing that could have stanched her blood, and the amount on your gown was negligible."

"I said I don't know, Detective. I only know you asked me up here to tell you if I thought anything was removed from her private suite, and I'm telling you I don't think so, all right?"

"If I showed you the contents of her jewelry box, would you know if anything was taken from that? In addition to things in her wall safe, she kept a jewelry box out in her bedroom on an antique chest of drawers—"

Kate fought for control and calm. He was right in her face now, despite his deceptively calm demeanor. "The only time I've seen her jewelry box open was when she tried to loan me a strand of pearls for last night, and I declined."

"For last night? And you declined because..."

"Because she'd already done so much for me, and I didn't want to take a chance on their being broken or lost. I've had things snag in stems and thorns more than once when I've bent over to work with my roses."

"I see," he said with a lift of his blond brows.

"I hope that's it, because I'm starting to feel I'm on trial here, so if you'll excuse me," she insisted more stridently than she'd intended.

"I didn't mean to stress you even more, Ms. Marburn," Rudzinski said, shifting so he stood between her and the hall door. He was short enough that she looked down at him slightly, but he suddenly seemed as formidable as a pit bull.

"Before you go," he went on, "how about answering my ESP question? You good at sensing things, maybe at psyching people out?"

"Not really, or I wouldn't have come up here without a lawyer today, Detective Rudzinski. And I would have known that my husband was a shyster who would stop at nothing to ruin our clients and friends, not to mention his daughter and wife. Excuse me, please."

She pushed past him into the hall—and bumped into Varina Wellesley. The woman's chunky gold jewelry clattered as they made contact, then stepped apart. Large-boned, the striking Varina usually wore her raven hair swept back in a twist that made her look older than Kate, although they were the same age. Against her severely cut pantsuit, and without her usual cosmetics, her complexion looked ghostly pale. Varina resembled her mother only in the bone structure of the face, not in size or style—and never in heart. A cold wave of loss rolled through Kate again.

"Once they're finished with you," Varina cried, pointing at Kate, "I don't want you back in here again." Kate saw her eyes were bloodshot. At least Varina seemed to be suffering, too. "And that includes moving out of the guest house."

"Hey, Mrs. Wellesley, please," Rudzinski cut in, stepping between them. "Of necessity, Ms. Marburn will be moving out, but the deceased would hardly want her thrown out before she finds someplace else."

"Unfortunately, my mother isn't here anymore, and Palmer and I are her heirs," Varina insisted, running a lacquered index fingernail under each eye to smear tears.

"Which makes you feel *how* about losing her, ma'am?"

Varina glared at him. "Deeply bereft. And ready to assume any duties to preserve all she and my late father worked for."

Kate forced herself to walk away. At least it appeared that the police were suspicious of everyone. If this did turn out to be a murder investigation, she supposed, Varina and Palmer could be suspects.

"Hey, Ms. Marburn, for your own best interests, hold up until I get an officer to walk you out," Rudzinski called after her. Kate wondered where his previously omnipresent partner was. She heard him order Varina in a softer voice, "Stand right there and don't go in yet, Mrs. Wellesley."

"Look, Detective," Kate heard Varina say, "all I know about Mother's antique furniture is that she was switching it around all the time—lending, selling, donating."

Waiting at the top of the stairs, Kate glanced out the bank of tall windows at the Maumee River glinting beyond the back gardens.

"Besides," Varina went on, "I thought you were going to get an expertiser in from that new Shaker village that's holding a lot of her furniture. Palmer and I want to get that back as soon as possible to reassemble her entire collection of the stuff."

Though Varina probably couldn't care less, Kate knew the Shakers had once been prominent in many areas. In gardening, design, and the liberation and elevation of women and blacks, the Shakers had left their mark. And Varina dared to call her mother's precious treasury of the Shaker heritage "stuff"!

Sarah's elderly lawyer cleared his throat and began to read. "'I, Sarah Clayton Denbigh, residing in Lucas County, Ohio, do make, publish, and declare this to be my Last Will and Testament, hereby revoking all Wills by me heretofore made.'"

Four days after Sarah's death, Kate sat with her silver-haired and steely-faced lawyer, Mason James, across a long, polished cherry conference table from Varina Wellesley and her husband Brad, the nervous Palmer, and their lawyer Pete Scofield. They were assembled for the reading of Sarah Denbigh's will by her lawyer, the portly but imposing Seth Myerman. As soon as Sarah's will had been probated, beneficiaries and the next of kin had been summoned by certified mail for this reading. Kate had been touched and surprised to be included; Varina was seething.

Kate was more apprehensive than pleased, though, for this haste, though entirely legal, seemed indecent. Sarah wouldn't even be laid to rest for two days, partly because the coroner had just released the body to the family and partly because the funeral had been set back a bit for out-of-town guests.

Through half-glasses, the lawyer peered down at the multipaged document, his jowls shaking as he talked. His voice was sonorous and impressive, as if it should belong to an evangelist or network news anchor.

"'I give, devise and bequeath the following items to the below named individuals as follows...'"

The Groveland mansion and grounds were deeded to the City of Toledo Metro Parks, with an endowment for upkeep of the house and gardens, the latter to be overseen by Katherine Marburn. Ms. Marburn was to receive a yearly salary from the estate of fifty thousand dollars with a three-percent per-year increase for inflation for as many years as she chose to remain in the position. If she wished, considering that the grounds and gardens would be open to the public, Ms. Marburn could continue to live in the guest house.

Varina's loud sniff—whether of grief or of contempt, Kate wasn't sure—punctuated Myerman's pause. Sarah's great gift and the admiration and love behind it moved Kate deeply. Sarah had mentioned her property becoming a park someday, but she'd never hinted at the rest to her. Perhaps Sarah's heirs had known, though, and accepted it because current death and property taxes could be ruinous.

Stone-faced, Varina shifted in her chair, though the balding, tanned Palmer glowered. "The bulk of the estate's still to come," Kate heard Varina mutter to her brother as she patted his arm.

There followed a long list of pieces of art or furniture—none of it Shaker antiques—to Varina and Palmer. Between the padded arms of their chairs, they grasped each other's hands, as Seth Myerman read off the growing list of endowments and bequests to various charities. Then came what they were evidently awaiting; both leaned forward.

"'Item nineteen. One-half million dollars to each of my two children, Varina Clarissa Denbigh Wellesley and Palmer Jones Denbigh.'"

That figure boggled Kate's mind, for her math teacher–father had never thought women proficient at handling money and had left her but ten thousand dollars when he died. But Varina and Palmer looked surprised and dismayed.

"Go on," Varina prompted, her voice shaking, when the lawyer paused. "How has she parceled out the rest to us? In stocks or bonds or the Shaker collection?"

"Not that I see," he said, flipping and scanning the last three pages. "There are two more bequests to Katherine Marburn," he said with a glance at Kate. He adjusted his bifocals and read, "'Item twenty. My collection of Shaker furniture, including those items in my home and those loaned to various museums (see list attached) as well as my core collection currently displayed at the new Shaker Run Village in southeastern Ohio, to my dear friend, Katherine Marburn, who admires the Shakers as I did.'''

"That's insanity," Varina spat out, smacking an open palm on the table. "Some of that furniture belonged to both my parents—and Mother's made decisions for everyone. And do you know what some of those pieces go for? Just the other day there was an online auction house sale for one work counter from the Sabbath Lake Shakers—a *work counter*. It went for $220,000, and some side chairs worth $20,000 apiece. So that can't be—be quite right."

"So you've already been checking on prices for your sale of what you call 'her stuff'?" Kate spoke up, unable to hold in her frustration any longer. "Perhaps your mother *knew* you'd unload the whole lot of her treasures the moment she died."

"And you won't?" Varina demanded.

"Never."

"Ha!" was all Palmer managed. The blood had drained from his face, and he still gripped his sister's hand.

The two of them began to whisper. All Kate could discern was Palmer's "Rina, can you believe that? How could she do that?" as Myerman plunged on.

"'And my antique rosebushes, from among the many others which shall stay in Groveland gardens, I bequest to Katherine Marburn should she ever leave this area.

"'In witness whereof, I have hereunto set my hand on the margin of the preceding twelve pages and at the end of this my last Will and Testament, at Toledo, Ohio, this fourth day of August 1999.' ''

"Wait, there has to be more," Palmer cried.

"Oh, there is," Varina insisted, yanking her hand free of his grip. "August 1999—this year? Mother just changed her will last month? And leaves a fortune in furniture and a longtime sinecure for gardening to a new friend who suddenly finds my—*our*— mother dead?''

"After," Palmer added, "her head hit one of the pieces of furniture which now go to Ms. Marburn?'' Varina and Palmer both spoke in low voices, but their frustration and fury seethed under that control.

"I know all this is a shock," their lawyer interrupted, "but in due time we can file—''

"You let Mother be taken in like this and didn't stop her," Varina accused Sarah's lawyer, who looked like an angry Buddha. "Why didn't you at least tell us she'd suddenly shifted the bulk of our heritage to a new employee? I cannot believe Mother changed her will so suddenly, so close to her sudden, strange death.''

"Now see here," Mason James countered. "Mrs. Wellesley, I'll not have you slandering Mrs. Marburn, even indirectly. That's a legal document and—''

"Which can and will be contested!'' Varina cried, half rising and leaning straight-armed on the table with both hands. "Isn't that true, Pete?'' she asked their lawyer, who nodded, just as Palmer kept doing.

"Quite true," Pete Scofield said, steepling his fingers before his mouth and nose. "The state of Ohio provides a four-month window for a will to be contested for fraud, duress, undue influence or incompetence—''

"Incompetence of our poor mother perhaps, for I must admit that Kate Marburn obviously has been skilled here—and not just at growing roses. I always said your resume must have read that you were clever at defrauding people and getting off scot-free yourself," Varina hissed. "But how daring of you to try it again after wriggling out of that embezzlement caper."

"Varina, that's enough," Scofield cried, and reached for her wrist. She shook him off. "It isn't," she insisted. "All that has to happen to freeze this will and take Kate Marburn out of it for life—*for life*—is for her to be charged and convicted of... certainly more than duress or undue influence!"

Kate's insides had been in free fall, but she wasn't just going to run. Mike had done that, and she hated him for it. She stood, scraping back her chair, and Mason did the same, evidently thinking they were walking out. But Kate simply wanted to face this woman eye to eye.

"Varina," Kate said, her voice steady despite her distress, "I can grasp how hard this is for you, but you'd better be careful before pointing fingers so publicly. Since you and Palmer obviously believed your mother's previous will was in effect, one which evidently made you her favorite charities, if I were Detective Rudzinski and his partner, I'd think that you two would have motives galore for—"

"Don't try to shift the blame," Palmer put in.

"By the way," Kate said, sitting back down again because her legs were shaking so hard, "Sarah never told me a thing about these bequests, though I knew she wanted me to care for the roses in the future."

Before Varina could reply, Kate went on, "All of

these generous gifts are a shock to me, although, in part, a pleasant one. However, I deeply grieve the loss of a great woman whom I shall always remember for her warmth and accomplishments—not for her stocks, bonds or fortune—as her own children evidently define her memory.''

She rose again now, slowly, to stand by Mason. ''At least someone who cares about her value,'' Kate said, ''and not what she was worth, will be able to oversee the two great loves of her later life—the furniture and the roses.''

For one moment, Kate regretted she'd come down so hard on them, but she had sworn to herself she would never again be left holding the bag for something she didn't do. At least, for once, even three lawyers were speechless.

But by the next morning someone had leaked details of the new will and Kate's defiance to the newspaper and TV stations.

Jack Kilcourse had never been a slave to money, but this job examining the authenticity and value of some great Shaker furniture—he was properly called an expertiser—was too lucrative and fascinating to pass up. Although he'd had to leave his own workshop where he produced authentic replicas of Shaker pieces—even though the CEO of a wealthy hi-tech Tokyo firm was waiting for his new dining room suite—he'd dropped everything to drive to Toledo. Besides, he figured he was doing it for a fine old lady who had loaned the struggling new Shaker village a big part of her collection to help draw visitors. The great Shaker heritage was worthy of honor and pres-

ervation, however strange some of the original Believers must have been.

Now Jack had set up bright lights to be able to
closely examine the pieces. He had opened his kit of
tools: magnifying glass, screwdriver, needles, plastic
gloves and envelopes, and specimen bags. He felt
something like the forensic guys who had finally
cleared out just ahead of him with the tools of their
trade. He'd eyeballed all the furniture in the suite,
picked the piece that looked most likely, and hauled
it under the lights for its examination.

"Hey, how's it going?" the young detective, Stan
Rudzinski, asked as he came back in. He had a folded
copy of the *Toledo Blade* in his hand. "Can I bring
you back some chow when I return? Got to run down-
town on this case." Rudzinski pointed to the headline,
which read What Does Kate Marburn Know—Again?
It was followed by a smaller headline that said something about a new will.

None of that meant a thing to Jack, nor did it interest him. He detested and avoided newspapers and
newscasts unless they presented a business item or
world news. He couldn't stomach the local domestic
tragedies the media fed on, so he pretty much kept
his nose to the grindstone, or, rather, to the wood. But
he had to admit, as he looked at Kate Marburn's photograph that even appearing frenzied and with a fold
right through her face, she was one good-looking
woman.

"I'll pass on the food," Jack told Rudzinski. "I'll
take a break at noon and grab some fast food around
here somewhere. So much of this is detail work that
I give my old back and forty-four-year-old eyes a
break now and then."

"Sure, no problem. Officer Cook will be right out here if you need anything. You know," the detective said, hitching up his pants as if that would give him a few more inches facing the six-foot-three antique furniture expert, "you're kind of a detective, too. See, I figure if there's some kind of funny goings-on with any of this furniture—like maybe some of it's fake— I got myself another motive to play with. Not that the cast of characters surrounding a rich, old lady won't keep me busy enough."

"Technically," Jack told him, rapping his knuckles on the desk, "I've found no fakes—but maybe one fraud so far."

"What do you mean?" Rudzinski asked, snapping to attention. "And what's the diff?"

"A fake is phony from the get-go—a complete fabrication," Jack explained, pulling a drawer out of the desk-bookshelf combination. "But a fraud is an antique that's been altered, disguised or misrepresented. Frauds are easier to pass off and, therefore, usually more lucrative to unload."

"This here?" Rudzinski asked, suddenly eyeing the cherry-and-butternut piece with suspicion.

"I'd bet on it, though I haven't done enough tests."

"Like what? It looks old to me."

"It's easy to dent, bruise or gouge such a piece to make it pass for old. It's called 'distressing.'"

"Good name. I feel that way half the time in this job."

Jack bit back a grin. "I'll have some lab samples done, but it looks to me as if someone's put random ink stains on this desktop and smoked the shelf wood to brown and dry it. Then they get rid of the burn smell with a saltwater soak."

"No kidding," Rudzinski observed with a shake of his head.

"Here's another telltale sign that they were thorough but not thorough enough," Jack told him, taking a darning needle from his kit. He easily ran the needle down several tiny holes on the side of the bookcase. "Worm holes, which are natural and expected with fine antiques, twist and turn. These worm holes were made by power drills."

"Frauds must be worth big bucks."

"Shaker grain sacks are going for a couple hundred dollars, and seed labels for at least that much. Compared to that, 'there's gold in them thar Shaker furniture.'"

"Got you," Rudzinski said. "And the rest of the pieces in here?"

"It'll take time, like I said. This one just stood out."

"What's so special about Shaker furniture?" the detective asked, crossing his arms over his chest so Kate Marburn's newsprint eyes stared at Jack. "Before this case, I didn't know that style, let alone the people, existed."

"That they did. There were once nearly twenty utopian Shaker communities scattered across the East and Midwest. They thrived as outposts of a unique group of people known for their wild style of dance in their worship services, but now more for their celibacy. They had a dark side, too, but don't we all?"

"In this job—tell me about it."

"But what's so special about the Shakers is their uniqueness, which shines through in all their products."

"Unique how?" Rudzinski pursued.

Jack didn't have much use for nosy people, but this guy was at least honest about what he didn't know. "Let me just put it this way since you're leaving and I've got a lot to do before giving you a decent report," Jack said, putting the needle away and going back to examining the dovetailing on the side of the desk drawer. "The Shakers were perfectionists in their work, but practical, too. Their female founder once said, 'Work as though you have one thousand years to live but might die tomorrow.'"

Jack wished he'd put it another way when he saw Rudzinski glance around the room as if Sarah Denbigh's ghost had lingered. "Or to raise it to another level, which they always did," Jack went on, "some Shaker furniture designers actually believed that their patterns came from heaven and were transmitted to them by angels."

"In short, they made practical things but lived in some sort of weird world of their own making. You know, Mr. Kilcourse—"

"Jack."

"Jack. I'd have to call that kind of people at least a little dangerous," the detective said, shaking his head and starting for the door. "I'll check in with you after I get back. And, like I said, I'm hoping your brand of detective work's gonna somehow jump-start mine."

4

You may break, you may shatter
The vase if you will,
But the scent of the roses
Will hang round it still.

—Thomas More
"Farewell! But Whatever"

Kate tried to calm herself and prepare for Sarah's funeral tomorrow by working with her roses. It was so great to be out in the open air instead of closed up in a lawyer's office or in a room with Rudzinski and his prickly partner—though it seemed Tina Martin spent more time with Varina and Palmer, while "Zink" had been assigned to her.

Kate kept pruning bush after bush and wheelbarrowing the cut canes to an enclosed trash pile, where Jeff, Groveland's handyman, would compost them. But she wielded her clippers with a vengeance, furious that Pete Scofield—Varina and Palmer's lawyer—had leaked word of Sarah's new will to the papers and put the worst possible spin on it.

The same article had quoted Rudzinski repeating that "Sarah Denbigh's death is still under investigation, though it appears to be an accident." But the man's tenacity was actually starting to make Kate fear otherwise. And if anyone had somehow deliberately hurt Sarah, Kate vowed, she'd make the Toledo homicide squad look like rank amateurs in an attempt to find out who was guilty.

Kate knew full well that she had filled a great gap in Sarah's life, but Sarah had been her salvation, too. "I can't think of a job I'd rather have than working with your antique roses while living on this beautiful estate," she'd told Sarah the day the elderly woman had offered her a future when she was still facing a possible trial for Mike's misdeeds. "But my stepdaughter needs some stability in her life right now," Kate had admitted, "so I'd hate for her to have to change high schools if we move into your neighborhood. Not to mention that the hours I could give you would be erratic at best for a while because of all the time I'm still spending with my lawyer and government investigators."

Sarah had nodded understandingly. When she took a step closer and put a thin hand on Kate's shoulder, the scent of flowers had emanated from her. It wasn't like that staggering smell of powder or perfume when certain woman sat too near in church or at a concert. Sarah Denbigh smelled fresh and real, which stunned Kate with a memory that came back with a bang.

Her mother. Her young, laughing mother she could barely recall had smelled like that. Of freshly turned loam and summer sun and clear sky. Of crisp breeze and mingled flowers. Her mother had loved to garden, and little Kate had toddled at her side to help her pick flowers...long before she had been swept away on the winds of time....

"Kate, are you quite all right?" Sarah's concerned voice had interrupted her thoughts. "You know, there's not a day goes by that either my maid or my yard man doesn't go on an errand into town, and when you are tied up somewhere, they could even bring your Erin back and forth from school. Or we have several cars, and she could borrow one to drive herself. She is a senior, you said, so she surely drives, and I'm sure we could get permission for her to remain at her same school.''

"I—yes," Kate had managed, blinking back tears that matted her eyelashes. At this point in her life, she'd given up crying over common cruelties, but moments of quiet kindness moved her deeply. "I'll talk to her about your generous offer, Mrs. Denbigh. And I can't thank you enough."

And now she'd never be able to thank Sarah enough, Kate thought as she kept working. For good or ill, gardening was always her best thinking time, and it made her miss Sarah, and her mother, fiercely.

She forced her mind to the tasks at hand. Besides using mulch to hill up the roots, she decided, she'd cover the beds with fir branches, too. A harsh winter was predicted, and the winds off Lake Erie could shake the roots loose if all of these were not properly pruned. Trying to calm herself, Kate cut and tossed and cut again, ignoring thorns and snags.

In the distance the buzz of Jeff's hedge trimmers stopped. He was not actually trimming, but was cleaning and oiling his various pieces of equipment. She'd rather liked the white noise of his machines. Today, her favorite classical music on her transistor made her think and grieve too much; it was as if even recorded music conspired against her.

She worked with a will, making sharp cuts on a slight slant to open the center of each bush to sun and air next spring. Bending to turn her radio off again when Jeff restarted his electric trimmers, she moved from the Chinas to the *Belle de Crecy* bush that would produce the most exquisite mix of cerise, violet and lilac-gray hues Sarah loved—had loved—so dearly.

Even through her earphones she heard Jeff come closer. Was he trimming, too, she wondered as she straightened and turned with her arms full of thorny canes. She gasped to see Varina hacking with the electric trimmer through the precious heirloom bushes at the other end of this long bed.

"Varina! Stop it!" Kate shouted. "Those are— were—your mother's roses, too!"

Varina merely glanced up, then plunged on. The fierce whine of the long trimmers with its moving blades drowned her out.

Yanking off her headphones with one hand, Kate ran toward Varina and, suddenly wary of getting too close to the woman when she had that determined, almost demented look on her face, threw an armful of cut canes at the trimmers.

Varina swung around with the electric tool, arced it once in the air toward Kate as if to hold her off, then bent to rip through the next Bourbon bush.

"Stop it, Varina!" Kate repeated, hoping the woman could hear her at closer range. "They were her roses, too!"

Again, Varina swung the heavy trimmers. Kate jumped back, and the tool thudded to the ground. Thank God, its blades stopped when Varina lost control. The moment Varina lunged to retrieve it, Kate tried to yank the cord, but there was too much slack to kill the electricity. It restarted in Varina's hands.

"I saw you trimming!" Varina shrieked. "I'm

helping! I'm showing I care about her roses, too, damn you!''

When Kate tried to dart behind her, Varina swept the trimmers at her again. The end snagged Kate's garden glove and ripped it off to shred the thick material. Crimson anger flooded her. She wanted to run for help, but refused to leave the plants to this—this butcher.

Kate strode to the main sprinkler control and yanked it on. Why didn't someone come out here and stop this woman? Who knows what Varina would do to these bushes. Could she get a restraining order on Varina to protect roses?

The extensive sprinkler system came on full force, spraying both women, as Kate charged back. She picked up her rake and shoved the metal tines in the blades of the trimmer. It jammed and jerked from Varina's hands. Too late, Kate realized the mix of water and electricity could have electrocuted them both.

Soaked, flailing, sobbing, Varina threw herself at Kate. Varina's weight took them to the ground. Kate rolled, heaved her off, and squirmed away. Varina lunged again, pinning Kate down until the woman's weight suddenly lifted away. A tall, dark-haired man Kate did not know held Varina upright with her arms pinned to her sides and her feet off the ground. Pushing her to her knees on the wet grass, he grabbed the long extension cord, yanked it to get slack, and firmly wrapped it three times around the struggling woman. Before he could help Kate up, she scrambled to her feet and ran to turn off the water and pull the plug.

Shoving her shirttails back into her soaked jeans, Kate headed toward him and his sputtering prisoner.

She knew she looked a mess; she pulled leaves and mulch from her hair and wiped mud off her face. What made matters worse was how good the man looked, even with water dripping off his nose, chin and earlobes.

His sodden shirt stuck to his broad shoulders and chest; stretched against strong thighs, his jeans bore big water blotches. At least he wore beat-up running shoes. Though she was tall at five foot eight, he towered a good six inches over her. His black hair, which was probably quite thick ordinarily, lay plastered on his brown forehead until a big hand shoved it back. Cocked at a devilish angle, thick eyebrows slashed above deep-set, dark blue eyes. His face seemed all planes and angles, and white crow's feet perched at the corners of his eyes, indicating he didn't wear sunglasses.

"I'm sorry that happened, but glad you came along," Kate told him, awkwardly wiping her palms on the hips of her jeans. He was looking her over with the same intensity that she had him. Their gazes, both nervous, snagged and held. She felt the impact of that down to the pit of her stomach.

"I glanced out the master suite windows and saw her go nuts with the trimmer," he explained. His voice had a rough timbre to it that fitted his rugged, square-jawed face.

"The master suite?" Kate said. "Oh, you're in forensics, working with detectives Rudzinski and Martin?"

"I'm Jack Kilcourse, an antique furniture expertiser specializing in Shaker. There was supposed to be a cop right outside my door, but I guess he took a break, or I would have sent him. You want this woman arrested for assault and battery?''

Kate was shocked that this stranger had almost made her forget Varina. ''No, though if you'd back me up on how she acted, I'll probably try to get her barred from these gardens. Pity, too, as her mother loved them so much, and she's just defaced about a quarter of them,'' she said, addressing Varina now instead of Jack Kilcourse. ''Pruning or trimming's one thing, but a chainsaw massacre's another.''

Jack unwrapped Varina and tried to help her stand, but she shook him off and scrambled up on her own. ''I don't care what it takes,'' Varina muttered, glaring at Kate. ''I'll get the things she meant to leave to me. And don't you show your face at my mother's funeral tomorrow!'' she cried as she backed away a few steps, her eyes darting once to Jack before she turned to hurry off.

''You sure you're okay?'' Jack asked Kate. ''You look—dizzy.''

''I probably look worse than that,'' she admitted, bending to pull the rake from between the hedge trimmer's teeth. She shoved her wet hair back from her eyes. ''I'm Kate Marburn, Mrs. Denbigh's rosarian,'' she told him as she straightened.

''Oh, right,'' he said, as if he either finally recognized her name or face. But with a hint of a smile, he extended his hand. Clean compared to hers, it was huge, callused, and so warm despite the quickening chill breeze that she clung a moment too long.

''Actually, Mrs. Denbigh left her Shaker collection to me, but the will is—obviously—being contested,'' Kate explained. ''I love her Shaker furniture,'' she added. She glanced toward the house, then riveted her eyes back on his piercing blue ones. "Shaker furniture is so lean yet strong and handsome..."

Her voice trailed off. She looked away from him and felt herself begin to blush. Of all the stupid, adolescent things. Why, when she knew better than to trust any man, was she confiding so much to this one?

"Again, I'm grateful for your help with—against Varina," she said as she started back for the guest house where she'd begun packing earlier today. Right now, she just couldn't face this man's scrutiny, nor the ruined roses. But as dangerously as Varina was acting, Kate was still going to Sarah's funeral tomorrow.

After the funeral in the church, people stared at Kate Marburn from the moment she got out of her car at Woodlawn Cemetery. Head high and shoulders back, she looked straight past the bereaved family, friends, television people and watchful police.

The western sky glared gun-barrel gray in contrast to the overhead sun that shot through the vibrant leaves of the gnarled beech guarding the burial site. But even larger loomed the gaping hole in the earth that would soon swallow Sarah Denbigh's coffin. The family plot where Sarah would be buried next to her husband lay in the shadow of the historic Denbigh mausoleum, which stood over the site like a massive tombstone. Beyond the grave, the sweep of lawns set with regularly spaced statues, pyramids and urns made the cemetery seem one giant chessboard.

Again, as so often, Kate's love for Sarah and her sense of loss over the older woman's death summoned a memory of her mother. Kate was holding her daddy's hand, standing at an open hole in the ground that looked so large. And they were putting Mommy in it in a pretty box and placing flowers all around the hole, not planting them but leaving them to die in the sun—and Kate didn't like that. She wanted to save each one, to put each in water the way she and Mommy had. And now she had lost Sarah, too....

"'Let not your heart be troubled,'" the minister began.

Heads turned toward the coffin again. Despite herself, Kate quickly scanned the crowd for the tall, dark-haired Jack Kilcourse. But then, why should he come to this?

"'In my Father's house are many mansions...'"

Kate frowned at the green plastic turf that stretched to the brink of the grave. That shiny rug, the hump of pink carnations and the ornate metal casket were all wrong. Sarah would have wanted a simple spray of her favorite antique roses on a plain, wooden coffin, lovingly handcrafted like a piece of fine Shaker furniture.

The stiff, gilt banner flared over the carnations pompously proclaimed, OUR BELOVED AND CHERISHED MOTHER. FROM YOUR VARINA AND PALMER. The ribbon tail with their names kept rapping against the top of the casket, as if Sarah were knocking to get out.

A shudder racked Kate. She couldn't bear for Sarah to be placed in a concrete vault in the deep grave. Sarah had loved to be outdoors under the vast sweep of sky.

"'If it were not so, I would have told you...'"

The two crimson Damask roses nearly vibrating in her grasp, Kate strode closer through the crowd. Sarah had filled the aching void in her life, just the way Kate had tried to fill poor, angry Erin's. And Mike's desertion of his daughter had brought back the fury Erin harbored over what—to a young child—looked like a mother's desertion.

"'I go to prepare a place for you...'"

Except for leaving her stepdaughter alone, Kate would gladly have died for Sarah, but no one evidently believed or understood that. Not when Sarah had been the uncrowned patron saint of the city and Kate the most notorious woman in it.

"'...that where I am, there you may be also.'"

Varina's stare stabbed at Kate from across the bowed heads, as the pastor began a prayer. Kate closed her eyes to shut out that fierce face and, next to it, that of the younger Palmer. Kate was so angry at both of them that she'd like to plant them in that hole in the ground. Yet Varina had known loss, too. And grief, no doubt, took different guises.

"'And now to Him who is able to keep you from falling, and to present you faultless...'"

Kate caught sight of Stan Rudzinski, hunched in a black trench coat against a large tree trunk, looking her way, too. Did he lift his eyebrows as if to ask another question, or was she imagining that, imagining all sorts of things again?

"'...now and forever.' Amen."

When people began to bid farewell to the Denbigh family, Kate moved around the back of the casket under the green canvas canopy. Despite the fact that she saw Palmer striding her way, she thrust the two fragrant Damask blooms, the last roses of summer, atop the heap of cloying carnations.

"In other words," Palmer said, "you want to make

a public statement we should have bought her roses? You know, somehow, that just doesn't set real well with Varina right now.''

Kate turned slowly to face him. "And who cares what Sarah's wishes would have been about it—about anything, right?'' she challenged before she could take the words back. "You were welcome to every single rose in her vast gardens, Palmer. But as you must know she hated the smell of carnations.''

He flushed right through his tan and could not meet her eyes.

"You're not making decisions for her anymore,'' he muttered, fingering the loose ribbon on the casket.

"And never was. You surely knew Sarah Denbigh too well to believe that.''

Yet, as if he were ten years old instead of thirty, he plucked her two flowers from the casket and dropped them back among the other arrangements clustered around. She felt some satisfaction when she saw he'd stuck his fingers with the prominent thorns.

"Is there a problem here?'' Detective Rudzinski said, stepping up to them. Kate had learned he'd recently been promoted to Homicide and was aching to make good, especially with this high-profile case. She felt adept at psyching out investigators, and this one scared her. He was out to make his own name, not save hers.

"I can't believe you'd show your face here after I told you to stay away,'' Varina accused under her breath as she emerged from the crowd. She wedged herself in to shut out the men and face Kate on her own.

"I came to honor a woman I deeply admired, who opened her life and home to me,'' Kate said, keeping her voice in check, as others looked their way and shuffled closer. "She was unique and wonderful. There is none—*none* like her," she said directly to Varina, then moved quickly away.

The buzz began again as Kate strode from the graveside. She heard the whir of the TV cameras even before Mandy Ross, one of the city's all-too-familiar top reporters, stuck a mike in her face and asked, "How are you answering the Denbigh family's charges, Mrs. Marburn? How—"

"The same way I answered the other false ones you people continue to resurrect and revel in. No comment."

Kate shouldered past the woman and picked up her pace. The reporter wore high heels, which bogged her down in the thick turf. She also had to drag her mike and cameraman with her. Kate had reached her car when a well-attired couple stepped swiftly forward, as if they'd been waiting for her. Some of Sarah's friends? She didn't recognize them.

"Mrs. Marburn, one moment please," the silver-haired man, older than the woman, called to her as they stayed politely a short distance away.

"I'm sorry. As you can see, I'm in a hurry."

"We're Dane and Adrienne Thompson, Board of Trustee members from Shaker Run. Mrs. Denbigh loaned us so much of her fine furniture," the man explained hastily.

Despite the way the television people were closing on her—another reporter from a competing network had appeared with a big mike on a handheld boom—Kate opened her car door but did not get in. "Shaker Run meant a lot to Sarah. How kind of you to come clear up from southern Ohio. I visited your village with her last winter.'' She remembered these people now; Sarah had spoken with them about where particular pieces of her loaned furniture might be placed in various buildings.

"We'd like to call on you, if that's all right," Adrienne said. "A bit of business, yes?" She was sleek and svelte-looking with a faint French accent; she sounded and looked completely out of place here, let alone how she'd look in a simple Shaker village, tourist attraction or not.

"I'm leaving the guest house at Groveland," Kate explained hastily as she got in, slammed the door, but cracked the window open. Just then, Mandy Ross appeared and thrust the microphone in, while her cameraman shot Kate through the glass. The other station's boom mike swooped before the front windshield like a bat. She'd be damned if she was going to give her new address only to have it recorded for the six-o'clock news, Kate thought.

"I'll just phone you at the village later," she promised the Thompsons. She rolled her window up, turned the ignition key and hit the gas pedal. The boom mike bumped away. Too late, Kate realized she'd caught Mandy's microphone in her window. In the rearview mirror, she gasped to see the cord snag the reporter's lapel mike from her suit, ripping her jacket open to reveal a white flash of bra and flesh.

Though Kate's life was in public ruins for the second time in two years, she laughed until the tears ran down her face, then dissolved in sobs so wrenching she had to pull over to the curb on a side street outside the cemetery. Finally, when she could calm herself, she heaved the mike out the passenger window into the gutter.

As she wiped her eyes and cheeks, she smelled on her hands the clinging scent of the Damasks she'd brought for the grave. And somehow she felt stronger and surer than she had since she'd found Sarah lying last week in that blooming pool of crimson blood.

"The new place is a cute little apartment with no view like this, but I got almost everything in it," Kate assured Erin over the phone, trying to sound perky.

"But you hate little places," Erin protested.

The day after Sarah's funeral, Kate had worked all morning to repair the rosebushes Varina had damaged; then she'd called her stepdaughter. Though Kate was ready to leave the guest house with her last carload of belongings, she had wanted to talk to Erin once more from this shelter where they'd tried to reconstruct their lives. Kate gave Erin their new home phone number and the address of the upstairs apartment in the big, old house she was renting from Sarah's maid's sister.

"No, really, this is fine," she told the girl. "I only needed to lease a small storage space for my bigger garden tools, not to mention those boxes of my rose books and my old client files, in case I ever try to get back into business."

There was a moment's silence between them. *But not in Toledo,* both of them thought but didn't say.

"With all the stuff we sold at the auction, I should hope you'd get most of it in," Erin said, picking up the conversation with a slight scolding tone, as if she were the parent now. "But even if Mrs. Denbigh left you that job, roses and furniture, do you really want to stay around Toledo, waiting for her will to clear?

Especially if Varina and Palmer are contesting it and trying to blame you?''

"If I go somewhere else, it may look like I'm running—and I can't stand that.''

"Can't stand what he did or just plain can't stand him anymore?'' Erin demanded, as if Kate had mentioned Mike.

She was shocked at the quick switch to Erin's strident tone.

"Never mind,'' the girl went on, calmer now. "Don't answer that. But the thing is, it's pretty neat to be away—to just be yourself and be free.''

To be yourself and be free, Kate thought. Yes, she'd always wanted that, and now it was being threatened again. She wasn't going to let that happen.

"Sweetheart, as much as I'd like to go away to college in a pretty, small town on the edge of the Appalachians,'' Kate said, describing Athens, where Ohio University nestled in the southern Ohio hills, "unlike you, I don't have anywhere to go. But as I said, I'll be down to see you as soon as I get resettled.''

After they said goodbye, Kate picked up her last packed box and glanced around at the guest house living area for the last time. But the phone rang again. Erin calling back? Her lawyer with more advice? Or Stan Rudzinski wanting another interview?

Putting the box back down, she glared at the phone, then snatched it up. "Kate Marburn.''

"Mrs. Marburn, it's Dane Thompson.''

The man from the Shaker village who had tried to talk to her yesterday at the funeral, Kate thought. She could hear the woman's lighter tones in the background, as if prompting him what to say. Behind all that was some sort of echoing buzz, maybe voices in a big room.

"You see," Dane went on, speaking quickly as if she'd hang up, "we're still in town and just took a chance you might not have left this number yet. We called Mrs. Denbigh's old number, and her maid gave us yours."

"I'm just on my way out the door—permanently, I'm afraid," Kate explained patiently. She could hear the muted, lilting, foreign voice of Adrienne again, as if Dane had partly covered the receiver with his hand. Then his voice came through clear and strong again.

"Frankly, Ms. Marburn, we have what we believe is a very attractive offer for you, one that we are certain you cannot afford to refuse."

That old threatening line from *The Godfather,* Kate thought, but she could not help being curious.

Despite her reluctance to talk to anyone about any business dealings, Kate decided to meet them. She hoped the Thompsons hadn't just read in the paper that she was to inherit the furniture currently on loan to Shaker Run and wanted to try to buy it. As she had vowed to Varina, she wasn't selling.

She agreed to talk about their offer at the Toledo Museum of Art cafeteria at four that afternoon. They knew the museum was a fine one, Dane explained, and, before heading back to southern Ohio, they'd decided to stay overnight to catch the Louis XIV touring display of *objects d'arts* from Versailles.

As Kate packed her final load in the car, she thought of Sarah again, and glanced at the Groveland mansion through the vibrant autumn trees. "Versailles on the Maumee," she whispered. She gazed at the tall, shining windows of Sarah's suite and wondered if Jack Kilcourse was still examining its fine furnishings.

Strangely, unbelievably, for she considered herself quite realistic and unromantic now, her stomach cartwheeled at the mere memory of the man. Shaking her head, Kate got in her car and drove away.

5

Rose leaves, when the rose is dead,
Are heaped for the beloved's bed;
And so thy thoughts, when thou are gone,
Love itself shall slumber on.
                    —Percy Bysshe Shelley
              "Music When Soft Voices Die"

Within the hour, Kate had changed clothes, and had driven to the marble, pillared, three-block museum. The graceful, Greek-style building had been donated to the city long ago by Edward Drummond Libbey, one of the glass barons who had made a turn-of-the-last-century fortune in Toledo. As she went in the back entrance, the interior felt cool. Her footsteps echoed even through the hum of distant voices.

Kate shook hands with the Thompsons as they indicated a table in the corner. While the women commiserated over Sarah's death, Dane left momentarily to get coffee and carrot cake for everyone.

When he returned, he quickly steered their conversation to business. "Since you've visited Shaker Run Village before and understand we are in the process of building it up to become not only a tourist attraction but an authentic piece of living history, let me get right to the point," Dane said. "Shaker Run is expanding its meager staff, and we need a rosarian to design, plant and maintain our flower beds and extensive future rose gardens—with the two, old-time roses the Shakers allowed, of course.''

That piqued Kate's interest immediately. A job away from here with a garden, antique roses...

''The two Shaker breeds would be the *Rosa Gallica Officinalis,* sometimes called 'Apothecary rose,' and a summer Damask,'' Kate said, recalling what she'd learned at the village during her visit. She gripped her coffee cup harder. ''Each rose has one big annual flowering, but the bounty of dried petals is a treasure that lasts all year long.''

''Precisely,'' Dane agreed with a nod, while Adrienne leaned toward him, apparently hanging on his every word. ''We would hope you could distill that famous Shaker rose water for the village to sell. That is, if you would consider accepting the position.''

It was a dream job, but Kate felt honor-bound to stay here to care for Sarah's roses—if she got the chance. Varina and Palmer's contesting the will could delay its bestowments to her or cancel them entirely. Besides, Sarah had wanted both Shaker Run and Groveland to prosper.

''And,'' Adrienne added, ''we'd like you to work closely with the part-time herbalist we have hired, yes?''

Not to mention the fact, Kate thought excitedly, that the Ohio University campus and Erin were just twenty miles from Shaker Run, instead of the nearly two hundred from Toledo! Kate bit her lower lip to keep from blurting out that she'd kill for such a job—though she dare not put it that way.

''We can discuss salary, of course, if you'd be willing to drive down to meet the others on the Board and the staff,'' Dane explained, shifting his feet under their small table where Kate had curled her toes so hard in excitement they almost cramped. ''We'd like to share our vision with you about the future of Shaker Run—a vision...'' he repeated, gazing toward the ceiling. ''Now that's a good way to put it, as the Shakers were so attuned to their visions from angels and those who had gone on to their rewards.''

His last words snagged in Kate's mind. She knew the Shakers were unusual, but obviously needed to know more. Imagine a life and place where people put stock in visions, angels and visits from the dead. And if they believed in angels, did they believe in demons, too?

''*Mon amour,* the apartment...'' Adrienne prompted her husband in the slight lull that followed.

''Oh, yes,'' he said, his voice steady again. ''Our offer to you would include spacious living quarters above the Trustees' Office, at least until you find some other place if you'd like. I'm sure it isn't quite up to Mrs. Denbigh's guest house and grounds, but it's—forgive me for putting it this way—but we believe it's a fertile opportunity for a woman with your interests and talents.''

''Your offer sounds wonderful,'' Kate admitted, still agonizing over whether to leave what Sarah had entrusted to her here. ''If I accept—and I repeat *if*— I could transplant my own bushes. The village wouldn't even have to purchase starts as most of mine are much more mature, and I could propagate others this winter.''

''How splendid,'' Adrienne said, beaming with apparent relief. ''Dane, isn't that splendid that she will consider it? I'm sure Mrs. Denbigh would approve, my dear," she said, addressing Kate directly at last, "for she obviously favored our cause."

"If you can assemble the board and staff, I'll come down this week," Kate promised, smiling at the thought of a new career she would love—and one near Erin.

"Didn't your mother ever tell you that if an offer seems too good to be true, it probably is?" Detective Rudzinski demanded, when she explained the job offer to him the next day. They were sitting in the small living area of Kate's newly rented apartment. Kate hadn't wanted Rudzinski here, but neither had she wanted to, as he put it, "make it a formal foursome with Tina Martin and her lawyer in his office."

"Look, Detective, I lost my mother when I was young and hardly remember a thing she said," Kate blurted, though she hadn't meant to share that with him. She knew her voice was too strident again, but he was really beginning to annoy her. "I know," she went on, trying to keep calm, "you didn't mean anything by the remark, but you can't understand how her loss still haunts me."

"Actually, I can. Someone shot my dad dead when he went out for a bottle of milk for us kids when I was five, and I can't recall one damn thing about him but his dedication to his job."

He looked away before going on. "He was away a lot on his job as a street cop who walked a beat for years." He heaved a huge sigh. "Then a stray bullet hits him 'cause a dairy store's getting robbed for a few bucks the week before Christmas."

"I'm sorry," she faltered, leaning slightly forward.

"I see." She really did see. That explained a lot about this man's doggedness.

"And here I thought you were dedicated to Mrs. Denbigh's gardens," he went on, obviously as eager as she to change the subject.

"I haven't decided to take the offer," she repeated. "I'm just exploring possibilities."

"You sound pretty excited about it to me."

"If the new will wasn't as frozen as the ground soon will be," Kate told him, gripping her hands in her lap, "I might wait it out here, hoping to get to care for Sarah's—hers and my—roses. But, as is, it might be years before I see that job her will leaves me."

"I'd stick around if I were you," he observed, throwing one arm along the back of the short sofa as if they had all the time in the world. "Why risk the windfall of a lifetime by taking off where you can't keep an eye on Varina—who, I think, ought to be darn grateful you didn't hit her with assault with a deadly weapon for her attack on you in the rose garden."

"The thing is," Kate admitted, not wanting to re-open their mutual wound of losing a parent, "I like to think that she is grieving her mother's loss and has just...well..."

"Lost it?" he put in. "You know, you and Varina seem like night and day, Kate, but maybe you're a woman who likes taking risks, too."

She noted he'd used her first name. If he thought he was going to pretend to get friendly with her, he could forget that ploy.

"You stand to be a rich woman if a judge rules this new will is valid," he pursued.

"Rich only if I'd sell the Shaker heritage, which I won't."

"Maybe these people at Shaker Run think you will—sell to them—or better yet, donate the furniture."

"It's not mine to donate, and I can't live my life in limbo, Detective, waiting for some judge's ruling or Varina's next lawsuit. My stepdaughter goes to college near Shaker Run, and, frankly, I could use the change of scenery. And I think—I pray—Sarah would understand. You aren't going to tell me I'm not free to go, are you, even to the interview?" she challenged.

"Why would you think that?" he parried, drumming his fingers on the back of the sofa. "Though, if you really do move down there, I just might have to learn a bit more about the Shakers with a visit or two."

Kate just stared at him. Surely he wasn't implying a personal visit. "Looks like cause of death will be ruled accidental," he went on, "though I don't know if that satisfies me. Does it you?"

"I think we've both said enough today," she countered. "Why don't you just continue this little conversation with my lawyer? I thought you had something to tell me, not that you wanted me to tell you all sorts of things again."

"You know, if I did visit you there, though," he went on as if he hadn't heard her, "I'd also drop in on that furniture expertiser we hired who lives near there. The guy even makes Shaker reproductions."

"Jack Kilcourse?"

"He said you'd met. Gave me a blow-by-blow of your encounter with Sarah's daughter."

Kate nodded grimly, then said, "You evidently had gone AWOL, and Mr. Kilcourse was kind enough to help me hold off Valkyrie Varina."

Rudzinski laughed. "She is hell on wheels and makes no bones about her feelings, which is why I just can't believe she's really a possible perp in her mother's demise. Can you?" he asked, suddenly leaning forward, his chin propped in his hands and his elbows on his knees.

"You never give up, do you, Detective? You're implying Varina would be more subtle if she were guilty?"

"Don't you agree? She's a hothead but not an idiot. She'd back off a bit from seeming to want control of the Shaker furniture and the fortune behind it. She wouldn't publicly assault someone near the site of her mother's death, however much she blames that person *for* her mother's death."

Again Kate's hackles rose; she stared Rudzinski down. He was right, but he was also much more devious than she'd given him credit for. And he obviously still considered her a—or *the*—prime suspect in Sarah's death. She sat up even straighter. If Sarah had been murdered, Kate might need this man's help to be sure the killer was brought to justice, but she trusted "Zink" less than she did other men—and that was not at all.

"I believe I've proved by now that I don't run from something—even the mere appearance of something—I am not guilty of," Kate said coolly as she stood. "But I do believe in running toward something good, and that's why I am going to seriously consider this job. Now if you'll excuse me..."

She marched across the room to open the door for

him. He went jauntily down the stairs, but he dared to call back over his shoulder, "Guess I'll have to tell you about the blood splatter evidence later. Best of luck with the interview for the great escape."

Though Kate supposed it seemed a crazy thing to do, she planned to talk to Sarah—that is, to visit her grave to say the solemn farewell she had not been able to say at the funeral. Before even going for the interview at Shaker Run, she was considering taking the job.

Kate decided to go to the cemetery in the early morning when no one else would be around. The last thing in the world she needed was to face Varina or Palmer at their mother's grave. But she'd miscalculated the opening time, and only the walk-through gate was open; the large, front Central Avenue gate accessible to cars was locked. She parked her car just outside, and went in the small entrance that evidently served the caretaker's nearby house. The gate's iron hinges screeched in protest.

Kate had brought two more roses with her, mere buds caught in the plunging temperatures she'd picked before she'd left Groveland. Perhaps they wouldn't even open, but Sarah would understand. New possibilities, ready to bloom but still a bit unknown.

Woodlawn was the grand old cemetery of the city. Kate had always admired the beauty of its mature trees and overall landscaping. Yet it seemed a heavy place, burdened with the weight of massive monuments to great Toledo families such as the Libbeys, DeVilbisses, Talmadges, Berdans and, of course, the Denbighs.

Though she hadn't seen it on the streets, a morning mist still hung here and the grass was damp with dew. She stuck to the main, curving entry road that passed the section on the right belonging to the Romany community of local gypsies. Several of the monuments were benches, for they often visited and communed with their dead, even picnicking there in celebration of their free-spirited, wandering lives. Right now, that struck Kate as appropriate and moving.

She took a turn to the left and walked over the bridge that spanned the narrow lake, for the Denbigh plot wasn't much farther in. The old crematorium sat near here. Kate shuddered in the morning chill as she cut up across the silvered grass, walking between stones and crypts under the thickening canopy of autumn beeches. The deeper she went, the thicker the drifting patches of faint fog.

Without people pressing in around it under the canvas canopy, Sarah's grave looked different. It was barren but for decaying carnations heaped, wilting and dying, on the replanted turf over her resting place. Kate closed her eyes to envision it abloom with heirloom Chinas, Gallicas and Bourbons. She would think of it that way—that Sarah simply slept under a beautiful blanket of roses and in the memory of those who truly loved her.

"Sarah," she whispered, placing the rosebuds atop the pile, "I've had a wonderful job offer. I'd have to leave the gardens at Groveland, but I'd be tending Apothecaries and Damasks I'd take with me to Shaker Run."

She felt foolish speaking out loud, and she glanced nervously around. The sounds of traffic were but a dull buzz. If it were warmer, she would have sat right here with her thoughts for a while. And then she saw that the door to the Denbigh private family mausoleum stood wide open.

It hadn't been open the day of the funeral, she was sure of it. And even if the family had been in there, or the caretaker, surely it would not have been open overnight. The cemetery hadn't had vandals that she'd heard of, but in this day and age, you never knew.

Thinking she would slam the door shut, Kate started around the grave for the mausoleum. She gasped to see a trail of rose heads, leading toward the stained and moss-covered stone building. It stood twice as tall as she and, like other monuments here, was built in a classical style. As she approached, a musty smell exhaled from its dark, gaping mouth.

She reached out with both hands to close the iron door. The lock had been broken, or at least neatly cut off. Then it must be vandals. She hoped things weren't defaced inside, but either way she should report it to the caretaker.

Instead of closing the door, she peered around it. No way she was stepping into the small interior to be sure everything looked all right. From here, the crypts in the wall looked undisturbed, though she saw someone had scattered rose petals on the floor. Varina or Palmer? But roses? And why break the lock?

Kate frowned as she studied the crimson rose petals in the wan light. No, not petals or full flowers but entire buds, just like the ones behind her. Quickly, she counted those inside the mausoleum and out. Twelve. Someone had evidently bought a dozen flower-shop roses, decapitated them, and thrown only their heads both on Sarah's grave and in here.

Kate was moving to close the door, when she heard

a muted slam. She jumped back, thinking it was a sound from inside. But it must have just echoed here against the building.

She spun around to see an old, black car had pulled up near the crematorium on the lane. A man had gotten out and evidently had slammed the car door. Wearing an unbelted, dark trench coat, his head and face covered by an old-fashioned fedora, he stood, bushes and monuments between them, just staring at her. Hunching his shoulders, he reached a gloved hand to tug the brim lower over his face.

She knew instantly it was not the caretaker. Was there something vaguely familiar about him? She wasn't sure—perhaps the set of the head or the way he raised his hand.

At least the gates must be open now, and others would be coming in. Squinting to see better at this distance, she began to walk toward him, around tombstones and trees.

For one moment she thought it might be Palmer. She couldn't imagine him in a hat like that, but then, who did wear those anymore?

"Hello," she called to him. "Is there a problem? Are you looking for a particular grave?" When he didn't answer, she added, "I was just going to get the caretaker." She hesitated, then stopped when he did not respond or move. "Who are you?" she demanded.

In reply, he opened his car door and got in. Kate wasn't certain, but she thought someone might be in the front passenger seat. She couldn't see inside because the car's window reflected sky and trees. She heard the engine rev. As the vehicle pulled away, she ran, hoping to catch a glimpse inside or at least get the license plate, but she saw now the windows were all tinted and there was no plate.

"People are so damn weird!" she muttered, and stopped running. After glancing back at the now distant Denbigh plot, she set a good pace toward the caretaker's cottage. Someone was going to have to fix that lock, and she was not going to phone Varina to tell her it needed repair. She even considered just leaving and calling the caretaker anonymously. She cut down the narrow, gravel lane off the main paved one, because it led more directly to her car. Walking briskly, she was soon perspiring and out of breath.

And then she heard a car behind her. She spun to squint into the rising sun. Crunching stones under its tires, the same antique, black vehicle—from the 30s or 40s?—was creeping much slower than the posted speed limit signs suggested. Kate glanced back over her shoulder, then moved to the berm and glared at it. For one instant she was certain two people were in the car, but the dark windshield obscured forms and faces.

It kept coming, edging over to this side of the lane, right at her. The front of it was studded with fancy metal grillwork, which seemed stuck in a toothy grin. Kate froze in disbelief and shock. The car windows were one giant mirror; she could see her own slightly distorted reflection in the dark glass.

Just before the car got to her, Kate cut up among the tombstones again. As though it could chase her through them, the vehicle sped up and barreled by on the lane, coming to a screeching halt a ways past. Was someone demented playing games with her? Down the lane, she saw the car slowly turn around in a crossroad and creep back.

Cutting deeper into the cemetery section, Kate broke into a run. She saw she'd have to skirt the far edge of the lake. At least she was nearly to the iron fence that ran along Central Avenue, and it was full of morning rush traffic. But she saw the black car along this outer loop of road, waiting, hulking down as if ready to spring when she crossed to the gate or caretaker's house.

She tore back up into the stones, darting around tall urns and crypts, then crouched to see what the car would do next. If it would just go by, she'd dash across the road.

"You'll be all right," she encouraged herself aloud, panting. "It's just some jerk harassing a woman he doesn't even know."

The car edged along the outer road, keeping pace with her, so easily, so smoothly, as if trying to wear her down. She ducked behind an angel monument and peeked out. The car stopped, its engine humming. She'd turn to go the other way. Even if it backed up, it would never get to her if she ran hard.

Huddled under the white marble angel, Kate sucked in two deep breaths. But when she stood and turned to run, the angel came to life before her, around her, all fanned white wings and shimmering robe, lifting, whirling, flapping. Something screeched at her and hit her, bringing pain and night.

6

When I am dead, my dearest,
Sing no sad songs for me;
Plant thou no roses at my head,
Nor shady cypress tree.
Be the green grass above me
With showers, and dewdrops wet;
And if thou wilt, remember
And if thou wilt, forget.

—Christina Georgina Rossetti
"Song"

"Hey, lady, you okay?" a man's voice asked. "You musta fell and hit your head."

Kate eyes flew open. She saw a burly, bearded man in jeans and a green sweatshirt squatting beside her. Despite her pounding headache, she was relieved he did not wear a black raincoat and fedora. Or had she dreamed the man and that black car after she hit her head?

Staring upward, Kate saw a stone angel, and beyond that the branches of an evergreen or cypress. The angel, at least, just hovered, unmoving now. She was in the cemetery, and this man must be a worker.

"I guess I fell and hit my head," she whispered. Had she said that a moment ago? *Sarah.* Sarah had fallen and hit her head. And died. Things were going in circles, and she was so dizzy.

"You're not supposed to be in here yet," the man said, as she struggled to sit up, then leaned back against the base of the angel. "The gates are just op'ning now."

"Then who was in that black car?" she asked, tentatively fingering her painful head bruise.

"Didn't see no black car. Nobody'd get in with the front gates locked, 'less they drove in the service entrance way at the back, and hardly nobody knows about that. The caretaker who lives on the grounds there—" he said with a nod in that direction, "drives a red van."

"It was a black car with tinted windows!"

"Can't help you, lady, but I can go get a car to take you to a hospital if you want that head bump looked at. It's gonna be a big one. Gotta watch out for concussions and all that."

Kate's mind darted after answers and kept hitting dead ends. She had seen a man in a car, and he had followed her and even tried to hit her. And then she'd hidden behind this angel monument and turned to run—

"Didn't you hear a screech of brakes a while ago? I'm not sure when but..." Her voice trailed off as the vision of that avenging angel swooping down replayed itself in her mind.

"The only screech I heard was that last white peacock we got on the grounds. You get near, she'll fan that tail and shriek like a banshee. Might even fly right at you. Rich folks in Europe used them for watchdogs on their estates," he explained importantly. "We had two of 'em 'fore one got kilt. But its mate was a coupla monuments away when I seen you. Let me just help you down to the caretaker's place—but he's not gonna be too pleased you trespassed on the grounds 'fore opening time.''

Big deal, Kate thought. That couldn't hold a candle to the other accusations she'd faced. ''All right,'' she said, getting to her feet with his hand on her elbow. ''I have to report a broken lock on the Denbigh mausoleum, anyway.''

''Denbigh? I knew I recognized you!'' the man cried.

His faced crushed in a frown, he folded his arms over his chest as if she'd insulted him. It was the same old story, and Kate was sick of it. She refused to let anyone drag her down as Mike had. Nor would she be cowed by the fact that she had, at least temporarily, lost the right to oversee the Denbigh gardens, or was probably under suspicion for Sarah's death.

At that moment, staring back at the angel she had hallucinated had come to life to attack her, Kate decided she would take that dream job at Shaker Run.

Two days later, on a crisp, sunny afternoon, Kate got out of her car in front of the Trustees' Office at Shaker Run Village and looked around at the panorama. She was so excited and on edge that she hadn't had to fight exhaustion while driving. Her insomnia had been in full bloom these past few years, and she'd often had to roll down her windows, sing and shout on long drives, to avoid falling asleep at the wheel. And ever since her visit to Sarah's grave she'd been glancing over her shoulder and in the rearview mirror to be certain she wasn't being followed. But not today.

She sucked in a fresh, free breath of air. The lawns and fields of this plateau stretched to the forests and foothills of the Appalachians. As it cut through the village, the stream that gave the place its name sparkled in the sun. No wonder some people had sought refuge here as the nineteenth century approached. It felt safe even on the edge of the new millennium.

Kate surveyed the neat wood frame and sturdy stone buildings of the 1820s-era dwellings, workshops and outbuildings. The village had once encompassed more than two thousand acres and had supported more than four hundred of The United Society of Believers in Christ's Second Appearing. That second appearing, they believed, had been the birth and ministry of their illiterate, immigrant founder, Ann Lee.

The Shakers, as they were more commonly called for their wild, trembling dances of worship, renounced sex and marriage. In their striving to create a celibate heaven on earth, they had increased their numbers only through converts. Under the philosophy set forth by ''Mother'' Ann, they farmed and traded with the outside world. A booming business in garden seeds, brooms, furniture and rose water helped the Shakers flourish but after the Civil War, Believers began to drift off and villages closed.

Finally, four years ago, the Thompsons had convinced some wealthy investors to finance the restoration of Shaker Run. It had only opened to tourists last spring and still had a long way to go. And, Kate thought determinedly, she and her roses could be part of that.

''I saw you drive in,'' Dane Thompson called to

her as he stepped out through what was no doubt the men's entrance of the double doors of the Trustees' Building. "Just looking around?"

"Exactly," she said, shaking his hand. "I'm seeing it through new eyes now."

"You will grow to love it dearly if you join us, I promise," he said fervently. "The outside world will never look quite the same."

"Exactly where is the perimeter of the village?" she asked.

He walked her away from the building and, despite the fact he wore no coat in the brisk breeze, began to point and explain.

"To the west, the way you came in on this Old Turnpike Road, which runs parallel to the modern highway, was the West Family Dwelling House and what used to be the school for what was called The Gathering Order."

"Where novices and new converts were prepared until they were ready to commit to the covenant," she put in.

"You have been reading up on us," he said, smiling. "We'd eventually like to buy those two buildings and their land—which are about a half-mile away—but they are owned by a very independent Shaker furniture designer who lives in the dwelling and uses the schoolhouse for his shop. Other than that holdout, all else you can see on this plateau is ours."

"What's his name—that independent builder?" she asked.

"Jack Kilcourse. Keeps to himself and has declined to join us in our efforts, though I must admit he makes some of the best, and most expensive, authentic Shaker reproductions in the world. Ah, you looked interested. Do you know the man?''

''I met him recently,'' she said, disappointed that Jack was not a part of things here, ''when he was expertising the Denbigh furniture collection in Toledo. So you were saying all these other buildings we can see belong to the village?''

''Indeed they do, though we're still in the process of restoring some. But the garden shops are ready for you and the herbalist. They're behind the Meeting House across that side lane, back toward the old burying ground and the holy ground where the Shakers sometimes worshipped outside. Why don't we go inside to meet everyone who's assembled, and I'll have someone show you those later.''

Kate walked back toward the Trustees' Building with him, admiring the neat look of the structure in which the Thompsons had promised her temporary living quarters. No one else lived here at night, so Jack would be her nearest neighbor; she found that both reassuring and alarming. But she had always wanted to live in the country, and this might be as close as she'd ever get. The Thompsons themselves lived twenty minutes away, and they'd told her that everyone else drove in from homes near Athens or up in the hills. Dane opened both doors and indicated she should enter through the one on the left.

''Here comes our newest convert,'' he called to the staff assembled at a long table in the front room. Everyone looked up from their meeting. ''And we hope and pray she'll agree to sign on the dotted line, just like in the old do-or-die covenants!''

Despite the way he'd put that, Kate felt right at home.

* * *

In addition to the Thompsons, there were four others at the table—the working staff for the place, as Dane put it. He introduced Kate to each in turn.

"This is Clint Barstow," Dane began, as a strapping man stood and leaned down the table to shake her hand with his beefy one. He pressed the flesh just a bit too hard, but she didn't wince. "Clint oversees a staff of four carpenters who do building maintenance and repairs but are also getting big-time into the Shaker reproductions we are going to start selling here when we reopen," Dane explained.

"So you have no relationship with Jack Kilcourse's work," Kate observed.

"He's a black sheep," Barstow muttered, "close to us only in the proximity of his workshop. 'Course, I guess he did put Dane and Adrienne onto you."

"Ah, yes," Dane said, glaring at Barstow as if he'd said too much. "Kilcourse isn't hostile to us, but usually isn't so helpful either. He mentioned Mrs. Denbigh had an antique rose grower who might be looking for a job."

That surprised Kate. Had Jack Kilcourse figured out all that while he was saving her from Varina, or had he wormed some information out of Rudzinski? At any rate, she owed her guardian angel two favors now.

But what really caught her notice was that Dane had lied to her, or at least misled her. Earlier he'd asked if she knew Jack, when clearly he was aware they'd met. She noted there was a slight lull before Dane said, "Of course, you realize that Adrienne and I serve as the movers and shakers here—"

Everyone laughed at his pun, though Kate sensed he'd said it before. "I act as curator, and chair the board," he went on. "And Adrienne buys for and oversees our gift shop in the Meeting House down the way. And this lovely, authentic couple are Ben and Louise Willis, volunteers—priceless ones."

"I like to think," Ben said with a little sniff, "that all true Shakers were volunteers."

It was only then, since the Willises were hatless, that Kate noted they were garbed in Shaker clothing. His big-brimmed hat sat next to his notes on the table. He wore a white, long-sleeved collarless shirt, and Louise was in a plum-hued long gown with the traditional kerchief crossed over her breasts. Her hat, a deep, tightly woven straw bonnet, hung by ribbons on her chair back. The couple were both brown-haired and nondescript-looking, somewhere in their fifties, Kate guessed. In a way, they looked as if they could be brother and sister, and not just Shaker ones.

"True," Dane was saying, though Kate had nearly forgotten what Ben Willis had said. "Anyhow, I was going to explain that the Willises are heading up a new effort to oversee some volunteer presenters."

"That is, Kate—if I might call you Kate—" Ben put in, "workers on the grounds will *become* Shakers, as it were, answer questions as the real Believers might have as they go about their daily duties, etcetera. That's done other places, such as at Jamestown and on the Mayflower, and it adds authenticity."

"As a matter of fact," Louise put in, her brown eyes flashing with purpose, "Ben and I were just going to introduce the suggestion that it would be marvelous if each of the presenters—all of us included—actually read some of the Shaker diaries—they were wonderful record keepers—and picked a person to become."

"It's a good idea," said the only woman who had

not yet been introduced, an attractive, young African American. "But no way any of us would want to do some of the things they did. It's kind of creepy, too, like becoming a dead person speaking from the grave."

"Well," Louise said, sitting up even straighter, "I certainly wouldn't look at it like that. Why do you always have to jump on other people's ideas, Tanya?"

"All right," Dane said, holding up both hands, "we'll get back to all that later. I was saving Tanya for last since she's our talented herbalist, and you'd be working most closely with her," he explained to Kate. "Tanya Dodridge, herbalist extraordinaire, meet Kate Marburn, rosarian extraordinaire."

"Come on now. Just let me show you the places that *really* count around here," her guide said.

After an hour's discussion with the Shaker Run staff—which had culminated in Adrienne's showing Kate the charming, top floor, four-room apartment and Dane again offering Kate the job—Tanya Dodridge took her outside to see the garden workshops they would share if Kate accepted. And Kate fully intended to do just that, if the financial offer Dane said they'd discuss before she left was even reasonable.

"That will be my main herb garden," Tanya explained, pointing out a bare, neatly tilled square of ground beside the Meeting House. It had obviously been planted in neat rows and sections during this past growing season. "You'll be free to put in one on the other side of the house to balance this garden and make whole hedges of rosebushes pretty much wherever you want in the village. As far as I can tell from my studies, they had them all over, even lining the lanes. I've seen a rambling remnant of them here and there on the grounds, though you'll have to pretty much keep them in lines—Shaker idea, you know.''

"So I see. It will be like an archeological excavation, finding where they used to put the bushes."

"Speaking of that, wait until you see the dig the university's going to do here," Tanya said, her expression and gestures even more animated as she pointed toward the other side of the village. "They're going to dig out an old well, and they predict they'll uncover all kinds of Shaker artifacts."

"I can't wait to look around and get going."

"I *thought* you'd take the job," Tanya said, looking not only pleased but smug. She had a habit of dramatically emphasizing certain words.

The young woman smiled often, displaying perfect teeth that made her entire face light up and lifted her sharply defined cheekbones nearly to the outer tips of her bright eyes and sleek eyebrows. Her hair was cut close to her head. She wore a floor-length denim skirt and jacket over western boots, a compromise between the Shakers and her own style, Kate surmised.

"These four buildings are the ones we'll share," Tanya explained. "I'm pretty sure they were for flower and herb work even then, though on the old maps of the village, they're labeled simply Sisters' Shops. That'll be us," she said with a raucous laugh, "two Shaker *soul* sisters, just *workin'* away."

Tanya's enthusiasm was infectious. Kate wished Tanya lived on the grounds, too, but she'd told Kate she kept the same apartment in Athens she'd lived in for her grad work. As Tanya gestured at the different garden shops, Kate noted her long, white-lacquered fingernails, an impractical luxury for any gardener. She shoved her own short fingernails into her palms, as Tanya walked her toward the cluster of buildings, still talking.

"That's the garden shop, then the herb shop, the extraction shop and the finishing shed," she recited. "The garden shop amounts to a tool and work area. Extraction is where you can distill rose water, and I plan to turn herbs to medicines—"

"Not for sale the way the Shakers used to?" Kate asked. "I know modern people are getting back into herbal cures and preventatives, but..."

"No, especially not some of the things I plan to grow, reproductions of what they *really* planted back then," Tanya admitted, her voice more clipped now. "In those days of desperate diseases, they used desperate cures—what they used to call 'heroic medicine.' Foxglove, aconite and belladonna, for example—but I'll grow the more common things, too."

"Foxglove is a curative but too much could be poison," Kate put in.

"But they knew what they were doing, and so do I. I'm even going to grow lettuce starts in these hotboxes this winter."

Kate had no idea how lettuce was used as an herb, especially a strong, "heroic" one, but she decided to ask later, since Tanya was demonstrating her composting hotbeds with their glass sashes made from small windowpanes. Authentic but antique Shaker again, Kate noted, even though other modern materials might have been better.

Kate studied the vibrant, young woman and hoped they would soon be friends. Tanya Dodridge's moods changed as swiftly as the expressions on her striking face. She was her own hotbed of emotions, ideas and opinions, Kate thought.

"As I said, straight rows, neat gardens, no weeds, no litter," Tanya explained, flinging gestures again as they walked toward the herb shop. "They had a lot of far-reaching ideas. They thought plants were nourished by what they called 'invisible forces in the air.'"

"Which shows they were way ahead of their time in realizing the importance of good aeration?" Kate asked.

"Not exactly," Tanya said, shaking her head. "I think they were referring to otherworldly beings that watched over everything. But, yeah—or *yea,* as they always said for *yes*—they were practical, too. They grew plants to be useful, not ornamental. You know, like when they picked a rose, they *never* cut the stem or leaves with it, so it could be used only for herbal cures or their precious rose water and not for worldly adornment."

Kate stopped walking at the single-doored entrance to the herb shop. The roses around Sarah's grave and on the floor of the Denbigh mausoleum had been beheaded like that—

"Do you agree with it?" Tanya demanded, turning toward Kate in the doorway.

"Not with that part of their philosophy."

"No, I mean, I thought you were staring at the sign I put up. See—?" she said, pointing a pearly fingernail.

Under drying clusters of pungent herbs hanging by little nooses was a sign lettered in old-fashioned, fancy script: *If you would have a lovely garden, you should live a lovely life.*

"Mother Ann," Tanya said, her voice almost proud. "I swear, that woman had more amazing things to say than my own mother. Come on and let me show you what else is inside, and then you'd better hustle back to tell Dane you'll take the job before he has a fit. He's like that, you know, way up and way down," she said with a roll of her eyes.

Kate wanted to ask her what she meant, but Tanya was already explaining something else.

7

In Victorian dining rooms, a rose motif on the ceilings recalled that to the Romans roses were a symbol of secrecy. To speak sub-rosa implies this since Venus dedicated her flower, the rose, to Harpocrates, the God of Silence, to conceal her sweet thefts.

—Peter Coats
Flowers in History

"Hello!" Kate called. "Anybody here?"

On her way to Athens, which was a mere twenty miles away, to see Erin, Kate had stopped at Jack Kilcourse's place. His large, vintage home and the building that had once been the Shaker schoolhouse had fieldstone foundations and timbered walls. Two of the smaller wooden buildings on the grounds looked as if they were used as a garage—the one to the far side of his house—and maybe a storehouse, since that one was closed up and even padlocked. The trim buildings sat neatly among gardens that, in contrast, were not neat. They had all gone to leggy riot, past their prime. Kate wondered if the insides of the tidy-looking house, shop, garage and storehouse were in the same chaotic state.

"Hello!" she called again, then leaned back into

the car to honk the horn. She heard the hum of a saw and realized it came from his furniture workshop. That door was wide open, so she walked to it.

As she took a step in, she smelled sawdust and felt a slight vibration on the wooden floor. She sneezed, but Jack didn't hear her, even at this close range. His back to her, he was bent over a band saw. She knocked on the open wooden door, then realized she'd have to wait until he was done to avoid startling him. His wide shoulders hunched, his head down, the tension of concentration—and intensity of the man—struck her again like a physical force. She tore her gaze away from him to survey the surroundings.

The interior of the large, one-room edifice was full of stunning wooden furniture, everything from a trestle table to a corner cupboard to slat-back rocking chairs with woven seats. Yet unlike his gardens, it all seemed ordered and aligned. Jack appeared to not be working on any of the massive pieces now; his hands held something small.

She glanced around and saw, just inside the door, a steaming tub of water with thin strips of wood inside. The haze of setting sun through the western windows and the sawdust aureole seemed to gild his dark silhouette—black hair, black jeans and a navy flannel shirt shoved up to show muscled, hair-flecked forearms.

Slowly, as if he'd sensed her presence, he turned her way. The saw slowly began to run down, then stopped. Wearing big work goggles that obscured his eyes like smoked glass, Jack seemed some sort of alien. He pushed his goggles up on his broad, brown forehead and pulled plugs out of both ears.

"I didn't hear you or expect you," he said. She

almost felt she'd trespassed. His expression was hard, his eyes narrowed.

"I've just accepted the job of rosarian at Shaker Run and hear I partly have you to thank—for that and lassoing Varina Wellesley the other day. I just wanted to say I appreciate it."

"Don't thank me too much," he said, putting the thin piece of wood he'd been cutting on his workbench. "That is, there are challenges with each new endeavor, including that Shaker Eden over there. They told you this is my place?"

"That's right. Beautiful furniture—but what are you doing now?"

"Shaker oval storage boxes," he said, and reached onto his massive workbench to select a large one from which he produced two other smaller ones, to show her a stack of variegated sizes. "They used them to store lots of things. You know the Shakers. A place for everything and everything in its place."

"They're little works of art and so delicate looking," she said, reaching out to stroke the gentle curve of one, then drawing her hand back.

"Actually, they're sturdy as heck," he said, pulling his goggles over his head, which mussed his hair even more. "Curves are stronger than corners, so you can stand on the bigger ones and they won't split. Want to try?" he asked with the first hint of a smile she'd seen from him.

She knew she must have looked surprised. "I believe you. Are you soaking the wood so you can bend it?" she asked, indicating the hot-water bath by the door.

He nodded. "You mold them around a form while they're wet and nail them in place—" He gestured slightly as he talked, and she found herself staring at his hands. Rough but graceful, strong but obviously capable of great gentleness. She shivered slightly, annoyed the man's hands, voice—all of him—affected her so elementally.

"I only do them," he was saying, "when I need a break from the big projects. Things were piling up, and I just needed a little downtime," he added awkwardly, as if reluctant to share even that much of a personal admission with her.

A man, Kate thought, who took a break from building big things by building small things. A man who worked himself too hard. To substitute for not having what? She recognized the symptoms, but was still looking for her own cure.

"So, you'll be working with Tanya Dodridge," he observed. "I hope you don't mind if I nail down these dovetails before this wood splits or warps the wrong way."

"No, go right ahead. Yes, with Tanya. Do you know her and the Shaker staff very well?"

"Not really, though I totally sympathize with their cause. But yeah, Tanya and I are friends."

"It sounds as if Clint Barstow and his boys, as he calls them, will be competition for you soon," she observed, realizing he'd said all he intended to about Tanya. She'd do better asking the talkative herbalist herself.

"No," he corrected her. "Barstow's shop does Shaker reproductions, but they won't be competition. I already have as much work as I can do building and trying to protect the integrity of my craft."

"Like quality control—quality assurance," she

said. "I suppose the Shaker builders were hoping you'd join them."

"I've made it clear I don't get invol—I work alone," he said, still hammering tiny copper tacks into holes he'd already drilled in the curved side and in the overlapping dovetails. "I know Tanya better than the others because her great-aunt is one of the foremost private collectors of Shaker furniture in the country, so she's especially interested in what I do, that's all."

"I see," she said, though that explanation didn't really satisfy Kate's curiosity about him and Tanya. She wondered if Sarah had known Tanya's aunt or vice versa. "Her great-aunt isn't Oprah Winfrey, is she?" she went on. "Mrs. Denbigh said Oprah's got a fabulous Shaker collection."

"Her great-aunt is the gospel singer Samantha Sams. Quite a few well-to-do African Americans collect Shaker because they admire the way the Believers treated blacks back when. Namely," he went on, as he tapped in the last tack, "even before the Civil War, they bought and freed slaves, then allowed them to rise as high as the whites in the Shaker hierarchy. Never heard of a Shaker with a prejudiced bone in his body. However strange they were sometimes, they were admirable, too."

Kate listened intently to him, but still kept her eyes riveted on his big, skillful hands. She was almost afraid that if she stared at his face, he'd look at her and she'd give away how insanely attracted she was to him. But she took a step closer as he fitted a lid on the box. It was perfect.

"Let me show you what I'm making for Tanya," he said, moving across the room. "But I told her delivery might take a while because my bigger orders have to go out first.''

He moved a tall, unfinished corner cupboard aside, and pulled out from the shadows what appeared to be a half-finished desk with many small compartments stacked above its work surface. Even in the dimmer light against the back wall, the unfinished wood seemed to glow with warmth.

''An herb cupboard made from butternut,'' he told her. ''These will all be separate drawers she can label.''

''It's great. Your own home must be absolutely full of unique, lovely things.''

She wondered if she'd said something wrong. Jack seemed to freeze, and a frown flashed across his rugged face.

Jack's heart had been thudding right in rhythm with his hammer. He'd actually been thinking of Kate Marburn when she'd appeared in his doorway, as if he'd conjured her up. He'd been trying to decide if he wanted to get involved in using her like—like another tool. Could he keep her at arm's length while he did? If he used her, she'd take some watching. Unfortunately, he was also attracted to her, and that sort of complication was the last thing in the world he needed. But, as if it were a sign, she'd come looking for *him.*

Jack knew where she was going with the comments about his house. He could scent an intrigued woman a mile away. He supposed he had to get all the chit-chat over without letting her know what he was really thinking. He stiffened his spine as she went on.

''I mean, your family is so fortunate,'' she was

saying. "They probably never have to see the inside of a furniture store."

"I'm not married," he said, wishing that didn't sound so blunt, "except maybe to my job. And these pieces I create are as close as I get to having kids."

"And, of course, you keep busy with the expertising, too," she noted as if trying to help him through this. He gave her points for not pursuing the family thing.

"I usually expertise only in my spare time," he said. "But your Toledo detective friend is very persuasive."

"If you mean Stan Rudzinski, he's not my friend. So did you find any of Sarah's—Mrs. Denbigh's— furniture was phony?"

"I'm not at liberty to say," he admitted, pushing the herb desk back in place. "But don't think I'm in league with him. It's just that I was asked to keep it confidential until all the evidence is assembled."

She nodded, looking suddenly forlorn. He had the nearly overwhelming urge to touch her, to comfort her. Kate Marburn was just the sort of graceful, sensitive—yeah, blond and leggy—woman he used to be intrigued by before all hell broke loose in his life.

So why was he taking this risk with a woman he could really grow to want, and maybe couldn't resist after all these years of living like a monk?

"Well," she said, breaking their awkward silence as they walked back toward his workbench, "I've got to get going. I'm going to see my stepdaughter at Ohio U., take her out to dinner, then head home tomorrow. I've got a lot to do to get ready to transplant roses and myself here. They may go dormant, but *I* can't afford to."

Her words blurred by as that old wound tore open. Kate Marburn had a child to go to—to love and watch grow. Andy would have been fourteen next week, into studies and sports in junior high school....

"Sure," he said, picking up the smallest size of oval box. "Let me walk you out."

At her car, he opened the door for her. Then when she got in and rolled her window down, he handed her the box. "A good-luck gift for your new job here." Damn, she looked like she'd cry.

"Oh, I can't accept that after all you've done for me. But tell you what—I'd like to make you a deal for it."

Better and better, he thought, entirely fascinated. Maybe she'd make this deceit easy for him. "Shoot," he said, when she hesitated, nervously licking her lower lip. He leaned closer, his elbows on her car as he leaned toward her open window.

"I see you've been too busy to prepare your beds—flower beds—for winter. I'll clean them out and do your autumn and spring yard work if you'll just let me put about a dozen of my antique rosebushes out back. They're beautiful bloomers, but they're not the breed historically planted on Shaker land."

"Great. I like antiques, even living ones." He looked deep into her smoky blue eyes. "Deal," he added, and thrust his hand in to shake with her.

"What do you mean she's not here?" Kate asked Amy Baldwin, Erin's roommate. Kate had just knocked on their door in Jefferson Hall, only to have Amy answer it. "Not here or not on campus? She knew I was coming late this afternoon."

"I mean, yeah, she will be back, and she did know you were coming, and she's not off campus," Amy replied, crossing her arms over her loose flannel shirt. "She's just gone out for a bit. Come on in, Mrs. Marburn. She'll be here in a sec."

Realizing she'd overreacted, Kate sat on Erin's bed rather than pulling out the chair from a cluttered desk. The girls had pretty much split the room in half to decorate it. Amy's bulletin board and sliding closet doors were adorned with a lot of family and friend pics, while Erin's side was conspicuously lacking in those. Instead, a poster of actor George Clooney and another of Leonardo DiCaprio with Kate Winslet on the *Titanic* covered Erin's closet doors.

"She didn't go to pick up a pizza or something?" Kate asked Amy, who offered her a fruit drink from their mini-fridge. "I told her I'd take her out to eat uptown."

"Oh, you know," Amy said with a shrug that bounced her straight, blond hair, "just the usual for a Sunday afternoon."

Kate didn't want to pry, but Amy was really nervous. Kate's stomach twisted tighter. "Nothing's wrong, is it, Amy?"

"Oh, no, no way. She's just dating someone and went out for a little while with him."

"I didn't know that. She probably meant to surprise me today. Is she bringing him back with her?"

"I don't think so. That's not what she said."

"Do you know him?"

"Ah—he's from home. Some guy she went with in Toledo, so you probably know him," she said, flopping on her bed but not meeting Kate's gaze.

"Mark Winslow? Mark drives down here to see her—on Sundays?"

When Amy nodded, Kate bounced up and started pacing, though there was little room for that. However minuscule this room, it was unbelievable that college kids lived so poshly today compared to when Kate had been in school. There was not only a mini-fridge, but a TV, a CD player, two PCs, printers, and an answering machine for the phone on the desk. Kate and her roommate had shared an electric typewriter, and there had been one hall phone for the entire floor, when she was at Toledo University in the good old days.

Kate pulled the curtains open farther to look out. The girls' room faced the Education building across the road at the bottom of a steep hill. Kate scanned the sidewalk and street, studying each walking or standing couple. Then she gasped and leaned so close to the window that she bumped her head on it. A black car with tinted windows was parallel-parked with others along the curb.

"If she comes in, tell her to stay put, and I'll be right back," Kate cried, and ran from the room. She hurried down the hall and burst out into the second-floor reception area, where she ran right into Erin.

"Oh, Mo—Kate."

"Wait here," she ordered, half hugging Erin, then quickly setting her back. "I have to see something outside."

"No, wait!" Erin cried, and ran down the staircase after her and out onto the street. "What is it? Come back!"

The car was still there: pastel Florida license plates with the Spaceshuttle *Challenger* on them. But she saw now that the vehicle—a Pontiac—was not the car from the cemetery. This was a newer, different model.

"What is it?" Erin demanded. "What did you see?"

"I thought this car belonged to someone I knew," Kate said, flushed with her exertion and embarrassment, as an elderly couple came along to get in it after hugging a girl who was apparently their granddaughter.

"And where have you been, young lady?" Kate asked, trying to force a smile and keep from looking like an idiot, as they started back inside. "What's this about Mark Winslow?"

"Amy had to tell you, huh?"

"Why didn't *you* tell me? And don't blame Amy," she added, when she saw the color drain from Erin's already pale face, "because I wormed it out of her."

"I—yeah, he just left a while ago. Since I've been away, I guess he's missed me."

"He's been coming down on Sundays? And then here I come to horn in on your time with him, huh?" Kate said, as they crossed the lobby.

"Don't say it like that. I'm glad to see you."

"Good, because you're going to see more of me. I've taken the job at Shaker Run."

"So it's 'Goodbye, Toledo.' Congrats and all that!" Erin cried, and they hugged hard in the hall before they walked back to her room.

"Surprises all around," Kate said. "You and Mark, me and—"

She was horrified that she'd almost said "Jack Kilcourse," but she caught herself. "—Shaker Run. Come on, I'm starved, so let me take you to dinner."

* * *

"Let's eat at the 7 Sauces again," Kate suggested. "You said it was your favorite place, and I'll bet you haven't been in there since the day I moved you into the dorm."

"Well—all right," Erin agreed, and Kate was certain it was reluctantly.

It was six o'clock as they walked up the steep hill into town. Kate loved the look of the campus, mostly redbrick, Georgian architecture with a central green where the chimes could be heard ringing out on the hour. The campus gate's inscription said the university was founded in 1804. That was at the beginning of the Ohio Shaker era, Kate thought, but there was probably no connection between early university students and the more isolated Shakers living about twenty miles away.

As they ate at the homey restaurant on North Court Street, Erin more or less just pushed her delicious *primavera* pasta around on her dish.

"You ate earlier with Mark, didn't you?" Kate asked. "You should have told me and just ordered a salad or something, or I could have just grabbed some fast food."

"Yeah, I did eat, but that's okay. You never really were the fast-food type, Kate."

Kate's insides felt hollow, despite how much she'd eaten. An invisible wall—what was that Tanya had said about the Shaker belief in invisible forces in the air?—seemed to stretch between her and Erin. And the girl was still calling her "Kate" instead of "Mom."

Kate recalled how devastated she'd felt when Erin had started that, as if her stepdaughter wanted distance from Kate after her father left—as if she blamed Kate, not him.

"You know, I don't disapprove of Mark's visits," Kate said, putting down her fork and gripping her hands in her lap, "but I do want you to have plenty of time to study. And it's hard to be on a campus when you're going with someone who's not there— local social life and all, you know what I mean."

Erin leaned back in the booth with a sigh. "I think I'm still trying to adjust to everything around here."

"Of course you are, so maybe that makes you want to hang on to Mark, a little bit of home, though I thought you'd been saying you're fed up with Toledo. It's been almost two years since your dad left and you broke up with Mark, and I was just a little surprised to hear he's back in your life," Kate said, and reached across the table to cover Erin's hand with her own. Erin's skin felt cold, and she didn't budge to return the touch. "You know, sweetheart, since you kind of cut him off—and since his uncle—"

"Stop it! I know, I know," Erin cried, snatching her hand back and throwing her napkin beside her plate. "His uncle, like half the population of Toledo, was taken in by Dad's scheming. Is that what you were going to say? Is that what you want me to admit?"

"Erin, I didn't mean—" Kate began, starting to slide out of the booth, as Erin stood.

"I'll be right back," the girl said, shaking her head as if to warn Kate off. "Got to hit the little girls' room, that's all."

Kate wilted back in her seat and stared at her nearly empty plate. She had prayed that her news of moving closer would bring *them* closer. Her head jerked up when their server, a tall young man named Stone, returned to their table.

"I think I'll take the check," Kate told him. "My daughter's a little under the weather."

"Or she's just had too much to eat," he said with a knowing smile as he took Erin's nearly untouched plate. "I saw her here earlier today. With that red hair, I remember her."

"And—not alone," Kate prompted.

"With a man. Can't recall him. Like I said, that red hair just draws attention to her. I'll have your check in just a moment," Stone said, and moved away just as Erin came back to sit down.

Rather than confronting Erin with what she'd just learned, Kate decided there was a bright side to all this. After all, Erin hadn't wanted to hurt her feelings by saying she'd already been to this place with Mark today; she'd come back in so Kate wouldn't be disappointed at this so-called celebration for her new job. Only now, Kate realized, she'd have to work as hard at rebuilding a relationship with Erin as she would at building new ones at Shaker Run.

Until Christmas and the millennial New Year, life was a blur for Kate. She transplanted her Apothecary roses to the village and her other, non-Shaker antique breeds to Jack's newly cleaned-out flower beds. More often than not, he was gone, overseeing the delivery of pieces people had bought for Christmas, even making a three-week trip to Japan at Christmastime, when most people wanted to be home near their families.

Despite spending more time with Erin, Kate took her own crash course in Shakerdom, concentrating on Shaker Run and its rosewater industry. She was part of much planning, especially with Tanya, for the all-important May first opening of the village.

Meanwhile, carload by carload, Kate settled her household goods in the spacious third floor of the Trustees' Building, overlooking the distant cemetery and holy ground. What she had stored of her and Erin's furniture in a rental space in Toledo, she had transferred to Rent-a-Room Storage just outside Athens. Most of her apartment was furnished in authentic Shaker items, and she felt as if she'd stepped back into the past. Despite the presence of her phone and PC, she didn't even unpack her TV, VCR or CD player. Had the entirety of modern life, Kate wondered, been reduced to abbreviations and anagrams? She couldn't wait to relax and really enjoy life again in this safe, simple setting.

During the last week of Erin's Christmas vacation, the two of them drove to Pensacola, Florida, and hit the beach. But for some reason Erin hadn't wanted to go, and had turned as prickly as a Rambler rose again. Kate could only pray this new millennium would mean a new beginning for both of them.

Unfortunately, Kate continued to deal with Toledo lawyers and Stan Rudzinski over the mess Sarah's will had made. If it weren't for wanting to honor her dear friend's wishes, Kate might have told them to chuck the whole thing, not that that would have prevented Zink from sticking like superglue. Sarah's officially ''accidental death'' still haunted Kate. She'd overheard Zink tell Tina Martin, ''Something's fishy, and I'll never let this turn to a cold case—never.''

Kate was cold now as she got in her car in late January, in bitterly subzero Toledo after her latest conference on Varina and Palmer's lawsuit. It had been a contentious meeting, with them and their lawyer present.

Before starting the drive back to Shaker Run, Kate leaned her forehead on her steering wheel, completely drained. She wasn't sure if she was racked by emotions or drained of them. No, she thought, knowing Jack had proved she wasn't drained of them. As austere and conflicted as he seemed sometimes, the man really got to her. She smiled as she recalled a recent discussion with Tanya over him.

"Don't you go giving *me* that all-knowing look, Kate Marburn," Tanya had scolded, when Kate finally asked her how well she really knew Jack Kilcourse. "You thinking there's something going on between him and little, old, celibate-Shaker me?" Tanya had rolled her eyes as she'd confided in Kate that her love life was nil right now. "We're not much more'n friends with a few interests in common, not partners in passion. And you been *dying* to know that, haven't you? Why didn't you just ask, girl?"

"Well—I didn't want to pry or maybe offend you."

Tanya laughed. "I just think you need another dose of Tanya's *terrific* herbal tonics, that's what I think."

"Right," Kate had countered, standing and stretching from bending over her rose starts. "All I need is a big dose of one of those good news–bad news herbs you're working with. The wonder drugs that may help you out with a little ache but may also kill you in the process," she teased.

"I could put a pinch of autumn crocus in that good valerian herb tea I mixed for your insomnia," Tanya had told her.

"Autumn crocus? For what?"

"You know, I often wondered if the Shaker herbalists slipped it in some of the brethren or sisters' food. For what?" Tanya had said dramatically and lowered her voice. "It lowers sexual excitement. But too much of it—just like sexual excitement—can be *deadly.*"

Tanya had gotten a good laugh out of that, and Kate had decided her new friend's sense of humor was pretty weird. But today as she began the four-and-a-half hour drive back to Shaker Run, she wished she had some sort of herbal cure for her exhaustion. If only she could be an insomniac when she drove and be this tired at night. If only—

Kate jolted awake as her car swerved into the other lane. Her heart pounded and she broke out in a sweat as she shook herself awake. Thank God this was a four-lane highway, and no other car was close.

She glanced in her rearview mirror. The nearest car was way back on this stretch through rural, flat land between Findlay and Columbus. Her heart still thudding, she slapped her face, then rolled down her window and let the icy air hit her full force. She could just envision the headlines now: Suspected Embezzler, Suspected Murderer Suspected Of Falling Asleep At Wheel And—

"Damn you, Mike Marburn!" she snapped as she rolled her window back up.

She never used to have trouble sleeping before Mike had deceived and deserted her. It had been months since Kate had felt so angry at her former husband, but at least now, she realized with relief, she no longer loved him. And maybe her anger would help to keep her awake. The psychiatrist who'd counseled her through everything after Mike left would be proud of her. She felt completely cured of him and of the terrible habit of thinking people were stalking her that had developed after he left. That unsettling incident with the black car in Woodlawn Cemetery would have made her absolutely paranoid before, but now she knew it was pure mischance that someone with a warped sense of humor had stumbled on her there.

She was a new person, her own person now, Kate told herself as she hit the power button of her car radio and turned up to full blast the first FM station that came on. Despite Erin's problems with it, Kate knew she'd done the right thing to divorce Mike rather than have him declared legally dead. The bastard was probably living on the French Riviera with a woman as young as Erin and the hunk of money he'd embezzled, suicide note or not.

At least she felt completely safe living at isolated Shaker Run, even if she was the only one on the grounds at night. Surely she'd start sleeping better soon, and be done with her past and with making this grueling drive alone.

As she glanced once more in her rearview mirror, Kate began to sing along with the music on the radio. She'd just consider it a good sign, for it was that bouncy, cheerful song "Everything's Coming Up Roses."

"Did you see her almost weave off the road?" the woman said to the driver. "She probably reached for something and looked away. At least we know where she's going, so keep this car back."

"Yeah, and she's staying put more and more," he muttered. "Right where we want her, thinking she's

home free. Having her out in the sticks, we can watch
her better.''

''If she doesn't cooperate, we'll have to do more
than hope and wait.''

''I know,'' he said with a deep sigh, taking off his
hat and tossing it into the back seat. ''We made a
mistake with Sarah Denbigh but—''

''But this time, no mistakes.''

8

The dreary wilderness must blossom like the rose.

—Mother Ann Lee

"Now, doesn't that gown make you feel a part of the Shakers, more than all that studying and work you've been doing?" Louise Willis asked, as Kate came downstairs from her apartment in the Trustees' Building.

For one moment, Kate stopped and stared at the others. It was like stepping back in time, to a darker, stranger world, to see Shakers looking up at her, assessing her, watching her. Kate wondered if everyone had driven in already costumed. Although Tanya lived twenty miles away on the edge of Athens, the others owned rural homes a bit farther out. Like the rest, Kate had donned her new Shaker costume for a group photograph.

"It's amazingly comfortable for walking and standing," Kate admitted, coming down the last few steps, "but I don't know about doing my gardening in it all spring and summer." When she saw she'd hurt Louise's feelings, for the woman had overseen the sewing of the costumes, she added, "But the gown's lovely and makes me able to get more inside their skin as well.''

"Of course, it does," Louise insisted as she adjusted her own small, white cape that the Shakers called the shoulder handkerchief. It crossed the bodice and, like the long, narrow apron and ankle-length skirt, obscured a woman's body to stem temptation among the brothers in the Shakers' celibate world.

If the weather was cold, as it was today when an early spring storm was lurking outside, the women also wore long, hooded capes, some in stunning colors. Their gowns, however, were muted hues. Kate's was a soft blue, while Louise's was plum-colored, and Tanya's and Adrienne's were brown and gray.

Kate carried her deep, woven sunbonnet with her rather than putting it on over the net cap the women wore, and she hadn't pinned her hair back the exacting way Louise always wore hers. And no way, Kate thought, looking over Louise's bent head as the woman straightened her apron, was Tanya ever going to like wearing one of these. Across the room, Tanya rolled her eyes. When Louise was on one of her we-must-do-everything-exactly-right missions, there was no stopping her.

"After all, it *is* April Fool's Day," Tanya mouthed to Kate with a little smirk.

"All right, everyone, please stand between the table and stove for one of the photos for the new brochure," Dane announced, as the professional photographer hustled in from outside with a gust of chill wind. "Then, storm coming or not, we'll be going out to have more taken with the men and women standing by the separate brethren's and sisters' doors."

"You know the Shakers," Tanya said, speaking up so all could hear this time. "Two sexes with no sex. Twin staircases, twin doors, two sets of workshops—the original 'separate but equal.'"

Dane just shot her a dark look and began arranging everyone before the photographer could. Like the other men on the staff, Dane was dressed in full old-fashioned attire of striped trousers, white, collarless shirt, vest and dark-hued frock coat. Plans for the Shaker Run staff to be presenters who dressed and spoke as if they were the original brethren had come to fruition during the past winter months of hard work.

Dane and Adrienne were taking the roles of elders, and the Willises the parts of deacons, or overseers of all that went on. Clint Barstow and his furniture makers would portray brethren, while Kate and Tanya were the sisters, although Louise and Ben had managed also to arrange for a rotating list of costumed docents to volunteer their time when Shaker Run officially opened a month from today. Though overworked, everyone was excited as they prepared for that momentous event. And Kate, though she shuddered in the chill and felt goose bumps suddenly sliding over her skin, was very pleased with the way her own life had been going since the new year. She told herself that again and again.

For one thing, she was sleeping better than she had in years, thanks to Tanya's valerian herbal tea, which she drank every night. "In just the right dose, a calmative," Tanya had explained as she showed Kate how to measure it out, "but more than a teaspoon, it'll keep you up, to say the least."

Kate had also been seeing more of Erin, who didn't seem to blame Kate quite as much as before for divorcing her father. And she and Jack Kilcourse had become friends, though an unspoken sexual undercurrent always arced between them. She was learning to almost trust him. Still, she admitted, she hardly knew the real man, and so little of their talk had been personal. Barriers seemed built between them as thorny as her roses and as solid as his furniture.

"Kate, I said, please line your bonnet up here with the other hats on the table for this picture," Louise was evidently repeating herself. Kate realized she'd been daydreaming again. "At least we have a lot of photos of the Shakers, so we can replicate how they looked and acted," Louise announced to everyone. "They surely weren't like the Amish who shunned the camera. Actually, I don't think they were so much reclusive as quite bold."

Kate had come to see Louise that way, too. However much of a nitpicker and complainer she was, the woman was dedicated to making the time warp that was Shaker Run absolutely authentic. Although retired from an insurance business they'd run together in Columbus, the Willises still kept an office and apartment there, where Louise's elderly mother also lived. They went back and forth a great deal, as well as putting in long hours for this dream of theirs. Kate wondered when they found time to sleep. For the Willises, just as for Dane and Adrienne, Shaker Run was a labor of love.

As she stood patiently for several photos, Kate realized she did feel *somewhat* Shaker. That is, she'd come here to join a group with a common cause, and they had become a bit like a family. She and Tanya were fast friends, if not quite sisters, with their very different backgrounds. As it had been for many Shakers, Kate tried to tell herself, this place where she could make her roses bloom was a safe, little Eden, hacked out from the wilderness of her past. But sometimes, as the only one on the grounds at night, with Jack a half-mile away—when he was home—the nights stretched out so silent, deep, and dark.

"Looks like we're in for a bad, late winter storm," Dane observed, squinting out the front windows. The staff, still in their Shaker garb after an hour of posing for publicity photos, were finally sitting down for their meeting. "I'll make this brief so you can be on your way if you need to—Tanya especially." Tanya was driving to Kentucky for her great-aunt's—soul singer Samantha Sam's—ninetieth birthday celebration held by her Baptist Church. "If you weren't going to be gone for a long weekend, Tanya, we'd have put all this off, but we've got to get this brochure to the printer. Which is why I need to bring up this next item of business—the main theme for the brochure."

"Don't forget to mention about the well," Adrienne put in, tapping her pencil on a notepad she always had with her.

"Oh, yes, that too," he said. It amazed Kate that Adrienne's interruptions to give advice or orders never seemed to faze Dane. If Kate had blurted things out to Mike when he was holding court, his Irish temper would have flared.

"Now that the weather should take a turn for the better," Dane said, with another rueful glance at the encroaching clouds outside, "the archeological team will be excavating the old well. I, for one, can't wait to hear and see what they discover in those depths. It's definitely a heyday-of-the-Shakers era well."

"And the other benefits," Adrienne prompted.

"The village is sharing in their grant money for the dig," Dane went on, "and we can bank on some good publicity from it, too. And that, at least until we get fully established, will be the name of the game around here. We are still operating on a shoestring, to use a phrase the old brothers and sisters might have known.

"Now," he continued, talking even faster, "to the reason I called this meeting. Since we've just come into a new millennium, Adrienne and I believe we should emphasize that the Shakers were also planning what they called a new millennium—in their case, not the turn of the century but a new age of unity and strength."

"But according to my reading," Kate observed when he paused, evidently to get their reactions, "the Shaker concept of a millennial age was a time to become stricter and more inward, more separated from the world—when we here at Shaker Run need to be opening our doors to it."

"Right," Tanya said. "All those millennial laws they had were rules and regs against just about *everything* in the world. Orders about the way people talked, how to eat at meals, mandates for rising and retiring, and, of course, what they called orders concerning *intercourse* between the sexes—"

"The old-fashioned meaning for that," Louise put in, glaring at Clint Barstow, who had dared to laugh. "The term meant just daily dealings such as simple communications to work together."

"True," Tanya admitted, "but it went so far as to include things like making the opposing sexes—"

"I think you mean 'opposite' sexes," Adrienne suggested.

"Well, if I was talking about men and women today, maybe I'd mean a little of both," Tanya insisted. "Anyway, their old rules say they can't so much as pass each other on the stairs, shake hands, whisper or *blink,* for heaven's sake. Their little, line-up-in-their-chairs chats at night were even strictly controlled. And I just read one millennial law the other day that said nobody can keep secrets from the elders. Is that where this is going, Dane?" she concluded with a teasing grin and overt batting of her eyes that was hardly Shaker. "No secrets from the elders?"

Everyone laughed, though Dane actually looked guilty of something.

"Yeah," Clint Barstow, who said so little in these meetings Kate felt she hardly knew him, added with a sly grin. "And that's why they have those little peepholes up high in the Meeting House. It's so the elders, or watchers, as they called them, could spy on the others meeting there or doing the sacred dancing."

Gooseflesh swept Kate again. She heard the wind pick up, whining around the building. No matter how much they bantered here or kept to business, she began to feel uneasy. Maybe, she scolded herself, it was just the barometric change from the approaching storm. She often got headaches and felt nervous when bad weather lumbered in.

"That is *not* why," Louise declared indignantly. "At Shaker Hill in Kentucky the elders had two watchtowers on roofs so they could be certain members weren't behaving out of union, as they used to say—but not here, not according to my extensive research. The holes in our Meeting House were built so that the deacons or elders could be sure the dancing did not get out of hand, especially when Believers had spirit visitations."

"Oh, right," Clint said, his voice openly mocking now. "Visits from dead folks could get things out of hand. That'd just be par for the course around here. There's always more to the Shakers than meets the eye."

"I wish," Ben Willis interrupted, "we could all practice not using these modern slang sayings such as 'par for the course,' since we've been working on being authentic, nineteenth-century presenters when our doors open to the world. Maybe we should all practice their favorite phrases so—"

"Don't change the subject," Clint argued. "And don't think I haven't read about those crazy doings out on that so-called back forty where they had their holy ground. But I'm just sticking to my furniture, especially if you try to get some of us to do dance demonstrations, Louise."

"I heard you all loud and clear on that before," she said with a sniff. "I'm bringing in some dance majors from the university, though Adrienne and I intend to instruct them and probably rehearse them in the Meeting House. Yes, Clint, you just stick to your precious furniture!"

"Speaking of which, Kate," Adrienne put in, "can we assume all is well with Mrs. Denbigh's furniture loans to us staying here? I don't suppose there's been any change in the litigation over it."

Kate was relieved to be able to swing things to a different subject, even that one. "The last word," she explained to everyone, "was that my lawyer has hopes Mrs. Denbigh's wishes to give the furniture into my care will stand, though her heirs are still contesting that.''

In the moment's silence, she heard only the ticking of the clock and howling of the wind. She shifted nervously in her seat.

''Well,'' Tanya spoke up, ''we're all on your side, Kate—in *everything*.''

Kate was surprised. She'd told them about the furniture and the will, but not about the fact that the heirs, and maybe the police—though, thank God, Rudzinski had not yet been here—might suspect she'd harmed Sarah. But no one asked what Tanya meant, so maybe the Thompsons, who'd surely seen the Toledo papers, had told everyone all that. Did they know about the earlier financial scandal, too? If so, as far as she knew, they had accepted her here without a look or whisper over it.

Sadly, Kate realized again, that she still couldn't trust anyone. It was mere illusion that this staff was pulling together as some sort of family. It made the storm, glaring at her through the tall windows, seem to blow right into her heart.

An alternately whining and howling snowstorm gripped Shaker Run to bring an early darkness. With everyone gone, the solitude oppressed Kate. And then, for the first time in the three months she'd lived here, the electricity went off.

It really annoyed her that she couldn't find where she'd put her flashlight when she'd moved in. Surely, she'd put it right here in this drawer by her bed.

She felt her way to the phone, but the lines were evidently down. There was no dial tone, no static—nothing. But that was not surprising in a wind like

this. Kate never used her cell phone around here, and
its batteries had run down. She hoped more than the
village was affected, so phone and electrical repairs
would be made soon. At least, living in Toledo all
her life with its lake-effect snow and winter winds,
she was quite used to this.

She fumbled for her stash of candles and matches
in the top drawer of the corner cupboard of her kitchenette. Although they used kerosene lanterns in the
village for appearance's sake, she still wasn't comfortable with them. All she needed was to burn down
this valuable building when so much money was going into restoring others.

The candle flared to life, and she lit three more,
one a fat, sturdy one. In the wan, flickering light, her
rooms seemed suddenly unfamiliar. Shaker walls
were uncluttered, all whitewashed with their traditional, head-high, dark blue pegged rail, on which
they used to hang garments and even chairs to avoid
clutter when they cleaned. *There is no dirt in heaven,*
Mother Ann used to say. But now Kate's rooms were
filled with shifting shadows thrown on the stark, white
walls by the furniture, much of it Sarah's. It was as
if her dear friend's spirit flitted from her furniture to
be with her. "Spirit visitations, indeed," Kate whispered as she put her candles on a table and stared out
the back windows from her bedroom. "You're starting to think like loony Louise."

The frosted panes partly obscured her view.
Though the trees were creaking with cold as their
limbs thrashed from the wind, now and then she could
catch glimpses of her and Tanya's workshops, and
beyond, the old cemetery and the plot called holy
ground, now lying pristine in a cloak of snow.

Snow was not falling now, but suddenly she thought she saw something sweep across the lane. Was that a cloaked figure, darting from the graves toward holy ground?

"No way," she whispered. "Just something blowing."

The bare branches of trees had whipped across her sight, and that had made her think something was moving out there, she told herself. Other branches knocked against the windowpanes as if someone wanted in. Still, if she squinted toward the holy ground where the Shakers used to hold special rituals, she could almost imagine a dark figure standing there against the snow. No, that was that young pine tree, whipped by the wind.

Shaking her head at her foolishness, she moved her candles back into the kitchenette. Then, since her eyes had adjusted to the darkness, she went to each window on all four sides of her apartment and peered out, just as the wind seemed to exhale its last breath.

In the sudden silence, the moon darted from behind the clouds, casting a pale light reflected by newly swept snow. And then she saw footsteps, clearly etched beneath her front windows. They must be fresh or the wind would have swept them away. They came almost to the front door of this building, then went on. Had she not heard a knock on the front door below? Could someone lost have been seeking help or looking in? If the candlelight was too dim to be seen, could the person have run around behind the building, thinking no one was here?

"Someone walking in here at night—ridiculous," she said aloud, pressing her face to the front window again. She held her breath this time so she didn't steam it up. This village road was a dead end, and someone coming off the distant highway looking for help would have to traverse too many fields and the ravine.

And then she saw that dark form again—or maybe another. It was by the furniture shop where Clint and his team worked in the large building that had once been the Center Family Dwelling House, across the lane from her and Tanya's realm. Half of it held his workrooms and the other half the infirmary and sample Shaker living areas.

Kate dropped to her knees and watched as the figure stopped, seemed to huddle there, then went in the right side—the men's—front door. She breathed a sigh of relief, which clouded the windowpane again. It must just be Clint or one of his men, but why now, and where was his car? Maybe he'd just gotten stuck on the narrow lane and left it, not wanting to bother her. But he didn't have any blankets over there, and could probably use a lantern. Heat and light were both minimal even when the electricity was working.

Blowing out her candles, Kate bundled up, took two blankets and an unlit lantern, and went out into the snow. It wasn't half as deep as it looked from the house because the wind had scoured much of it off this plateau. And it was amazingly light out here compared to in the house. She always preferred the outdoors to being cooped up. That was why she'd refused to "go to ground," as her psychiatrist had suggested when she'd been obsessed with being followed after Mike left. Even if someone could be watching her, she'd choose being out under God's open skies over being trapped in a building anytime.

Crunching the stiff grass, she followed the tracks

across the lane. Large footsteps, big feet—no doubt Clint. Maybe he'd have some idea about how to get the lights back on.

But she hesitated outside the square stone-and-frame building. Its double doors glared at her like dark eyes in a vacant face. What if it wasn't Clint, and she went barging in on a stranger, especially one who was breaking in?

Feeling strange at being the watcher, Kate walked around the right-hand side of the building. She knew two places she could peer in, either the back steps or the slanted, wooden root cellar that leaned here to match the one on the other side.

The cellar looked too slippery, so she decided on the steps. Someone already had a light inside, a moving beam, maybe from a flashlight. And she could see that the intruder was playing it along various pieces of tall, standing furniture.

She thought of Rudzinski's theory, which she'd finally figured out on her own, that someone had been selling Sarah fake furniture. The fact a Shaker antique expertiser had been called in by the police and not by the appraisers for Sarah's will meant that it was somehow tied to her death. If Sarah had found out she was being swindled, Kate had surmised, and was going to accuse someone, maybe that person had paid to have Sarah killed. It was a wild idea, but so was the concept that her own husband could bilk hundreds of people out of millions of dollars and get away with it.

If only her phone were working right now, she'd call the local police, or at least phone Jack, she thought, peering in the back window. And then, when she saw the man inside set his light on a tabletop and bend to examine something nearby, she gasped.

The intruder *was* Jack.

9

Change in a trice
The lilies and languors of virtue
For the raptures and roses of vice.
                    —Algernon Charles Swinburne
                                        "Dolores"

Kate nearly knocked on the window, then hesitated. How did Jack get a key? Surely, he hadn't broken in. And why was he coming here at night during a storm? He could probably finagle an entry in here with his fellow furniture makers, or ask her if she could get him in to look around. She had a master key.

Her curiosity to know what he was doing got the best of her, and she tried her key carefully, quietly in the back sister's door—force of habit from Louise always preaching they should follow tradition on that. One of the first things the village would purchase from early entrance fees this year, Dane had said, was an electronic security system for the buildings, despite the fit Louise had had over lack of authenticity.

Now the door creaked briefly, but then so did old houses and furniture in the cold, so she didn't worry Jack would hear her. Putting the lantern down outside, but holding the blankets to her chest, she slid in the half-opened door and closed it quietly behind her.

At least Jack was making enough noise in there to cover her sounds. She heard a tapping, cupboard doors opening and closing, and drawers sliding in and out. What could he be looking for, and why now?

Kate shuffled through what had been the pantry but which currently held tools. Slowly, she peered into a vast, dark room, once the big kitchen, its old counters now converted to workbenches. She saw the light across the room, and stepped in.

Suddenly, hard arms clamped around her. Her breath whoofed out as she hit the floor, a big body on top of hers.

His hand over her mouth bumped her nose. Furious, she bit his fingers.

"Damn!" he cried, and yanked his hand away.

"I'll scream!" she choked out instinctively.

"Who's going to hear? I didn't know it was you and didn't want the intruder to scare you by screaming in a supposedly deserted village."

"Oh, how thoughtful. But you're the intruder here!"

"I'm assuming you knew it was me before you walked in, because this would have been an even more stupid move on your part, otherwise."

"You're the one into stupid moves tonight! Get off!"

He only stopped shaking his hurt hand. "Why were you sneaking in, if you saw who it was?" he demanded, frowning.

"You still have no right to be in here. I wanted to see what you were doing."

They glared at each other at breath-tingling range in the dim, reflected gleam of his distant flashlight. As crazy as it seemed, she realized they had never argued before, hardly said anything emotionally charged to each other, though she felt that way around him all the time. Somehow, for her, his presence was always overwhelming. But they had never been this close.

Kate still held the blankets, but shoved them away to try to get up. "You brought bedding?" he asked as his eyebrows lifted to widen his dark gaze.

Her heart began to beat even harder. "So, what are you doing here and in the dark?" she demanded.

He shifted his weight and sprawled next to her, one arm around her waist, one foot still over her ankles. "I'm more or less holding you, which is something I've been wanting to do for a while, but I wasn't ready for the complications."

"Give me a break and don't be ridiculous. Or change the subject," she said, but her voice quavered. "And you've got complications of another kind now. Who gave you the key to get in here?"

He sighed, rose and helped her up. It was only then she realized that, as startled as she'd been, she had believed he would not harm her. But she didn't need to be trusting any man—getting into complications, as he put it. Especially not this one, with his quiet charisma that both built up walls but somehow invited her to try to scale them.

Though a long bench and several rocking chairs were nearby, Jack blocked her between the backs of two tall cupboards set sideways against the wall. Of necessity, they stood close together in the small space. The warmth of his breath caressed her face in the chill air.

"Let me explain," he said. "I want to trust you."

"Isn't the line that you want *me* to trust *you?*

You're the one on thin ice. I came over here because I thought Clint or one of his workers had a car that had acted up in the storm and he'd need these supplies. You aren't here trying to see what your competition's building, are you?''

"I told you they are not my competition. But all right," he said and cleared his throat, "I'm checking whether some of this furniture matches some fine museum and collectors' pieces and so could be switched with those authentic antiques. It would be a great place to make and hide fakes and frauds.''

"So would your workshop," she accused, feeling defensive about the village staff. "But—run that by me again. And why are you here in the dark during a storm?''

"I thought blowing snow would help cover my tracks, and knew no one would be out now.''

"Is the electricity off at your place?''

"Not that I know of, and I wasn't planning on using it here. Then, too, I just recently came into possession of a key. I'm not desperate enough for breaking and entering—yet.''

"And then the wind quit blowing, and I followed your tracks," she told him. "But where did you get the key? And who are you suspecting of furniture forgeries? You aren't still working for Stan Rudzinski, are you? Does he think there's some theft ring at Shaker Run that could tie in to Mrs. Denbigh's death?''

"Whoa. Slow down," he murmured, lifting both hands as if to hold her off in the small space, but the gesture made him nearly touch her breasts. "I'm working for myself, Kate. I had some furniture stolen last year, not from here but hijacked from an airport warehouse while still in shipping cases. Later, they were substituted for authentic pieces that were stolen from a couple of Shaker villages.''

''But not here? Not Mrs. Denbigh's things?''

''Not unless she'd donated pieces to villages on the East Coast. No one would have noticed the switch for years if I hadn't become suspicious and gone looking,'' he explained. ''I never do exact replicas, but I do what I call 'inspired pieces.'''

''Inspired? Now that sounds really Shaker.''

''Yeah, but I'm not making fake identical pieces to allow thefts of the originals. Kate, the reason I've been gone so much this fall is that I've been in England as well as Japan. A British museum curator who discovered he had a well-made replica and not the original Shaker desk they'd purchased years ago traced the replica to me. Hell, that wasn't hard. I'd signed the piece as I do all of mine—that was one thing that helped exonerate me. Anyhow, international customs authorities were going to arrest me until I convinced them I was clean. I don't know,'' he added with another shrug, ''they probably still suspect me.''

Kate didn't say so, but her heart went out to him. She suddenly understood perfectly what he was going through. If only she could help and comfort him, however much little warning signals about trusting him went off in her head.

''Go on,'' she urged.

''Customs is working on it from their end and told me to stay out of it, but I figured I'd try to cover some bases here to see if I could turn up something.''

''But Shaker furniture stolen from England?'' she marveled.

"It's admired all over the world," he insisted, his voice tinged with pride. "And one of the best European collections of Shaker is in the American Museum in Claverton Manor near Bath."

"So," she said, "you're thinking Clint Barstow might be behind a worldwide, lucrative, switch-and-steal scheme?"

"Or someone pulling his strings is."

"Jack, no one pulls Barstow's strings. If you ask me, he's not the brightest guy in the world to mastermind anything, but he's fiercely independent and doesn't like taking orders from anyone."

"Yeah, but you don't really know what someone is like until a crisis hits," he argued, shifting his weight so he leaned on his forearm close to the side of her head, still blocking her into their small space. "Or until you deal with them up close and personal."

She nodded as if she were drugged by his closeness and the raspy timbre of his voice. The faintest halo from the flashlight illuminated his tousled head, though he hardly seemed angelic. With his craggy features and big shoulders, he seemed a darker spirit, a compelling, luring demon.

But she managed to merely nod. *Until a crisis hits, you don't know someone...* It sounded as if he were describing her marriage, but she wondered if he was thinking of his own. The only personal revelation he'd made to her before tonight was that he also was divorced, but he'd volunteered nothing else.

"So," she said, pressing back against the solid wood, "even though you have to take risks, you're determined to discover who is behind all this. And you're working alone and undercover."

"In a nutshell, that's it."

"Alone—not with or for Rudzinski or some other law agency?"

"Kate, this is not *Mission Impossible*. Besides, I always work alone."

"But now you've been found out," she said, "and confessed to an outsider. Perfect place for it, since the Shakers used to confess all their sins."

"You gave me no choice. The only other thing I can do is silence you."

His words and piercing gaze made her tense up even more, but only because she was certain he was going to kiss her. He shifted his shoulders, and his mouth hovered close. But she was wrong.

"You could have lied," she insisted, clearing her throat, "and are still lying, for all I know."

"You *are* a tough cookie," he said, his voice getting even huskier. "I wouldn't risk lying because I want you to cover for me—or, at least, to not tell anyone you found me in here tonight."

"So I'd really be abetting your actions, then. Which, Jack Kilcourse, returns me to my oft-asked but not answered question—how did you get in here if you didn't break and enter?"

He shocked her by leaning even closer across their small space, tipping his head and covering her mouth with his.

Though it was a careful kiss, Kate felt it down to her lower belly. She knew she needed to hold him off instead of pulling him to her, but she wanted him. Still, both palms flat on his leather jacket, feeling amazingly out of breath, she set him slightly back.

"I just wanted to get that in at least once," he whispered, "in case you won't accept my next confession."

"Which is?" she whispered.

"Being a builder of old-fashioned furniture, I used the old-fashioned way of copying a key," he admitted, bending his arms so he leaned closer against her, barely touching, not pressing her back into the wood. He shrugged so slightly that she felt, rather than saw, the movement. "I made a wax impression of a master key and had a copy made."

"From Tanya's?"

"From yours. Last week, when you were out back checking on your rosebushes and left your stuff on my porch."

She shoved him hard. Sliding out from their nook, she picked up the blankets from the floor and started for the front door before she realized she needed to get him out of here, demand his key and relock both doors. One hand on the cold brass knob, she turned back to face him. He stood in the middle of the open work space, hands thrust under his armpits, his face etched in the meager light, all unreadable angles and lines.

"The bottom line for all these—these 'complications,' is that you've been using me," she accused.

"No more than you've been using me."

"I haven't lied to you and stolen your property."

"I don't know about the lying, but your roses are on my property."

"Hostages for my silence, I suppose?"

"Kate, you do understand why I'm trying to get to the bottom of this grand-scale furniture scam, don't you?"

"Yes. I really do. And if I help you, it's because I believe Stan Rudzinski thinks that if Sarah Denbigh was murdered, it could be linked to such a scheme.

Sarah was very dear to me, almost a second mother. It's like Tanya says, I guess, that you have to take some bad to get to the good sometimes."

"Tanya's talking about herbal medicines. Besides, that can backfire," he said, his voice bitter now. Kate was amazed to see his eyes tear up; they glinted not in the flashlight glow but in reflected moonlight off the glaze of snow outside. She realized he must be seeing a sort of mental vision, remembering something else.

"Look, Kate," he said as he sucked in a deep breath, "I don't know if what I'm trying to discover could lead to information about whether someone harmed Sarah Denbigh, but some of her furniture was fraudulent. She was too savvy a collector to buy a fake in the first place, so I'm thinking, like the other examples, hers were substituted *after* she purchased them."

"So—someone might have broken in, or just walked in that night, with all those people at the party, to examine or switch some of her furniture," Kate reasoned aloud. "Maybe Rudzinski believes that now, too, and that's why he hasn't been down here grilling me as he hinted he would. Or else he's got someone spying on me here."

"It's not me," Jack declared, slowly coming closer. "And city police don't hire spies or do long-distance stakeouts, especially in a place like Shaker Run. Don't get paranoid about this."

Relieved Jack didn't know she used to be exactly that, believing she was being watched, she insisted, "You don't know Rudzinski. He's like a leech—masquerading, of course, as a friendly, helpful leech."

He gave her a tight smile. "But then, as you said,"

she added, "you never really know people, even the ones closest to you, until you get in a crunch."

"I'm in a crunch now, Kate, and asking for your help. Give me an hour or so to look over this furniture. I won't harm anything, and Barstow and company will never know I was here."

"If I don't tell, it's because you—or we—might turn up something that would help me, too, not because of your forged kiss, thinking you could soften me up. Talk about trying to use someone to—"

"That kiss," he interrupted, his voice adamant, "was entirely authentic. But I should have done a much more thorough, inspired job of it. Are you any good with a darning needle?"

"What?"

"You can save me some time by lighting that lantern you left outside—"

"So you did see me coming. You said before that—"

"And start checking wormholes in this wood. I'll show you how."

Damn, Kate thought, as she put the blankets down and stomped out to get the lantern. Even if he was taking her in, she was willing, right now, to go along for the ride.

"Come in," Kate called, when someone knocked on the door as she tended her Apothecary rose seedlings two days later. She'd been working hard all winter to propagate them under growing lights in this so-called garden shop. "The door's open," she prompted, when no one entered. Her stomach was still in free fall at the thought it might be Jack.

"It's not really open, but unlocked," Louise observed as she came in, scraping mud off her feet onto the mat.

"Hello, Louise," Kate said, trying to sound cheerful. "You look different in modern dress—well, not really a dress but slacks and a slicker."

"*Touché,*" Louise said with a hint of a smile. "I hope you don't mind my popping in."

"Not at all. I can use some company, with Tanya still gone."

Tanya's great-aunt had become ill so she wasn't back yet. And Kate should have known it wasn't Jack—he'd gotten what he wanted for now here at Shaker Run.

He'd found two large cupboards of Clint Barstow's furniture he was quite sure were being painstakingly, fraudulently aged. But he admitted that wasn't illegal, and it didn't mean a thing until he could prove the pieces were going somewhere to be switched with the real, priceless articles. And that would take some time. Besides, who knew that Barstow wasn't just trying to make authentic, antique reproductions? Kate, like a fool, had said she'd try to find out.

"What can I do for you, Louise?" Kate inquired, when the woman just looked around at first, her high forehead crumpled in a frown.

"I wanted to be certain that you plan to have all this modern equipment out of here before we open in less than a month. Visitors will pretty much have the run of the place, you know, and we can't have a rosarian in Shaker garb using phosphorescent tube lights, fertilizer, etcetera."

"If I could have done old-fashioned air or soil layering instead of this in the middle of winter, I would have," Kate explained patiently. "But since *Rose*

Gallica Officinalis is the only authentic Shaker rose allowed on the grounds..."

"I thought I read that Damasks and Apothecaries were used for their rose water, too."

"A little learning is a dangerous thing," Kate said, amazed anew that Louise knew as much as she did about so many aspects of Shaker life. "Both of those are old-fashioned names for this very breed. And as I was saying, if I didn't give them a jump start, even the twenty mature bushes I have, and these I've got started, wouldn't give us much of a show this year."

"The Shakers were most certainly not interested in show," Louise said with a noticeable shiver.

"I know that, but modern-day tourists just may be. Besides, transplanting bushes can really stress them, and I want to have enough blooms to distill some Shaker rose water this June. And you, Sister Louise, will be presented with the first bottle."

She cocked her head suspiciously. "Why me?"

"Because I think things matter more to you than anyone else here. More even than to Dane and Adrienne. And I appreciate that."

Louise looked relieved. "Then I'd like to walk you out back to holy ground. I take everyone there sooner or later, when I think they're ready. You see, I can't bear for anyone to think that the Shakers were evil or one bit mad, when they were only different—strange in a good way. I want you to understand them."

"All right," Kate agreed. She clapped soil from her hands and quickly watered the rest of the peat pots containing her precious seedlings, which she'd plant outside as soon as the last threat of frost was gone. "But I've already read a lot about holy ground," she assured Louise. "I know it used to be enclosed behind a taller fence and adorned with fir trees. The so-called holy procession was once a year, with the Believers accompanied by the spirits of departed village members and an angelic host. Spiritual gifts were given out, and it was a day of soul-searching and awesome judgment, I believe I read."

"So, you have done your homework. The yearly official visit to holy ground and the Midnight Cry were their two happiest, holiest, if wildest events."

"The Midnight Cry?" Kate asked, her head snapping up. "I don't recall reading about that."

"I shall save that for another time," Louise promised. "Let's just enjoy Shaker Run in all its silent beauty before we're inundated with those well-diggers tomorrow, not to mention the volunteer workers and dancers."

They walked together down the gravel lane and stood between the cemetery and the perfectly square piece of well-tended spring grass called holy ground. Both were set off by fences of piled, flat stones. Kate had more than once explored the old cemetery, its brothers and sisters buried in separate sections, just the way—but for some tasks, such as relegated social time and worship—they had kept separate in life. Here, only their first names were carved in limestone, slowly being washed away by the elements. One day Adrienne had even pointed out the headstone of long-time rosarian Sister Jerusha, whose diary Louise had wanted her to read but could not find.

"Believers used to sing two particular songs when they processed out here to holy ground for their special day," Louise said, her eyes narrowed, her voice almost a whisper as she gazed at the other section across the way. "One was 'Brethren, We Have Come to Worship' and the other was 'Ye Watchers and Ye Holy Ones.' Both songs mention angels, as they believed this holy ground was guarded by an avenging angel with a flaming sword, just as the entrance to Eden was, once Adam and Eve were thrown out. And angels were the ones who sent the Shakers their dances, their furniture designs and their visions.''

Turning their backs on the cemetery, they approached the nearby holy ground. Kate nodded at Louise's lesson, but her thoughts skipped back to the statue of the angel in the cemetery in Toledo. She shivered and wrapped her jacket closer. "So the Shakers thought they had to rebuild that lost heaven-on-earth here to get into the eternal one," Kate mused. "I can't say it wasn't a lovely idea, but impossible since they were dealing with people. I'm afraid Mother Ann had some very misleading visions at times.''

"Don't let me hear you telling any visitors that. A sister would have been cast out of union and condemned by the whole village for such talk back then," Louise insisted.

"I know you love the past, Louise, but I'm rather glad we're living now," Kate said, unwilling to back off.

"Then, just recognize that this is the spot where they sincerely believed that their dear departed, including Mother Ann, came back to dance with them and impart visions," Louise said, her voice almost pleading. "I sometimes wonder if it wasn't why the founders of Shaker Run built their holy ground so close to the cemetery." She glanced toward one and then the other. "The holy ground in most Shaker villages is more remote. You know, Kate, you are probably the only person in the world to have a box seat, as it were, to watch the goings-on here."

"You don't mean to imply that you believe there are actually ghosts—"

"I only mean," Louise interrupted, turning toward her, "that I am going to ask Dane if we might not have a sort of festival once a year, among our other annual events, where the dancers I'm training will come out to holy ground and reenact some of the visions and spirit visitations. I'd very much value your support when I bring it up in a staff meeting. By the way," she said, starting back toward the village so Kate had to hurry to keep up, "has Tanya phoned? With our grand opening barely a month off, she's sorely needed here."

"No, but I hope her great-aunt's all right—even if she has lived a good, long life."

"A good and long life, yes, indeed, that's something to be hoped for," Louise said as she quickened her steps.

"How is your mother doing?" Kate asked, trying not to slip in the mud as they cut off the lane toward the garden shops and Trustees' Building. "I know both you and Ben go to see her quite a bit. I lost my mother early and think you're so fortunate to have yours for so long."

"I'm sorry to hear about your mother, and it is kind of you to inquire. Mother's up and down. With her," Louise explained, as they paused by the garden shop, "it's that her spirit is willing but her flesh is weak. Rather sounds like something Mother Ann would say, doesn't it?—and my mother's name is Ann, by the way. Now you just drop by the dancing some late afternoon, Kate, and see how everyone's doing," she repeated as she disappeared around the corner as if she'd simply vanished.

Kate realized she should have thanked Louise—or should she? When Louise opened the door to Shaker Run's past, it was intriguing, but also downright disturbing.

10

Sweet is the rose but grows upon a briar;
Sweet is the juniper but sharp his bough;
Sweet is the eglantine but pricketh near;
Sweet is the nut but bitter is his pill;
And sweet is moly but his root is ill.
So every sweet with sour is tempered still...

—Edmund Spencer
Sonnet 26
"The Amoretti"

The next morning, Kate took only a moment to watch the team of archeologists from the university excavating the old well near the Center Family Dwelling House that was now Barstow's furniture shop. They had erected some sort of drilling apparatus to widen it and had suspended a metal-and-canvas cradle to lower things, or perhaps themselves, into its depths. Fascinating, but she had no time for that today.

Kate felt a sense of urgency she hadn't had since arriving here in the village. Tanya had called to say her great-aunt was still ill and had asked Kate to tend her herbs and run a few errands. At least one of the favors Tanya asked had fit in perfectly with Kate's desires to get some information out of Clint Barstow.

And despite feeling like a liar and a spy, she was on her way to do it.

"Hi, Clint," she called as she stopped in the open front door of the busy furniture shop. Though he was standing by the window apparently just looking out at the well excavations, she could see three of his workers bent over various tasks.

She had to raise her voice to be heard above the sound of hammering and high-pitched whine of an electrical circular saw. The Shakers had always adapted current technology, whether it be water, steam, wind power or electricity, but Kate wondered if Louise scolded these guys for not sticking with hand tools of the early 1800s era of the village. And had Louise dared to tell Clint he'd have to get rid of his "unauthentic" tattoos Kate could see wrapped around both strong forearms below his un-Shaker-like T-shirt sleeves?

"Hey, what's up?" Clint asked as he ambled toward her. "Just been watching the treasure-hunt guys. Told me they'd be using tiny brushes and dental picks, but looks like they're going at it big-time so far."

"I noticed. Clint, Tanya's great-aunt is still ill so she asked me to bring you this lemon balm oil," she told him, putting the large bottle of it in his callused, dirty hands.

"Yeah, great. We're almost out. We mix it with beeswax to give us a real close polish to what they used to use."

"So you really are striving for replicating the original pieces," Kate observed. She nodded, hoping to show him she approved. "It amazes me how antique some of your furniture looks when the pieces are obviously brand-new.''

''Bigger demand for reality,'' he explained, looking pleased. ''Still, it does take some getting used to when I take a chain or hammer to new wood to make it look old,'' Clint said, bouncing the bottle of lemon balm hand to hand as if it were too hot to handle. ''It's the main difference between us and Kilcourse's workshop. He uses old techniques but doesn't go out of his way to age the stuff like we do—not that we get a lot more profit per piece than he does. But we will, once we get our reputation built up, once this village really thrives and visitors see what we got to offer.''

Kate tried to remember everything Clint had so freely told her. But the fact he'd been so forthcoming meant he wasn't trying to hide anything, didn't it? Keeping an eye on Barstow and his boys, as Jack called them, could be a dead end. Either that or she wasn't much of an investigator, because she'd believed from the first that Clint Barstow wasn't capable of enough cleverness to switch furniture, let alone lie about it.

Kate headed back to work at a good clip, then stopped in her tracks and gasped. Getting out of a black, unmarked car parked in front of the Trustees' Building was Stan Rudzinski.

''I can't really say it's great to see you, Detective,'' Kate said as she walked Rudzinski out to the garden shop. She had no intention of anyone overhearing whatever this man had to say to her.

''Now, don't go making snap judgments, Ms. Marburn. Maybe I'm here with some real good news.'' It annoyed her that the man actually looked glad to see her.

"If so, I'd love to hear it," she prompted, as he stared up at Tanya's quote, *If you would have a lovely garden, you should live a lovely life.*

"Interesting people, the Shakers," he observed as he came in and stood at the end of her potting worktable, only to drum his fingers on it nervously. "I've been reading up on them."

She decided not to bite on that lure. "So *are* you here with good news for me, Detective?"

"I don't suppose you'd want to call me Zink."

"I don't suppose so."

"Look," he said, and smacked his palms down hard enough to make her clay pots rattle, "I don't like being treated like some sort of pariah. And here I read that Shakers always showed great hospitality to visitors."

She sighed and turned to face him down the length of the cluttered worktable. "I don't want you to think I have some sort of guilty conscience," she insisted, "because I don't. But it's hard to feel real chummy toward someone who pretends to be a friend but could well be waiting to fry me."

"Fry you? Sounds like you're having visions of electric chairs, Kate. Surely you want answers—the truth—about what happened to Sarah Denbigh."

"Of course, I do. But I can see in your eyes that you are out to blame m—"

"I'm not! Look," he said, thrusting out both open hands in supplication, "I admire your backbone, but I think because of what you've been through before, you're overreacting."

"No, I think I'm reacting to a homicide detective's

driving way down here to see me over what's evidently a hot case to him. You still think she was murdered, don't you?''

"You ever get a gut feeling about something?'' he challenged, hitting his chest with his fist.

She sensed she had him on the defensive for once. "Of course, I do. I told you I had that feeling when Sarah was up in her suite the night of the party, even before I found her there.''

"So I recall,'' he said, nodding. "It's one of the things, along with the fact that you called for help the minute you found her there, that makes me believe you're innocent. You're a bright woman, and with what you went through before with the investment scandal, you're a cautious woman. No way you'd do anything to land yourself in the negative limelight again. So if you'd harmed Sarah, you'd never arrange to be the one to find her and call for help. Unless...''

"I've been waiting for the other shoe to drop, Detective.''

"Unless you got her blood on your gown and figured you couldn't explain it any other way.''

"You never change, do you? I'm going to have to ask you to leave and take your next little field trip to see Mason James, my lawyer.'' She walked over and yanked open the door. He didn't budge.

"Kate, the point is, having thought all that out, I believe your story,'' he plunged on, speaking even faster. He made no pretense of calm nonchalance now. "There's only one thing I'd like you to tell me, so I can close all this in my own mind. I hear you went to a shrink after your husband left—which sounds really reasonable to me.''

"Detective Rudzinski, we are finished talking. It

may be public record I sought counseling, but it's none of your business for what reason I went. Are you going to try the approach that I'm mentally off and didn't even recall I hurt Sarah, or that I'm some sort of pathological liar? I don't know where you get your information, but—"

"You'll kill me when I tell you, but I'm going to level with you, anyway," he said, still holding his ground, though he was now fidgeting and shifting from foot to foot. "After you first went to live at Groveland, Varina evidently pried out of her mother that you were at a shrink's."

"Varina again!" is all she managed to say.

"And I wanted to warn you that she also let slip that her lawyer found some precedent for the last will being overturned, since you were living on her mother's property at the time and had, as they're claiming, alienated the woman's affections from Palmer and Varina."

"And you came here claiming to have good news?" she cried, flinging out both hands.

"Now hear me out. In addition to Mrs. Denbigh's death being officially deemed accidental, I also have good news for Jack Kilcourse—I finally brought the check the city owes him," he said. "But as for the case, yeah, the blood splatter evidence is inconclusive. Mrs. Denbigh could either have fallen hard or been thrown into that blanket chest. She could as easily have removed her glasses, and placed them at arm's length, as lost them if she were shoved."

"Then that's it, right?" Kate queried, with a shudder at the visions of Sarah's death his words evoked. "Case either closed or at least shelved?"

"Kate, is it true you used to have hallucinations and that's why you went to that shrink?"

"You know, Detective," she said, completely exasperated, "I almost fell for your helpful routine that time. But if you don't get out of here, there's going to be blood splatter when I smash a clay pot over your head. Now *that* will give you an open-and-shut case!"

He forced a tight smile and shook his raised index finger. "If you did that you'd ruin my main theory that, unlike Varina, you don't have a volatile temper. And then I'd have to start following you around again until you made a slip," he said, and finally stepped outside with a half wave over his shoulder. "And I'm sure I'd never blend in with the roses here, or—" he glanced at the little cemetery out back "—with the tombstones."

Kate stared wide-eyed at him. Was he hinting that he'd been the one following her in the Toledo cemetery? That black car he drove today was not the one, but she had been certain there had been a woman with that driver, and it could have been his partner. Kate had observed that he always drove when he and Detective Martin were together.

To be sure he left, Kate followed him around the Trustees' Building. He strolled back to his car as if he hadn't a care in the world, got in and drove away. She watched until he turned into Jack's distant driveway, then, distraught at all he'd told her—or had he intentionally, helpfully warned her?—hurried inside to call Mason James.

Late that afternoon, Kate checked on Tanya's herbs, which were drying in the distilling shed where

Kate would also make rose water this summer. With her own rose starts taking up a lot of room in their main garden shop, Tanya's work had spilled over from the herb house to this small building, too. Usually working with plants in any of this cluster of sister's shops calmed Kate, but not today.

On top of everything else, Rudzinski's visit had set her on edge. Standing here in this silent, fragrant shed, she pictured tourists she didn't know wandering in to watch her making the double-distillation rose water, which early Americans used not so much for fragrance but for a common cooking flavoring, much the way people today use vanilla. But even those warm thoughts couldn't take away the chill of picturing strangers staring at her as she worked. "Ye Watchers and Ye Holy Ones," began one of the sacred songs for the holy ground Louise had mentioned.

And now Rudzinski had reminded her of her stalking obsession and suggested he, too, had watched her for wrong moves.

"Tanya," Kate said aloud, "wish you were here to buck me up."

"Talking to yourself already, or communing with the old Shaker spirits?" a man's voice behind her asked. Startled, Kate spun to face a smiling Dane Thompson.

"Just wishing Tanya were back," she explained, as he stepped into the small space. "But even with all the work here, I'd never want her to be called away from comforting her aunt. I know how much I wish I'd had time with Sarah Denbigh before she died, to thank her again and tell her how much she'd meant to me."

"The great bounty she left you in her will shows

she knew you cared,'' he said, his voice comforting. Dane always did sound half professor, half preacher.

"I'll always treasure that," Kate admitted, "even though I had a visitor today who told me things may have taken a turn for the worse in the heirs' challenge. Evidently, Sarah's daughter's lawyer has found some loophole to overturn the last will. I swear, I'd like to be rid of that woman."

"That's terrible news," he commiserated with a frown furrowing his high brow. "You're in Adrienne's and my thoughts all the time in this difficult situation."

"I appreciate that. But what can I do for you?"

"Tanya said that she had a couple of things for the display on old-time Shaker herbal drugs over at the brethren shop we're using for the infirmary this year. I hope you can be more accommodating than Clint. He just had a fit when I reminded him we needed an adult-size invalid cradle for the display. You know, those things actually look like modern-day coffins, but Shaker nurses found rocking adult patients as good as rocking babies to comfort them."

"Never underestimate Shaker ingenuity," she said, reaching for her flashlight. She'd restocked it with fresh batteries so she'd be prepared next time the lights went out. It was quite dim back in some of Tanya's herb bins. "Let me see if I can help," she offered. "What's needed?"

"Belladonna, for one."

With a shake of her head, Kate surveyed the way Tanya had taken over this shed with stacks of drying racks for her herbs. Kate was going to have to get them out of here soon, or the distillations would put humidity into them, not dry them. While Dane waited,

Kate shone the light on canvas rack after rack, and scrabbled through the drying layers of leaves and roots looking for what was labeled *belladonna*.

"Too much can be toxic, she says here," Dane explained, evidently reading from Tanya's notes. Kate heard a piece of paper crinkle. "She says that the Shakers used and sold it as a relaxant and narcotic. Hmm," he went on, "I guess they were ahead of their time on that, too. Today it's used for digestive tract relaxants, like Donnatal. But it says here that Southern belles used to use drops of it to dilate the pupils of their eyes when that was in style, even though mere daylight then gave them piercing headaches. You believe that?"

"I'm continually amazed at the arcane things Tanya knows, but not at the lengths to which people can go," Kate admitted.

Kate finally found the belladonna and took out a large piece of dried leaves and root. "It's probably one of Tanya's pet herbs," she told him as she wrapped it in a piece of paper towel. "Too much is poison but a little can help. What else?"

She dug out henbane, which smelled terrible and was used to produce a deep sleep in patients. "It kills insects like crazy," Dane explained, "an early pesticide."

"Maybe I could use that to protect my roses," Kate observed. "What's next?"

"Hmm, this is a good one. Angel's Trumpet. Perfect name for the Shakers with their angel visitations and all. Says here it used to be a form of opium to relieve pain."

"A pretty name, but it smells about as weird as henbane," Kate said as she located it and took a handful. "It doesn't say any of this is a contact poison, does it?"

"No, all ingested, I think," he said with a little laugh.

"Thanks a lot."

Kate couldn't find lettuce seeds until she'd gone through several small tin cans on what served as Tanya's desk.

"Here it is," she told Dane, who hovered over her so close Kate wished he'd give her a little breathing room. "Tell me what these were for, because I was wondering when she showed me the lettuce starts in her hotboxes."

"Ah, says here they allay coughing and are a good sedative for hypochondria, nervous complaints and— get this one—nymphomania," he said, and chuckled. "Let's not let Louise in on that. Can't imagine they'd need a cure for that in a celibate Shaker village. But it says here they used to collect a milky substance from incisions in the lettuce stalk with a piece of cotton, then make an extract of it to produce a false kind of opium, too."

"I'd be the last one to criticize Tanya's fascination with harmful herbs that can also be helpful," she admitted. "I've often planted white lobelia between roses for the visual impact, and lobelia can cause death if overingested. And I've read the Shakers planted rue among their roses as a natural insecticide, and that can cause everything from rashes to abortions. People just have to be careful with all this."

As they spoke, she carefully wrapped the tiny seeds in paper amidst Tanya's array of corks, funnels, scales and an herb press. "She's even going to write a book on it someday," Kate added.

"Someday?" Dane said with a little snort of surprise. "Last time I asked, she was halfway through it. Thanks, Kate. I know her being away has put an extra burden on you. I think having the opening so close is making us all a little crazy."

He patted her shoulder on the way out. So her friend Tanya, who had already begun her book, had lied to her, just the way Jack had the other night. But then, not everyone could be as painfully accurate and as truthful as Louise and Clint Barstow.

"So, do you have a favorite place to eat in Athens?" Jack asked Kate as he drove them into town for dinner the next night.

"Not really, though I know the 7 Sauces has great pasta."

"Sounds good to me, though it seems we should be eating Greek food in a place called Athens. So Clint sounded like he had nothing to hide, huh?" he circled back to their earlier conversation.

"A few years ago I would have staked my life on the fact he was telling the truth, but I realize I'm not such a good judge of people anymore," she admitted.

"Since me, you mean?"

"Do I hear a guilty conscience speaking? No," she said, shifting slightly sideways to see him better, "I mean since my husband ran out on me and Erin."

"Sorry I brought it up. I'd like to meet Erin, though."

"I thought maybe you didn't like kids, or at least teenagers. You've never asked about her before."

"It's not that I don't like them, but just that I don't know any," he said. "You know—have any in my life."

A long pause followed where his silence seemed to scream at her. Why didn't he even try to follow up on what she'd said about her husband deserting her—unless he somehow already knew all about that? Or did he think such a conversation would mean *he'd* have to make confessions, too.

"Did Rudzinski tell you he'd been to see me first?" Kate asked.

"He did. I think he admires you and wants to help."

"Oh, right. Now that makes me think you're not such a good judge of character, either," she insisted.

A tight grin twisted his lips. "The guy's fascinated by the Shakers, so I showed him a lot of furniture and explained how they lived and thought."

"Did you confide in him about your furniture thefts—I mean, the thefts of your furniture?"

"No, I let him confide in me that he's still working on that angle in Mrs. Denbigh's death." Kate sat up straighter and leaned toward him. "He asked me quite a bit about my furniture again, and what was being made in Shaker Run."

"I *knew* he hadn't given up on her death!"

"Kate, if she met with some sort of foul play, thank God for someone like Zink, however plodding or annoying he is. Besides, I've been an insomniac for years, and he killed some of the dark hours, as I've come to think of them. We had breakfast at four a.m. before he headed back to Toledo. I really think you may have misjudged the guy."

"Maybe, but I have something better to make you sleep than staying up with Zink Rudzinski all night. I've had trouble sleeping for years, too."

He gave her an intense look before returning his

attention to the road, then put a hand to the seat back behind her head, slightly snagging his big fingers in her hair. Vibrations feathered down her nape to her spine. Too late, she realized he thought she was coming on to him. And had she meant it that way? She was very attracted to him, though that was the last thing she needed in her life right now. Or maybe it was exactly what she needed.

"I'd like to hear about any cure you have," he said with a grin that lifted his thick eyebrows. He kept glancing from her to the road—full face to aquiline profile. She was so close that, though he was clean-shaven, she could see the outline of where his beard would be. He emanated the slight tang of pine as if he'd been out among fresh fir trees all day.

"Don't get any ideas," she said, laughing but hitting his shoulder with her fist. "Tanya's valerian herbal mix tea is the antidote for insomnia. I know others have used melatonin pills or popped seda-tives—"

"I don't take anything like that," he interrupted, and put both hands back on the wheel. His teasing, open expression had slammed shut; his voice had gone sharp-edged, his face stony. She was amazed at how swiftly he could change moods and close the invisible door on his thoughts and emotions.

"Not even vitamins?" she pursued.

"You got it. By the way, I meant to tell you," he went on hurriedly, "I found out more about why the lights went out at Shaker Run during the storm."

For once she was relieved when he changed the subject instead of stonewalling her. "You said earlier that the wind had snapped a pole in front of your place that carried both electric and phone lines to the village," she reminded him.

"Not exactly," he admitted, shrugging his big shoulders. "I ran into one of the guys from the repair crew at the gas station in town. He says the wind didn't topple the pole—a car snapped it."

"Snapped a telephone pole—then just backed away and disappeared in that storm?"

"This guy saw definitive tire tracks in the mud where the wind had scoured the snow away. He said it was really strange that there was no scattering of plastic from broken headlights, which is always expected from low-slung cars today. The vehicle's fender hit the pole higher than most cars would, too, so he figured it might have been a truck or four-wheel drive, until he saw that the tire tread imprints were from a car."

Kate's stomach cartwheeled. If it wasn't a modern car and wasn't a truck, maybe the vehicle that hit that pole, plunging her into the dark, was the one she'd seen. "Are those tire tracks still there?" she asked, trying to keep her voice calm and sound merely curious.

"No. I looked. The warmer weather's turned it all to mush again. A mini-mystery, Ms. Marburn, but we've got to keep our minds on fake Shaker furniture—and dinner. I'm starved."

With his right hand, he reached over to squeeze hers clenched on her lap. Staring straight ahead, Kate saw not the sleek, silver hood of his car. In her mind's eye, she saw that antique, black car from the cemetery ramming the pole as it had meant to ram her.

Kate remembered the waiter she and Erin had had a few months ago, more by his unusual name than his face. "Hi, Stone. The redhead's mother—remember me?" she asked when she and Jack were seated in a back booth.

His open face showed surprise, but he smiled, looking slightly embarrassed. "Oh, yeah, sure. She's been back in on Sundays as regular as can be. Is her name Angel?"

Kate laughed and was relieved to see Jack smile. He'd been really uptight since they'd arrived, and she'd almost started to regret this formal date she'd accepted with him. She needed a break from tensions at the village, not a roller-coaster plunge into even more.

"No, you misheard—unless he's nicknamed her that," Kate said. "It's Erin."

"Oh, that suits her, the Isle of Erin and all that," Stone said as he gave them their menus. "And the guy's name is an *M* word, uh—"

"Mark."

"Oh, yeah. Glad to see you again, Erin's mom."

Jack buried his nose in the menu. "Jack, I was really looking forward to this but do you think we're making a mistake?" Kate asked.

He put his menu down and leaned toward her. "I have made a lot of those in my life, but if you're a mistake for me, I don't ever want to know it."

"That's hardly one of the nicest compliments I've ever had. We can just call this quits now and—"

"Kate, Zink is not the only one who admires you and hasn't let you know about it because he—I'm just not good at...feelings anymore."

Stunned at the admission, she nodded. He had just told her so much. "Then it's not just insomnia we have in common,'' she assured him. "There's nothing like the blind leading the blind, but I'm willing to pursue a relationship—friends, at least, if you are.''

Kate was aching to ask him, *You're just not good at feelings since when? Since what happened?* But instead, her gaze riveted on his, she nodded in a silent pact.

Stone returned to find them shaking hands across the table.

11

Persian legends maintain that the rose's red complexion came about because a nightingale loved the white rose too much and grasped it tightly to its breast. The thorns pierced it and the blood turned the white rose red.

—Peter Coats
Flowers in History

Kate had returned to the village late, since she and Jack had eaten a leisurely meal and driven back to sit in front of his fireplace with snifters of brandy. And yet, she realized when he returned her to the Trustees' House in the village, as much as they had discussed family—his retired parents lived in Florida—current events, careers and plans, he had avoided his personal history again.

Kate wondered if it could be because he didn't want to make her feel that she must discuss her own painful past. She loved being valued for herself for once, with no questions asked. Or was Jack's avoidance of such revelations simply to protect himself? And could she really know and trust a man who was certain where he was going, but who wouldn't say where he'd been?

Now, this mutual good-night kiss in his car was enough to make her push all that aside. It could not just be her imagination that his kisses were as dark as they were delicious, and therefore as mysteriously luring as Jack himself.

She feathered her fingertips through the slightly silvered, dark hair at his temples, then cupped her hand around the back of his neck as if to hold the kiss. As dizzy as she felt, he made her want to soar. Though he had restrained himself when they'd sat before the fire, it seemed now that something had snapped in him. He trailed frenzied kisses down her chin to her throat, his hands pulling her across the seat toward him until the gearshift stopped them.

"Darned new cars," he murmured, his breath warm against the hollow of her throat. He kept kissing her there, his hair tickling her chin. Slowly, he lifted his head. "Right now, I'd much rather be driving one of my dad's old-fashioned ones with one big front seat." He reached back to click his seat belt free, then leaned over her, as if he were embracing her, to undo hers.

"What's that line from an old movie?" she said, her voice husky. "'Fasten your seat belts, everyone. It's going to be a bumpy ride.'"

"Or was that 'It's going to be a bumpy night?'" he whispered, cradling her closer and kissing her hard again.

"I, for one, intend to sleep tonight," she said when their lips parted. "No bumps if I take some of my herbal tea, though maybe that brandy will be enough. Are you sure you don't want some of that tea to take with you?"

"No medicinal tea, nothing like that," he insisted, and set her away from him.

"You aren't a Mormon or Christian Scientist, are you?" she blurted.

"Kate, I'm not a health nut. Used to be but no more. I'm—was a Methodist, before..."

He paused and looked past her in the darkness.

"Before what?" she prompted.

"Before I had to rebuild myself. Like you said, it's late, and I'd better get going."

She had a hundred questions now, but he opened his door and got out, slamming it after him. Cold night slapped her back to reality. Was it worth it, she wondered, to become intrigued by this Jekyll-and-Hyde? She should forget it right now, but she couldn't. At least she knew what she was up against. Mike, the once beloved betrayer, had always seemed so open and up-front, but he and Jack were like night and day—thank heavens for that, she thought, as he opened her car door.

He walked her up to the Trustees' House and watched while she used her key. He had given her back the master he'd had made, though that didn't mean, she knew, that he hadn't made a second one. And she was just too tired to demand to know that tonight.

When she'd turned the lights on, he left and drove away. Silence settled like a cloak on the village, as Kate made her way up to the third floor of the large building, turning lights on, then off, behind her, as she went. This sturdy dwelling creaked like an old person's bones at night, and sometimes it seemed to breathe with muted memories and voices of the past. Maybe, she thought, that's what they meant by Shaker spirits. They had put so much into this village that they never quite left it, even in death.

The moment she went into her apartment, she heard the beeper on her answering machine, telling her she has a message. Not even taking her coat off, praying Erin did not have some emergency, Kate hurried over and pushed the play button.

"Kate, it's Tanya, still in Covington. Aunt Samantha died late this afternoon." Her voice snagged. *"It was a* blessing *since she was suffering. Please tell everyone I'm* sorry *but there's no way I'll be back till at least Sunday evening, as the calling hours and funeral are noon Saturday at her big Baptist church here. Thanks for doing whatever you can to cover for me—you know, take care of the herbs and all. Uh, let me give you my phone and address here in case you need it..."*

Kate played the message back twice and copied the information carefully. If it weren't so late, she'd call the Thompsons and Willises right now to let them know.

As harried as things were here, she wanted to go to the funeral. She knew how Tanya felt, and she wanted to be there to support her.

Erin heard the phone ringing as she came into her dorm room. She'd just taken a shower down the hall; Amy had already snatched up the phone.

"Oh, hi, Mark. Yes, she's coming in right now. Just a sec."

Erin's pulse started to pound. She put her plastic bucket with her soap and shampoo down and took the receiver from Amy. She closed her eyes to picture him.

"M-Mark?"

"Hi, baby. Just wanted to be sure we're on for Sunday."

"Oh, yes, sure. Is everything okay? I mean, you don't usually call this late."

"So why are you just coming in, then?"

"I haven't been out, just taking a shower. This is not the plush life, you know, and I have to go clear down the hall."

"Life's tough, huh? I just wanted to tell you I might not be able to call you on Saturday to set up our Sunday, because I've got to take a little business trip. But same time, same place, okay?"

"Sure. It seems like everyone's heading somewhere this weekend. Kate's going on a trip, too, to a funeral at some Baptist church in Covington, Kentucky, for some once-famous gospel singer."

"Is that right? Well, love you, angel. Gotta go."

Before Erin could say more, the line went dead. She put the phone down slowly and just stood there.

"Not problems?" Amy asked as she scooted down in her bed where she'd evidently been studying. The covers were wrinkled, and an open book was half buried.

"No. No problems."

"Why don't you ever bring him up to the room?" Amy asked, stifling a yawn. "We'd all like to meet him, your 'phantom lover.'"

"He's not my lover."

"Well, if he was, I wouldn't tell your mother."

That jolted Erin back to the here and now. She put her things away and yanked her covers down on her bed.

"Or you could at least ask him to the spring dance,

or get him to stay for a whole weekend," Amy went on.

"He has a long drive to get here, and he's got a— a job as well as classes there. We decided Sunday is our day, and that's that."

"Okay, okay. Does he still look like his picture?"

Erin glanced at the old picture of Mark she'd taped on her closet door over the poster of Leonardo Di-Caprio and Kate Winslet windblown on the prow of the *Titanic*.

"Yeah, he hasn't changed much. Just like all of us, a little older."

"He always sounds that way. Nothing like an older man. Don't forget to set your alarm, or you'll oversleep again." Amy's voice became muffled as she hunched into the covers again, her book over her crossed knees.

Yes, *Mother,* Erin almost said, angry at Amy's bossiness, but she bit her lip. Lately, she'd been unable to sleep at night, as if insomnia were suddenly in her genes, her *Y* ones, at least. She didn't think her father had ever lost one wink of sleep over anything, not even when his world fell in. But her mom used to be a real mess.

Erin shut her eyes and pictured her stepmother darting around their living room like a trapped animal in a cage that night Erin had tiptoed downstairs. It had been a few weeks after the embezzlement scandal broke and her dad had disappeared. As usual, Erin had cried herself to sleep, then woken up suddenly panicked and sweating, only to find Kate's—her parents'—bed empty.

Like a crazy woman, Kate was rushing from one living room window to another, peering out into the darkness. As Erin stared aghast from the staircase, Kate also darted from one piece of furniture to another, looking under things peering, up into lampshades, rummaging through drawers she yanked open. She was pawing through her houseplants in the front bay window by the time she noticed her stepdaughter on the stairs.

"Oh!" Kate had shrieked, jamming her fists against her lips, knocking a plant onto the hardwood floor. The ceramic pot cracked, spilling soil and an African violet at Kate's bare feet.

"What's the matter?" Erin had cried, gripping the banister. "What is it?"

Kate's eyes had looked sunken, haunted. Though she'd always been slender, lately she looked gaunt, especially bare-legged in one of Dad's big T-shirts. She crossed her arms and clasped her elbows as if to hold herself up.

Sucking in a breath, she lied, "It's nothing, honey. Can't you sleep, either?"

"I just wanted something to eat—crackers or a cookie. But—*what* are you doing?" she demanded, slowly going down the last few steps.

"I...I just wanted to be sure no one was outside—you know, a reporter or someone upset about what happened."

"At midnight? And what are you looking for in here?"

"You just never know if they've put in a hidden camera or bugged this place, since they follow me everywh—"

Kate had stopped talking, evidently realizing how nuts she sounded. And then, sobbing into her hands, she'd collapsed beside the broken pot. Scared of maybe losing Kate, too, Erin had held her and rocked her like a baby. And she'd made Kate call a doctor to get help the very next day.

Now, Erin jumped as her roommate slapped her textbook closed and clicked off her light. Erin sighed, set her clock and turned her lamp off, too. She'd better get her head together, because her grades were starting to suffer. She snuggled deep under her comforter. Maybe she could pray herself to sleep, because, despite increasing stomachaches and restless nights, she had a lot to be thankful for lately.

Waiting in the long line to greet the large number of bereaved family members at the Covington New Hope Baptist Church, Kate listened intently to the recordings of Samantha Sams, in her prime, singing gospel songs. Kate tried to let the swells of "Swing Low, Sweet Chariot" calm her.

I looked over Jordan, and what did I see,
Coming for to carry me home.
A band of angels coming after me,
Coming for to carry me home...

Although no one in the throng recognized Kate, she saw some reporters and TV people. This whole situation was starting to remind her of losing Sarah, and her heart flowed out to Tanya again. The family had even brought in several pieces of the deceased's Shaker furniture and placed some of the huge floral displays on them, up by the altar. Sarah would have loved that, but, of course, Varina and Palmer couldn't have cared less. Still, the flowers and the furniture were not making Kate feel at home here.

"Thanks so much for coming!" Tanya greeted her, when Kate got to the front of the line. They hugged hard, something they had never before done, but death always brought the living closer. "It means a *lot* to me."

"To me, too" was all Kate managed at first, tears blurring her vision. Despite being gone such a short time, Tanya looked thinner. Her beautiful chocolate-hued skin was tinged with gray, her eyes were bloodshot. She wore not the black worn by most of her large family, but a striking jade wool suit with a long skirt.

"I couldn't *not* come," Kate told her. "I wanted to honor your aunt, even if I didn't know her, and just be here with you."

"You came alone?"

Kate nodded. "Jack wanted to come, but he has clients in from the East Coast. Some guy he says always knows exactly what he wants him to make." Everyone at Shaker Run had asked her to make excuses, but she didn't want to launch into all that, and she knew Tanya understood.

"I promise," Tanya went on, blotting under her eyes, "that the service will be a blessing to you. I'll see you in the church Fellowship Hall for the meal after the interment, okay?"

"Yes, I'll be there."

After Kate shook hands and introduced herself to a few of the many family members clustered around the closed casket, she moved on, examining the various flower arrangements. One, mostly roses which she wished could be her own flowers, read, The Staff and Your Friends at Shaker Run Village. She shook her head. The Shakers would probably have sent be-

headed blooms so that they could not be used for
ornamental display. She remembered the flower heads
thrown on the Denbigh graves.

Kate edged toward the back of the crowded sanctuary, looking at the photographs. Stretching back de-
cades, events in Samantha Sams's life included singing everywhere from churches to the *Ed Sullivan
Show,* the Grand Ole Opry, and the White House during Kennedy's presidency. Kate heard someone say
that Samantha had "helped break down the color
lines in this country—just one step behind Marian
Anderson, singing at the White House..." It was an
impressive and moving display.

But however Kate tried to distract herself, she kept
feeling she was being watched. She glanced at Tanya
to see if she was looking her way, but her friend was
still greeting people. It was probably just the fact that
local media were covering this, that set her on edge,
Kate thought. But she made her way toward the back
of the sanctuary, from where she could survey the
room better. She sank gratefully onto the end of a
pew.

Two elderly African-American women were sitting
two pews ahead of her, both fanning themselves with
the memorial programs, though it wasn't that warm
in this high-ceilinged room.

"Can't believe it came on her so fast," the heavier
of the two finely dressed matrons confided to the
other, though she talked loudly as if she were hard-
of-hearing. "I mean, I knew she was getting up there,
but I always thought she had a cast-iron stomach."

"You live that long, somethin's gonna get you, too,
Bessie, don't tell me it won't. I'm just wondering
who's gonna get all her collections of things. Why,

they could make a paying museum out of all that woman had, signatures and gifts, photos of famous people, not to mention all that Shakes furniture.''

''*Shaker* furniture,'' Bessie corrected her friend. ''Shakes is those rough-cut kind of shingles like to blow off roofs in a storm. Well, the storms of life are over for our Sammy Sams. And the good Lord's gonna be glad to see her coming to join her voice to those angel choruses. Just wish her homegoing could have been a bit more peaceful, I do. Pains and convulsions from complications of food poisoning's no way for one of the Lord's earthly saints to go, not if you ask me.''

Food poisoning, Kate thought. Tanya hadn't mentioned that.

As moving as the funeral was, it seemed to blur by for Kate. She wondered if Tanya had tried to help her aunt with her healing herbs in the end. Although Tanya hadn't mentioned food poisoning, why should she? With a person as old and frail as Samantha Sams looked in the latest photos, any complications could be fatal ones.

The entire congregation sang Samantha's favorite hymn, ''Amazing Grace.'' The pastor and several other speakers paid their tributes to ''the amazing Samantha.'' The large choir raised their voices in a rocking rendition of Samantha's beloved gospel songs. Often people broke into rhythmic clapping and occasionally shouted, ''Amen! Praise the Lord!'' It was a far different service from those Kate knew, but wonderfully exuberant and spontaneous—so real. Maybe, she mused, this was more like the Shakers, who used to let their emotions run their worship. Kate sensed she knew now what Louise meant when she kept after her dancers to "start out in control, then just let it run away with you."

Everyone rose while the casket was carried from the church and put in the hearse at the front of the long procession. Cars with purple-and-white funeral flags snaked twice around the old church and disappeared down a side street. Kate's car was about halfway back in the outer line.

Like everyone else, she got in and sat with her engine idling. There were so many family members of the deceased that they got in the limo, several cars behind it, and scattered into others throughout the first part of the long line. Kate lost sight of where Tanya was riding, but it was somewhere up ahead.

Finally, the hearse and the family limo pulled out, and then the cars in the inner line began to move, passing her. She sat mesmerized by the faces, yet seeing Sarah's and remembering the large turnout at that funeral.

An idea hit Kate so hard that she jerked her hands on the steering wheel and hit the horn. When the people ahead of her, who couldn't possibly move yet, turned to glare she tried to signal them that it was an accident. But was it an accident that Kate had lost Sarah and now Tanya had lost Samantha? Kate wondered if Tanya would inherit her great-aunt's Shaker furniture and bring it to Shaker Run. If Dane and Adrienne were trying to orchestrate that, they wouldn't even have to recruit Tanya the way they had Kate. Worse, had someone tried to take some of Samantha's valuable pieces of furniture but decided to get rid of the old woman when she became suspicious or caught them at it?

"You're nuts," Kate told herself aloud. "You're getting absolutely paranoid again. There is no pattern here, and no one is following you."

And then, as the unwinding coil of cars snaked by, her worst nightmare sprang to life.

"We're going to go right by her car," the man said. "These dark windows better hide us."

"You know they darken in full daylight. Duck down if you have to."

"Do we need to do this to keep her in line?"

"Not in line, but off balance. She's begun to question others, when we want her to just question—doubt—herself."

The woman slouched in her seat, but the man only tugged his fedora lower as they drove by.

"It's them!" Kate cried. "It wasn't in my head!"

The old-fashioned black car with tinted windows looked so proper—so perfect—in this procession for the elderly Samantha Sams. Though Kate's insides tensed, she did not physically react at once. After all, the black hearse and black limo also had tinted windows. But this one—

They were two cars past her now, and she was still stuck without enough clearance front or back to get out of line. The cars behind the black one kept her from seeing its license, from even seeing it anymore. It was as if she'd imagined it.

Kate unhooked her seat belt and jumped out. Leaving her car idling, she darted between it and the one ahead. The people she had honked at were still looking askance at her. Ignoring them, she darted between the moving and stationary lines of cars.

She could see the old black car again. It was four or five ahead, and the entire entourage was accelerating now. Kate ran faster, trying to catch up, to see. Surely this could not be a coincidence: that someone in Samantha's community of elderly friends had a car like that. If so, it would have a license plate. When she caught up and knocked on its door or window, they would stop or roll it down, and she could see their faces—their normal, real faces.

Her blood roared in her ears. She was out of breath and maybe out of her mind. Far ahead, as the line of cars turned right onto the main street, she could see the police motorcycle escort had stopped traffic. The officer was saluting as the cars came out and rolled by. But he got back on his vehicle and sped away, just as Kate reached the street.

She began to run along the sidewalk. Her high heels were tripping her, killing her, but she pressed on, darting around occasional pedestrians. She could see the top and side of the black car now, but not its plate. When she realized she wouldn't be able to catch up, she darted into the parking lot of a strip mall, trying to find a better angle from which to read the plate.

Unlike before, there was a license plate this time, white, but she could not read it from here. With a stitch in her side, she turned and ran back toward the church. She'd get back in her car—catch up with them that way.

At the church, the procession had moved away to leave her car first in line, but the cars behind her were so closely parked, they couldn't budge.

"I'm sorry—sorry," she called to the driver behind her, and got in, trying to ignore the glares. Thank God her keys were still here. She hit the accelerator and sped up to the car that had been ahead of her.

Should she keep her place and try to find the car and its inhabitants at the cemetery? Or if they had spotted her running after them—she always thought of the occupants as them, a man driving and a woman in the passenger seat—would they leave before she could get there? This was taking forever, and she had no idea how far the cemetery was. But city traffic was heavy even though the procession was moving through red lights with the motorcycle escort. Should she try to tell the policeman that a black car like that had followed her before in another cemetery?

No, she told herself. *He'd think you're crazy—and maybe you are.*

But it all seemed so unreal—just like when she had been sure someone was following her everywhere after Mike had screwed half of Toledo out of their savings. She could easily understand why someone would have been after her then, but now...? Unless it was someone Varina hired, someone paid to harass a rose grower from a rural southern Ohio Shaker village.

It seemed an eternity before the procession turned into the cemetery. As they wound their way around the various plotted sections—the vintage of the place reminded her of Toledo's Woodlawn—she decided not to get trapped in this long line again. She had to park where she could get out easily, and in a place from which she could see that car.

She turned out of the procession, pulled over under a tree near a hand pump, and got out, locking her car. Sprinting down the gravel lane, she stood back to spot where the car must be in the procession. Unless it had gotten out of order, it wasn't there.

More frustrated than fearful now, she strode toward the cars. Again, her eyes skimmed over to where she was certain it should have been. Even during the short graveside service, she stalked up and down the entire lineup of parked cars. Finally, out of breath and with her heart pounding, she leaned on a tall tombstone and tried to stop her legs—her whole life—from collapsing.

Kate hoped she wasn't making even more of a fool of herself than she already had. During the buffet dinner back at the church in the basement of Fellowship Hall, and after she had spent some time with Tanya, she forced herself to go from table to table, asking people, "Did you see an old, black car with dark-tinted windows in the funeral procession today? Friends of mine have a rare car like that, and I thought it might have been them, though I couldn't find them later."

Finally, a thin, well-dressed young man with a wife and four cute kids said, "You're the lady who honked at us, and then got out and ran."

"Yes, I'm sorry. I hit the horn by mistake when I was so surprised to see my friends drive by."

"But you didn't see them at church during the calling hours or at the graveside?" he asked disbelievingly. He stopped eating chicken to stare up at her.

"Uh, no," she admitted, feeling sheepish as well as silly.

"And they're not here now?" he pursued. "What's their names?"

"Sorry to have bothered you," Kate said, realizing

she'd have to go about this some other way. Maybe
she should tell Stan Rudzinski what had happened in
both Toledo and here today. Maybe he could check
it out somehow, and it would help convince him that
someone hostile was out there. But since she couldn't
even give him a license plate number...

"Didn't say I didn't see them," the young man
said, as she started away. Kate turned back. She could
have hugged him.

"So you did see them?"

"Saw the car, if not the folks in it. Not many old
Packard sedans still around. This one's prob'ly vintage late '40s. My grandpappy had one like it once,
when everybody else in the 'hood was buying Cad-
dies."

"Oh, thank you. Did you notice anything else
about it—a license plate?"

He squinted as if trying to envision it again.
"Maybe an Ohio plate—white with that funny,
peachy-colored blur on the bottom of it—but sure
don't know none of what it said. In it though, think
it was two people. Yeah," he said, stroking his chin
in thought, as if he had a beard. "And a man with a
real bad, old kind of hat was driving."

Kate thanked him profusely and even got his name
and address in case she needed corroboration later.
Though she still hadn't eaten, she went to the back
of the hall and skimmed every name in the guest
book. Nothing hit her as familiar or unusual.

But *Ohio* plates! And the car *had* really been
here—surely the same one that had followed her before.

But why? *Why?* If it was the last thing she ever
did, she was going to find out.

12

All things uncomely and broken,
All things worn out and old...
Are wronging your image that blossoms
A rose in the deeps of my heart.

—William Butler Yeats
"The Lover Tells of the Rose in His Heart"

As she left the church to head home, Kate knew she had to get hold of herself. But driving through busy Covington, then the Cincinnati traffic across the Ohio River, she kept glancing in her rearview mirrors for that damn black car. The traffic was too thick, and vans and trucks obscured her view. Once she almost rear-ended the vehicle in front of her. Though she forced herself to concentrate on traffic, she missed a turnoff and had to circle back.

"That's what I've got to do—circle back in my mind," she said aloud as the revelation struck her. "And not panic."

She took the next exit off I-75 when she saw the signs for several chain restaurants. It was still mid-afternoon, not dark for hours yet, thank God. She needed to take a break and try to discover who could be harassing her with that black car. It could not be mere coincidence. And she meant to figure out why.

Kate drove into a Wendy's Restaurant, locked her car, and went back to *check* that it was locked. Looking all around to be sure the other car hadn't come into the lot, she hurried inside. With a coffee and chicken sandwich in hand, she chose a corner table and sat with her back to the wall so she could see both building entrances, her car, and the field beyond the parking lot. Still, it bothered her that it was a dark day and brightly lit inside. She felt as if she were sitting in a fishbowl, if anyone wanted to watch her.

To force herself to focus, she flipped her paper place mat over and wrote on it, *Suspects 1—Varina & Palmer.*

They would benefit the most, Kate thought, from making her crack up, either in her car or in her head. ''Or,'' she muttered, ''they meant to hit me in the cemetery and are looking for another chance to finish the job.'' Running her out of Toledo wouldn't be enough for the Denbigh heirs, because she could still inherit Sarah's furniture. Varina, especially, was so vitriolic that she'd love to see Kate as dead as Sarah.

But that could not be all of it, she scolded herself silently. They obviously weren't simply out to kill her. Then why would they have appeared in a crowded funeral procession? No, they were sending her a message. She sat up straighter as a new possibility hit her. The fact they—she still felt there was a couple in that car—harassed her at cemeteries or funerals was a threat in itself. They enjoyed tormenting her, scaring her…perhaps before they did more.

Kate shuddered and drank more coffee. She'd had very little food back at the church, so she forced herself to eat some of her sandwich. For what she had in mind, she was going to need her strength.

*Evidence—Varina told Zink I went to psychia-
trist & she could know why—could want to make
me feel watched, followed to set me off again.
Then my death could look like an accident. Jeal-
ous of Sarah's feeling for me, wants to make me
suffer first—or thinks I'll break under pressure
& she & Palmer will get Sarah's goods.*
*Evidence—never seen any of them, but Sarah
said Palmer collects vintage cars—1940s Packard sedan?*

She underlined *vintage cars* repeatedly until her
pen point slashed through the paper.

Kate knew she could call Rudzinski and tell him
all this, ask him to find out if Palmer Denbigh had
such a car in his collection. It was one of the things
Sarah had said her son valued. "My children have,
at least, inherited the urge to collect," Sarah had told
Kate. "Palmer loves his classic cars—and beautiful
but brainless women, whom he trades in as often as
he does the autos. Varina has her jewelry and horses.
I don't fault them for that or for their disdain of my
'old furniture and flowers,' but they ought to at least
understand my passion for my collections..."

Kate shook her head to clear it. Sometimes Sarah's
voice came back so sure and strong, unlike the broken
and worn-out memories of her mother that she still
clung to. Yes, that old car had to lead her to whomever was behind the dark windshield and windows.
And if she could prove it was Palmer and Varina, then
she'd call in Stan Rudzinski.

"But there could be others," she whispered as she
craned her neck once more to scan the parking lot
and street outside. There could be other candidates

who wanted to observe, scare or harm her. She scribbled haphazard lines through all she'd written about Varina and Palmer, then wrote at the bottom where her spiderweb of lines didn't reach, *Zink.*

Zink might want to watch her, to pressure her until she was willing to confess something or other to him, but she couldn't believe he'd do it in an old car. And he must have had her under extensive surveillance to find her that early morning in Woodlawn Cemetery and then at a Kentucky funeral, for heaven's sake. Although he'd suddenly appeared at Shaker Run recently, the man couldn't spend that much time away from his job, unless to stalk her *was* part of his job. That's why she couldn't—wouldn't—go to him for help on this, at least not yet.

The Mike connection, she wrote next. She supposed there could be someone from among her ex-husband's defrauded clients who was wealthy, weird and vindictive enough to harass or hurt her. And then, she thought with a chill that racked her so hard she slopped coffee on the table, there was the missing Michael Marburn himself.

Rubbing her arms to stem the gooseflesh that swept her, she realized she had no doubt that he was out there somewhere on the run, probably blaming and hating her for testifying against him, and then divorcing him. Mike liked classic cars, and they'd been to an outdoor show or two to see them, but he'd neither owned one nor said he'd wanted to—at least, while she and he had been together. Yet Mike could have found out she'd been traumatized by all he'd done to her and Erin, and could be hoping to take advantage of that. Would Mike stage something as elaborate as a phantom car gliding in and out of settings related to death?

Kate sucked in such a loud breath that the couple at the next table turned to stare at her. She hastily gathered her things. She'd had a sudden memory—a vision—of that shadowy form that had glided from the Shaker cemetery toward holy ground during the snowstorm the night a big car had rammed the light pole. *Was* all this a message? A threat? Why? Even if it was, she wasn't running away from it but toward it. She was determined to find out what was going on.

Kate hit the rest room, then stood in line to get more coffee to take with her. She had a long drive ahead. Despite the fact they were expecting her back tonight, she'd call Dane and Adrienne and let them know she'd return tomorrow instead. Whatever it took, she was going to get some answers about her prime suspects.

Kate strode out of the restaurant with new purpose. But as she approached her car, she saw something splattered on her front windshield. She gripped her coffee cup so tightly, the plastic cap exploded off. Nearly scalded, Kate dropped the coffee, jumped back, and stared aghast. In the short time she had not been watching her car—rest room break or standing in line—someone had evidently been watching her. And he or she—they—had broken a wicker basket of flowers against the front windshield. One windshield wiper caught a tattered ribbon, which fluttered forlornly in the breeze.

Kate glanced between adjacent cars to be sure no one lurked there, then kneeled to look under hers.

Carefully, she edged closer to the front of her car, which faced an open field.

The smashed basket still held some stems and wilting rose leaves, but the blooms had been cut off and evidently thrown elsewhere. Perhaps they were strewn on Samantha Sams's grave, just as others had been thrown near Sarah's. Then Kate realized this was the basket of flowers that had been sent to the funeral from Tanya's Shaker Run friends—including herself.

Her hands pressed to her mouth to keep her from being sick, her legs shaking, Kate leaned back against her car and again scanned the weedy field, parking lot and busy street beyond.

Nothing amiss.

Nothing but more beheaded roses stolen from a fresh grave as another warning.

However fearful Kate was, she was furious, too, and she was not turning back. She'd start by driving by Palmer Denbigh's place. Though she knew where Palmer lived in Sylvania—a northwestern, affluent suburb of Toledo—she'd only driven by his house once before. The maze of streets in his neighborhood confused her at first. Finally, about six o'clock that evening, she found his home, a sprawling, gray stone house sitting on a good-size, treed lot. She was not surprised to see that his landscaping consisted of clipped taxus and yew bushes, without one hint of the crocus and daffodils that adorned the other early spring lawns.

But it was his deep, three-door garage that interested her now—and one of the doors was open. She was hoping, as well as fearing, she'd find an old Packard sedan in there, with its motor still warm from its drive back from southern Ohio and northern Kentucky. Maybe a car with a dent in its big front fender from knocking down a telephone pole. Maybe one with remnants of butchered funeral flowers on the seats or the floor.

Kate coasted by the house twice, then parked on the cul-de-sac one street over. It had looked as if no one was home, but that didn't mean anything, and she was not about to do a frontal assault. Though it pained her, she was going to use the same stealth and spying tactics that Palmer and Varina were probably using on her. Of course, the Denbigh heirs had enough money that they might have hired someone to do their dirty work. Even so, the car would be the link.

Since Kate had changed into comfortable clothes at a gas station when she'd filled up the car, it was easy enough to look like a neighborhood jogger. She tied a silk scarf over her head, knotting it under her hair at the nape of her neck. It was at least a minimal disguise, in case Palmer looked out a window. Glancing around again, she stuck the keys to her car in the pocket of her sweatshirt jacket and started to walk back toward Palmer's.

Though the weather was fairly mild for early April in northern Ohio, Kate felt flushed even before she picked up her pace. Her keys jangled, and her heart beat much harder than her exertion warranted. At least, she thought as she approached the house again, one of the three huge garage doors was still up. She wouldn't dare to break in, but she was planning on entering. She grimaced at the thought that she was acting just as deviously as Jack had that night he got into the Shaker Run furniture workshop.

She ran back around the block and located the

house directly behind Palmer's. She jogged up their driveway as if she belonged there. She was going to sneak in through the adjoining backyards with her eyes peeled for Palmer, so she could become a watcher, a phantom gliding in and out. Turnabout was fair play.

She hoped it was a good sign that she'd chosen a house with an as yet bare rose garden surrounding a fountain, one that had not been turned on yet this year. And as she had seen from the street, there was no back fence separating this house from Palmer's.

Kate slowed as she looked for a good spot to get through Palmer's hedges. Still, she scraped her legs and snagged her nylon running pants. Making no pretense of jogging now, she kept close to the side bushes and headed for the garage. Despite its lack of flower beds, the yard had several bulky stone statues, modernistic ones that suggested the human form.

Suddenly, this place reminded her of the cemetery with its monuments. All it needed was a strutting peacock guarding the grounds, instead of the crows cawing at her to get away as they pecked something from the spring grass.

Keeping on the far side of the attached garage, which fortunately could not be seen from the house, Kate scanned the front street and yard, then peeked in. The garage was so big that it had places for six cars. One of the two parking spots next to this open door was empty, the other held a low-slung red sports car, an old Corvette. That was certainly not what she was searching for. The next two garage doors were closed, but a large auto—maybe a vintage Cadillac— was parked behind the middle door, and next to it, what she would call a Model-T. Farther down behind the third door, and closest to the house, she saw what looked like another empty space and then a covered car. But in the dim depths, she wasn't sure.

Yes, she thought as she stood on tiptoe, the one parked back against the inner wall was covered with some sort of tarp. It had a hulking shape that could be the car she sought. Hearing nothing, seeing no one, she darted farther in and, keeping to the back wall, headed for the covered car—

She nearly jumped through the roof when she heard an engine start. No, not start, but come closer from outside. Headlights shone on the back wall. A car coasted into the parking spot, the open garage door began to descend behind it and ceiling lights sprang on.

Kate scurried deeper into the garage. Crouched behind the Cadillac, she peeked over its hood to see Palmer with a blonde. Their vehicle was one of those squat, camouflaged Jeeps from the Gulf War called Hum-Vees. Quickly, with the noise of the descending garage door to cover her, Kate darted farther away, around the Model-T's far side, and opened the driver's door. She dove inside and crouched on her hands and knees on the floor. The garage door's descent and the woman's voice covered the click of the latch behind her.

"Now, that's a fast, fun ride," the woman was saying. "I'll just pretend you're some sheik who abducted me during the 'mother of all battles' and swept me off to his desert tent."

Palmer boomed out a laugh. "Then step inside, my darling, though I hadn't planned on a battle."

"Mmm," the blonde murmured, as sounds in the lighted garage told Kate they were getting out of the

Hum-Vee and coming closer, toward the house, "maybe just the battle of the sexes."

At least Kate had a lot of floor room in this uncluttered, boxy, old car. She held her breath, praying they'd just go by and into the house. She wanted to peek under the tarp on that car, then get out of here. All she needed was for Palmer to find her on—in—his property.

She heard keys clink but the house door did not open. Where were they? Why didn't they talk again so she could get a fix on their position?

A throaty feminine laugh suggested the woman and Palmer might be kissing. The Model-T bounced a bit. Damn, but they must be pressed against it. It was a rhythmic rocking, making her feel sick to her stomach. Surely they weren't...wouldn't...

Kate recalled a scene in the movie *Titanic,* which she and Erin had seen together here in town last year. Erin had been so swept away by the tale of fated love that she'd seen it several times, but Kate had gone only once. While the villains searched for the young lovers, they were hiding and making love in a vintage car below decks in the belly of the big ship, the very night the *Titanic* went down. Kate envisioned that poster from the movie in Erin's dorm room. And she desperately wished Jack—that had been the hero's name in the movie, too, the one who drowned—her Jack—were here.

"Let's take it inside, my lord and master," the woman murmured. "That hood ornament's branding my bottom."

"Don't want to do that—not with a hood ornament," Palmer murmured.

Kate rolled her eyes as she heard the keys again,

then the door opening. The couple went inside, and closed it behind them.

Kate forced herself to stay put for a minute, then sneaked a look. The coast was clear but the timed ceiling light went out and, with all the garage doors shut, it was suddenly pitch-black. She would need to get out of this place but she wasn't sure where to find the garage door opener, or the light switch.

Carefully, quietly, she got out of the car, which bounced each time she shifted her weight. She didn't quite close the door behind her, afraid the latch would make a sound, however distracted Palmer and his friend might be inside.

Kate felt carefully along the garage wall for a switch, but wasn't sure if the one she found would trigger the door or the light. So she felt her way past the draped car, past the Model-T and, holding her breath, opened the door of the next automobile, the big Cadillac. As she had hoped, a light popped on inside.

Though the bulb was distant and dim, with her eyes now accustomed to the dark Kate managed to see well enough to get around. She tiptoed back to the covered car and tried to lift the tarp. It didn't budge. Tied at the bottom?

Feeling more hurried now, she yanked at the heavy material. It came free over the front bumper where she stood. She lifted the canvas to bare the hood. A dark color! Hard to tell which color, though, in this wretched light.

She freed more of it. A four-door. It could be *the* car, but she'd always seen it before at a distance. This close, in the dark, it was so hard to tell.

She pulled the canvas away from the hood ornament, hoping to find the name of the car somewhere. Where would it say Packard? She'd never noted the car's make. She was just trusting what some strange man had told her.

She felt and rubbed the hood ornament but could not tell what it represented. A flying bird? A woman's flowing garments? The make of the car was not written here. She dashed toward the back and skimmed her hands over the cold, metallic skin of the trunk. Yes, a word was here, a fairly long name. She touched the raised metal script as if she were reading Braille. It seemed longer than the name *Packard,* and she was sure the first letter was an *O.* Oldsmobile?

Hoping Palmer was too deep into other things to hear her, Kate went back to the switch on the wall by the entrance to the house. Sometimes garage doors opened of their own accord, she thought, especially if someone with a similar switch nearby hit their opener. If she got out of here quickly and no one saw her, maybe Palmer would never know—except for the mess she'd made of the car cover, but some kid could have done that.

She hit the switch. The garage door she'd come in through lifted with a steady, loud *hum.* Every light in the long garage sprang on. She still made herself stop to read the make of the sedan—Oldsmobile—and to see that the color was maroon. Then, without even taking the time to replace the tarp, she ran out the door. She tore around the side of the house toward the backyard, this time pushing through the prickly hedge into the next-door neighbor's yard before hurrying to the other street.

She was scratched and frenzied; she was also furious with herself at first for her failure to find proof.

But, she thought, gasping for breath as she started her own engine, this didn't mean Palmer didn't have another car that wasn't here right now. There was a spot for one, and Sarah had said he was always trading them. "Or," Kate said aloud, "it could mean I'm still looking for someone else."

"Jack, is Kate here?" Tanya called up to him, when he opened up a second-floor window at his house that evening.

"Tanya?" he called down. "You're back already? No, she's not here? You mean she's not in the village? She should be."

He shoved the window closed and hurried down the stairs to open one of his two front doors.

"I was *sure* she'd be back by now," she told him, out of breath. She was still dressed formally in a green suit, but she looked as if she'd been through the mill.

"I mean, I saw her at the funeral, and she got a good head start back but she seemed really nervous. I've got *tons* of stuff to do and needed to get out of there, anyway—family overload," she told him, and rolled her eyes.

He nodded, understanding full well what she meant. Despite having lost his immediate family, his parents' continual consolation had worn him ragged before he'd finally moved here to find some peace and quiet. But he'd found neither.

"You surely took the same route Kate did?" he observed, shoving his fingers through his hair. "You didn't see any road accidents or—"

"No," she said, almost scoldingly. "Don't worry. She's a big girl, but I guess you've noticed that. Who knows—maybe she stopped in some garden store or whatever.''

''Or a restaurant. She's probably with her daughter at O.U. Listen, Tanya, I'm sorry I had clients scheduled here and couldn't come to the funeral.''

She patted his arm, then grasped it a moment. ''The card and flowers were *really* nice. The village staff sent a big basket of roses, too. I didn't expect you or them to attend, since you didn't know her, so it was special that Kate was there. Well, got a lot of work, like I said. You guarding my writer's workshop?''

''Sure. Even if the village rents that building, I keep an eye on your things. Dane comes and goes fairly often, usually at odd hours, getting or stashing something, but I'm sure he doesn't disturb your work.''

''You know the village would like to rent or even buy your entire spread here,'' she reminded him with a glance around the grounds.

''Too bad, because it's perfect for me. You want to check on your stuff while you're here?''

''Might as well,'' she said with a huge sigh. ''With the village opening up soon, I have *no* idea when I'll get back to that book of mine. Got some other experiments to complete before I write more, too.''

He walked her toward the back building, beyond the one he used for his garage, on the other side of the house from his furniture workshop. When Dane Thompson had rented it, they'd agreed Jack would have a key, too.

''A Shakerabilia treasure trove,'' Tanya said, as Jack unlocked the padlock and shoved the old door open on its rollers.

''I think of it as the biggest Shaker storage box

I've ever seen,'' he said with a grin. ''That reminds me, I'm hoping to have your herb desk ready for the opening of the village, but I just can't promise.''

''No,'' she said, playfully punching his arm. ''Whatever the real reason you're supporting my writing project, Mr. Jack Kilcourse, I know you're not one to be making admissions *or* promises.''

Not one to be making promises. The words echoed in Jack's mind. Since he'd lost Andy—and then Leslie, too, damn her—he'd been unwilling to get close to any woman, and he'd certainly steered clear of commitments. But now with Kate, the temporarily missing and somehow always elusive Kate...

''Would you *look* at this *mess.*'' Tanya's voice cut into his agonizing. The setting sun illumined the stacks and piles of Shaker goods that were not currently being displayed or stored in the village. Some of it was furniture too damaged to be used until Barstow's men got around to fixing it. Two small crates of new things that Dane must have brought over sat here too, Jack noted. Maybe he'd just have a peek in those when he got a chance, since they were the sort of crates that furniture was best shipped in, despite their diminutive size.

Tanya's makeshift writing desk sat beneath the single window. She used an extra light, and in the cold months Jack would bring out a space heater when she came here to write in private. He didn't want to discuss with Tanya why he was really helping with her project; she was writing, but he was underwriting it.

At first, he'd been staggered to hear her book would focus on how overdoses of medicine and drugs could harm and kill. *Cures Can Be Killers* she was calling it, though it had some longer subtitle, too. At least she never pried about his passion to see her book in print. He'd tell her someday and ask her to help him expose a murder—the tragedy that had devastated his life.

Within this storage area also sat stacks of old wicker, extra bricks, and a large, plastic, airtight box of Shaker memorabilia that Louise Willis and Adrienne had yet to sort through. And, of course, the classic antique touring car that had belonged to the last Shakers about the time they closed Shaker Run.

13

Roses have thorns, and silver fountains mud;
Clouds and eclipses stain both moon and sun,
And loathsome canker lives in sweetest bud.
All men make faults.

—Shakespeare
"Sonnet 35"

Shock drained the color from Erin's face as she saw who stood at the door of her dorm. "Mo—Kate," she gasped. "Is everything all right? You look like—I don't know, you've seen a ghost or something. Uh, come on in."

Kate had forced herself to get some sleep in a motel last night, then she had headed straight to Athens. She needed to see Erin, to be with her, and to get her to quit calling her "Kate" instead of "Mom."

"Honey, I know this is your day with Mark. I thought he might be here already, but I just couldn't wait any longer to have a real good talk with you. And it's about time Mark realizes I approve of him, if that's been worrying you. So I thought I could take you both out for dinner, after you and I have a talk..."

Kate realized she was rambling and flinging gestures. Conflicting emotions flitted across Erin's face:

annoyance, surprise, confusion, maybe even fear. "But," she told Erin, hauling her into her embrace for a long, hard hug, "if that doesn't suit you, how about if I come for you tomorrow after your last class? I'd love to take you over to Shaker Run to see the dancing rehearsals I've been telling you about."

Blessedly, Erin hugged her back. She'd been losing weight; Kate could feel the girl's ribs and backbone.

"Sure. Why not?" Erin whispered, before tugging loose and stepping back into her room to indicate Kate should follow.

Kate was relieved Amy wasn't in the dorm room for once.

"Actually," Erin said, "the reason I was kind of upset when you arrived was that Mark can't make it today, anyway. He's a little under the weather."

"Oh, then this is perfect," Kate cried. "Let's get out of here for a while, see the Shaker dancing, then just hang out and talk without everyone around."

"It was that funeral you went to, wasn't it," Erin asked as she grabbed her jacket and threw some other things into her backpack. Kate was amazed at how hurried Erin seemed to be to leave. "The funeral?" Kate repeated, puzzled.

"Tanya's great-aunt you told me about. When you lose someone, it makes you think about all the things you regret, like mistakes. I thought maybe that triggered your just showing up like this."

"Loving and needing you is what triggered my just showing up like this," Kate said, but she realized Erin had read her well. Not that it was the funeral itself, so much as her fear and her failure to pin down the person who was after her. She had to be certain they weren't after Erin. She was sure, at least, that she hadn't been followed to Toledo or here. She'd nearly sprained her back rubbernecking, and almost ran off the road staring in her rearview mirror. Of course, if the people following her knew where she'd be, that was another problem, she agonized, glancing nervously out Erin's windows.

Kate waited as Erin glanced at her watch, scribbled Amy a note, then hustled Kate out the door. "Let's go down the side stairs—it's closer," Erin said, leading her to the exit at the end of the building.

"You don't even know where I'm parked. And don't you have to sign out?"

"Not just for the day, and Amy won't worry now."

Erin hurried Kate along, leading her downstairs and out the side entrance. Still, even as they got in the car and Kate headed out of town, she saw and sensed Erin was looking around as anxiously as she was. It made her want to shelter Erin at Shaker Run, to feed her, and to distract her from the strange mood the girl was in. Kate wanted to pull a roof over both their heads to keep them safe and sane.

"I make you kindly welcome, for the Believers used to allow 'the world's people' in to see their worship," Louise Willis told Erin, as she and Kate sat on the sisters' bench to observe the rehearsal later that day. Louise and all her performers were in full Shaker attire. "All right now, brethren, sisters," she called to the dancers and her husband, who made the third man in the troupe despite his slight limp, "let us begin at the beginning, if you kindly please."

Everyone had been trying to "speak Shaker" in preparation for being presenters at the village opening, and Louise was still the guardian of the frontier for all things authentic. But Kate was coming to admire greatly both the Willises. Shaker Run was their dream, and they were giving it their all, including hosting a working dinner for the staff at their home tomorrow evening.

As the Believers used to do, Louise and Ben had cleared all furniture from the polished wooden floor, pushing the benches to the sides of the room. Their dancing, of course, was all individual—nothing with partners in this celibate world. Louise and Ben seemed such rigid personalities that Kate found herself wondering if they even went so far as to abstain from what the Shakers used to call "marital relations."

She recalled the peepholes high on the walls, accessed by narrow, hidden stairways where the elders used to observe what went on here. As she tipped her head back, she glanced up, and in the sun filtering through from outside she could almost imagine someone staring down right now. But she didn't *feel* she was being watched, not as she had at the church before the funeral. Besides, Dane and Adrienne were at their home today and the Willises were in plain sight, she thought smugly, so who could be up there spying?

Kate was grateful that Erin seemed interested, even excited to be here. Erin knew one of the female dance majors from among the eight women and two men from campus. Or maybe it was just the fact that Kate had fixed the two of them their old comfort food of macaroni and cheese with a side salad. Kate had coaxed every bit of what was on Erin's plate into her, and Erin seemed a bit calmer now. Actually, it was also the first time in days that Kate had felt like eating.

She and Erin had spent a little time with Tanya. Kate had been so pleased to hear Erin express condolences to her bereaved friend, whom she herself hadn't had the time to talk to privately since the funeral.

But having time to get through to Erin about taking better care of herself was more important. The girl had admitted that she was still having adjustment problems, and that her grades were slipping. But Kate knew they had much more to cover than that today. Just a little while here, and then she'd get Erin off alone again.

Beginning the dancing slowly, in an intricately patterned wheel, the women and men sang as they moved and swayed,

> *Awake, my soul, arise and shake,*
> *No time to even ponder,*
> *Keep awake, keep awake*
> *Lest ye be rent asunder...*

"That's a good one," Erin whispered to Kate. "I've been keeping awake too much lately. I think," she said, leaning even closer to be heard over the shuffling steps and singing, "I've caught your insomnia."

Kate put her arm around Erin's shoulders. "Too much worrying about grades," Kate whispered. "Maybe you're actually working too hard. You're not falling behind because Mark's taking up one of your good study days every week, are you? Are things all right between the two of you?"

"Kindly hush, Sister Jerusha!" Louise hissed as if they were speaking too loudly in a library. "You should know better and set an example. All right now, everyone, let's go right into the 'Angels Watching' pattern." Louise conducted the singing as if she were a choir director, swaying along with the dancers. Kate had noticed that Louise often joined in.

"Step livelier, keep it moving, moving," Louise called to her dancers. "It's not called an 'endless chain' for nothing. Keep weaving, weaving."

"Let's step outside," Kate suggested with a nod at the open double doors.

"Just a sec," Erin whispered. "I've got to see this when it gets crazy."

Kate had described to Erin how the movements became wilder as the dancers broke away from the slow, set pattern to mimic receiving heavenly gifts with out-stretched hands. Some of them were already making the motions of sweeping the devil from the room. Even now that the slower dancing called "laboring" was ending, individuals began the jumping steps that symbolized flying up to heaven, and the trembling movements that indicated visions of angels. It was all choreographed by Louise, of course, whom Kate suspected of seeing some Shaker visions of her own.

But what surprised her the most was Ben Willis, whom Kate considered quiet and circumspect. Not only did his weak leg not stop him, but also he had a beautiful baritone voice that soared with the Shaker songs. And he looked almost...dazed.

The regular singing—they had just finished the best-known Shaker song "Tis a Gift to Be Simple"—was breaking down into shrieks and shouts. Faster, jerkier, the dancers spun off into the spontaneous displays of whirling, leaping and shaking that had given the Shakers their name. The more dramatic of the young women seemed frenzied, as if seeing things that obviously were not there.

Evidently awed yet embarrassed, Erin indicated they should step outside. They skirted the edge of the large, echoing room, and went out the sisters' door into the brisk wind and gentle sun. Though muted now, the noise chased them outside through the doors set ajar.

"The Shakers were pretty weird," Erin said, tossing her red hair. Kate had always thought her step-daughter's pale beauty a cross between that of an Irish princess and one of those pale classical nymphs emerging from the sea in a painting by Boticelli. But, thinner and wanner now, the girl seemed more like a wraith or woodland sprite who could dart off in the wink of an eye.

"That dancing," Erin went on, "was starting to remind me of that Arthur Miller play the high school did when I was a junior. You know, *The Crucible,* with all those Puritan girls flipping out because they thought witches were everywhere around them, or were pretending they saw them just to pull the wool over people's eyes. But back in the Meeting House, it seemed almost like they were *on* something."

"Not around Sister Straight-and-Strict, they weren't," Kate protested with a little laugh, but she realized Erin had been quite observant. Kate sometimes thought the so-called angel visions the Shakers claimed could have been something far more scary. It always amazed her that the peace-loving, quiet and celibate Believers could suddenly turn loud and passionate.

"That's part of the mystery about the Shakers," Kate told Erin. "They careen between light and darkness, simplicity and depths. And speaking of the depths, wait till you see this old well the university is excavating over here,'' she added, glad to shift subjects as they strolled across the lane.

Though the progress made in the old well near the Central Dwelling showed Kate that the crew had worked long hours since she'd been away, no one was here on Sunday afternoon. Carefully, standing outside the rim of flimsy wooden fencing they'd put up to protect the site, Erin and Kate peered at the digging equipment and the slightly widened hole.

''Any money or treasure?'' Erin asked with a nervous laugh.

''Things like combs, buttons and bottles so far, I guess, but that doesn't mean something significant won't turn up.''

''Yeah, like the body of somebody who croaked dancing that way. Or of someone who fell in forbidden love here in this 'do ask and do tell place.'''

''You've been doing a lot of deep thinking about all kinds of things lately,'' Kate observed, looping her arm around the girl's waist. ''Being away at school, even this short time, seems to have changed you, matured you.''

''But that's good, right?'' Erin demanded. She shrugged away, and they walked through the village to the fence that ran beside the frothing stream called Shaker Run. It was still full of spring rain from the surrounding hills, churning more wildly than Kate had ever seen it. Erin perched on the stone fence, so Kate did, too, though the stones hurt her rear. The strange songs and cries from the ''Shaker high'' going on inside the Meeting House drifted to their ears on the wind.

"You seem very upset," Kate began, choosing her words carefully. "Tell me if there's anything I can do to help." She wanted to hug Erin again, to reach out to touch her hand or knee at least—but she didn't.

"It was too late for that once Dad left. You know, all that water over the dam," the girl said with an awkward little laugh as she pointed to the swollen stream.

Kate was shocked that Erin had instantly referred to her dad's desertion. She'd expected to hear about grades and school. "Erin, I know I'll never fill the void your dad left, but I'm here for you," Kate said simply.

"You should have been there for *him.*"

"Do you still think I turned on him? Honey, don't you think he turned on us first?"

"He was trapped by circumstances," she insisted, frowning at her fists on her knees. "Would you like to face spending the rest of your life—years of it, at least," she added, looking up, "in prison, when it wasn't really your fault that all the investments fell in like a house of cards?"

Kate's jaw dropped, but she quickly recovered. Mike's guilt had been proven and widely published. Kate thought Erin had come to accept it. But *like a house of cards* was exactly the way Mike had described the financial mess he'd "fallen into," which "had collapsed on him through no fault of his own." That's the way he'd always talked and precisely what he'd written in his farewell letter to them.

"Erin," Kate said, "I know it's so hard to accept that someone you love and need—"

"You used to love and need him, too. You said you did."

"—could be deceitful or betray you. But he ran, Erin, and left other people, including me, holding the bag—a bag he made sure was empty when he took off."

Erin jumped down from the fence as if it had turned hot. "He had to keep from starving if he was driven away," she shouted at Kate, hands on hips. "And it's hard to accept that a person fighting for his financial life—his very life, considering some of the threats he got—could just be dumped, jettisoned by his wife, who was supposed to stand by him for richer, for poorer, and all that."

Kate slid down from the fence. She felt it had just fallen on her. She could not believe this explosion of emotion. She'd thought Erin had moved on from their family catastrophe, as Kate was trying to do. But Erin had failed to do that—and she'd failed Erin. Yet above all else, one thing the girl had said snagged in Kate's thoughts.

"'Threats' he got?" Kate repeated Erin's words. "'Fighting for his very life'? No one ever suggested to me that someone threatened or endangered your father's life. Is that what you mean, Erin? Did you somehow hear about that, but didn't tell me? I've got to know."

"Don't!" Erin shrieked, turning away and flinging up her hands as if to hold Kate off. "Don't try to tear him down any more. He's not here to defend himself, and I just can't talk about it. It's your problem, your fault, Kate, and I've got enough on my mind with getting my grades up and—"

Kate tried to pull Erin close, to stem the rising hysteria. To Kate's surprise, Erin let Kate wrap her arms around her, but the girl stood stiff and cold in her embrace. Then Erin pulled away and strode back to stand in the door of the Meeting House, as if fascinated by the wild dancing.

"You *look* like I *feel,*" Tanya told Kate, when Kate dragged herself into the garden shop early that evening. It wasn't dark yet.

Kate had taken Erin back to school, stunned and sick at heart that the girl was barely speaking to her. She'd decided to give her a little cooling-off period, then insist they see a family counselor together if things were still so bad between them. Somehow, she needed to convince Erin to explain the threats made against Mike. That could be the link to whomever was after Kate. On top of everything else, this emotional crisis with Erin was all she needed.

Tanya gave Kate the warm hug that Kate wished she'd had from Erin. "I'll bet you're exhausted, too," Kate told her as she took the rake she'd come in for. She almost told Tanya about the flowers from her aunt's funeral being thrown at Kate's car, but that would lead to a full confession of all that was wrong, and Kate didn't want to upset her friend even more. "Why don't you get a good night's sleep and start over tomorrow?" she suggested.

"No can do 'cause too much to do," Tanya said with a shake of her head. "And I don't just mean around here. I'm supposed to be back in Covington late next week so the family can divvy up Auntie's Shaker furniture with the church."

Kate leaned on the rake. She ached all over, but that comment grabbed her attention. She'd been agonizing about whether to discuss a possible pattern between her loss of Sarah and Tanya's loss of her great-aunt—and the fortune in furniture involved. And now Tanya had given her the perfect opening.

"Her collection will be divided up?" Kate asked, trying to keep her voice calm. "So evidently there will be no surprises like the kind I had with Sarah's," she mused aloud, hoping Tanya would add more information.

"Since she had no kids of her own, the church will get the bulk of her estate," Tanya explained, continuing to sort herbs. "But my mother says all her nieces, nephews—great-nieces and great-nephews, too—will be getting some Shaker heirlooms. She also said Auntie left me some special pieces since she was so *proud* of my efforts here."

Kate nodded as her mind raced. She decided to try to lead Tanya into the other topic she wanted to discuss. "Then it was a special blessing you were there to help her in the end. Tanya, I overheard she died of food poisoning," Kate blurted, "and..."

She hesitated, when Tanya knocked over a small sack of dried leaves, then hurriedly brushed them up. "And," Kate went on, "I was thinking that was ironic. You know, with your work and all, the curing herbs and the book you're going to write," she prompted lamely.

She'd done it now, Kate thought, gripping the rake handle so hard that her hands went numb. By setting a trap for her best friend, she'd sunk lower than she had when spying on Palmer Denbigh. But Dane had said Tanya had half her book written when she'd told Kate something quite different. And though Kate hated herself for so much as suspecting Tanya, she was dying to know if her friend had tried to dose her great-aunt back to health.

Kate watched now as Tanya continued to scrape crushed leaves into her hand, then dumped them back in the sack. A bitter scent drifted between them.

"When someone's as old as Auntie Sams," Tanya said as she kept busy with her back to Kate, "you think they're *indestructible*. But when they're that old, even something as small as indigestion or food poisoning—which the doctor put on the death certificate—can be a big thing. And yeah," she said, turning to look Kate full in the face, "can you believe I tried to dose her with peppermint tea? Too little, too late, I guess."

"I'm sorry," Kate said. "But she had a long, rich life."

"And right when she died," Tanya went on, her gaze going past Kate to fix on the wall as if she saw a scene there, "her eyes opened real wide, though she'd earlier had them scrunched shut in pain. And when I leaned over her, I heard her say, 'There are angels here, and they are the prettiest ones I've ever seen.' It seemed so—so *Shaker*."

Kate reached out to touch Tanya's hand, and her friend grasped it hard. "Her happiness—acceptance—at the end must be a great comfort," Kate said as goose bumps skimmed her skin. She decided then that she had been wrong to mistrust Tanya. So what if her friend hadn't told her the truth about her book. Or perhaps it was Dane who hadn't told the truth.

"I'll let you get back to work," Kate told her as she edged out the door, holding it ajar. "I'm going to rake mulch off those transplanted roses. Time to uncover their canes so the spring sun and air can do their thing." Still feeling guilty that she had sprung so much on her bereaved friend for her own purposes,

Kate added, "Let me know if I can do anything to help."

"Oh," Tanya said, following her to the door and leaning through as Kate started away, "I meant to ask you if you ever found that car you were asking everyone about at the funeral—some old sedan. Why didn't you ask me?"

Kate just stared at her for a moment. Tanya suddenly seemed angry. "I thought," she said simply, "you had enough on your mind."

"So who would have been at Auntie's funeral that were friends of yours?" she pursued.

Again Kate almost spilled everything to Tanya, but something held her back. She needed to reason things out just a bit more, maybe see what Tanya inherited from her aunt before she told her everything. Besides, what did she really have to share but some suspicions with no proof, no clear motives?

"I thought it might be some people I met in Toledo," Kate said, tipping the rake handle back and forth. "I knew it was crazy to think it could be them, but the car was so distinctive."

"Probably just one of Auntie's elderly friends still driving their old junker," Tanya said. "I don't recall seeing it, not that I was looking. And if it just disappeared," she added with a sharp shrug and sharper laugh, "maybe you've just been hanging out with Louise too long—and you're seeing things."

Though Jack Kilcourse had permission to enter the Shaker storage shed on his property and had done it before, he felt a little guilty this time. But he couldn't afford to pass up this opportunity right under his nose. He had to look in those two, small boxed crates, just the sort, if not the size, in which he used to ship furniture. These looked more like wine crates.

He sneezed at the dust as he entered and slid the door shut behind him. Light flooded in from the window above Tanya's writing desk. The odd thing was that the other items stored here were tattered, broken or generally unused—including, he now noted, the car Dane used and had evidently dented. But these crates were pristine.

Then it hit him. Dane must have been out in that car in the snow and slid into that light pole, and he was too ashamed to tell anyone. That would reassure Kate, but it might get Dane in trouble if anyone else found out. He wondered if the electrical repair crew would charge the driver for the repair costs.

He edged around the old Shaker vehicle that Dane kept in good shape but refused to put on display. "The vision of Shakers we want for the village is circa 1840s, not 1940s," he'd told Jack one day when he'd driven it back after a fill-up or tune-up. "Louise says someday we'll do an End of the Shaker Era display, and then we'll haul it out."

Jack quickly put his small crowbar to work on the first crate. He'd opened and sealed hundreds of these. It would be a joke if they actually held wine that Dane just didn't have room to store at home for that French wife of his—the one who loved the good life but didn't really have it right now. That, Jack thought, made the Thompsons worth watching on this furniture fraud thing. Kate had mentioned that though Barstow and his guys were doing the construction, Dane Thompson was overseeing the marketing.

With a groan and a creak from the protesting wood frame of the crate, Jack pried his way into the first box. Expensive wooden shavings rather than foam or newspapers were packed around whatever sat inside—maybe wine bottles, indeed. If so, he'd seal this up without a mark on it and get back to work.

Jack lifted out handfuls of the shavings until the carved finial of a chair back appeared, and then another. It was Shaker for sure, but so small. A child's? And was it the traditional Shaker rocker?

He uncovered the rest of the rocker, then thrust it quickly back into its protective nest. He'd never made one for a child, wouldn't want to, even though they were rare and that made them expensive. His appraisal of originals would be sky-high.

Quickly, he restuffed the packing and hammered the crate closed, then cursed himself that he hadn't checked the chair for authenticity. He turned his attention to the other, same-size crate. It was identically sealed and packed.

Another child's rocker? No, he bared a flat wooden cherry surface the moment he pulled out a handful of wood shavings. He had to lift this piece out a ways to see what it was.

A small washstand, obviously a child's height. Could these be stored here close to his house because it had once been the so-called gathering order, where they took in children to make new converts? he wondered. Were Shaker Run's modern-day leaders collecting furniture they'd use if they ever got this property from him? Dane did seem awfully secretive about things sometimes.

He checked the dovetailing, the wormholes, the finish on the washstand's single drawer. The underside was haphazardly stained where someone had cleaned a brush against the wood—waste and carelessness of which the Shakers would never be guilty. And the finish had not weathered darker where it had been exposed to the air. Fairly new wood, then—a replica, but one that would pass a layman's examination.

He repacked the washstand, puzzled and angry. He could hardly go storming after Dane and demand to know what was going on, because he'd give himself away. Should he tell Kate what he'd found and ask her to keep her ears and eyes open even more? She'd said she was going to a staff party tonight at the Willises' house.

And then he realized why he had to tell Kate about the furniture, even if he didn't betray Dane's dent in the car. He'd seen the authentic matches for these two Shaker fakes before—in Sarah Denbigh's suite at Groveland.

14

If neglected or in hardship, a rose refuses to flower until it is severely cut back and weeded.

—Sister Jerusha Lockhart
Shaker Run Diaries

"Oh, Jack," Kate said, surprised. She was in her silk bathrobe when she opened her apartment door. "I thought you'd be Tanya. She's due here to pick me up for the staff party."

"This will only take a minute. I thought I'd stop by rather than calling, since I was out walking—thinking. I came over the back way past the cemetery," he said in a rush.

He had been taking a long walk, trying to decide whether to trust Kate enough to get her more deeply involved. But in more ways than one, he guessed, she already was.

"Come in," she said, and closed the door behind him.

Her silk print robe, tied tightly to her slender form, accentuated her curves. He tried not to stare.

"What is it?" she asked, her voice agitated. She might as well be, he thought, because *he* was. The woman really got to him. She obviously was partly dressed under the robe, but she was barefoot. Her hair was damp and disheveled as if she'd just taken a shower, and she had on only some of her makeup, which conveyed a certain intimacy. She appeared sleepy, kind of tousled, and...

"Kate, I've stumbled over something that makes me think it's possible that Sarah Denbigh's furniture was being tampered with or, let's say, was about to be tampered with. I've discovered that identical fake pieces to two of hers exist."

"In Barstow's workshop? But you gave me back the key to it."

He shook his head. "In another storage area that belongs to the village. I'd rather not say where right now, because I don't want you insisting that you or the police go through it yet. I'm hoping you'll trust me on this."

"Is it at Rent-a-Room Storage where they keep other things?" she demanded. "I know where that is. I have my extra furniture and other things there."

He looked surprised. "The village rents storage rooms in town?"

She nodded. That, he thought, opened another whole Pandora's box. What if Barstow, or even Dane, were keeping furniture there until they could switch it with authentic pieces? Maybe the children's pieces were the overflow or en route to the Athens storage.

"I didn't realize that," he admitted, crossing his arms over his chest so he wouldn't reach for her as he so badly wanted to do. "Look, I know you're heading for the staff dinner, so I'm just hoping—without giving yourself or me away—that you can keep an eye out, maybe even steer a conversation to children's furniture pieces. I'd better get going before I really get in your way."

"But I need to know more. Which pieces? Why children's?"

"A small rocking chair and child's washstand— you know, what some collectors call a commode. The washstand is cherry, the rocker butternut-and-ash with a dark blue-and-beige woven tape seat. Can you recall if those were the colors of Mrs. Denbigh's taped child rocker?"

"Yes," she said, nodding. "I know the exact pieces you mean. She said that children's furniture is difficult to find. I guess they were harder on the furniture than adults were."

"That's why they'd be especially valuable as fakes. But the forgers don't dare flood the market with such rare pieces."

"But, Jack," she said, and reached to touch his arm, "what do you mean by perhaps they were 'about' to be substituted for Sarah's furniture? Do you mean that very night she died?"

"I don't know. But it would explain intruders."

"Whom she stumbled on. But to kill her over substituting pieces of furniture? And the thing is, they *didn't* substitute them. But maybe because she caught them at it, and they panicked..." she reasoned aloud.

Her words were half conjecture and half question, but they seemed to shake her. When Kate gripped her arms as if to hug herself, Jack took a huge step forward to finish the job.

He crushed her to him, but she held him tight, too, her face pressed into his shoulder. Her body seemed to fit so perfectly against his. She was soft and supple where he was solid or angular. When she clung closer, he cradled her with the top of her head nestled in the hollow of his throat. And then she lifted her head, offered her lips, and he was lost.

Jack held her close and hard. His mouth slanted over hers crazily and hungrily, but she held to him, both taking and giving. His hands moved over her supple back and soft bottom; his heart pounded against her breasts. He lost the sense he was a separate being as he shifted his stance to bring her closer, never breaking the kiss. They breathed together, belonged together.

It had been forever since he had felt so open and needy. Kate seemed to feel the same, stoking the wild, devouring emotions he had exiled to some dark place. It shook him to his core knowing how strong he felt, and yet so weak.

He heard the doorbell ring—darn Tanya. No, it was a telephone to shatter both reality and the dream.

"Better get it," he managed, out of breath, his lips buried in her hair. She smelled like roses, but he set her back, desperate to rebuild the barriers he tried to keep between them. "Tanya could be late, the party canceled. Don't I wish."

At first she didn't move away, but held to him. He wanted to smash the phone and lift her in his arms. When it kept ringing, she pulled back and knotted her sash tightly. The moment she stepped away, he tried to tell himself he was fine now, self-controlled and contained again. That it had only been his body reacting, not his mind or heart.

Kate stepped over to her desk and picked up the phone. "Kate Marburn here," she said, her voice uncharacteristically throaty. "Oh, hello, Mason. How's the world of big, bad law in Toledo? Any new word on Sarah's death?...I know you're not the police, but I said it's more important that I know about any developments on Sarah's death than details about the legal ramifications of Palmer and Varina's claims.... What? Tomorrow?''

Her voice sounded exasperated now. ''But I'm buried with work here. With everyone there? Palmer and Varina, too? Yes, I understand. One o'clock tomorrow at your office it is, then. You know, I'd do anything for this to be over—except give in to them against Sarah's last wishes. Yes, I'll try not to worry,'' she said, shaking her head and rolling her eyes at Jack. ''See you.''

''Not good news,'' he observed, as she hung up and leaned a moment on the old Shaker desk she used.

''Probably not,'' she admitted, still frowning. ''A joint meeting of all parties involved in the dispute over Sarah's will. Though the Denbigh children are about the last people in the world I'd like to see, it will be a chance for me to tell them to keep out of my life. And I have other things to discuss with Mason.''

He sensed she wanted to say more, but didn't. ''Do me a favor,'' he said in the awkward silence, ''and don't tell him about the lead we have. I'm not making accusations yet.''

''Yes,'' she said, nodding slightly as their gazes met and held again. ''I understand.''

They both jumped at a rapid knocking on the door. ''Kate, we're gonna be late,'' Tanya called. ''And Louise will probably refuse to feed us if we're not there on Shaker time!''

''Go ahead,'' he said, and nodded toward her bedroom. "I'll talk to her until you're ready. Sorry I slowed you down."

"I'm not," Kate said with a pert smile that made him feel he'd ridden a roller coaster down a drop-off. If Tanya hadn't been rapping on the door again, he might have tried to get Kate to go along for the ride.

"Now everyone is to 'Shaker your plates,' and that means eating every bit of food here!" Louise announced as she put the finishing touches on the buffet table. Ben had summoned them all into the Willises' living room.

Despite her worries, Kate had been enjoying herself. The support of the village staff always bucked her up. Everyone had been solicitous when she'd been asked to update them about the state of Sarah's will and she had mentioned the meeting tomorrow.

"Give 'em hell!" Clint Barstow had said, best summarizing everyone's feelings.

But now they were *ooh*ing and *aah*ing over the lovely, unique spread of food Louise had prepared— authentic Shaker, of course. They'd been drinking fruit shrubs, a delicious mix of pureed strawberries and made-from-scratch lemonade, while Dane conducted a rather informal meeting during which each person had explained what he or she had yet to do to prepare for opening day—a scant three weeks away. Now steaming cups of ginger tea awaited them with the other offerings. It was quite a spread, both in selections and quantity. But then, with Clint Barstow and six others to feed, the bounty was necessary.

"The corned beef and cabbage was one of their old standbys," Louise was explaining as she pointed out the dishes and uncovered the hot ones. "This is blue flower omelette made with early chive blooms to lend color and flavor. Buttermilk herbed biscuits with apple paring jelly here..."

Smiling, Ben put in, "They used every bit of their apples, especially during hard times."

"These are watermelon pickles they actually sold from time to time," Louise continued. "And the salad, which they called sallet, is lamb's lettuce they kept covered in hotbeds all winter. It's flavored with basil and other herbs."

"Have you helped her with this?" Kate mouthed to Tanya.

Her friend shook her head. "Louise was the village's herbalist before they hired me," she whispered, "but I don't think she knew much about it."

"Evidently she knows enough. She's amazing," Kate replied, shaking her head, "just amazing."

"And last but most certainly not least, we have Mother Ann's Cake for dessert," Louise was saying. "The Believers celebrated her birthday with this cake—probably scores of them—on March first every year, so we've missed that special day, but this will have to do."

"You'll never be able to place the gentle, fabulous flavor of it," Ben noted, pointing to the pale peach-colored, iced layer cake. "The master chef said I could give her secret away. It's flavored with rose water, which we hope Kate will provide fresh for us next year so we won't have to buy it at an import shop. But the key is in the beating.

"You beat the batter with peach twigs," Ben explained, "which are cut and bruised so the flavor imparts itself very subtly."

Across the room, Kate saw Adrienne whisper

something to Dane. She was stunning but over-dressed for this gathering in a long, print silk skirt and blouse.

"I think," Dane said, "we all owe the Willises a round of applause."

Everyone clapped, while Louise and Ben beamed. "And we don't insist you eat silently, despite how the Believers did it," Louise put in. "Sometimes rules, like those peach twigs, are meant to be broken."

After dinner, while the men huddled downstairs, Louise proudly showed her three female guests around their home. Although Kate would term the decor Early American, it wasn't strictly Colonial; several fine Shaker pieces of furniture were in evidence.

"Beautiful furniture, Louise," Kate observed. "Did Clint and his workers make it or are—"

"We have a few authentic pieces. Several, no doubt, came from this area, as we found them years ago in estate or yard sales before things got so pricey."

"You know," Kate pursued, "since the Shakers took in so many orphans and entire families to swell their celibate numbers, why don't we find more Shaker furniture for children?"

"Well, for one thing," Adrienne said rather huffily, "around our Shaker village, at least, the children's order buildings and property were sold off early and never came back to us. And your friend Jack Kilcourse apparently isn't about to sell. But as Dane says, we have a lot more important things to worry about before we can find the time or money to deal with that."

Kate frowned. Adrienne had put that final remark in a threatening tone she'd never before heard from her. The lilting, charming French accent had never sounded less captivating. Kate filed that away to tell Jack.

"I imagine," Louise put in as if it were her hostess duty to smooth things over, "children's furniture would fetch a pretty penny, as they used to say. We really should suggest to Clint that his men make some of it."

"Good idea," Kate said, "if they haven't already. I'd like to ask him."

"But, my," Adrienne said, "what you've inherited, Kate, and Tanya, too, evidently, is a real treasure. Why, if I had just a few real, rare Shaker pieces today, children's or adults', I'd be able to afford my dream home, my *pied-à-terre* in the south of France. Provençal, that's my favorite style in everything, yes."

"I had *no idea* you two would want to move to France," Tanya said.

"We 'two' don't, but I'll manage it someday," Adrienne insisted, looking quite smug. "Dane loves France, too, you see, as he was attaché at the French embassy—a vice-consul—there when we met."

"Vice-consul," Louise repeated. "It almost sounds as if he were in charge of something illegal, doesn't it?"

Adrienne shot her a quick glare before going on. "My point is, you know men in love and lust will promise the moon, but he vowed we'd have a getaway home someday, and I shall pick the place, you just wait and see."

"Getaway, you say." Louise kept at it, looking appalled. "But I thought Shaker Run was in your blood, too."

Kate's mind drifted as the two women sniped at each other. *Love and lust*, Adrienne had said. Though it revealed a lot about her and Dane, did the woman have to put it that way? Weren't the French supposed to be more romantic and subtle? Kate had always thought Adrienne so smooth, but tonight she had actually said more than she realized.

The tour ended in the large, country kitchen still strewn with the remnants of Louise's preparations for the meal. "Let's all us sisters just pitch in and Shaker this place up," Tanya suggested. Soon, over Louise's protests, Tanya had her hands in dishwater, while Adrienne cheerfully dried dishes. Kate put them away, while Louise covered and stored leftovers.

Their conversation was freewheeling, and Kate managed to work in another question that she thought might help Jack. "I have some things stored at the Rent-a-Room in Athens. Does anyone know if that's a good, safe place?" she asked of no one in particular.

"Oh, dear," Adrienne answered, "you'll have to ask Dane, but I know the village has at least one cubicle rented there, maybe more. But I'm sure they're reputable, don't you think, Louise?"

"With our large cellar and attic here, I really wouldn't know, but isn't that the place they had some vandalism? You know, so many doors there and some terrible young people with no respect for things spray painted graffiti all over?"

"Yeah, I heard that," Tanya said. "The college newspaper covered it—the news, not the doors," she said with a little laugh. "It was a year or so ago, but they never caught the guys, I think."

"Maybe it wasn't guys," Clint Barstow put in as he entered the kitchen. Kate wondered how long he'd been listening in on them. "You got a few toothpicks, Louise?"

"What do you mean, maybe it wasn't guys?" Tanya asked as she hauled another clean serving dish out of soapy water. "Who else would do it, extraterrestrials?"

"I mean," Clint said, starting to pick his teeth, "it takes a bunch of women to want to blame men for things. Maybe girls did it."

As he went back out with the box of toothpicks, Adrienne just shook her head. *"Liberté, egalité, fraternité,"* she muttered. "If Clint and his 'guys' had the chance, they'd be the first of the unwashed rebels over the barricades around here, yes."

Tanya and Kate gave each other looks that said simply, *Huh?*

As Kate placed dishes on shelves in the pantry near the back door, she glanced out the single window to see a lighted room that extended toward the backyard. She could see office shelves, and a glowing computer screen with a moving screen-saver that looked like flying birds with huge, beating wings. The room must be connected to the dining room, but the common door was closed. Other than the attic and basement, Kate had thought Louise had shown them about everything.

"I see you keep a large home office here," Kate observed, as Louise popped into the pantry to place a chafing dish on a high shelf.

"Ben's never really gotten completely out of the business—insurance," she added hastily. "He may seem an authentic Shaker antique, but he's good at planning for the future, too.''

Fascinating, good-hearted, real people, all of them, Kate thought. If she could only handle the mess her own family life was in, maybe she could appreciate this group a little more.

Again she fingered the card in her pocket lettered in old-fashioned script. Louise had placed one at each person's place at the table. Kate's quote was by Jerusha Lockhart, whose diary Louise said she had misplaced, evidently after she'd copied several passages, including this.

If neglected or in hardship, a rose refuses to flower until it is severely cut back and weeded, it read. After the quote, since the rose grower was the persona Kate would be assuming as a presenter, was lettered, *Kate Marburn is Sister Jerusha Lockhart.*

''Thank heavens that's over, and we're still standing,'' Kate told her lawyer as they left the meeting in Toledo the next day.

''Since they believe, erroneously, they have won, they are in their gloat mode instead of goad mode,'' Mason whispered, and she had to laugh.

Kate and Mason had not even mentioned that she intended to contest their latest claim of ''undue influence and intentional alienation of affection under duress.'' Mason had assured Kate that Sarah's longtime maid Marie—from whom Kate had rented her short-term apartment after Sarah's death—was willing to testify that Kate was guilty of none of that. And Dane had told Kate last night that the Shaker Run staff would assist her with legal funding to fight Sarah's heirs if she would agree to keep Sarah's furniture

where it was for at least the next five years, should
Kate win the case. Though Kate was a bit annoyed
that Dane had dealt directly with her lawyer and not
with her on that, perhaps it was just so she would not
be embarrassed, she thought.

That term *alienation of affection* kept haunting
Kate. Yes, she'd seen Sarah turn to her almost as to
a daughter, but then Sarah had been like a second
mother to Kate. It was Varina and Palmer who had
alienated their mother's affection, not her.

At that thought, Kate's mind turned to Erin, her
own daughter. What had happened to turn Erin more
and more against her?

Mason and Kate huddled together in the cul-de-sac
in front of the Denbigh lawyers' building. It was set
in a new office park out on Secor Road, and Kate
intended to get directly on the nearby outer-belt to
head back home. Strange how Shaker Run was home
now, she thought.

"So you'll call me as soon as you've deposed Marie?" Kate said, with a glance down the street at Varina and Palmer. They, too, were standing in the cul-
de-sac with their lawyer, Pete Scofield, in the sweet
spring sun, talking, not yet getting in their cars parked
down the way. Palmer had driven his red sports car
today. Kate could see Varina gesturing dramatically
toward them, as if they were plotting more dire things
against her. This was not over yet, Kate vowed, as
she turned her back on them.

"I'm also going to try to find some other character
witnesses, since it's come to this," Mason said, pulling out a small leather notebook and flipping it open.

"That's a good one, isn't it," Kate said with a
rueful little laugh and shake of her head. "Character

witnesses for the hated scapegoat of the Marburn Securities scandal. Can't eat lunch in this town no more.''

"What?" he asked, frowning up at her into the sunlight.

"Nothing. Just a book I read once, something like that title.''

"Anyone else besides Marie you can think of who observed you with Sarah on a day-to-day basis?'' Mason pursued.

"I wish I could use the staff of my current employment," she admitted with a sigh, "as I feel so valued and appreciated there. But yes, I'm sure the Groveland gardener, Jeff Petersen, would testify for me and against Varina, as she's the one I'd like to jettison the most...''

Her voice faded. Erin's angry words about *jettisoning* Mike when she should *have stuck by him for better or worse* danced through her mind again. Damn, she had to get back to Erin and work on a solution to their problems. If only there were a healing herb for that—

As Mason droned on, Kate heard a distant squeal of brakes. An engine revving made her turn to look at what Mason had already seen down the court over her shoulder.

Kate gasped. The car—an old black car—was coming straight at them.

15

Prick not your finger as you pluck if off,
Lest, bleeding, you do paint the white rose red,
And fall on my side so, against your will.
                                        —Shakespeare
                                        King Henry IV

Kate screamed. The car leaped from her worst night-mare, growing, blocking out the sun.

At first it seemed to hurtle toward her, then veered toward Palmer and Varina. Kate watched in frozen horror as—it seemed in slow motion now—Varina, Palmer and their lawyer shouted, then scattered. But it plowed into them. Kate screamed again as Varina flew over the hood and Palmer disappeared. Only their lawyer was able to scramble through parked cars onto the sidewalk.

Mason shoved Kate away in the split second the car careered closer. It brushed by so close she could feel its breath, but she was sure it tried to miss, not hit her. It screeched into a U-turn around the curved end of the court. Kate rolled once on the sidewalk, got unsteadily to her knees, then to her feet.

She gaped as it swerved to miss another car, turned the distant corner onto Secor Road, and disappeared.

Tears blurred her vision. Everything had begun and ended so fast. The entire, seemingly-eternal horror must have happened in less than a minute.

"Are you all right?" Mason demanded, taking her arm. "I'm going inside to call a medical vehicle. See if you can help them—no, you go call. We don't need you bending over your fallen enemies."

Kate nodded. Varina and Palmer were down, with Pete Scofield leaning over them. She had been so certain Palmer owned that car, or at least had hired someone to torment her. She shuddered with a new possibility, more dreadful than what she'd believed before.

Whoever was in that death car had meant not to hurt or hit her, but help her.

The receptionist in the lawyer's office had heard the accident, run outside, and had already called 911. But Kate demanded the phone and dialed it again.

"I can read your telephone number on my monitor," the woman who answered said in a monotone. "If you are calling from the same number about the same accident—"

"It wasn't an accident. It was a deliberate hit-and-run, attempted murder," she insisted, her strident voice rising. "I want you to call Homicide Detective Stan Rudzinski and get him over here. Tell him Mrs. Marburn is waiting for him and needs his help. And the car that hit them is a black one with tinted windows, probably a 1940s Packard. It turned left onto Secor Road. The police have got to find it!"

Without hearing what else the 911 operator would say, Kate handed the receiver back to the astounded receptionist and ran outside. A crowd had gathered;

a man she didn't recognize was trying to hold them back. Both lawyers knelt by the victims. On trembling legs, Kate ran toward them.

Palmer had been thrown onto a strip of grass and wasn't moving. Unconscious or dead? Varina was lying sprawled in the street on her back, still but apparently alert, her face and arms covered with blood.

Kate ripped off her suit jacket and bent to cover Varina with it. Both lawyers gaped up at her but let her do it.

You, Varina mouthed when she saw Kate. She didn't look in pain; maybe she was beyond pain. "My mother..." she said, but her voice drifted off in a rasping sound. She sucked a slow, shallow breath. "My moth—"

"Your mother loved you very much," Kate told her, her voice breaking. "She told me so more than once. She just wanted to spend more time with you and Palmer."

Varina gave a barely perceptible nod. Her eyes closed tight, then her entire face relaxed. She opened her eyes and stared blankly straight up at the sky, as still as a statue.

"Get back," Mason warned Kate, pushing her away as she tried to kneel by Varina. "I hear sirens. Let's just all stay back."

He stood and pulled Kate away, his arms around her. Scofield moved from Varina to bend over Palmer. He felt for the pulse at the side of his neck. "He's alive—I think," he called to them.

Screeching sirens, a medic and a fire engine raced into the court, then a second medic and a police car. Though Kate was certain Varina was dead, they took her in the first medical vehicle. Palmer had a concussion or was in a coma—Kate wasn't sure what she heard—and they took him in the second ambulance.

Two more police cars arrived. Officers taped off the scene and drew crude chalk lines around where the bodies had been. One ran a long-handled tape wheel along the skid marks to measure their length. Kate knew the car had only put on the brakes to make the turn to escape the court, not to avoid hitting anyone. An officer began to take statements from eyewitnesses. Then from a fourth car, a plain black one that had just pulled in, Stan Rudzinski and his partner, Tina Martin, emerged.

"Is this *déjà vu* all over again?" Kate heard Tina Martin ask Rudzinski out of the corner of her mouth.

But when Kate cried, "Zink, I'm glad you're here. I have so much to tell you!" Rudzinski threw an arm around her and led her—with Mason James in quick pursuit—back into the building.

"You should have told me you'd seen that car twice," Zink said a half hour later. Kate and Mason faced both police detectives across a conference table Zink had commandeered from Varina's lawyer.

"I am telling you," Kate insisted.

"Should have told me *before*."

"Get off it, Detective," Mason cut in, holding up both hands. "or we're out of here right n—"

"It's all right, Mason," Kate said, turning to him. "I want to get this thrashed out. I'll answer their questions because I want them to find that car and whoever's in it."

"I didn't tell you about the car before today," she explained, looking straight at Zink, "because it—they—hadn't done anything illegal. And I was trying to figure out who it was before I told anyone. I didn't tell Mason, either. And I'm not going to crumble to some—some stalking terrorist.''

''You're not some damn detective!'' Zink shouted so loud that his partner jumped. ''You want to get yourself killed next?''

''No, and I wouldn't want to be some *damn* detective!'' Kate shouted back before Mason could protest again, though he threw up both hands and turned away slightly. She stared down Zink, and he glared back as some strange feeling leaped between them. Mutual anger? Attraction, on his part? Kate had to admit they were starting to sound like bickering mates.

She rested her chin back on her hands, elbows on the conference table again. ''Sorry, I'm just shook and starting to imagine all kinds of crazy things.''

''Of course, you are,'' Detective Martin put in. ''But we've got to go back over all this again before we let you go.''

Kate nodded as Zink resumed, in a calm tone. ''Despite the fact you and Mr. James say the car seemed to intentionally swerve away from you, we can't be sure of that. It still could have meant to hit you instead of them. Police investigators outside and the witnesses say that old car had up a pretty good head of steam for a dead-end street. It may have been out of control in more ways than one.''

Kate nodded again. It didn't make sense that it would have been terrorizing her but then hit Palmer and Varina—unless it had simply careened out of control and not accomplished its intent to kill her— yet.

''So, is there anything else you haven't told us,

besides that you've seen that car before?'' Zink prompted, his voice on edge again. "Tina and I want to help, Kate. And I still say we need to run you in to the ER or a doctor to get checked out.''

"No, I'm all right, physically,'' she insisted, though she'd been shivering, even wrapped in Mason's suit coat.

"Okay, like Tina said, let's rerun some of this,'' Zink repeated. "In Woodlawn Cemetery, the driver actually got out of the car, but you only sensed there was a woman beside him and never saw him otherwise, so there's no way you could pick him, or either of them, out of a lineup.''

"That's right. It was distant, and he pulled down that old-fashioned fedora-type hat. I don't know, maybe it goes with the car.''

"You're sensing things again,'' he said matter-of-factly. "Like you *sensed* that Sarah Denbigh was up in her suite that night you found her dead.''

Though she ached all over, Kate sat up straighter. She had almost been lulled into trusting Rudzinski because she had needed him to help her figure all this out, maybe even to protect her. But if he was going to put her on the defensive about Sarah's death again, she'd just go on the offensive.

"I can't believe the police couldn't find that car,'' she said, glaring at both Zink and Tina. "It had to stick out, and I gave them the direction it was going.''

"Look, Ms. Marburn,'' Tina said, as Mason started to protest again, then just slumped back in his chair. "The perp's vehicle could have turned into any nearby garage. Maybe the driver knows Toledo well. If this is as calculated as it sounds, the escape must have been planned, too, so we may have to go at it another way besides the old cops-chase-robbers. For starters, we can try to trace those dark-tinted windows every eyewitness has mentioned. That kind of dark glass is illegal in Ohio and most other northern states.''

"Illegal?" Kate repeated.

"Yeah," Zink said. "Officers of the law really don't need to be approaching a stopped car when they can't see what and who is on the other side of the dark glass. Limited light tinting is okay, but not that black one-way mirror glass.''

Words her grandmother used to say spun through Kate's brain: *Now we see through a glass darkly but then face-to-face.* She had to figure out whose face was behind that black mirror glass, watching her, stalking her. And that meant she had to know why. So, on her own, without telling these people or anyone, she had to become what she'd just taunted them about: a damn detective.

"But it's legal and common in other states, mostly down South," Tina was explaining. "Zink, we can hardly canvas every shop that darkens windows in this country to see if they did an old Packard. We'd be better off just going back through the list of the investors her husband swindled.''

"My thought exactly," Mason agreed.

Kate knew she should follow his lead, but she added, "That's too long a list." She was intrigued that the detectives seemed to be taking her into their confidence—or was that some sort of ruse to get her to trust them even more? Zink had been wanting that for so long. Today she'd finally caved by calling him for help. She felt he'd always liked her, but she couldn't afford to start liking him.

"It's a mile-long list," Zink agreed. "I've already looked at it, thinking someone might have wanted to frame you for Sarah Denbigh's death—but nothing jumped out at me."

Kate knew she could help narrow that list if she could get Erin to give her the name of, or details about, the person she'd evidently heard had threatened Mike. But she didn't want to tell Zink that yet. The last thing Erin needed was to be grilled by the police. Kate was just going to have to get it out of her.

"Then, too," Zink said, downing the last of his coffee, "we can start at the other end of the suspicion spectrum, so to speak, and go looking for a party of one—not that the law hasn't already tried that."

"Yeah," Tina agreed, leaning back in her plush leather chair, "but that's like looking for a needle in a haystack, too, unless someone can give us a hint about what part of the haystack to start in."

"What do you mean?" Kate asked, staring at Zink, daring him not to tell her.

"We mean," he said, standing and stretching, "you're on record as saying you didn't think your husband would really kill himself. But maybe he'd kill someone else."

"But Varina?" she demanded. "Surely, you don't mean Sarah, too."

"It would make you look guilty," Tina said, "or, on the other hand, help you get the Denbigh furniture inheritance. Maybe Mike Marburn thinks he could blackmail or coerce it out of you once the contesting heirs were eliminated."

"I'm afraid," Zink went on, leaning toward her on stiff arms across the table, "your husband—"

"Ex-husband!"

"—would know your habits well. He could be watching or following you."

"Unfortunately, that's highly possible," Mason added.

None of this was news to Kate, but she was not going to let on that the possibility terrified her more than any car bearing down on her. Her insides lurched as a dreadful thought uncoiled itself in her brain. Not just that Mike could be involved, but that he could have secretly contacted Erin and turned her against her stepmother. Who but Erin could tell Mike where to find her at each place she'd gone? Kate had told Erin about this meeting with the hostile heirs, though she'd told the entire Shaker Run staff, and Jack, too, for that matter.

"I—I don't know—" Kate floundered. "Mike would be crazy to hang around me, even covertly. I swear to you he hasn't contacted me, and I'd never take him back. That can't be."

"Weirder things have hap—" Tina began, just as Pete Scofield rapped on the door and opened it.

"We've just heard from Flower Hospital," the lawyer told them, his face ashen. "Varina Wellesley was DOA. Palmer's critical but he may make it. Thought you'd want to know, Detectives. And, Mrs. Marburn, considering that I'm sure you would have liked her out of your life, that was nice what you said to Varina there at the end, whether it was true or not."

Tina Martin shook her head, and Zink hung his, though he watched Kate out of the corner of his eye. Mason blew his nose. But Kate cried, especially since Sarah was not here to mourn for her children.

* * *

"Varina dead and her brother hurt badly?" A wide-eyed Erin repeated Kate's words. They sat together the next morning in a corner of the Jefferson Hall lounge on campus. "By some old black car that's—been following you around?"

"A car that's known where to find me from time to time, at least," Kate said. "Oh, I don't mean the car itself as if it's some demonic being, but whatever idiot is driving it. And that's what I have to find out."

They were sitting knee to knee on a sofa, but Erin had not hugged her, so Kate didn't push her luck touching her stepdaughter, either. Kate was just grateful Erin had agreed to come with her to talk. But she could tell, once the girl had heard what her news was, that she was not eager to stay.

"And you came here," Erin said, seeming to grope for words, "to tell me this in person to make up for not coming to see me about Sarah's death before the reporters called?" She looked pale and her hands trembled, though she had gripped them in her lap.

"I came straight to you from Toledo because I thought maybe you could help me figure out who would want to terrorize me like that. And then either try to kill me in a hit-and-run, or kill Sarah's children."

"Me help? How can I help you figure it out?" Erin demanded in a shrill voice before getting hold of herself. She glanced over at the main desk to see if they'd been heard—they had—and back to Kate again.

"Because it could have something to do with someone's sick vendetta," Kate said. When Erin's high brow crushed in a frown, Kate thought for a moment she didn't know what *vendetta* meant. "Revenge, Erin, over what your father did."

"What *he* did?" she repeated, and wrapped her arms around herself. "Oh—you mean someone thinks you were in on everything no matter what you claimed in court, and they want to scare or—or hurt you."

"That's one of the theories the police are working on. But there is another, isn't there."

The girl stared at her mutely, but Kate read fear in her eyes. Surely not just a reflection of her own, even though she knew kids could sense a parent's emotions without being told.

"Erin, I desperately need your help." Kate took a deep breath and decided to just spit it out. "Your father hasn't contacted you, has he?"

Erin gasped as if she couldn't get her breath. "You're going to try to blame it on him?" she cried, her voice rising again. "Hasn't he gone through enough? You think he's driving around in some old, black car trying to run you down?"

"Or just scare me and run down my enemies so I get the fortune in Sarah's furniture. Either way, it could be him, and you haven't answered my quest—"

"Of course, he hasn't contacted me. Thanks to you, he's on the run somewhere, just—"

Kate seized both Erin's wrists as the girl started to stand. She could see and smell fright in her eyes, her body. "Honey, think. Don't just feel for a minute— think! I'm not the one who worked covertly for years to set up those dummy investments, I'm not the one who took off when it looked like there was no choice but to take responsibility. Just listen to me a moment so—''

Erin wrenched free, flinging Kate back in her chair. "No! It's stuff like this that drags my grades down, drags me down. I've got to go to class, or I'll flunk out and waste your hard-earned money to keep me here. Just leave me alone if all you ever want to do is upset me!''

Kate started after her across the large room as Erin hurried away, banging the door to her hallway behind her. The two student receptionists at the desk were staring. Kate glared back and stalked out. But she was not leaving any of this alone, however much it upset anyone, or everyone.

Kate began to work her Shaker Run rose beds with a vengeance, but her mind was miles away. She'd always done her best thinking like this. As she agonized over everything, it was now the terror of Mike's returning and turning Erin against her that scared her the most.

"Oh, so glad to see our Sister Jerusha back at her roses." Louise's voice floated to Kate. "But I do hope, when our visitors start coming, you'll use the village's antique rose cutters and not those shiny, new ones of yours.''

Kate nodded, waved and went on working, hoping Louise would leave her alone. Thank God the woman went on about her business. On her knees, Kate pruned deadwood and weeded even harder. But she did stop work when two big boots and jeans-encased, long legs appeared on the other side of the rows of bushes. She looked up to see Jack.

"What are you doing here?'' she asked bluntly,

shading her eyes to see him better. As if to help her out, he shifted slightly so she was sitting in his shadow. It wasn't the way she'd meant to begin with him, but it was too late to take back the brusque tone. She just wasn't ready to face him—or the way she was coming to feel about him. Sensing he wanted to help her up, she quickly got to her feet.

"Thanks for coming by or calling to let me know you're back safe and sound from that meeting in Toledo with Sarah's heirs," he said, his voice edged with annoyance.

She wanted to tell him about the car hitting Varina and Palmer, but no words came. She'd completely lose control out here, so she'd just have to tell him later.

"I should have called you or stopped by," she admitted, "but it was a—dreadful, draining experience. I meant to come see you—to tell you about it."

"All right. I just thought you should know the police came." He sounded calmer now, but she could tell his emotions were still pent up. His big body was rigid but for his fists, which he kept flexing at his sides. She had the urge to hurl herself into his arms, but trusting a man too much was dangerous.

"They took a paint scraping off that broken pole across from my house," he went on. "When I walked over to talk to them, one said you were the one who had tipped them off about a car taking down the pole. You didn't happen to tell them I was in Clint's workshop that night, did you?"

"Of course not. But it was the Toledo police? Was Zink with them?"

"Now why should he come all that way for a piece of paint? Besides, I thought you went up there for a

legal meeting with Sarah's heirs, not to see Zink.
What's the deal?''

"You're starting to sound just like him with your
parade of questions,'' she cried, throwing down her
pruners and ripping off both garden gloves. *"Is that
your* final *answer, Kate Marburn?"* she mimicked.
She knew she was overreacting, but she felt pressured
and panicked by too many things, including her own
emotions everytime Jack Kilcourse so much as looked
at her.

"Kate, I am not the enemy,'' he said, holding up
both hands as if to ward off an attack. "I thought we
were working together on probing this furniture scam
and Sarah's death. And it was the Athens police,'' he
went on, "though, of course, they admitted the Toledo jurisdiction requested the search. You know,
sweetheart, I think you've got a lot to tell me, and
you've suddenly decided not to.''

"It's just that I have some serious, personal problems with Erin right now,'' she insisted, nervously
wiping her palms on her jeans. "I realize, since you
don't have kids, you might not appreciate or understand but—''

"Sure, I get it,'' he threw back, his voice even
harder. He clasped his arms over his chest. "What
would I know about raising or protecting a kid, right?
My own, let alone anyone else's.''

"What?'' Her hands shot to her hips. "You're the
one who's chock-full of secrets about your past, no
matter how much you pretend to tell me what's going
on in the present.''

"Don't tell me anything else, then,'' he said over
his shoulder as he started away. "Because I'd want

to help and then I'd get involved, and that's the last damn thing I need!''

Kate was appalled this had gotten so bad so fast between them. She gaped after him as he strode away. For such a private, controlled man, that was a tirade. But one that, finally, had given her a glimpse into his explosive emotions. The trigger had been the mere mention of a child and the hint he was being shut out, even though that was exactly the way he operated. Worse, she feared she could not help him when she was so volatile and needed so much help herself.

Kate burst into tears and hurried in the other direction, to the garden shed. Sucking in great sobs, she tore in and slammed the door. But she was not alone; to her surprise, Tanya was bending over the worktable, crushing herbs in an old-fashioned mortar and pestle.

''Hey,'' her friend said, then caught Kate's expression. ''What happened?'' she asked, dropping the heavy marble pestle.

Although Kate had not cried on anyone's shoulder since Mike left, she soaked Tanya's, spilling out to her about Varina and Palmer, the black car's most recent, deadly appearance, her sudden blow-up with Jack, and her fear that Mike was back and using Erin.

''You told anybody else here about Ms. Denbigh's daughter being dead?'' Tanya asked, when Kate got control of herself again.

''I'm going to tell them all, of course, but Dane and Adrienne aren't around, and I've only seen Louise—and Jack—just now. And no, I didn't tell him—yet.''

''Or go crying on *his* shoulder.''

"Of course not," she said, sniffing back tears. "Do you know if he ever had a child?"

"He had a stupid wife who left him, but if there was a child, he never said, and I never quite asked. Why?"

"Just a feeling. I can't believe how badly I'm screwing things up with people I really care about."

"You *do* know that Varina's loss," Tanya went on, "might make things easier for you in getting Sarah's goods? I don't mean to say it's a break for you, but..."

"Don't even breathe something like that!" Kate protested as she blew her nose. "I'd never want things to end this way. But I think my ex might be behind Varina's death. It's a wild idea, except that someone's turned Erin against me. It's possible Mike could think he would profit from my inheritance. As for Jack, I'll try to explain to him, but there are two things I have to do first."

"Which are?" Tanya prompted as Kate dabbed at her eyes.

"I've got to try to keep up with my responsibilities here, but start spying on Erin. I've been stupid not to put two and two together about her before now."

"Like what?"

"Like the fact she supposedly spends Sundays with an ex-boyfriend I've never seen—at least, not since she broke up with him two years ago."

"You don't have me convinced yet, girl."

"She's swung back to believing her father did no wrong and that I have. She adored her father, used to worship him, mostly because he wasn't there much for her, like some distant god from Olympus who swooped in from time to time, smiled and bestowed his bounty on her. You know," Kate mused, "he even used to call her angel—"

Kate slammed her fist on the worktable, making the mortar and pestle thump.

"What? *What?*" Tanya demanded.

"The guy who's a server in a restaurant where Erin meets her boyfriend, Mark, told me that Mark calls her 'angel.' And I'm the one who said his name was Mark, when the server looked like he was going to say something else. But he might just have accepted a name from me that sounded like Mike…"

"But Erin wouldn't call her daddy 'Mike,' would she?"

"I don't know. But she calls me Kate, and maybe he told her not to call him 'Dad' in public. Tanya, if you can cover for me here, I'd be grateful because I've got to go back to campus and do some—well, some undercover work."

"Now, you listen," Tanya scolded, wagging a finger in her face. "I'll cover for you here, sure, just like you did for me when I was away, on *one condition.*" She gripped Kate's upper arms hard; they stared face-to-face.

"Tell me," Kate said, not willing to commit to anything but finding out about Erin.

"You discover it's your ex, you call the police or you get me—maybe Jack—but you don't go facing that man alone."

"All right. Unless it means Erin's safety somehow, I'll get help. But not until I know I'm right. Not until I turn over a few rocks to see if he's hiding under them."

"Yeah, well you just watch out," Tanya warned, frowning, "'cause cornered snakes can bite, and some of them are *poison.*"

16

The roses fearfully on thorns did stand,
One blushing shame, the other white despair...
But, for his theft, in pride of all his growth
A vengeful canker eat him up to death.

—Shakespeare
"Sonnet 99"

"Is Mark Winslow there, please?" Kate asked the young girl who answered the telephone. It was early afternoon, but Kate figured she'd just talk to his mother if he wasn't in. She was calling long-distance from Shaker Run to Mark's home in Toledo because she needed answers now.

Though the child evidently walked away from the phone, Kate could hear her yell, "Mom, it's not for you! It's another girl for Mark!"

Another girl? Kate thought. In addition to Erin? Someone he was dating in Toledo?

"Hi. This is Mark."

"Mark, this is Erin's mom, Kate Marburn. Listen, if it's okay with you, I thought we'd throw her a little surprise party at the 7 Sauces this Sunday when you come on your regular day."

"Ah—okay. But it's not her birthday, is it?"

"No, you're right about that," she said, fighting to keep her voice in check. She wound the phone cord so tightly around her index finger, it turned red, then white. Mark merely sounded cautious, not shocked or caught off guard, so he must be the one visiting Erin on Sundays. Could Kate be completely crazy?

"It would just be to kind of cheer her up," Kate went on to get past the awkward pause, "to get her mind off the pressure on her right now. What time do you usually arrive?"

"Oh, it depends." He sounded more than cautious—wary now.

"I've got to tell you I was really surprised you two were back together, but pleased about it, really. I'd love to stop by and see your parents when I'm in town next, so do you mind if I talk to your mother about it for a moment?"

"She's not here."

"Oh, I thought I heard your sister say she was."

"No. Maybe she thought she was."

"Let me ask you one more thing. Do you think Susan's a good roommate for Erin? I guess I just wanted someone to reassure me. I know you've met her." Out on a limb here, Kate thought. If he'd been visiting Erin, he'd surely know her roommate was Amy, so he'd correct her.

"Yeah, I think she's fine. They get along and all. Are you sure you want to surprise Erin, though? Maybe she'd look forward to it if you'd tell her ahead, do it on her birthday."

Was Mark lying for—with—Erin? Kate agonized. If she had to guess, she'd say he was, but there was still no positive proof, and she didn't want him tipping Erin off that her stepmother might be swooping in for a surprise this Sunday. No, she wanted to head that off for sure.

"You know, Mark, I think you're probably right about not trying this out of the blue. I think I will just wait for her birthday to do it. Besides, I'm *so* busy at work here in southern Ohio," she added, trying to sound light and spontaneous. "But don't tell her, because I will do the party later, maybe invite her dorm friends as well as you. But it's great to talk to you, anyway, and thanks for being such a support to her."

"Oh, glad to. I—so you won't be calling my mother back or anything?"

"I think I'll just let you pass on my good wishes since she's not there right now," she said, shaking her head at how she'd gotten into, then out of this conversation.

As they said goodbye and hung up, she thought Mark sounded more than nervous. Yes, scared. But not as scared as she was starting to feel.

Kate dressed in jeans, T-shirt and denim jacket to blend in with the campus crowd, but it made her feel even more conspicuous instead. She did, at least, have Erin's schedule for this semester, shared when they had been getting along better. Keeping her distance, she followed Erin up the hill to her eleven o'clock class, then decided not to wait the whole time until it ended. She'd go uptown to see if she could talk to Stone at the 7 Sauces. Soon, she thought perversely, she'd have every young man who'd ever known Erin thinking her mother was nuts.

The restaurant manager told Kate that Stone would not be in until the dinner shift, but suggested she might find him at the Beta house. She thanked him and went back out onto Court Street. But fraternity houses were not on her campus map. She asked a student on the street for directions, and shortly afterward located the white-facaded, pillared house with its statue of a dragonlike creature peering down from the roof.

Within five minutes of her asking for him, Stone came down the staircase, stooping first to look at whoever was waiting for him in the first-floor foyer.

"'The redhead's mother,' the guys said," he greeted her with a nervous grin. "Now you've got them thinking I'm in trouble with some girl's mother."

"I couldn't think of any other way to let you know who I was. I don't mean to invade your privacy, but I would really appreciate your help," she told Stone, as he congenially shook her hand. Tall and thin with an open, pleasant face framed by coal-black hair, Stone looked as much at ease here as he had in the restaurant. She could use some of that calm demeanor right now.

"My name's Kate Marburn," she explained, still unsure about how to go at this. Yet Stone had always been accommodating, so she decided to risk honesty. "You see," she said, "I'm afraid my ex-husband has been visiting Erin when he—well, he isn't supposed to. I recall you said the man Erin eats with on Sundays calls her 'angel.' I told you his name was Mark—but could it have been Mike?"

"Tell you the truth, Ms. Marburn," he said, cocking his head as if in deep thought, "Mike's what I thought it was, but I'm not sure. The guy looks older than someone she'd date, though he's in great shape, good-looking and all. But I never overheard her—Erin, that is—call him 'Dad' or anything like that.''

Kate almost told him that Mike was on the run and might have told Erin never to call him that in public, but she wasn't up to sharing that. ''He's not a redhead, too, is he?'' she asked, gripping her purse strap.

''Naw, if that settles your mind. He's got hair almost as dark as mine, but he's got a mustache, and his skin's pretty pale for the hair. He always has a big roll of bills, leaves great tips. Well, actually,'' he added, shoving his hand through his hair, ''it's in a neat gold money clip, kind of old-fashioned.''

Kate felt as if the floor had given way. Mike loved his money clips and had a big collection that he'd taken with him.

Kate shadowed—actually, she admitted to herself—stalked Erin to her mid-afternoon class, then waited and walked behind her in the crowd from Scripps Hall, following her across the green and down the hill to her dorm. She saw nothing unusual, but then why should she? If Mike was coming to see Erin, it must be on those sacrosanct Sunday afternoons.

That's why Erin had been so nervous when Kate had shown up last Sunday, Kate reasoned. The girl had been disappointed, probably because her stepmother was there to wreck her weekly reunion with her father. Then she'd lied about Mark's not coming that day when, in fact, he probably never came, though Erin must have had Mark covering for her. Erin had hustled Kate out of the dorm, practically running down the back steps. The girl had been a nervous wreck as they drove away. And then she'd exploded at Kate about forcing Mike away.

But now Kate was torn about lurking around the campus. She couldn't ignore the fact that things had to be ready for Shaker Run's big opening in just over two weeks. What if Amy saw her and told Erin? Kate decided not to confront Erin's roommate because she might tip off Erin, who would then tell Mike. Sunday was the key: she'd be back then...to see if Erin's caller was Mark or Mike.

"You realize you're keeping to the same schedule the Shakers went by?" Tanya asked, as they crossed paths en route to their separate gardens the next morning.

They were running themselves ragged, trying to prepare for the village opening. Frenetically, Kate tended her bushes as the new reddish shoots popped with buds. She'd been up at four-thirty; she couldn't sleep, anyway. By lantern, since the staff was trying to become adept at using those, she'd done duties in the garden shops until dawn, then headed outside.

"Maybe you *are* Sister Jerusha, like Louise says," Tanya teased, though Kate wasn't in the mood for it. "The diary I've been reading says *my* Sister Faith had prayed, washed up, aired the sheets, swept the floor and wiped the woodwork for both the men and women's retiring rooms *before* breakfast, which they fixed before seven-thirty. I think that makes them kinda hardworking but kinda crazy," she concluded in her best rendition of Louise's starchy Shaker voice. But Kate just couldn't laugh, however relieved she was that Tanya was up-tempo when Kate herself was down in the dumps.

"There's supposed to be a diary by a brother who used to be an herbalist," Tanya went on, "but it's

missing just like that one of your Jerusha, so I'm
stuck reading about dirty sheets..." Tanya's voice
trailed off.

Kate shook her head. Let Louise look for the lost
diaries. But Kate managed to give Tanya a grateful
smile and a quick hug, before Tanya trudged back to
her workshop.

She knew Tanya was almost as frenzied as she was.
For the division of her great-aunt's furniture, she was
heading to Kentucky tomorrow—Friday, two days before Kate would return to campus to watch for Mike.

How Kate wished she'd had time to ask Tanya for
one of her soothing herbs. The efficacy of the herbal
tea she drank every night seemed to be wearing off,
and she wasn't sleeping well. As a result, despite how
revved up she felt, she nearly nodded off while working. Sometimes her brain just seemed to slow down.

Startled from her stupor, Kate jerked as a thorn
pierced her hand right through her glove. Someone
behind her had spoken. She stood and straightened. It
was Dane, his arms full of new color brochures, and
Adrienne, hers with hand-wrapped packets of Tanya's
herbal teas for the gift shop.

"You've been making up for lost time," Dane observed with a nod at the rows of rosebushes.

Lost time, Kate thought. So much lost time with
Erin, maybe with Jack, too—time she could never
make up, never get back. Adrienne stepped forward
and squeezed Kate's arm. "We heard about the tragedy in Toledo—the latest one, yes."

"You should have told us everything the moment
you got back, even phoned us from there," Dane
commanded, his voice suddenly hard and accusing.
Kate marveled that, for someone who had been in the

diplomatic corps, he could at times be so blunt and harsh. When Tanya had once said he was either up or down, she must have meant his moods.

"I fully intended to when I returned, but I've had other concerns and didn't realize you were back," Kate explained. "I don't know if the tragedy will make any difference in my inheriting the furniture, if that's what you're wondering. I'm praying that Palmer will recover, and I certainly know better than to try to go to Varina's funeral Saturday. Again, I'm grateful for your offer to help pay my lawyer's fees if this drags on, but your continued understanding and support is even more valuable to me."

Kate felt as if she'd made a political speech, but Dane's expression seemed distant, as if he were thinking about something or someone else.

"We knew we were right to hire Kate, weren't we, Dane," Adrienne prompted, elbowing him.

He started, then nodded. "Absolutely. Despite the fact Jack Kilcourse first mentioned you, it was my decision and a good one."

"I love it here and hope to help build things—or should I say, grow them?—over time," Kate assured them.

"You see, we weren't primarily concerned about the furniture, but about you," Dane said. "It must have been dreadful for you to have to go through seeing that hit-and-run after losing Sarah Denbigh, too."

However stilted this conversation seemed to Kate—as if it had been staged somehow by the Thompsons—she was relieved they seemed to understand. "Did someone call you about the car accident in Toledo," she asked, "or—?"

"Dane read it online in the *Toledo Blade*," Adrienne explained with another little squeeze of Kate's arm as she stepped back next to her husband. They started to walk away. "If there's anything we can do, just anything," Adrienne threw back over her shoulder, "let us know. And please keep us informed."

That evening as the sun sank, Kate ate a peanut butter and jelly sandwich—downed some breath mints—then showered, picked a small bouquet of white violets and bloodroot from the edge of the forest beyond holy ground, and set out toward Jack's. The way they'd parted had been eating away at her.

Although it was for its pale, pretty flowers that Kate had picked the herb bloodroot, she had a real affection for it, too. When Erin was little, it had grown in their backyard. She and her friends had cut it to make "Indian paint" on their faces, for the stalks, when sliced open, bled a bright red-orange liquid.

When Kate had mentioned that memory once, Tanya had said that American Indians had used it not only to dye their skin but to treat breast cancer. But, she'd warned, like so many things in nature, too much of a good thing could be harmful.

"You mean it's poison?" Kate had yelped. "And I let Erin play with it as a kid?"

"Don't worry," Tanya had assured her. "You'd need *toxic* doses of it, lots and lots ingested. You go ahead and keep your happy memories of it. Just be sure your grandkids don't make a salad of it someday."

"What would happen if they did?" Kate had asked.

"Oh, intense thirst, burning in the stomach, vertigo, collapse and paralysis—the *usual,*" Tanya had said with such a smug look that Kate hadn't been sure whether she was kidding or not.

But knowing Tanya, she was not.

Jack saw Kate coming up his drive with measured steps, carrying a nosegay in front of her with both hands the way a bridesmaid might. He'd had an ache in his gut since their argument, but it infuriated him—actually, scared him—how she turned him upside down emotionally. She made him want to resurrect and share all sorts of things he thought he'd buried for good.

As he opened the front door, she thrust out the little bouquet of pale flowers.

"Truce?" she said, and smiled. It lit her face, which helped because she looked so pale and drawn—so defenseless, though he knew better.

"Come on in."

"Let's just sit here in the rockers for a few minutes. And don't drink the water you put this bloodroot in. It's one of Tanya's pets, if you know what I mean."

He laughed. "I don't think a woman's ever given me flowers before, so I'm desperate enough I'll even take poison ones. Thanks, Kate, for coming over."

Though he wanted to pull her onto his lap in one of the rockers, he went in the house and came back out with a pint jar filled with water for the flowers. The water turned pink.

"Now tell me about where you've been and what happened," he said, and pulled the second rocker close to hers. "And how Erin's doing at O.U."

"She's got problems, maybe some piled as high

and deep as her stepmother's," she told him. "I want to explain all that to you sometime, but as you've never told me much about your—your family past—I feel funny unloading about mine."

He flinched but forced himself to return her riveting stare. "I'm bitter about my divorce," he said.

"Thanks for trusting me enough to share that," she said, but her voice was not sarcastic or bitter as he'd expected. "Jack, divorce is a bad thing and means someone or something failed, but it happens. It happened to me. And my marriage and divorce was public knowledge, whereas at least yours was private."

"We lost our son," he stumbled on, still scared to say more when he hadn't told a soul here even that much. "After that, things fell apart, and Leslie—left me. That's it. End of story."

Unfortunately, she waited, poised on the edge of her chair for the rest of it. He could tell she wanted to ask what happened and why. He thought about lying, saying crib death or a fall down the stairs. He knew people had different ways of running from their grief, and, sitting stone still, he knew he was still running.

"Jack, thank you for telling me. I didn't come to put you through all that, really. But any time you want to talk about it, please tell me. The loss of your child—that's got to be devastating. I'm so sorry and I would love to hear about your child. Was it a boy or a girl?"

"Andy. He would have been just a little younger than Erin."

She took his hands, and he held hers hard. They rested their wrists on their touching, trembling knees.

He wanted not only to haul her into his lap, but to sob on her shoulder.

"Tell me why you came," he insisted. "I'm not just changing the subject. I want to know."

"I think my timing's terrible, but that seems to be the way things are lately. I came to tell you something before Zink shows up on your doorstep again to fill you in on the latest Denbigh death."

"More evidence on Sarah's?" he asked, rocking toward her, grateful for a new topic, a different death to dissect. When she shook her head, and her eyes teared up, he asked, "What? You don't mean something happened to her crazy daughter?"

Kate jerked erect. "Did you...know—or just guess because of what we've been saying?"

"I didn't know," he insisted, reaching out a hand to stroke her damp cheeks gently with his callused fingers. "It's just that the one time I met Varina up close and personal, she seemed wacked out to me. Come on, Kate, give. Now you tell me what happened."

It both helped and hurt Kate to share the nightmare with him. It was like living it all again, but at least he knew now. And he seemed to listen intently, to really empathize. She described Varina's death, her two previous encounters with the Packard, and her latest interview with Zink. But she did not tell him her suspicions about Erin and Mike. Besides, she kept praying she was wrong about Mike being back and Erin siding with him.

"You're not thinking of going to Varina's funeral," Jack said, his voice adamant.

"No, though I'd go for Sarah if I could."

"It's horrible that someone would do that so deliberately," he said with a sharp sniff. "Life is precious, then here comes some accident. You're sure they didn't mean to hit you instead of her and Palmer?"

"Why do you say *they* hit them? I didn't say there was more than one in that car."

"Just a figure of speech, a sexless way to refer to the driver since you don't have a clue who it is. You don't, do you?"

"I'm working on it, but—"

"It sounds similar to the old, black Shaker car Dane keeps here, but he said he never takes it farther than the shop or gas station in town—and it's not a Packard."

She stopped rocking and jumped to her feet.

"Dane keeps a black classic car? That the Shakers had? I've never seen it. Is it at his house?"

He reached up to pull her back into the chair, but she didn't budge. "Kate, it can't be the same car. Not only is it a different make, but it doesn't have black-tinted windows. When the village closed in the '40s, the Shakers sold it. I heard it was pretty much kept in mothballs until someone donated it to the village a year or so ago."

"Where is it?" she demanded. "Or if you don't know, I'm going to see Dane right now. Okay, it's not the same one, but maybe if I could see it I'd learn something about the other. Jack, I'm getting desperate."

"It's here, in storage," he said, standing and cupping her shoulders in his big hands.

"Here, where?"

"If I tell you—even show you—you cannot let Dane know. I happen to have a key to the place, but

I'm not supposed to let anyone in there, though Tanya uses the shed to write in sometimes. I don't need him or anybody else knowing I keep an eye on the furniture they store in there, and that I'm in and out as much as I am.''

"Shaker furniture? Children's Shaker furniture?''

"Yeah, that's where I saw the copies of Sarah's pieces. Do I have your word? I'll help you get to the bottom of this, but I can't have you blowing the new way I have of keeping track of Shaker Run furniture.''

"I promise,'' she vowed, craning her neck to stare in the direction he'd first glanced when he'd mentioned the shed. "You mean that old shed out there—the one that you said was too full when I wanted to keep my tiller there?''

With a sharp nod, he went into the house and came out with a single key on a large ring.

"Tanya writes her book out here?'' she asked as she followed him through the graying dusk toward the shadowed shed. The red sunset silhouetted it.

"So if you tell her what you know,'' Jack went on, "I'm in as much trouble with her as I'll be with Dane. I'd make you wait until after dark, but a light in here at night might be seen more easily from the road or village.''

"How often is Dane in and out of here?'' she asked, sticking close to him as he turned the key in the padlock. *Dane.* Could Dane somehow be related to the death car? It didn't make any sense.

"I actually don't know,'' he admitted as he shoved the big door on tracks to the side. "And I'll show you why else I'm not sure.''

Kate stared into the dim, crowded shed. It was hard

to see at first. When Jack stepped in, she stayed right behind him.

"I'm trusting you here," he said as he rolled the door closed behind them. "Though I'm at odds with village staff sometimes, I've forged ties to Tanya and even Dane."

"So have I, and I don't want to endanger that, either," she said as they stood close to each other. Slowly, her eyes adjusted to the dim interior. It would have been very dark in here if the sunset through the single window had not bathed the place in a pinkish glow.

Though anxious to see the car, she was suddenly afraid. Not of Jack, but of what might happen between them because she felt so needy and vulnerable. She had not had someone to lean on since she lost Mike, and he'd turned out to be as damaged and deceptive as his business.

They stared at each other in the warm glow of sunset. Even when something scurried away on tiny feet in the back of the shed, they didn't move.

"Trust me," he said.

Kate knew better, but she wanted to, desperately. She leaned toward him, and he toward her. She wanted to yield, to let him take over, but that had been her fatal mistake with Mike.

"When you really trust me, too," she blurted. Taking a step back to look in his eyes, she saw rage surge in him, but he mastered it.

"I could just toss you out of here right now," he said, "but I have a feeling you'd find a way back in. Come on, Kate Marburn, but you owe me."

He led her past a makeshift, messy desk that must have been Tanya's. Books about herbs, yellow legal pads of notes, a mechanical typewriter. The stacked, typed pages lay open to one labeled Angel Trumpet, Also Known As Jimsonweed And Devil's Trumpet. Her friend had indeed lied about not having started her book, but Kate had other things to worry about now.

They walked around boxes and a knee-high, very un-Shaker-like clear plastic bin with a snap-on top, filled with what appeared to be paper and books. They passed furniture, most of it broken, draped piles of something or other, and a few stacked crates.

"It's gone," Jack said, and stopped so abruptly she bumped into him.

"The car?"

"Hell, yes, the car. Do you see one here?"

She peered around him into the space at the back of the shed. "When he does take it out," he said, calmer now, "he goes out the back sliding door, which he has the lock to. This used to be a hay shed, so they once drove wagons and tractors straight through. Sometimes he even drives out around the old cinder lane to the road, instead of using my driveway."

But none of that mattered to her.

"And it is black?"

"Yeah, I said black. A lot of the early ones were."

"And you're positive it isn't a Packard?"

"Give me some credit," he said, as they both stared at the oil spot on the packed dirt floor. "It was a Buick from the end of World War II when they started making cars again. Listen, if you don't overreact, I'll ask Dane where it is and let you know what he says. Maybe he just took it to get the dent pounded out of the front grill."

Dent, Kate thought. From a telephone pole or from Varina? She pressed her palms to her temples. For one moment she thought her head would explode: dented grill and black paint, but no dark windows and the wrong make. Yet right now, tracking down all the old black cars in the universe was not going to distract her from finding out who Erin was seeing on Sundays. Her worst fear now was that Mike would drive up to Erin's dorm in a vintage black Packard. Which would mean not only that he could have been driving the death car, but that Erin could have been the one on the seat beside him.

"We should come back another time, maybe tomorrow night," she told the man. "They say these darkened windows don't obscure the view looking out, but at twilight or dawn you don't have really clear vision if you don't turn the headlights on."

"I'm hardly turning them on here. Who's to say they won't glance over this way."

"With us hidden in this thicket? But why do you suppose they went into that shed? They even closed the door behind them."

"Meaning hanky-panky?" he said with a little snort.

He started the engine again but still didn't turn on any lights. At least these old classics didn't have headlights on day and night like new models, he thought.

It annoyed him that she was giggling. "Hanky-panky?" she repeated. "*Hanky-panky?* That's a good one."

"Cut it out. But I agree we back off now. I want her alone to shake her up or shut her up. We've got to do more watching to find out how much she really knows. This isn't going quite like we planned so we might have to improvise.''

"I'll get out of her what she knows one way or the other.''

"I'll drop you off, then stow this car. Who knows, maybe cops all over the state are looking for it, even though I switched plates again and got the dent pounded out. If I wasn't so attached to her—this car, not our dear Kate—I'd deep-six this big baby for good.''

He pulled out slowly and didn't turn the headlights on until they were almost to the main road. He loved the dark satin night, so slick you could slide right into it and disappear.

17

As soon
Seek roses in December, ice in June;
Hope constancy in wind, or corn in chaff;
Believe a woman or an epitaph,
Or any other thing that's false...
　　　　　　　　—George Gordon, Lord Bryon
　　　　　"English Bards and Scotch Reviewers"

In the dead of night, Kate sat straight up in bed. The red glow of the digital clock read 3:04 a.m. Something had awakened her, but now she heard nothing but the whine of wind and the normal creaking sounds of the old building.

She threw the covers off and stood, feeling she moved in slow motion, not nauseated or dizzy but slightly disoriented. She was just groggy from sleep, that was all, she assured herself. Wracking her brain for what she'd eaten at dinner, something that could have upset her, she recalled nothing suspicious.

Then she remembered the dream she'd just had. Erin had been throwing calendars at her as if they were Frisbees, but not ones with the usual pictures of animals, landscapes or flowers. Each page of each month had displayed a big, black car with gleaming front grills like metal teeth.

"It can't be Mike," Kate muttered as she clicked on a light. She shoved her feet into slippers and pulled on her terry-cloth robe. "And it can't be Erin—never, ever."

But she forced herself to do what she'd been dreading. Digging Erin's class schedule out of her purse, she went into the other room and sat at her desk. From the top drawer of the Shaker antique, she looked for her current calendar—the one with new breeds of roses for each month. Where was it? Why wasn't it where it should be?

Finally she found it in the right drawer, but it had been neatly placed under a stack of envelopes and another of paid bills. She couldn't remember straightening the drawer, but then, she'd been so distracted lately....

She flipped back to the small calendar for last year, then figured out the three dates she had seen the black car. Why was she having such trouble remembering? She had to get more sleep. Finally, she wrote down the date the car might have hit the pole near Jack's knocking out electricity to the village.

She scribbled the dates in order, then stared at them on the page because the letters seemed to swim into each other. She squinted and tried to concentrate. The car had first appeared in the Toledo cemetery near Sarah's grave on Tuesday, October 5, 1999. The other two dates she'd actually seen the car were this year: at Tanya's aunt's funeral on Saturday, April 8, and the day it killed Varina on April 11, a Tuesday. If it had struck the pole down the road, it would have been during the storm of April 1, a Saturday.

"Its visits are getting closer together," she whispered.

She shook her head. The car was not a living, demonic entity in itself, but a machine driven by someone perverted and evil. At least one pattern emerged. The dire events had all occurred on a Tuesday or a Saturday. With trembling hands she smoothed open Erin's current class schedule, then rummaged through her desk until she found the girl's first-quarter schedule.

It annoyed her how small they were printing something as important as a class schedule now. The words seemed to waver on the page, too, but that must be because she was so tired.

Yes, as she had thought. Erin had no classes on Saturdays; she had Tuesdays off her first quarter, back in October, so technically she could have been in Toledo at Woodlawn Cemetery that first day Kate saw the car.

But Erin surely, would not betray her like that even if Mike had come back into her life.

As for Erin being off that second Tuesday—just a few days ago when the car hit Varina—it could not be. Erin had an English class at one on Tuesdays, Thursdays and Fridays. Her bad grades couldn't be the result of skipping class to go wheeling around with her father looking for revenge, could they?

"Oh, Lord, please don't let Erin be involved, even if Mike is," Kate muttered, lacing her fingers tightly together. "She's all I have left. Don't let him pois— hurt her that way."

But, she thought as she stood and snapped off the light, right after the staff meeting this morning she was driving back into Athens to talk to Erin's English professor. She prayed he kept attendance; she had to know if Erin was in class the day that car killed Varina.

Kate was suddenly so chilled that she went to lie back down under the covers in her robe and slippers, curled in a fetal position. But she soon heard a strange sound again. Was that what had awakened her or was it the nightmare of Erin throwing calendars—her own subconscious telling her Erin could be involved in this horror?

Lying still and stiff, Kate strained to listen. Singing. Outside. She had one window slightly ajar to suck in the sweet spring breeze.

She lifted herself on one elbow, though that made her a bit dizzy. If it was a melody, it was a dissonant one, like some of those Shaker laboring songs that accompanied the dancing. But perhaps it was her imagination, or her exhausted, overworked brain playing tricks on her. Now she heard not only the music, but her name.

She jerked alert and listened again. A man's voice that time? Could Jack be outside, calling to her?

Wrapping her robe tighter, she hurried from window to window, stooping or kneeling to peer out. She heard no one now, saw no one. It was her imagination that was betraying her. Just the way it had when Mike had deserted her and Erin, when she had thought someone was stalking her everywhere and she'd lost control to—

"No, you're all right," she told herself fiercely. "You are not going to lose control again."

But she was certain she'd heard music. As she peered out the back window of her bedroom, she saw someone dashing—or dancing—from the cemetery toward holy ground, lit only by the glimmer of the cold half-moon.

"Oh, Mark, I'm go glad you called," Erin whispered into the phone, cupping her hand around it. She'd had to scramble out of bed to get it before Amy woke up.

"Who is it?" Amy mumbled from the darkness of the dorm room.

"I've got it. Go back to sleep. I'll take it out in the hall." They sometimes found more privacy for personal calls by threading the phone cord under the door and closing it on roommates or visitors.

"Just a sec," Erin whispered into the mouthpiece, then yanked her quilt off her bed to wrap around her. No way was she turning on a light to find her robe.

"But who is it?" her roommate repeated.

"It's just Mark. Go to sleep," Erin said, and finally got situated, sitting on the floor in the hall with her back to the wall.

"You surprised to hear from me this late?" he asked.

"I'm just so glad you called! You should have given me your number so you don't always have to phone me."

"Not a good idea. I don't need this phone number recorded anywhere it could be traced."

"Oh, right. But the thing is, I think Mom—Kate's on to us."

She heard his sharp intake of breath. "Tell me."

"She came here and asked me flat out. Actually, accused me."

She waited until two girls, obviously up late studying, passed in the hall.

"Then let's do our little car trip early."

* * *

Kate was as furious as she was fearful. She had definitely heard singing and had seen a human figure out there. Perhaps that person had called her name. Who was doing this to her? And damn Dane Thompson for not installing flood lights and a modern security system here, no matter how unauthentic they would be. As soon as Shaker Run had its opening, she was going to look for someplace to live in town, even if Erin didn't want her so close.

She huddled at the windowsill, peeking over it, squinting out into the moonlit scene. Perhaps that snow-cloaked figure she'd thought she'd imagined two weeks ago had been real.

Refusing to be terrified, she stripped off her night-clothes and yanked on jeans and a sweatshirt. She donned her parka, hoping its downy filling would stop her trembling, though it was not really cold out. Maybe the fresh night air would clear her head.

Taking a flashlight and a hammer, she went down-stairs and let herself out the back. She had almost phoned Jack first, but then decided she'd just stay in the shadows and look around. The last thing she needed was for him to think she was wacko.

She stood quietly in the moonshade of the ever-green near the back door, peering through its branches. It was never as dark outside as it seemed inside. And now she'd turned the tables on whoever was out here; she was watching for them—him.

Then she heard the singing again, louder, clearer. It *was* a Shaker song. When the breeze shifted, it seemed to emanate directly from the cemetery or holy ground out back.

Then she recognized the song and smiled in relief. It was that "Awake My Soul" song that Louise had taught the dancers. It might even be Louise's voice.

Carefully, looking all around and not using her flashlight so as not to call attention to herself, Kate edged out from the Trustees' Building and headed toward the Meeting House. The moment she passed Tanya's herb garden, she could see the downstairs windows were dimly lit.

Louise should have told her she was practicing late. Everyone was harried trying to get things ready for the opening, but this was above and beyond the call of duty, even for someone as obsessed with perfection as Louise and Ben were. Perhaps that had been Ben she saw darting toward the Meeting House. Could he even have called her name, thinking she could critique or participate in the dancing?

Feeling like a felon, she stood on tiptoe to peek in the window of the large, lighted room. But it was Adrienne who danced and darted about the floor to what must be a tape recording of Louise's voice. And the French woman was not attired in Shaker dress or her own usual striking garments.

Adrienne Thompson was stark naked.

"Pick you up Friday—hey, that's today already—instead of our usual Sunday," he told Erin, his voice at first authoritative, then, when she hesitated to agree, wheedling. "Hey, it's not good for us to get into a set schedule, anyway. Pack some things. If she can't find you, she can't blame you, and your temporary disappearance will give you more leverage to deal with her."

"What about school? I don't want to flunk out."

"You won't flunk out. You may only be gone for the weekend, and if not I'll clear it with your profs."

"Mark—Mike—this isn't high school anymore, where dads just write an excuse for days missed, you know."

"I told you not to say things like that. Not unless we're really alone. And we will be soon. The usual place, one o'clock, okay?"

"Okay," she agreed with a sigh, "but I'll be cutting English for it. I'll tell Amy I'm going to see friends for the weekend and leave it vague. But I don't really want to do any more than we already have to hurt her."

"Trust me. See you tomorrow, with no bells on. In short, just be sure no one hears about this. And don't worry about Kate. I'll take care of everything, angel."

Smacking her hand over her mouth in surprise, Kate ducked, as Adrienne cavorted nude past the window. She was whirling, leaping and singing off key, along with a recording of Louise's song. Could the usually elegant and self-contained woman be drunk? Kate shook her head and smothered a laugh.

And then Kate realized how she'd heard the song and music, however distant and walled-off she'd been. This window was slightly ajar, perhaps forgotten earlier when the university dancers had been practicing under Louise's eagle eye.

Kate knew she should tiptoe away. How embarrassing if Adrienne or Dane knew she'd seen this. And where was Dane? If it weren't for Adrienne's outrageous display, Kate would love to corner him right now about his old Buick. Perhaps that had been him running around out back. Maybe he was even getting an erotic kick—Kate giggled as she saw Adrienne kick her way past the window—out of watching this from outside. But if so, he might spot Kate spying.

Kate had just headed back to the Trustee's House when the shrill voice stopped her. "You naughty peeping Tom!"

Thinking Adrienne had spotted her through the window, Kate whirled back, only to hear Dane's voice boom out from somewhere. "A peeping Dane, you mean." His words echoed. "I kind of like it up here. It's a great place to watch from."

Totally intrigued, Kate tiptoed back to the window. Now draped in her black slip as a sort of Isadora Duncan scarf, Adrienne was waving up at the ceiling. Scooting down, Kate saw Dane peering through one of the high observation slits overlooking the meeting room.

"I'm coming down for an up-close-and-personal look, my love," he called out, and dared to wave his fingers through a slit.

Kate quickly headed back toward her apartment. Maybe she could hold it over Dane's head to get better security and lighting, or to make him tell everything he knew about the black Buick. But if *he* was in the tiny upstairs room spying on his wife's display, who was that man out back?

Kate was downstairs early the next morning. The staff meeting was to start at nine, and she had much to do first. She let herself in the small, unlocked office at the back of the building and turned on the PC and printer there. A fax machine hummed away in the corner as something came in. None of this was off-limits, and most of the staff had used it from time to time. Louise had been on a campaign to have it all removed, but Dane had stubbornly refused. Why she hadn't done this before, Kate didn't know, but she hadn't thinking clearly lately. But then, why hadn't Zink thought of it if he was so hell-bent on solving this case? Maybe he thought it best not to tell her everything. After all, she'd held things back from him, especially to protect Erin. And she hadn't told him about the old Buick the Shakers had owned because she didn't need him questioning or accusing the village staff when she had no proof anyone was involved in anything.

Kate heaved a huge sigh as she did an Internet search for PACKARD. When she'd pulled up a lot of useless information on the modern company Hewlett-Packard, she went back and tried PACKARD CARS. The screen filled with car clubs and personal sites. It didn't take her long to find, on a page labeled 1947 Packard Automobile Page, the picture of the car.

"'Packard Clipper,'" she read aloud, her voice solemn. She printed the page off. It was somehow like finally having a wanted poster or police drawing of a criminal. She faxed it to Zink with a scribbled cover page of explanation, then sat back down again.

In the search box, she typed in BUICK CARS. It took a lot longer, but she found and printed a picture of a 1947 Buick. She stared aghast at it: it looked amazingly like the other car in shape, and it also had heavy front grillwork. Still, the Packard's grill was a bit broader, more wraparound. However frenzied she'd been each time she'd seen the car, it had been the Packard and not the Buick—hadn't it?

"What's happening?" the man's voice behind her asked.

She spun in the wheeled chair to face Dane. Although Jack had said he'd broach the subject of the Buick with him, she might be caught now, anyway. She quickly shuffled the Buick picture under the one of the Packard, though she knew the Buick ink wasn't quite dry.

"I wondered if I could locate online a picture of that car that hit Varina Palmer," she explained hastily. "I did, and faxed it to the Toledo police to be sure they are looking for the right vehicle, since I never was really sure of its year or make."

"Good move. Kind of like looking through mug shots, huh?" He came in to hang his coat on the wall peg. Kate wondered if Adrienne was sleeping in for obvious reasons. In addition to her wild display last night, like everyone else, Adrienne Thompson had been burning the candle at both ends.

"Actually," Kate said, "I was going to show it to you because someone said the last Shakers here had an old black car that you're carefully preserving—so I thought you might know something about old cars—in general." She hoped playing dumb would get her some information from him, though a few moments ago she'd decided not to give that old black Buick a second thought.

"The one we—the village, that is—owns is a '47 Buick Eight, a beautiful thing," he said, leaning in the doorway as she hurriedly rose and gathered her material from the desk.

At least she knew now he wasn't going to explode at her. And if he was guilty of anything, which was as wild an idea as Mike and Erin in the death car, he was hiding it well. She remembered to bend down to click the Buick site off the screen, not sure if he'd noted it.

"I'll show you the car sometime," he went on, still blocking the door. "We'll even put it on display, I imagine. And, Kate," he added, his voice almost sonorous as she edged closer to the door, "Louise has several old pictures of it filed somewhere. If you want to see it before I bring it back from getting its yearly overhaul, just ask her."

Before she could react, he reached toward her and pulled the smeared picture of the Buick out from under the one of the Packard she'd showed him. "If we can't be up-front with each other, this place doesn't have a snowball's chance in hell," he told her, his voice hard-edged now, "and our days will be numbered."

He pushed past her and sat down at the PC as if she'd been keeping him from doing something essential on it. She felt fortunate that he hadn't demanded to know who had told her about the old Buick. Neither, evidently, had he wanted to confront her on why she'd printed and hidden the Buick picture when she'd implied to him she hadn't seen it.

And since it wasn't the same car, why was she in a sudden sweat over the Buick? Just because it had been stored nearby? Yet Dane's last words to her had sounded like a veiled threat. She was getting so paranoid, she didn't believe anyone.

"I'd like to formally introduce all of you to Dr. Myron Scott, though I know most of you have already spoken to him, as he led the archeological dig of our old Shaker well," Dane announced to the staff later that morning in the meeting room of the Trustees' Building. "I've asked him to give us an initial report about some of the exciting things they've turned up in its depths."

Though Kate was interested in the findings, she was so shaken and exhausted that she had to force herself to concentrate. And she had the wildest impulse to giggle when she saw Adrienne sitting at the head of the table, so serious and—so dressed.

"It has indeed been a fascinating excavation," Dr. Scott said. He had spread before him on a card table several artifacts, some covered with a white cloth. "Not that we're finished. But we have turned up some real surprises so far that I want to share with you Shakers."

A small ripple of laughter, but a stern nod from Louise, who was sitting right in Kate's line of sight.

"Some of this we could have predicted," the man went on. He hardly looked the part of a stereotypical professor, Kate thought, with his golf shirt and a single earring barely showing under his straight, longish hair. But his hands looked like those of an archeologist: large and rough, even a little dirty.

"However," he went on, "let me start with the surprises we found by looking closer than ever at the commonplace and the familiar. For example, let's peruse the bottles we found down the well, something I guessed we'd discover. But I hardly would have predicted what sort and what the final conclusion might be."

Kate saw Dane frown and sit farther forward in his seat. Clint Barstow looked fascinated. Tanya was totally on edge, fiddling with her car keys in her lap; she was leaving for Kentucky as soon as the meeting was over. Kate leaned in a bit to see past everyone else, as she sat at the foot of the table, hoping no one would notice how bad she looked in this bright window light.

"Here we have the well of a group of strict people who have renounced what they think of as 'the world,'" Professor Scott went on, "but what kind of bottles do we get? I present to you this brown one clearly marked in the glass, World's Hair Restorer. I'll pass it around. I don't have to tell you to handle it carefully."

"But it doesn't have to be a product used by a Shaker," Dane protested. "Anyone could have thrown it down there."

"That's why we are very careful with the dated layering of artifacts, Dane," the professor explained. "I can show you bottles from the later periods after the Shakers had departed, but the things I'm sharing with you today are definitely Shaker and definitely eye-opening. There were even several early-era bottles that once held perfume."

"I don't believe it," Louise snapped. "I'm afraid you're so-called layering work has been a bit shoddy."

"Now, Louise," Ben put in, as Dane shot her a glare. But nothing seemed to faze Myron Scott as he displayed his artifacts.

"Here's my other favorite," he went on, passing a cobalt-blue bottle around. "Note on the back of that one the raised words PAIN KING. Order pain out the door."

"Amen to that," Tanya put in, "though I'd like to think that our belief the Shakers used traditional—

that is herbal—cures was the true story. Do you have any other bottles of cure-alls?''

''Only,'' he said as he pulled a cloth off what he'd kept covered, ''if you count these, which once held wine, beer and whiskey. Obviously, it's not an accident that these were all down the well. I'd say the early, supposedly disciplined, Shakers were as rebellious and secretive as most of us are today.''

That seemed to be the general signal for chaos. Louise kept tut-tutting, while everyone else put in their opinion all at once. Dane looked furious that he'd ever allowed the dig. Clint Barstow laughed; Adrienne was arguing with Ben; and Kate slipped away when Tanya went out to get in her car.

As Kate watched Tanya head for Kentucky to meet with her family, she decided she couldn't wait one more moment to check up on Erin. It might be two days early, but she had the strangest feeling Erin needed her.

In her casual collegiate clothes, Kate waited outside Erin's dorm, figuring the girl would soon be heading to her one-o'clock English class after her lunch in the dorm cafeteria. Kate hoped she hadn't missed her. If so, she'd head directly to the class and pick Erin up there.

But at a quarter to one, out came Erin, her red hair gleaming in the spring sun to give her away among the clusters of other blondes and brunettes. Kate had dropped back and followed her up the hill to the main green before she realized that the girl was pulling her wheeled overnighter carry-on suitcase.

Kate's stomach lurched. Going where? Away for the weekend? Going directly from her last class?

Kate turned around abruptly when she saw Erin glance back. She'd looked back before, but Kate had been mingling with the other kids and hadn't worried Erin would spot her. On the green many students walked its cross paths, and she felt more visible. She cut over to another walk that ran at an angle to the direction Erin was walking, but saw the girl look back again.

Her heart went out to her beloved stepdaughter. Kate knew how it felt to be watched, pursued. Poor Erin, like her, wasn't sleeping well, and that took a terrible toll.

To Kate's surprise, Erin stopped at the small, single-spired and pillared chapel wedged between two large buildings, Ellis Hall and the hulking Memorial Auditorium. Was Erin so distraught that she was going to go in to pray or meditate—or just to ditch someone she sensed was after her? She watched as Erin went in and the chapel doors swung shut behind her.

Ignoring the web of brick paths, Kate cut straight across the green toward the chapel. She opened one of the double doors a crack and peered in one direction, then the other. The interior was bathed with light pouring in windows onto the emerald carpet. She did not see Erin, at least in this small foyer that lay outside the small nave itself, which she could partially see through double doors. The appearance of the place almost calmed her foreboding.

Kate darted inside and held her hand against the door until it closed quietly. A plaque on the wall told about this chapel being donated by a man named Galbreath, who had met his now deceased first wife on the same spot. A paper sign by the open doors announced a poetry reading. Could Erin be having her English class here today? But it seemed so silent, deserted.

And then Kate heard a strange humming inside. It reminded her of last night, of hearing music but not being able to place it. To peer in without entering, Kate moved behind a door that stood ajar between the foyer and the nave. Perhaps Erin was sitting in a side or back pew and had begun to sing a hymn.

Looking through the crack where the door was hinged, Kate tried to get hold of herself. Perhaps it was time this charade ended. It could even be a sign that Erin had come to a church, looking for help and security. Kate loved her and wanted, above all, to help her. Enough of this lurking. She was going in to find out exactly what was going on.

But Kate jumped back when she heard a distant door close, maybe one at the front of the nave somewhere near the ornate pipe organ. A man's voice echoed, but she still saw no one. Gooseflesh gilded her arms. Dark-haired with a mustache, he stepped into her view, his arms held wide before the small silver cross on the altar, as if he were the welcoming minister or a living tableau of Jesus Christ himself.

"Angel," he called, as Kate saw Erin rush down the aisle to him. "There's my girl."

18

Marriage is like life in this—that it is a field of
battle, not a bed of roses.

—Robert Louis Stevenson
"Virginibus Puerisque"

It was Mike! Disguised, her ex-husband had finally
appeared. Kate gasped in shock, then she was sure
they had heard her. But they were already intent on
each other.

"No phone calls from Kate, no problems?" Mike
asked Erin.

He looked heavier. His dark hair and mustache did
a lot to change his appearance, too. As she stared at
him through the crack between the open door and the
doorway, he jammed a baseball cap on his head. He
also wore a bright green-and-white O.U. athletic
jacket, probably so he'd fit in with the students and
not be spotted. But Kate thought it made him stand
out like a parrot among sparrows.

"No problems," Erin said, "except I'm still scared
to do this. What if she thinks I'm kidnapped and calls
the police?"

"You just let me worry about that. Besides, the
weekend may be all we need to settle things."

"How? What are we going to do?"

"Erin, let's get out of here and talk on the way, okay? I'm parked illegally behind the Alumni Center across the street and don't need to be towed. Get your stuff, and we'll go out the other door."

Kate let Erin walk toward the back of the nave to get her suitcase, then turn toward Mike, pulling it. When the girl was several steps down the aisle, Kate darted out and grabbed Erin's arm, thrusting herself between the two of them.

Erin shrieked and froze; Mike, instead of running as Kate had hoped, moved forward to block the aisle. They stood about twelve feet apart.

"Long time, no see," Kate said, "though you've been watching me, haven't you."

"That I have. You've been a busy little bee."

"Dad, I didn't know she was here."

"It's all right, angel."

"Oh, of course, it is," Kate said, amazed her voice sounded strong when she was shaking so hard. "Everything's just absolutely peachy. No sweat about embezzlement, financial disaster for people who knew and trusted us. What's theft, or desertion of a wife and child? So no problem with running from the law or illegally taking Erin off somewhere when I'm the one who has custody—not to mention menacing and maybe even hitting—"

"Just shut up," he interrupted, slashing the air with a flat hand. "You've done enough damage to Erin and me."

"I cannot believe your arrogance." She stood her ground, her hand still hard on Erin's arm. "And once again, I see you're going to run, this time with Erin, so you can disrupt and ruin her life even more."

"I'm her father, Kate. You're just the ex-wife and ex-stepmother, and you're the one who chose that."

"The one who chose not to desert her."

"Hurry up," he ordered Erin, yanking the brim of his baseball hat down harder.

Kate gaped at him. The tilt of his head or the way he'd lifted his hand—was Mike Marburn the man driving the old car in the Toledo cemetery? If his cap were a fedora and the bright jacket a dark trench coat, she could be certain it was Mike.

"Erin," Kate said slowly, trying to stare Mike down, "go back to your dorm and your life. You are right to question going away with your father. He's a man on the run who could get dangerously desperate if—when—he's caught."

"'Dangerously desperate,'" he mocked. "That's good, Kate, very dramatic. You want a demonstration of that? Move, Erin!"

"No!" Kate cried, but Erin yanked away and Mike stepped between them. When he backed up, following Erin to keep an eye on Kate, she advanced.

"Let's sit down and talk about this," Kate said, trying to sound calm and rational.

"Oh, sure," he said. "I'd love for all of us to put ourselves on public display."

"No, we can stay in here. Don't involve her anymore, Mike. Last time you left her, you broke—"

The moment Erin was out the door behind the altar—Kate could hear it close—and before she could scream or run, Mike lunged at her, one hand clamped hard over her mouth. He dragged her toward the door where Erin had gone out, but then veered off into the small room behind the pipe organ and altar.

He must have been here before, Kate thought. He'd

cased this place, probably been everywhere she'd been, too, waiting to retaliate. He'd admitted he'd been watching her.

She struggled and kicked as he shoved a handker- chief in her mouth. Instantly, she began to gag.

"Quit fighting, damn you!" he muttered. "I'm just going to tie you up."

Shoving and holding her, her face against a small pillar, he somehow unbuckled and yanked off his belt. He pulled her hands down at her sides, belting her to the post. Gagging, she could hardly breathe.

"You'll wiggle out of that as fast as you do every- thing else. Listen to me, 'cause I gotta go." He stepped around the post to seize her face so hard her mouth puckered, even with the gag. "We'll call you, so stick by the phone at the village. I'm willing to take you up on that little talk—just the three of us, though. I swear, you bring your cop or village friends, and you'll never see her again."

Though she couldn't talk, Kate shouted through her gag at him. About those threats. About what he'd done to Erin and her. Frustration and fury poured from her, even as he turned and hurried away.

She scrambled to twist and writhe out of the belt, scraping her skin. Stumbling, she ripped out her gag as she ran, though she knew she'd be too late to stop them. She pictured them pulling away in a big, black Packard.

But as she raced out the back of the chapel and looked frantically up and down the street, she saw only a gold compact car turn the distant corner.

The phone call came just two hours later: Erin's voice. It was obvious from the background noise that she was calling from a public phone. Kate stood, leaning against her desk, hoping it would hold her up because her legs were trembling so hard.

"He wants to talk to you, Kate."

"Honey, are you all right? Are you sure this is what you want?"

"To be with him? He's sorry for being too busy for me before and wants to make it up to me. And none of this is his fault so—"

Her voice stopped abruptly, as if Mike had covered the phone. She came back on.

"See, these are the kinds of things we can hash out if you meet us," Erin said, obviously repeating what he'd just told her.

"I don't trust him enough to meet him someplace alone, and I won't—"

"No, this is a public place, a peaceful place," Erin insisted, sounding on the verge of tears. Kate's love for Erin roared through her. The child might not have been born from her body, but she was always hers in her heart.

"Where are you?" Kate asked calmly, raking her free hand through her hair.

"Kate, it's me." Mike's voice. "Let's make plans."

"Please, please, take her back to school."

"Not until I have that talk with you, make a deal about how we can share her—without you turning me in."

"You said you've been following me. You mentioned the police and my friends at the village."

"You still psychotic about being followed, Ms. Marburn? Kept your name—that *disgraced* name— didn't you, even when you cut me loose."

"How could you just run and leave us to face all—"

"Save the questions. Here's the deal, take it or leave it—and take Erin or leave her. We're in a busy public park on government land, so that sounds safe enough, doesn't it? Lots of campers, hikers, even park rangers. Old Man's Cave at Hocking Hills State Park, not more than a half hour away. Meet us here at four today or I'll take Erin to get her schooling, life and a new mother somewhere else."

"Mike, I won't just—"

"Be here or just wish us *bon voyage*. And no cops, Kate, or else."

The phone went dead in her hand.

Kate had less than an hour to get to a place she'd never been and didn't know. If Zink weren't hours away, she would have called him, no matter what Mike said. But it would take too long to phone the Athens police and explain it all. Besides, then it would be in their hands, and she couldn't take that chance.

She had to save Erin from Mike, make the girl realize that he was the one who'd stalked Kate and killed Varina. She should have told Erin all about seeing that black car in the cemetery and at Tanya's great-aunt's funeral. Maybe she could get Mike to admit it. With his arrogance, it was worth a try. But even then, would Erin realize he wasn't some betrayed hero? Or worse, did Erin know about the appearances of that black car because she'd been right with him all the way?

Kate grabbed her keys, purse and Ohio map, and ran for the stairs. If Tanya had been here, Kate would have taken her, had her stay in the background, perhaps, to blend in with the other hikers.

She was terrified to go alone.

Downstairs, she flew past Louise and Adrienne, who were huddled in conversation.

"I thought you said you didn't feel well, yes?" Adrienne asked. Kate hated to lie, but she had just wanted them to stay away while she waited for Mike's call.

"Got to go to the doctor's," Kate cried, and ran for her car. "I'll be happy to go with you!" Louise called, following her to the door of the Trustees' House.

Pretending she didn't hear her, Kate started her car and pulled away. Whether they were still watching her didn't matter. Down the road, she turned a sharp right into Jack's driveway, honked twice and got out.

He came to the doorway of his workshop, a table leg in hand. One look at her, and he threw it down and came running.

"What is it?" he yelled. "Something at the village? That car again?"

"My ex-husband has taken Erin to the Hocking Hills State Park and demands I come talk to them. I'm afraid he's dangerous and I've got a deadline and orders to come without the police. Do you know where it is?"

He pushed her back in her car, on the passenger side, and ran around to the driver's door. "I've been there more than once," he said, putting his hand on the back of the seat behind her and craning his neck to back out. "Tell me everything while we drive."

Jack drove just slightly over the speed limit on the highway. Kate kept looking in the rearview mirror.

Not one car—especially a black one or a pale gold compact—was anywhere behind them. But what if this was a trap to see if she left the village with anyone? Erin and Mike could have lied about being at the park to test her.

Kate fought back tears of fear for Erin, tears of gratitude for Jack. "You can't come with me at the park," she told him. "Mike may have spied on me, and I can't risk it. He may know what you look like if he's been spying on me."

"The mystery man in the deadly black car. Then he could be doubly dangerous, but I'll go in way behind you and keep back. Now it's time you listen to me," he insisted. "Try to picture everything I'm describing."

They turned south off Route 33 onto 668 when they saw signs for Old Man's Cave, but she closed her eyes to try to concentrate on his words.

"We'll leave the car in the main parking lot, and you'll follow signs northwest to where the trail starts over a stone bridge," Jack told her. "You're going to descend into a fairly rugged gorge, a hiking area with waterfalls and caves. Old Man's Cave is beyond the bridge. Hang right—the trail is well marked—and cross a creek, then climb up to it. You can't miss the cave because it's huge."

Her eyes flew open. "What if I can't find them? No, I guess they'll find me. I think they're good at that."

"At the cave, try to stay out of its depths. It goes back in about—I don't know—over a hundred feet."

Kate pictured the depths of the dark Shaker well, yielding up its surprises.

"Is it dark inside?"

"Way back in, but it has a large mouth, and even if the gorge is all in shadows by then, the sun won't be down. Don't go back into the cave and don't stay in the park after dark, or I swear I'll come after you."

"You'll be hiding somewhere nearby, hanging back?"

"I'll try to locate a park ranger. We may need him if anything goes wrong. And the footing can be dangerous in there," he warned, seizing her wrist as he stopped in the parking lot.

"I'll be careful," she insisted as she reached for her door handle.

"Kate," he said, holding on to her a moment as she started to get out. "Stay on the path, in sight of people—and not just because of Mike and Erin. Hikers have fallen to their deaths in there."

America's Discovery Trail one sign read, as Kate hurried across the parking lot in the direction Jack had indicated. She looked back only once. He was out of the car and already striding after her, though taking a roundabout way and keeping his distance. She skirted the check-in station and found the trail, marked by blue blazes. No one seemed to be going in at this late afternoon hour, but the parking lot suggested a few visitors must still be inside.

Ahead stretched the stone bridge Jack had mentioned, and beyond and beneath that, a gorge hewn from bone and buff sandstone. Waterfalls thundered from cliff to cliff beneath the bridge. It took her breath away, but she started across. Sharp shadows crept into the crevices and lurked in jagged rock faces. Cold and dampness seemed to seep from the rock walls.

On the other side of the bridge, she stopped momentarily at a signpost with arrows that listed park attractions: Old Man's Cave, the Devil's Bathtub, Cedar Falls, Ash Cave. All she cared about was Old Man's Cave, so she moved on.

She was relieved to see sporadic groups of hikers, though most were on their way out. Another sign about Old Man's Cave explained how the elderly hermit who came here years ago in search of game was buried beneath the ledge of the cave. Kate shuddered and hurried on, trying to watch her steps on the slick rock. The wind whined through hemlocks huddled along the trail.

A ways beyond the bridge, she turned right as Jack had said, though the path was clearly marked. Bluffs and cliffs towered over her as she descended toward a rock-strewn stream. Fortunately, someone had lashed three heavy logs across it, or she would have had to ford the thigh-deep water. Though she knew it was rude, she rushed to the makeshift bridge and crossed it before the campers who were closer could reach it.

"Sorry," she said, and hurried down the trail, not stopping to read the entire sign about violent flooding wiping out other bridges.

The rocky surface here was even slicker with spray, and she slipped, going to her hands and knees. Quickly, she got up and hurried on. When she looked up to see Old Man's Cave stretching above her, plunging back into the sandstone cliff face, she hesitated.

What if Mike was amusing himself by sending her

on a wild-goose chase? Or what if he'd laid some trap
for her here?

She glanced at her watch: ten minutes before four.
She'd made such good time. Surely, if he was waiting
for her here, he'd never suspect she'd brought someone with her.

Jack's thoughts roared like the nearby waterfalls as
he crossed over the stone bridge and took the blue-
blazed trail about five minutes behind Kate. He felt
cold without his jacket, and these smooth-soled western boots slowed him down. He hadn't even gone
back into the house when he'd seen how distraught
Kate had been.

It scared him how much he'd come to care for her
in a short time. More than that, he was panicked that
her stepdaughter, whom he'd never met and used to
avoid in conversation, was in danger. The last thing
in the universe *he* had wanted was to hurt his own
child; evidently, the same could not be said for Mike
Marburn.

As he hurried down the trail toward the stream, he
cursed himself for not stopping at the check-in cabin
to locate a park ranger. He thought he'd find one out
here—but, even if he did, should he risk having Mike
Marburn see one? At least there were still hikers in
the area, and a few were heading into the gorge—like
the guy not far behind him. Jack had already checked
him out and he didn't look a bit like Kate had described Marburn.

Jack picked up his pace but got really annoyed
when the man bumped him just before he crossed the
stream on the lashed-log bridge.

"Hey, watch it," Jack told him, swinging around to make sure the man stayed back.

But the burly blond with a backpack stepped even closer. Jack's muscles tensed; the back of his neck prickled. He had to locate Marburn, so he couldn't see bothering with this guy.

But suddenly, he *could* see bothering with the snub-nosed gun the man pointed right at his chest.

The roof of Old Man's Cave—actually, a deep, eroded recess in the cliff face—loomed above Kate. As she climbed to its floor level, it opened before her, vast and dim. Daylight still grayed its mouth, but its throat was dark. She stayed put, not going deeper in, looking all around. Where were they? Could she have beat them here?

She strained to listen. Someone's shout echoed down in the gorge, but this place seemed so empty. She heard a scuff of stones from someone on the path she'd just climbed, though she'd seen no one behind her. Could Jack be this close and, seeing no one else, was he coming up?

She backed onto the cave floor. When she saw who it was, her heart thudded and she wanted to flee, but she stood her ground. Besides, as far as she could tell, there was only one way up here, and Mike had emerged on the trail, cutting it off from her.

"You screwed up again," he accused without preamble as he stopped about ten feet from her. He was no longer dressed like a student but as a camper in jeans, flannel shirt, down vest and hiking boots. "You think I wasn't watching? I saw, in the parking lot, you brought a damn posse."

Her pulse pounded even harder. "That's just a

friend of mine who knew how to get here when I didn't,'' she tried to explain. ''There are no cops involved. Your phone call and deadline panicked me. I was too upset to drive when I had no idea where this was—where's Erin?''

His clenched features relaxed; perhaps he believed her. ''Later for that, but I will tell you where your friend is.'' He looked smug now, folding his arms over his chest but not coming closer. ''Back a ways off the trail with a friend of mine.''

''What do you mean?''

''I mean, I hired a guy—one with a very convincing gun—to be sure you and I got this chance to chat alone.''

''A gun? Are you crazy?'' she cried, smacking her hands to her sides, then gesturing wildly. ''He'd better not hurt him.''

''Maybe a real close friend of yours, huh?''

''The point is, you don't need any more trouble.''

''Not with you back in my life, I don't. And Erin's here. You'll see her on our way out—all of us, together—unless you want to keep fighting me. But let's get down to business. Exactly how much is that furniture worth you killed Mrs. Denbigh for?''

''You bastard!'' She could have launched herself against him, but she lowered her voice. Besides, maybe he had a gun, too. She wouldn't put anything past him now. ''I didn't kill her,'' she said, fighting to keep her voice steady, ''and I want to see Erin right now.''

''You seem to think you're in charge here. I'm a wanted felon, but you could be, too, and for murder. Seems I recall from before I left,'' he said, dramatically stroking his chin, ''you told me all about a plan to get in tight with the old lady, worm your way into her affections and her will, then knock her off. I'd hate to testify to that the way you did against me.''

Kate realized she hated this man. She'd never really known him. "Oh, come on," she said. "I hardly knew her when you left, and everyone knows you're a liar, except your poor daughter. But you're even more despicable than I imagined. My hurting Sarah Denbigh is as obvious a lie as the ones you told about loving me or Erin. It's all about you, isn't it?''

"Or, tell you what—rather than us going on the run together," he went on maddeningly as if she hadn't even spoken, "Plan B is I'll take Erin for 'insurance,' and you can start supporting both of us in the manner to which *you* used to be accustomed. With Mrs. Denbigh's heirs disappearing, you can sue for that furniture, then start to sell it off and send the funds our way—to Erin and me. When you've paid me enough for what you put me through by testifying against me and divorcing me, I'll tell you where to find Erin so that—''

"So that I can try to pick up the pieces of her life again? You're demented. I want to see her right now or none of this is going to happen—ever. And I want to know if she's been with you in that car.''

"Sure she has.''

"The old, black car? Where did you get it?''

"What old, black car? I meant here, today.''

He was so skilled at lying and shifting subjects. Surely, he had been the one in the old Packard, though that didn't mean Erin had been with him. He just didn't want to have anyone know he'd done the hit-and-run that killed Varina, that was all.

"Okay, okay," he said, holding up both hands, "I

told Erin to get way back in the cave and wait for us. Come on, and we'll all talk things over.'' He stepped past her toward the cave and motioned her into its depths.

"I'm not going in there with you," she said, not budging. "I don't need to get yanked around any more. Get her out here."

"You're not calling the shots here, Kate, never were," he said, advancing on her for the first time. "When are you going to get that through your stupid, stubborn head?"

"I've been stupid, all right. To ever have loved you. To not have realized you were making another attempt to ruin Erin's life by horning back in on her after she'd gone to make a fresh start at the university."

"She wants me back in her life!" he roared, and rushed her.

Though Kate had tried to stay on guard, the sudden attack after all this talk surprised her. She ducked, circled him and scrambled for the trail down. Erin probably wasn't even here. Or, what if both she and Jack were being held by his friend with the gun?

"Not up toward the cave," the blond ordered Jack and jerked the barrel of the gun downstream. "Family reunions need to be private. This way."

Scanning the deserted area, waiting for a chance to get rid of the gun and the guy, Jack had no choice but to do as he was told. The waterfall roared so loud in his brain that he knew he'd never even hear that gun if it went off, echoing up and down the cold rock walls.

But he figured it was now or never. If Mike Marburn had run down Varina Wellesley and her brother in cold blood, he probably didn't choose or hire accomplices who were nice guys.

Jack pretended to slip on the slick rocks along the stream. He cried out as if in pain and rolled directly at his captor. When the guy jumped away from Jack, he slipped, too, and Jack lunged at him.

Jack had been wrong, because he did hear the crack of the gun. For one minute he expected to feel the agony of a bullet, but the man had missed. However furious he was, what came back to him was his high school football coach's patient voice: "No, Kilcourse. Tackle him low, take out his feet and you get the whole guy."

But he could not be patient and deliberate. His boy Andy would never get a chance to play football, never have a girl to love or a child of his own. Jack slugged the gunman, again, again before he could even hit back. The man lay gasping.

Panting, exhausted, Jack heaved the gun in the stream and hit the man in his gut one more time. He didn't even take the time to tie him, but stumbled to his feet and tore in the direction from which he had come, praying he was not too late.

19

Oh, no man knows
Through what wild centuries
Roves back the rose.

—Walter de la Mare
"All That's Past"

The path down was impossible for Kate to handle at a run. Mike caught up, grabbed her arm, swung her back around to him on the narrow path. For one moment, she was sure he'd slam her into the rock face or try to throw her over. But Erin stood on the next turn down.

"Let her go!" Erin shouted. "She could fall."

"He'd like that," Kate cried, trying to keep her balance and shove him away, "except he'd lose his future meal ticket. Have you already spent all the money you took off with?" she demanded from Mike as she tried to yank free. "Finally bought an antique car you used to just look at, right? Have you seen his classic black car, Erin?"

"What? Stop it," Erin screamed, "both of you."

Mike cocked his head. "Now you've done it. Someone's coming—running."

One hand in a fierce grip on her wrist, he yanked Kate down the path, forcing Erin to retreat ahead of them. Kate went willingly, glad to be coming down off the cliff, trying to pick a level spot to get free from him. But she was not going to leave Erin with him again. And someone *was* running somewhere in the gorge.

"Help! Help *meeeee*..." Kate screamed, before Mike slapped her across the face so hard her ears rang.

"Dad, don't! Let her go!"

Though her jaw stung, Kate wasn't going to let him shut her up. She had to make Erin see her father for what he was. But Mike bent her arm behind her back to make her walk with him deeper into the gorge.

"Dad, don't, don't," the girl cried, jerking his arm. "I heard some of what you said up there. You're acting wild. I'll go with you if you just leave her alone."

"Shut up!" Mike hissed at Erin, but it was Kate's arm he wrenched. She almost blacked out as the shaft of pain pierced her, but she staggered on her tiptoes. The path was uneven, and dark devoured the bottom of the gorge. The sound of roaring water became louder again. Why was he taking them deeper into the park?

"He's been hurting you, too, Erin—whether or not you know it," Kate muttered from between gritted teeth.

Her eyes darted wildly to take in her surroundings. At least they were still on the blue-blaze trail, so if she had a chance to grab Erin and run, she'd know where to go. A blur of a sign went by with large letters, The Devil's Bathtub. Under a small bridge, Kate saw a gaping hole in the rock, a sandstone pothole with white water frothing so furiously it looked like a boiling cauldron.

"You're either with me—us—or not, Kate," Mike said, gasping for breath between words. "Plan A or B, like I said before. Which is it going to be?"

"I said stop it!" Erin cried, and jerked Mike's arm until he partly loosed Kate's.

It wasn't until he freed her that Kate realized Erin had hit him with a small rock. Kate heard it bounce away, over the edge. Leaning against Kate, he went down on both knees, holding his head, then grabbed for her legs when she tried to shove him away. She kicked but slipped. Sitting down hard, she bounced against him. Mike seized her again. They rolled and landed sprawled on the edge of the rock basin, with Erin screaming, "Stop it, stop it!"

When Mike tried to push Kate over, Erin grabbed Kate's legs to hold her back. This time when Mike rolled, he took Erin down. She slid even closer to the edge than they had.

"*Er—in!*" Kate screamed. She fought like a wild woman to free herself from Mike. Didn't he see Erin could go over? Kate butted him with her head where Erin had already turned his forehead bloody.

A man's boot stepped on Mike's neck, and a big hand grabbed him by his hair. She looked up. *Jack!*

"Get Erin!" Kate screamed. "Erin!"

"Where?"

Oh, dear God, she'd gone over. She was gone.

"Here!" the girl screamed from someplace close.

"Hang on!" Jack yelled, then ripped Mike's weight away from Kate.

When Mike swung a fist, Jack hit him twice, a left to the gut, then a right to the jaw. Mike flopped back, hitting the bridge stones and backing out. Jack was already on his stomach, reaching over the ledge for Erin. Kate scrambled to her hands and knees, gasping for breath, peering over. It was so dark in that hole, but she could see Erin clinging above the rocks and churning water, her upper torso on the lip of a narrow ledge, her hips on the edge, her legs dangling. Beneath her was a twenty-foot fall into the Devil's Bathtub.

"Kate, go back on the trail for help," Jack ordered, ripping his shirt off and knotting one sleeve around his wrist. "If I can't reach her, we're going to need help. Can you walk?"

"I can run," she vowed.

"Come on, Erin," Kate heard him say in a calm, coaxing tone, when she herself wanted to scream the cliffs down. "Reach up and try to grab this sleeve. I can't get to you otherwise. Come on...come on."

"I'll be right back, Erin!" Kate cried, and loped away, shouting for help. She couldn't bear to leave, but she saw instantly that Jack had the best plan. It had been years since she'd trusted a man, but she had to now.

Jack knew his hands were slick with sweat and blood, and Erin's were probably wet with spray. But if his flannel shirt didn't rip, she could hold on to it. He'd knotted it around his wrist and grasped it tightly. He had to pray that Mike didn't come to and shove them both over.

"No, don't look up at me because that tips you back," he told Erin. "Keep your head down, your weight forward on the ledge."

"I'm slipping."

"Just let your legs hang there. Stop trying to get back up. I've got a shirtsleeve dangling almost by your right hand. Just lift that hand from the elbow, not the whole arm. Okay, great. Open your hand—I'll put the sleeve right in, and then you grab it."

She did. The shirt went taut, yanking his arm down. He wished he wore a belt. He tried to find a solid, comfortable position on the rock above her, but there wasn't one.

"Can't you pull me up?" she cried, her words muffled as she kept her face down on the ledge. The constant hiss and rumble of the water in the big pothole below also muted her voice.

"It might tear. But I'm going to hold you right where you are until your mom brings help. All you have to do is keep as much of your upper body on that ledge as you can. If you start to slip, I can pull you back onto it." He had no idea if that were true, but it was all he had. "The shirt won't lift you up here," he tried to explain, keeping his voice calm, "but it will hold you there, okay?"

"Okay. Please talk to me. Please don't let go."

"I won't. I swear it. Just like your mother never wants to let you go."

"She's my stepmother, you know."

"I can tell she loves you more than most mothers love their kids."

"Is she okay—Kate?"

"She's been through one hell of a lot, Erin. Was your dad the one in the black car that's been stalking her?"

"What? I don't know. He's been hiding—he wouldn't."

"Wouldn't try to shove your mother over a cliff and delay helping you, either, would he?"

Only a sucking, sobbing sound.

"Just hang on, Erin. I'm right here with you, and I'll never let go. I've got strong arms, honest. I work with wood all day, making furniture. I'll get Kate to bring you over to see it. Will you come visit me?"

"Okay. By the way, I can swim," she said, her voice even weaker.

"Great. How about rock climbing?"

"Anything to get out of here. Whatever happens, thanks."

"What's going to happen is that you're going back to school and get your grades up. I had a terrible time my first year at college. The sudden freedom kind of makes you drunk, you know, turns into all kinds of strange rebellions."

He felt her slip; he thought he heard—felt—the flannel rip somewhere.

"Erin," he said when the shirt pulled even tauter, "I don't mean to be preaching about what I did when I was a kid. I hate to be preached at myself. The point, believe it or not, is that adults like your mom and I can understand some of your problems. She wants to be here helping you right now, but you got me for just a little longer—as long as you need..."

He choked back a sob, not of terror but for the memory he had of hanging on to his son. He'd held his little hand in that coffin and had not wanted to walk away, even at the funeral, until they'd all insisted it was time for him to just let go.

"Erin! Erin!" Kate cried, leaning over the edge next to Jack. The park rangers pulled Kate away and soon flooded the scene with portable lights.

"I'm okay…okay now" came the faint voice down the ledge.

The park rangers looped ropes between Erin's legs and another around her waist just in time, Kate thought, for she saw how much her stepdaughter had slipped.

Erin kept quiet as they pulled her up, but it was Jack who was talking. "I was scared that with no leverage I wouldn't be able to keep her from going over," he told the rangers. "Thank God you're here."

Kate saw he stood back in the glare of portable lights, watching as one ranger cuffed and arrested a groggy Mike, while the others pulled Erin up. Summoned by park rangers, two medics soon appeared with a stretcher.

"I can walk," Erin insisted, even as she hugged Kate. "How's—how is he?" Erin asked the ranger who pulled Mike to his feet.

"Fine, for someone who's dumb enough to try assault and kidnapping on State Park land," the ranger muttered, and pulled Mike away. Erin took two steps after him, then stopped. His face bruised and swollen, Mike looked back at her.

"Blame her," he muttered through a split lip as he glared at Kate. "I sure as hell do."

They marched him away, while another ranger wrapped Erin in a blanket. "Thanks, but I'm not cold," she told the officer, shrugging out of it. "Actually, I'm still sweating bullets."

"Luckily not bullets," the ranger said. "We've got the accomplice under arrest. He had bullets on him."

"I meant to tell you about that guy," Jack spoke up. "Sorry, but I threw his gun in the stream. So much for evidence."

Kate wondered if Mike would admit he'd been the one watching and stalking her. Since he'd no doubt go to prison for years, anyway, would he confess that he'd killed Varina and tried to kill Palmer that same day? He'd said enough to her to indicate he was guilty, including mentioning that the Denbigh heirs were "disappearing" to allow her to inherit that furniture he intended to benefit from. Despite this dire predicament tonight, Kate concluded, it had been worth it to be free of being harassed and threatened by Mike Marburn.

"You still need to see a doctor, Erin, even if you can walk out of here," Kate said. "I'll go with you. I can't thank all of you enough," she said to everyone. "I'm so grateful, to Jack, especially."

He nodded. She wasn't sure, but it looked as if he'd been crying. His eyes glinted in the artificial glow of the rescue lights. Despite not wanting to let Erin go, Kate walked over to Jack and straight into his arms.

He held her hard. Despite the pain in her arm from Mike's wrenching of it, nothing mattered now but that Erin and she—and Jack—were safe. She held him tight, too, her arms linked around his waist.

"How can I ever thank you?" she whispered, her words muffled against his shoulder.

"Helping her—saving her—meant a lot to me," he choked out. "But besides that," he added, clearing his throat, "we'll think of something."

As if in celebration, Kate's antique Apothecary roses began to burst with blooms in the bright spring sun over the next few days. The flowers so far were few but stunning with their flat, full ruby petals and

stark yellow stamens. Their sweet fragrance assaulted
the senses, though it was nothing compared to the
overwhelming scent that would fill the air later when
more buds opened. These were the harbingers of all
that was to come, for the non-Shaker breeds in Jack's
backyard would bloom much later.

The early display of the once wild roses took Kate
unaware, because the spring had been early and mild,
and they were much farther south in the shelter of the
Appalachian foothills than on the shores of Lake Erie.
Most of the bushes had been transplanted, and they
seemed ready to rejoice in her freedom from fear.
Besides, who knew what heirloom strains like these
would do? What defiant, deviant tendencies were hidden in them that could suddenly explode, just like in
people?

Mike had been handed over to the federal prosecutors, with additional charges of assault, battery and
attempted kidnapping. Charges of murder and attempted murder were still pending, and Kate was hoping Stan Rudzinski could prove Mike had killed Varina. Zink was to be able to interview him about that
as soon as he got permission from the feds. But in
her heart she knew that Mike was guilty.

"I gotta hand it to you for flushing him out," Zink
had told her on the phone earlier this morning. "It's
going to save me a lot of time, because I'd actually
begun calling and visiting shops that do all kinds of
window tinting, hoping to track the driver of the car
that way. It's not illegal *per se* to darken passenger
windows in Ohio vehicles, because commercial ones
like limos or trucks can have it. And cars are allowed
up to five inches of fifty-percent tinting on a front

windshield, but none of it is as extensive or dark as you and other eyewitnesses have described on that Packard that hit Varina.''

"Sounds as if you've become an expert on this.''

"If that's a compliment, I'll take it. I'm on another case—have been for weeks—but I can't let the Sarah–Varina one go. My gut still tells me they were both murdered.''

Kate had slumped over the phone at her desk. Surely, Mike would not have killed Sarah, too, or contracted to have it done, even though he'd shown himself capable of hiring help. At least they could question his accomplice, too. The thing that scared her now was that he'd threatened to accuse Kate of planning to kill Sarah.

"I have to tell you something," she told Zink.

"Shoot.''

She bit her lip at his wording. "In addition to the hints Mike gave me that he was the one driving the Packard, he also swore he'd testify I set Sarah up and then—got rid of her.''

Silence.

"Zink, none of it's true. I should never have told you that without telling Mason James first, but I'm trying to level with you. I want this nightmare over— all of it, for Sarah and, yes, for Palmer, so Erin and I can pick up our lives again.''

"A life with Jack, too, maybe? He called to give me his read on your ex, so I know how deeply he's gotten involved.''

"What else did he say?''

"Ask him. He's the boy next door, isn't he? But if Mike Marburn accuses you of anything, I'll consider the source. And if he's behind the Denbigh deaths, Palmer's coma and your troubles, I'll get it out of him. And thanks for the heads-up on the pic of the Packard and now all this. We'd make a hell of a detective team. Now run by me again everything Mike said that made you believe he was the one driving the Packard. It'll give me ammo when I do get to question him.''

She closed her eyes, then opened them to stare out the side window at her roses. "For one thing, the moment I asked if he'd been watching me, he said, 'That I have.'''

"What else?"

"I tried to pin him down on the fact he slipped up when he asked if I brought my cop or village friends.''

"He knew about me?"

"I guess he could have gleaned all that from the newspaper or Erin, but she says he spent his time talking against me, not inquiring what I was doing now. I just feel he's the one who's been watching me.''

"Anything else?"

"He asked if I was still psychotic about being followed.''

"You realize you just told me what you refused to share before," Zink said, his voice soft now. "Why you went to a shrink.''

"Maybe I'm trusting that you're trying to help me now, not do me in.''

"Praise the Lord and pass the ammunition.''

"Zink, the only reason I don't want it to be him in that black car is that he might have coerced Erin to go with him. I'm just hoping and praying you'll be able to come up with some other woman who was with him in all this—through fingerprints or hair samples—if you can trace that car.''

"The paint sample the Athens police sent us from the phone pole across from Jack's isn't paint but chrome alloy, and most cars of that era had the same stuff on their grills and fenders. Our sample won't differentiate makes or models, so we'll have to go at it another way.''

"You *are* going at it another way. You'll get it out of Mike Marburn, I know you will.''

"Don't overdo thanking the local hero for helping save your daughter," he'd said, his voice suddenly sounding almost bitter. "Meanwhile," he'd added, "I'll try to clear her mother once and for all. Talk to you or see you soon.''

Now, encouraged by Zink's help, Kate continued to examine her roses, looking for pests or problems on their buds, but her mind still drifted. Despite Zink's continually teasing her about Jack, Kate felt her relationship with "the boy next door" had gone to a deeper—or was that a higher?—level. Best of all, a sadder but wiser Erin had agreed to counseling and was back in school this Monday. She would soon be answering a lot of questions from investigators, but they'd agreed to go to Athens to talk to her. Erin and Kate hadn't reconciled, but the girl was seeing chinks in her father's armor. It was the most she could hope for now, Kate thought, because noses seemed out of joint here at Shaker Run.

"I cannot believe you just ran out without telling us the truth," Louise had sputtered, when Kate had explained everything to the staff. "And here I offered to go with you! You had to go to the doctor's, indeed," she'd concluded with a sniff.

"Kate," Dane had remonstrated, "you should have come to me for help. We've got to be able to trust each other. I knew where that park was, so you hardly had to go running to Jack Kilcourse. I stress again that we are a family here and can trust each other."

"It wasn't that I didn't trust you or anyone here," Kate had countered. "I was just in a hurry to get to Erin. You've all been great to me, but..."

"But Jack Kilcourse has been greater," Dane had concluded, and went on to other business while Adrienne glared at her. Kate hoped Tanya would come back soon, because she might be the only one who understood.

Now, as Kate noted the first signs of aphids on her baby blooms, Dane and Ben Willis walked toward her. It looked as if Ben, who was two steps behind the bigger man, was actually propelling him. Ben usually lagged, walking not quite with a limp but with hesitation in one leg. Kate always thought of Ben stepping hesitantly through life with Louise pushing him, so this was a big change.

"They're looking great," Dane said, folding his arms over his chest, staring at the roses instead of at her.

Kate nodded and waited for what was coming next. Surely, they weren't going to fire her, not with the opening of the village just thirteen days away.

"Aren't they?" she finally said. "I'm thrilled at their early progress, though I see a few signs of aphids. I'll probably be able to make some rose water next month, but I must admit I'm going to hate the Shaker practice of picking roses without their stems."

"A little sacrifice for authenticity," Ben put in. For

one moment, with Dane looming and blocking out the thinner man, Kate had almost forgotten he was here.

"Kate," Dane said, looking quite uncomfortable, "I don't want you to think I, or we, are not supportive of you through your troubles. I thought I should tell you something I've just admitted to Ben and Louise."

Waiting, holding her breath, Kate stared at him. *Admitted* implied some sort of guilt.

"It was me driving the antique Shaker car when it slid into a light pole and knocked the lights out in that snowstorm. I was so annoyed and embarrassed, I just kept going and didn't tell anyone about it. I've paid to have the dent on the grill hammered out myself, and it will soon be good as new. It's in a shop in Columbus, but if you want to see it sooner, Louise and Ben have some photos of it."

"I'd love to see them, but I realize I overreacted about the car. Although I've learned that a '40s Buick and a '40s Packard can look a lot alike, I hear your car doesn't have dark-tinted windows like the one I was looking for."

"Tinted windows?" Ben piped up, his voice incredulous. "Back in the '40s?"

Dane cleared his throat and shifted from one foot to the other, glaring at Ben instead of her. He obviously had something else to say. "I don't appreciate your even thinking that our village car could have been involved in something dire, but I realize your past makes you—shaken and suspicious," he said.

"I think the nightmare's over now," she said, trying to assure herself as much as him.

"Maybe not—the publicity fallout, I mean."

When he hesitated, Ben added, "The thing is, we covet publicity for Shaker Run's opening—but the right kind. The capture of your husband is kicking over the beehive in the papers and other media.''

Dane held up a hand and took up the explanation. ''We've gotten numerous calls in the office about reporters wanting to come here to interview you about your husband—''

''Ex-husband.''

''Well, yes. I've told those reporters to stay away, but the press and TV people are not known for following protocol or propriety. I'm just warning you they might try sneaking in or following you if you leave the premises.''

''That's the last thing I need!'' she admitted before she got hold of herself. ''I know they're good at that, but I don't want to see them, and I'm grateful if you've turned some away. If we only had more security here at night when everyone's gone but me, it would help. I mean, I realize someone on the staff might come back for dancing or singing practice late, but...''

Dane's eyes narrowed. She could tell he wasn't sure if she was implying she'd seen him and Adrienne.

''You tell Louise it's going to come to that, Ben,'' Dane muttered huffily. ''Security lights and alarms, however un-Shaker-like. Meanwhile, I've got enough problems around here.''

He glared at Kate before relaxing his expression again, but in that unguarded moment he'd looked absolutely malevolent.

20

Rose, shut your heart against the bee.
Why should you heed his minstrelry?
Refuse your urgent lover, rose.
He does but drink the heart and goes.

—Humbert Wolfe

"I hope you're proud of me, Louise," Kate told her as she gently washed aphid scales with soap and water from the tips of her budded Apothecary rosebuds. Louise, in full Shaker garb to meet with the volunteer presenters, had come out to see what she was doing. After Kate's earlier visitors, Dane and Ben, she was almost glad to see Louise for once.

"I'm being straight Shaker here in fighting these aphids," Kate explained. "Otherwise, I'd be using a modern nicotine sulphate product. The soap-and-water cure was in one of those old diaries I read, but since you keep insisting I'm Sister Jerusha Lockhart, I wish you'd relocate hers for me."

Kate almost inquired if it could be with the loose, stored papers over in Jack's shed, but she dared not give away that she'd seen in there. Again, she thought of Jack and how much she owed him.

"I've been searching everywhere for that journal," Louise said, sounding either disgusted with herself or

Kate. "But I came out to ask if you'll be here to kindly lend a hand when I give the volunteers a tour of the village. Sister Jerusha, are you listening?"

"Sorry. I'm still so exhausted from everything. Did you ever get so tired that you have little dizzy spells or just nod off?"

"Not since I pulled all-nighters when I was in college," she said, but she came closer and looked in Kate's eyes. Their bonnet brims bumped. Louise had been right about one thing. The Shaker sisters might not have used or permitted sunglasses, but these bonnets were cool and shady. Lately, Kate had worn hers quite often; Louise almost never took hers off, at least around here.

"You'd best ask someone to go with you if you need to drive to see your daughter," Louise added, suddenly quite motherly herself as she patted Kate's arm. "She's a lovely girl, and she was quite interested in the dancing. I'd like you to have her back sometime so I can show her around more."

Kate almost retorted, *She doesn't need your tour of the graveyard and holy ground,* but she said only, "Even if she decides to go to summer school, I'm hoping she'll be here much more, maybe even help me with the flowers or assist Adrienne in the gift shop, if it works out."

"I'd like that. We would all like that very much. I hope she appreciates the Denbigh Shaker furniture heritage as you do."

Kate nodded, thinking how fortunate she was that Erin thought the furniture was "way cool," unlike Varina, who had thought so little of what had been Sarah's pride. Kate hoped that she didn't have to continue to fight for what Sarah had wanted to share with her, and that somehow she and Jack could find out who was switching and stealing precious pieces of it.

"Instead of helping with my tours, you'd best go in and drink some of Tanya's herbal tea and take a nap," Louise ordered, squinting as if Kate were some specimen under a microscope.

"I just might. Both Sister Jerusha and Kate Marburn are dead on their feet, even though they're relieved to have a lot of problems solved and questions answered."

Louise patted her arm again and headed back to her duties. She was probably right, Kate thought, about not driving until she got some more sleep. She could just walk over to Jack's and check on her rosebushes there, though since they'd bloom much later than these, they would hardly need pest poison yet. But she needed to thank Jack again.

She stowed her anti-aphid ammunition of pail, old toothbrushes, and rags in the garden shop. It seemed quiet and lonely without Tanya here, and Kate hoped again that her friend would be back soon. Besides, she needed some other kind of herbal bedtime tea, though she fully expected to sleep better now that her stalker, and Varina's murderer, was locked up. It would just take a little while to unwind.

She changed to a fresh blouse and long skirt, her and Tanya's compromise with Shaker style when they weren't in costume. She changed her bonnet for sunglasses and walked down the road toward Jack's. It was such a stunning spring day that she seemed to be drifting, flying. No wonder those eccentric Shakers thought they were having angel visions, she thought as she whirled once around, flinging out her arms, then, dizzy, stopping to steady herself.

Jack came out of the furniture shop to meet her; he must have seen her coming. "Is everything all right?" he asked. "Have you talked to Erin today?"

The man had done a one-hundred-eighty degree turn about Erin. Whereas he used to avoid so much as mentioning her, now he'd made Erin's safety and happiness his cause. Wasn't there some Indian legend, Kate tried to recall, that when you saved someone's life you felt responsible for them the rest of yours?

"I talked to her before breakfast," Kate assured him. "She was looking forward to hard work and getting her grades up. And she said, yes, she'd love to see your furniture shop this weekend."

"Good," he said, his rugged face lighting. "Then she can chaperon us at dinner here Saturday evening. We can pick up something in town when we go in to get her. And how's her mother today? Kate, you haven't been drinking, have you?" he asked, cupping a palm on one shoulder and tipping her chin up in his other hand. "You look a little tipsy."

"I'm fine—just exhausted. I haven't been better in weeks, though go ahead if you feel you must give me a Breathalyzer test," she said with a smug, little smile.

"You mean the mouth-to-mouth type, I hope, because that's what I was planning."

He stepped closer and bent to kiss her. His lips were masterful and strong, but it seemed a mere taste of him before he pulled slightly back.

"Hmm," he said. "Inconclusive. I'm going to have to try again."

"I, of course," she went on, linking her arms around his neck and swaying them slightly as if they would dance, "only came here to see how my rose-bushes out back are doing."

"Yeah," he said. "Let's get out of this front yard with the village view. They might need binoculars to see us down here, but you never know. Sometimes I think the old Shaker ghosts still have eyes."

Despite the disconcerting way he'd put that, no way she wanted to be spied on, ever again. They half walked, half waltzed behind his house, and strolled back among the clusters of her Damasks and Bourbons. She wished they could burst into full bloom this very moment, just the way she felt she was doing. But she had no desire, for once, to look at or touch them. She only wanted Jack, as they came together in a vibrant kiss.

The entire garden, maybe the whole world, tilted and spun. Kate couldn't breathe apart from this man and didn't want to. His strength both stoked and sapped hers until she leaned into him and held to him.

It was good that he held her up, for his hands were urgent on her back and waist, making her more dizzy yet. Her brain buzzed, or was that the early summer bees back here? But all such random thoughts stopped as she kneaded his powerful back muscles and propped her trembling legs against his thighs. His lips slanted over hers, both devouring and feeding her. Tipped back in his arms, she tilted her head to bring him even closer. Finally, they broke the kiss and simply stared, inches apart, into each other's eyes.

"At first I didn't want this," he whispered.

"Do we now?"

"I want you, yes. Let's go in. If I make a phone call right now, then take the phone off the hook, I can stop a client from coming, and we can have some time together.''

They went in the back door, holding hands. As he made the call, she heard him say, ''Yeah, sorry. You're my favorite client, Mick, because you always know precisely what you want, but I'm just gonna have to reschedule. I'll call you tomorrow, okay?''

He crossed the kitchen to reach for her again. She raked her hands through his hair. ''Mmm,'' he murmured, nuzzling the hollow of her throat, ''you smell like roses.''

''They've started to bloom at the village.''

''I saw them, even in the dark.''

She pulled slightly away, looking up at him.

''You came over in the dark?''

''Kate, I've walked Shaker Run for years at night when I can't sleep. And I wanted to be closer to you after everything that's happened.''

''I'm very sure that Mike was my problem—and that's over now, thanks partly to you.''

''Since you haven't had a thing to drink, let me get some wine,'' he whispered in her ear, warming her, though it also gave her gooseflesh. ''We can go in the other room.'' He banged around in a cupboard, then closed it. ''I've got some glasses in here somewhere.''

She watched him open sparsely filled cupboards, slamming them shut as if he were in a stranger's kitchen. He finally produced two glasses, then opened a nearly bare refrigerator and pulled out a bottle of white wine. He began a rattling search through a utensil drawer, evidently looking for a corkscrew. Kate felt so finely wired she could have pulled the cork out with her teeth.

"I'll take the glasses," she volunteered, realizing he was so nervous he might break them, though she wasn't sure she wouldn't. She walked ahead down the center hall of the big, old Shaker building and saw both front doors stood ajar, though there were screen doors, too. How wonderful to live out here in the country now, she thought, without a shred of fear.

But she jumped when someone peered in the left-hand door. It was Tanya, shading her eyes as she looked through the old sisters' entrance.

"Oh, sorry, guys," she said. "I yelled for Jack in the shop and turned up the music 'cause I was so excited to tell you both what I've got."

"Tanya, hey," Jack said as he came up behind Kate, but his voice carried his disappointment that she'd shown up now.

As they all stood there, Kate could hear the music she'd mentioned, a gospel song with Tanya's great-aunt's clarion voice singing about *leaning on the everlasting arms*. It was pouring from Tanya's car, behind which she was hauling a large, bright orange U-Haul trailer.

"*Wait* till you see the *great* furniture I got," Tanya cried, as Jack opened the screen door and they went out. "I'm hoping you can store some of it here, and I'll offer a few pieces for the infirmary for the opening, and maybe use that Rent-a-Room storage, since no way I can handle all this in my apartment."

Kate saw Jack's body stiffen as if he scented something on the wind. She wondered if Tanya had any pieces that were fake, because surely that's what he was thinking.

"I'll get another glass," Kate said, "and we'll drink to Tanya's inheritance."

"Oh, no," their friend cried dramatically, smacking her forehead with her hand. "You guys and a bottle of wine, and here I come crashing in. Sorry, but I was just so thrilled—"

"And so are we," Jack assured her, giving Kate a silent sigh and slight shake of his head behind Tanya's back. "Let's see what you brought."

Tanya went out to the U-Haul with Jack. Kate stomped back into the kitchen to get a third glass. She was not angry with Tanya but with herself for resenting her friend's arrival, when until now she'd been eagerly awaiting Tanya's return. And worse, Kate had once suspected Tanya might have had something to do with the death of her elderly great-aunt. Mike might have killed Varina and maybe even Sarah, but surely Aunt Samantha Sams had just died of old age. And with those larger questions settled in Kate's mind, she could focus on helping Jack solve the furniture fraud—maybe now with Tanya's help.

But as Tanya drove the U-Haul behind Jack's shop where they could examine her bounty in privacy, Jack told Kate, "I don't necessarily want her to know everything about the forgeries. I'm going to look closely at these pieces, and if some of them are fake I'll try to explain to her."

Tanya got out of her car with a big grin. "All right," she said, "take a look. Auntie donated about half to her church. All family members got a few pieces, but she had written a note that I was to have more because of my work with the black Shaker heritage. What do you think? It all means so much to me because *she* meant so much."

Kate put an arm around Tanya and squeezed her

shoulders, as Jack let down the makeshift ramp, then strode up. "That's why I'm fighting for Sarah Denbigh's pieces," Kate explained. "It's like still having part of her—her beauty, love, talents..."

"Tanya, you've got a real treasure here," Jack said excitedly, peering into the depths of the U-Haul. "If I lift one end of these pieces, think you ladies can help handle the other end so we can take a better look at all this?"

Into the sweet spring sun and breeze, they unloaded six large pieces of furniture and four rocking chairs, which Tanya had carefully packed in the trailer with towels and blankets to keep them from bumping or rubbing the fine patina of wood.

"Look, this one's a bigger herbal cupboard than the one you're making for me, Jack, though I'm not going to part with either of them," Tanya said. "But I think I'm going to make the Thompsons and the Willises nearly as happy as I am, because I want *this* and—" she darted over to a work counter "—*this* to go in the Shaker Run infirmary for the opening. All they have in there so far is a table, corner cupboard and that adult invalid cradle that looks like a coffin."

"This piece is cherry, ash and walnut," Jack observed of the work counter. As his big hands stroked it, Kate held her breath, for she could still feel those hands on her. She saw him slide open the top drawer and bend to size up the dovetail molding and probably check the wood for weathering. "It looks great," he added, to her relief.

Kate's favorite piece was a tall food cupboard with twenty-four elaborately pierced tin squares set in a wood frame on the front and sides of it. The metal had provided ventilation within during the days of pre-refrigeration.

"And look," Tanya said, leaning closer to it. "I didn't notice this before, but the designs punched in the tin look like stylized *angels* blowing horns! It almost makes it look Christmasy."

"I've seen another piece similar to this," Kate said, frowning. When she was this tired, it actually made thinking difficult at times. "I think it's in Sarah's collection, but it's been on loan in the East for years, in some museum. I've never seen it in person, but it's on the inventory list of other pieces I inherited, with a photograph of it."

"Maybe there was once a matched pair that somehow got separated," Tanya surmised. "You know the Shakers—two of lots of things, one for the brethren and one for the sisters."

Kate's eyes met Jack's over Tanya's head. Evidently he wasn't going to tell Tanya about identical fake pieces; he must think hers were all authentic.

"Or else," Kate put in, "more than one Shaker furniture designer or builder was inspired by the same angelic vision."

"More like a hallucination," Tanya muttered.

When they both looked at her, she said, "One theory I've been working on—and *don't* you two go telling the so-called elders or deacons of Shaker Run— is that, at least at this Shaker village, some pretty strong and strange herbs were used to keep people in line. Or," she added, "to get them *out* of line with hallucinogens—so they'd see visions."

"That's why you've been focusing on curatives that could become injurious," Kate said.

Tanya nodded firmly but her voice was tentative.

"That's one reason, anyway. It's kind of been a theory that's an offshoot of my other studies, and I'm trusting you two to keep my secret till I can get to the bottom of this. I trust you guys, and maybe you can help me think it through."

Jack's gaze snagged Kate's again; he raised his eyebrows as if to say *Why not?* Realizing he'd finally decided to take Tanya into his confidence about the possibility of the furniture scam being tied to Shaker Run, Kate nodded.

"Tanya," he said, his face and voice solemn, "I—we—have something we want to tell you. Let's sit down in these rockers, and just listen a minute, okay?"

To Jack's surprise, Tanya was furious when he explained his theory and asked for her help in return. He saw her emotions crash from exhilaration over her furniture to outrage over his and Kate's theory about the thefts.

"Then—this wonderful gift from my great-aunt," Tanya stammered, "could all be worth—nothing."

"Tanya," he said, "the few pieces I've looked over so far seem authentic. I'm not saying your great-aunt knew any of it was fake. I don't know if it is fake, so it wouldn't change the intent of her gift."

"But *she* believed in it, so someone's ripping off her memory, let alone my heritage from her. Jack, please, can you expertise these pieces here right now?" she asked, leaping up again. "Even if you think they look real, be sure, okay?"

"Not and do a decent job," he admitted. "But maybe the two of you can help narrow it down if I tell you what to look for. Then I can focus in on a suspicious piece. It's worth a try. There are telltale signs, definite clues, however subtle.''

He knew Kate was still exhausted, but she seemed energized by Tanya's anger. Though he'd been upset when Tanya had shown up when she did, this was better. He shouldn't have been plying Kate with wine when she was already so tired, though the idea of time alone with her, even in the middle of the day, made his pulse pound.

''Where are you going?'' Tanya's tense voice demanded when he walked away.

''To get my doctor's diagnosis kit,'' he threw over his shoulder, then turned back. ''Hey, girl,'' he told her, ''you've got to calm down.''

''The whole thing's insulting,'' she said. ''And I'm mad as hell at the two of you for not telling me before. I could have found out something for you—at least, whether Clint Barstow or other village staff are in on this.''

''I've been careful because it's an undercover operation that's needed here,'' he tried to explain, ''not some seek-and-destroy mission. Don't make me—us—sorry we told you.''

But he was sorry when, during his perusal of the furniture, he discovered that the unique piece Kate loved most, the tin-and-wood food pantry with angels, was a modern fake.

''And that means the similar one Sarah owned could be, too,'' Kate whispered, half to herself.

''Or it could mean,'' he said, ''that this one was originally made to be substituted for that one, but then the fakers saw a chance to sell this to an elderly woman as an original. The possibilities boggle the mind.''

"They don't boggle mine," Tanya declared, hands on hips. "There's three of us working on this now, and you two just better keep me informed."

That afternoon, Jack drove Kate to see Erin, and the three of them had dinner, but not at the 7 Sauces, though Erin said she'd been in to thank Stone for his help and explain a bit more about what had happened. He'd asked her out for coffee, but she'd said she'd take a rain check.

"So don't worry," she'd assured Kate. "I'm not going to have any time for men right now, any of them, because I'm hitting the books."

"Not even time for the one who's asked both you ladies to a Saturday-night tour of a furniture shop and take-out Chinese?" Jack had asked.

Erin still had not warmed up to her again, and the girl playfully hit Jack's shoulder with her fist. Time, Kate thought. I just have to give her time and love.

And, she decided now as she finally stretched out on her own bed at night, she had to give herself some sleep. Why couldn't she just unwind, let go and relax? Jack would surely get to the bottom of the furniture fraud. Her harasser had been Mike. It made perfect sense. Her ex-husband had betrayed her before, and she'd learned to live with that. Her tough times were finally over. She had a wonderful man in her life, Tanya was back and the village would open soon.

Kate lifted herself on one elbow and took a final swig of tepid tea—she had added slightly more than a teaspoonful, figuring she was getting resistant to the stuff—and lay back on her bed. But when she closed her eyes, the room seemed to spin. It was as if she whirled in Jack's arms again or—she was a Shaker sister, dancing, dancing.

Yes, she was better with her eyes open. She glanced at the few early roses on her bedside table. She had not been able to resist cutting them, stems and all. They, too, seemed to move, to shake.

Her phone shrieked once, then again and again. She got up slowly and walked barefoot into the other room, wishing she'd had a phone jack put in by her bed. She fumbled for the receiver, not turning on a light.

"Kate Marburn."

"Kate, Tanya. I'm on my cell phone, just leaving the storage place in Athens. Call Jack and tell him I'll meet you both at Barstow's workshop. I've found the tin angels! And it all may tie into their horns and Angel's Trumpet!"

"You're losing me. You mean we're going to get into Clint Barstow's workshop? Jack told you that we already did that—"

"I've got the master key to the building and the master key to this mess," she insisted. "I'll explain everything in ten minutes!"

As soon as Tanya hung up, Kate dialed Jack. Though it was nearly eleven o'clock, his phone rang and rang, then his answering machine came on. He was either working late in his shop, making a racket, or hadn't heard the phone, because she knew he didn't sleep soundly at night. Maybe he was on another after-dark walk. Perhaps he'd come over to the village again.

"Jack, this is Kate at 10:56 p.m.," she said, leaving a message. "Tanya needs to see us pronto, at the village wood shop. I'm going over now to find out what's going on. See you there, or we'll fill you in tomorrow.''

Kate stripped off her nightgown, and pulled on slacks and a sweatshirt. Her stack of clothes on the shelf in her closet looked more neatly piled than she remembered. Louise or Adrienne must have had that local girl who cleaned downstairs pick things up here, too, so she'd have to remember to tell them she'd do it herself and try not to sound as if she wasn't grateful. Kate had said the girl could sweep and dust up here, but she must have gone beyond that. Louise had just been preaching last week about how the Shaker sisters always pitched in to help each other like one big family—but privacy still mattered to *this* Shaker sister.

Kate took her flashlight and keys and started carefully down the women's side of the stairs. Tanya had said she had a master key. Given to her by Dane or "borrowed"? Kate wondered. And Tanya had been to the storage place in Athens, so maybe she had the master key to the village's Rent-a-Room there. That could be the missing link, Kate thought, a place for someone in the village to store the duplicate pieces of fake or authentic furniture. How Shaker, she thought: perfect pairs of furniture. But since they were ones used to deceive and defraud others, it was a scheme of which Mike Marburn himself would be proud.

Though still exhausted and dizzy, Kate went out into the blowing spring night to meet Tanya.

21

Then glut thy sorrow on a morning rose.

—John Keats
"Ode on Melancholy"

"Tanya. Tanya?" Kate cried as she crossed the road toward Clint's wood shop.

She turned back when she heard the motor of a distant car. Either she'd beaten Tanya here, or Jack had received her message and was driving over. She hoped it wasn't Dane and Adrienne in the village again tonight, because she was starting to think they were prime candidates for masterminding the furniture scheme.

But where was the car she heard? Maybe Tanya was driving in with her lights out for some reason. Surely, a car on the highway would not sound so loud at night.

Kate stepped into the narrow road, glancing up and down, then realized that the car she heard wasn't coming into the village, but going out. It must be behind her.

She turned. A car came at her, dark as the night. So close. Just like when Varina was killed. Kate screamed.

Its headlights came on, slashing into her. Like a

deer in the double shafts of blinding brightness, she stood, staring blankly. The headlights, big, wide-set, round. Not modern.

The car! *That car here!*

She turned to flee, and it seemed an eternity—but so fast, too. Her scream echoed, echoed. She thought she heard another scream. The vehicle roared three feet past her, evidently with the windows down, because someone threw something at her. She put her hands up as it pelted across her face, scratching her arms.

Too late she thought to click on her flashlight, but it would have done no good. Like two red animal eyes, the taillights peered at her as she gaped after the car. Had it meant to hit her, or was it only trying to escape the village and she had been in the way?

Kate crumpled to her knees. She had been so certain that it had been Mike watching her, trying to terrorize her. She had felt so safe since he'd been caught.

She blinked back tears and squinted into the night to make sure the car left the grounds. It kept going, over the bridge that spanned Shaker Run, past Jack's house, where it either turned its lights off again or disappeared. Had it gone straight or turned? Could it have been the old Buick Dane drove? As black as it was out here, with the car's side windows rolled down, she wasn't sure if it was a car with dark-tinted windows.

Expecting Tanya to come running out from behind the wood shop to demand what had happened, Kate got to her feet. Feeling dizzy again, she walked a few steps and sank onto the front stoop between the double doors. As she propped her head in her hands, she realized she had indeed been scratched by something.

She fingered slightly raised marks on her forearms and felt a trickle of blood. Looking all around, straining to listen, she walked back to the edge of the road to see what had been thrown from the car. Her flashlight illuminated about a dozen of her full-budded Apothecary roses, the thorny stems cut off separate from the beheaded crimson blooms.

"Zink Rudzinski here." He finally answered the phone.

Kate's call hadn't been picked up at the home number he'd given her, or at his office. At last the dispatcher had patched her call through to his cell phone. She was grateful Zink had left word she was to be put through, day or night.

"It's Kate," she told him, stretching her desk phone cord to enable her to look out her front windows over the now deserted street. "I've just seen the antique black car again, here in the village, but it's gone now."

"Damn! You all right?"

"Physically."

"That sure beefs up Marburn's alibi for not being implicated in Varina's death," he muttered. "You call the Athens police?"

"Zink, what can they do now?"

"Get somebody there to help, look around, guard you. You should go to Jack's or something. No, sit tight. I'll call the police and get them there."

She thought she could hear Tina Martin in the background, whispering something to him, but he evidently ignored her.

"I thought for sure it was Mike," she admitted.

"I was willing to believe you until I got a chance to talk to him, which the feds haven't let me do yet."

"The people in the car whizzed past me—shades of when Varina was hit." She thought about explaining that there was an old car kept nearby, but she didn't want to implicate Dane—yet. Besides, he had said the Buick was in a shop in Columbus and that she could see photos of it or the car itself. No, however much she didn't want to admit it, that must have been the Packard.

"They threw some of my roses at me, out the passenger window," she went on, "so I'm certain someone was sitting on that side. And it means someone's been watching me closely and recently, because they've just begun to bloom." She closed her eyes and swayed against the window frame. It could mean the village staff was involved, and that thought sickened her. Shaker Run had become her home and haven, until tonight.

"Kate, you there?" Zink's voice brought her back to reality.

"I'm okay. I only hope their little visit this time was not to hit me but strictly to harass me more, this time by beheading some of my roses."

"Like you found at the Denbigh crypt, and the ones ripped off from that gospel singer's grave," he said with a huge sigh. "Sit tight, and I'll get the local cops there fast."

"But where are you?" she demanded, before he could hang up. She couldn't bear to be alone again, and Jack hadn't called.

"On an all-night stakeout. I'll get you some help, then call you back in a little while, since I don't know what's coming down where I am now."

With a click, he was gone.

* * *

Kneeling in her second-floor roadside window to wait for the police, Kate shoved up the sash to listen for their sirens. That might bring Jack. As she stuck her head out, for once she was grateful screens were not authentic Shaker. They hadn't put them in here, another of many reasons she had to move into Athens when the warm weather came with its flies and mosquitoes. She wished that were her only worry. It would upset the Thompsons and Willises if she moved, but it had to be done. She could not stay here alone anymore. Unless the police would stake this place out, she was not staying one more night.

But as she strained to listen, she was sure she heard a voice calling her name—a woman's voice. Oh, no, she thought, she wasn't going for that again, whether it was a naked Adrienne cavorting through the grounds or just her imagination. But it sounded like Tanya, and her friend had to be out there somewhere. The police would surely be here soon. But what if the car had hit Tanya and she was lying out there calling for help?

Resolutely, Kate went down and out the sisters' front door again, looking both ways on the deserted Shaker street. Tanya had lied about not writing that poison herb book. But she'd seen so much of herself in Tanya, especially with her friend's joy then outrage over the inheritance of her Shaker furniture. And they had been friends working together almost as Shaker sisters, however different their pasts and personalities.

Kate walked around the Center Family Dwelling with its furniture workshop occupying the right of the building and the smaller infirmary on the left side. As she turned around the back of the large edifice, she gasped. Tanya's car was parked there, hidden from the street.

Kate hurried to it and shone her light inside, though the window glass reflected most of its wan beam back at her. No one inside, nothing odd looking or apparently out of place. The car was unlocked, so she opened the door and reached in to pop the trunk lid. No one and nothing—not even Tanya's purse—was in the car or trunk. Tanya had come here to meet her but had parked where her car wouldn't be seen, then had gotten out and gone...where?

Peering around the other back corner of the building toward the excavation site, Kate saw nothing amiss. Picking up her pace toward the well, she played her light before her. She gasped to see the wooden barrier that guarded the well was broken, the jagged wood shoved inward.

She opened her mouth to call Tanya's name, but as in a nightmare, nothing came out. Earlier when she had tried to flee the car, she'd felt her feet were lead and she couldn't run. This whole thing was a dreadful dream she wanted to wake from.

"Tanya?" she whispered, then called her name loudly. *"Tanya!"*

She walked inside the broken barrier. It was slippery footing because the archeologists had lined the well with layers of sheet plastic in case of rain. Holding on to the metal arm they used to swing themselves into the depths, Kate leaned closer to the widened well to shine her beam down.

At the bottom, partly swathed in clear plastic as if she were under ice, Tanya lay crumpled in the hole, not moving. Kate heard sirens coming close—or else it was her own screams.

Gesturing frantically, Kate met the cruiser the moment it roared into the village. The officers called the medics.

Jack showed up just behind the police. After the paramedics worked on Tanya at the scene, Kate and Jack followed in his car as the ambulance rushed Tanya into Athens Memorial.

"I tried to call you," she told him. "I couldn't believe you didn't answer."

"I must have been in the shower. Thank heavens I checked my messages before I went to bed."

"I know I heard Tanya calling me, but then she was unconscious when I found her," Kate explained, as he drove even faster. "I guess she could have slipped into the well, but she knew where it was. And why would she crash through the wooden barrier?"

"Tell me again what she said on the phone," he insisted.

"That she was just leaving the storage place in Athens. She has to mean that Rent-a-Room where some village things are kept. I rent a small space there, too."

"We've got to get in the one the village owns. What else?"

"That she found the tin angels—something about Angel's Trumpets."

"Maybe she found a third food cupboard with those angel designs," he suggested.

"I think it's time to stop trusting the entire village staff. Oh, yeah, Tanya also said she had the master key to everything."

"So she must be able to link what she found in Shaker Run's storage unit to a particular person. If she doesn't regain consciousness soon to tell us what she knows, we'll have to retrace her steps."

"Not until I know if she's all right."

"They're doing what they can," Jack assured her. "I heard one paramedic say they were trying to stabilize her."

Kate closed her eyes to picture Tanya immobilized, her head and neck restrained in case she had a neck injury. Her skin had looked gray.

"She wasn't hit by a car, was she?" she had asked the medics.

One, an auburn-haired, freckled woman, frowned at her. "And the car threw her into the bottom of a well?" she asked incredulously.

Kate knew she sounded crazy. She had come to think of the car itself as some demonic entity. Everything was falling apart again. At least she had Jack to trust—and Zink, who'd called the cops.

"I know you said you hate hospitals," Kate told Jack as they parked and headed in together. "But thanks for bringing me. I never could have made it on my own."

"I keep seeing Erin hanging over that ledge," he said with a shudder. "And this night-run into a hospital—I've done that before. I mean, not here, but years ago…"

It took this tragedy, Kate thought, for Jack to even mention his own.

Kate and Jack waited all night in a room for families and friends of those in surgery. They had called

Tanya's parents, who were now on their way from Kentucky. The doctors were putting pins in Tanya's shoulder and doing a spinal fusion to stabilize her back. She'd received a compression fracture and a concussion, but they were grateful since it could have been so much worse. Not, Kate thought, that what happened to Tanya wasn't attempted murder.

"It's like she's some piece of furniture who can be patched," Kate told Jack, shuddering at the idea of metal pins and spine fusions holding her friend together. She was so strung out, she didn't even know if she was making sense. "Thank God her injuries aren't life-threatening."

"I just hope her head's okay when she comes to," Jack said, handing her another styrofoam cup of coffee as he sat back down beside her on the well-worn couch. At least this stuff was clearing her head, Kate thought, sipping it despite its bitterness. "The doctor said," Jack went on, "that the concussion could develop into brain swelling, and then there's the general anesthetic that might keep her from recalling what happened right away. Sometimes after a traumatic event like an accident the memory never comes back."

"I only hope she'll tell us she slipped on that plastic sheeting and fell down there herself," Kate said. "I can't bear it if the idiots in that car hurt her and then roared past me to escape. Maybe they drove back in to cut some flowers, and she was already there waiting for me, then she accosted them and they— did that to her."

"Don't beat yourself up by imagining things," he said so forcefully that she swung around to face him.

That was exactly what her psychiatrist had said so many times.

"I'm not," she insisted. "I must have heard Tanya shouting for me before she blacked out, so I'm not imagining things."

At least he didn't argue about her instincts the way Zink usually did. Jack sighed, slumped to lean his head back against the couch and rubbed his eyes with thumb and index finger.

"The thing is," he said, "it doesn't help to want things to be different. It doesn't help to keep playing things over in your mind a million different ways, blaming yourself, hating yourself..." His voice trailed off.

He sat up suddenly, hunched over his knees. She reached out to rub his back between his shoulder blades, but his tense muscles did not relax.

"I really did kill my son, you see," he said, so quietly she was certain at first that she hadn't heard him correctly.

Leaning closer so their shoulders touched, Kate forced herself just to listen. "My son was only four and wanted to be like his daddy," he whispered. "I was on a real health kick then, jogging, weights, power boosters. Anyway, he found my vitamins, got them off the bathroom counter. Just vitamins...good for you, right?" he asked, his voice cracking.

He turned to look at her, his eyes glazed with unshed tears. "You know the iron in vitamins can kill a kid?" he demanded. He flung one hand out helplessly. "When he was dying of systemic poisoning with all his organs shutting down, he said, 'Daddy, I knew if I took more than you do, I can get big and strong like you.'"

She stared at him. All she had been through was nothing compared to that. Everything about him made sense now. Even why he let Tanya do her writing, on her strange topic, secretly in the shed.

"But it wasn't—" Kate began.

"Just cut the phony, psychobabble, feel-good lines!" he exploded, getting up to pace. "Sure, it wasn't my fault. I didn't tell that little boy to take an entire bottle of my pills. It was just an accident," he mocked.

"And she—your wife—blamed you and left you," she said.

She thought he would be angry at that, but he simply nodded and crunched his cup before flinging it in the trash can.

"Case closed," he said. "No one at fault. If I'd been a judge I would have put me in prison for life."

"And that's exactly what you've tried to do to yourself," she insisted. He didn't look at her for a moment, then nodded jerkily. He rubbed his jaw. "No," he said slowly, "not exactly prison. More like I tried to bury myself alive before a few things dug me out."

As she began to rise, he walked quickly to her, pushing her back in the seat. He sank down beside her again, his hands clasping hers. She wanted to hold him, shelter him.

"One," he said, "I found a cause in fighting some brilliant, nameless bastard who's screwing with my life work through fakes and frauds. Two, I found a woman I care for deeply when I really thought I never wanted that again."

He hesitated and cleared his throat, squeezing her hands even harder than she squeezed his in return, as

if by her sheer strength and love alone, she could hold
him up. He was crying openly now, but so was she.
Tears blurred her vision, making two Jacks leaning
closer to her.

"And three?" she whispered, her heart pounding.

"She's nothing like my Andy," he said, and
winced as if it pained him to say his son's name, "but
I helped save Erin."

He pulled Kate into his arms, and they embraced a
long time in that waiting room, holding each other
hard.

"Let's lay out our plans to prove who's behind all
this," Jack said, as they sat at his kitchen table in
mid-afternoon. They'd just returned from the hospital
and were eating what amounted to breakfast, though
Kate was picking at her food. Neither of them had
slept, having kept a vigil until Tanya's parents had
arrived.

The surgeon had told them Tanya might regain
consciousness today, and Tanya's mother had promised to phone them if she did. Kate had called Dane
and Adrienne this morning; Dane had said they would
go over to sit with Tanya's parents as soon as they
could.

"First of all, I think you ought to move in here,"
Jack told Kate as he reached across the corner of the
table to take her hand. "Or, at least, stay here at night
now. As much as I'd like that to be some sort of
come-on, it isn't. Shaker Run's obviously not the
great escape you thought it would be."

"I know," she said, lacing her fingers through his.
"And as much as I wish we had time for us, this is

deadly serious. Do you know if the Buick's back in
the shed yet?''

He sat up straighter at her sudden shift of topic.
''It wasn't yesterday—but that seems ages ago. You
want to check the tires for mud, match tracks, or
what? We could get Zink down here to do fingerprints.''

Kate pictured her tormentor, the driver of the Packard, swathed in a trench coat and hat, as she'd seen
him that first day in the cemetery. And he'd worn
gloves. She'd tried to question him but he'd said nothing. Now, somehow, she had to make him reveal himself.

''I think this person—persons—is clever enough
that he would leave no prints, and the rest is police
work,'' she said. ''Actually, if the Buick's there, I'd
like to search it for Shaker Apothecary rose petals. I
think it was the Packard last night—but maybe not.''

Nodding, he got the shed key and they hurried out
to unlock it. Even as they passed Tanya's messy writing desk and the large plastic container of Shakerabilia, they could see the Buick was back. They rushed
to it and quickly checked all four doors. The car was
completely locked.

''Can you open this back door of the shed he drives
in and out of?'' Kate asked, trying to peer into the
front seat, then the back. ''It's too dim to see inside
the car.''

''Dane's the only one who has the key to that...''
Jack's voice trailed off as they looked at each other.

''And Tanya said she'd found the master *key*. Certainly she meant not to a car but to whomever might
link the car to the fake furniture.''

''In other words, Dane? Yeah, I've thought of him.

I never did believe Barstow had the brains to orchestrate an international furniture scam, but he could be working with someone else.''

"I've got to start suspecting all of them, but Dane's in first place right now,'' Kate said. "After he and Adrienne made me the offer to come here, maybe they thought they'd better scare me out of Toledo to make sure I took the job. So they followed me until I gave them the perfect spot—the cemetery near Sarah Denbigh's grave.''

"But why appear at Tanya's great-aunt's funeral in Kentucky?''

"Just another warning associated with a death of a Shaker furniture collector? I don't know!'' she cried. "Sorry,'' she added, and hugged him. His arms crushed her to him, but the luxury of that moment couldn't last. "What if,'' she reasoned aloud, her face pressed in the hollow of his throat, "Dane and Adrienne wanted me here because of Sarah's furniture and not my roses. That could be why they tried to eliminate Varina and even Palmer—to make sure I inherited the furniture they want here.''

"Or which they want to substitute with fakes. Then they could sell the originals to buy Adrienne's dream house in France that you mentioned. Granted, they've left Palmer Denbigh alive, but he has no heirs, and who knows when he'll regain consciousness.''

"Tanya and Palmer both—there is a sick pattern here. And as important as Tanya is to the village, they figured she had to go when she learned too much.''

"Or they figured now that her Shaker furniture was here, they could keep it here if she died.''

"Or they were here last night to harass and hurt me and simply stumbled on her,'' she said with a shudder. She stepped reluctantly back from his embrace.

"The thing is, we can't just wait for the other shoe to drop," he said.

"Exactly. Can you go get a flashlight, maybe a couple of them? We can at least look into this car, though I'm tempted to break in. But I am going to look at what's stored in this plastic bin. If you can open their few furniture crates here, I can open that."

Though he looked surprised, he nodded. He started out, then turned back. "And somehow, we're going to look in that Shaker Run storage space at Rent-a-Room," he vowed. "That has to be where Tanya found furniture, the Packard, something. I don't believe Dane when he says that a car can't fit in that storage space. Look what's crammed in here."

"If Tanya somehow got or made a master key to their storehouse," Kate said, "it might be with her things at the hospital."

"Which has probably been given to her parents as part of her personal property. The hospital and her parents wouldn't know what keys were what. But Dane and Adrienne might, if they get there before I do."

Jack tore into the house for a big flashlight and handed it to her. As she shone the beam into the car, he searched his pockets for his own car keys. She could not see one rose petal on the seats or the floor. But some might be obscured by that trench coat thrown across the front seat.

"A trench coat, Jack!" she cried excitedly, as he produced his car keys. "The driver of the other car wore a trench coat."

"What does that prove?" Jack challenged. "Zink wears one, and I've got one, too."

She was suddenly so frustrated she wanted to throw herself across the hood and windshield of the Buick and literally punch its lights out.

Not Zink, she thought. Not her protector, even if from afar. She knew he liked her, and wanted to be trusted and called on for help. And he was obsessed with solving his cases, and must be a mastermind when it came to stalking and stakeouts. But surely, he could not have some fatal attraction to her. She was going right over the edge with all this agonizing, that was all.

"Go on to the hospital," she urged Jack, when he hesitated, watching her closely. "Besides getting Tanya's keys, maybe you can ask for a police guard for her. What if someone tries to sneak in to finish what they evidently started when they threw her down the well? I'm going to look through this plastic bin of Shaker papers, and we'll check that storage unit as soon as you get back."

"All right. I'll keep my cell phone with me, so call if you figure out anything here or need me."

Or need me. Despite his hurry, he kissed her good-bye. For one moment, she felt afraid to have him leave. But he'd be back soon, and this was best. Even if they went down separate paths for a while, they were working as a real team now.

As she heard him drive out, she unsealed the bin and pulled out the books and letters on top. If anyone caught her going through this stuff, Kate thought, she could always say she was looking for Sister Jerusha Lockhart's lost diary.

She put the pile of things on Tanya's desk. Yes,

some early records of the village—typed letters signed by Dane, dated just a few years ago, apparently all about rebuilding and redecorating. But these books looked older.

She opened one and smelled its age before she noted the yellowed pages and spidery scrawl of old-fashioned handwriting. It appeared to be a business record about plants and flowers, not by Sister Jerusha, but by some Shaker brother named Benjamin Owens who must have been an early herb gardener. Surely Tanya could use this for her research.

With a silent prayer for her friend's recovery, Kate touched the papers on Tanya's desk as if she could reach out to touch her. Then Kate took in what she had glimpsed before, what was staring her in the face now in Tanya's bold handwriting:

Jimsonweed, Nightshade, Mad Apple, Devil's Trumpet. But the Shakers called it Angel's Trumpet.

And farther down the page in script:

In small quantities Angel's Trumpet is medicinal to control pain. Large doses bring wild hallucinations and death.

22

Footfalls echo in the memory
Down the passage which we did not take
Towards the door we never opened
Into the rose garden.

—T.S. Eliot
Four Quartets

"Angel's Horns—Angel's Trumpets," Kate muttered to herself. "That's what Tanya said was the key. But to what, exactly?"

Puzzled and awed, she read more of Tanya's notes about the Angel's Trumpet herb. Some of the early signs of ingestion were rapid pulse and breathing, restlessness, depression, dilated pupils and insomnia. "Also, polydipsia," she read slowly, sounding out the strange word, but at least Tanya had annotated it as "extreme thirst."

Angel's Trumpet, alias Jimsonweed, Kate read on, had originally been dubbed the "Jamestown Weed" because eating it in a salad had caused British soldiers at Jamestown to "take leave of their senses." Some cavorted naked, most danced and whirled about, and all were in a "frantic condition" until they were confined. Because their doses had evidently been minimal, they did not die, but after eleven days of hallucinations "returned to themselves again, not remembering anything that had passed."

Kate pictured Adrienne dancing naked in the Meeting House four days ago. What if someone took the drug willingly for the dangerous high it gave? Or worse, what if someone was secretly dosed with it?

She covered her mouth with both hands. Mother Ann's work, as the Shakers used to call it, led to riotous dance sessions, some out on holy ground, where the brethren and sisters claimed they'd seen visions of angels and other departed friends and famous people. Could it be because they intentionally took or were covertly dosed with something like Angel's Trumpet? And maybe it was kept inside a special herbal cupboard decorated with angels. Could *that* have been the missing link Tanya referred to on the phone—a link in her own theory—rather than the car being linked to a murderer?

Kate scooped up Tanya's notes, the old herbal diary, and as many of the other loose papers from the plastic bin as she thought she could carry. Stuffing them in a large canvas bag that must be Tanya's, she went out and clicked the padlock closed. Hefting her pack like a Shaker peddlar, she walked as fast as she could toward the village.

"Dane, how long have you and Adrienne been here?" Jack asked, coming to a halt as he hurried into the hospital waiting room.

They stood like sentinels, as if guarding access to Tanya's parents. Jack realized he hadn't seen Adrienne for a while. She looked really wiped out from all the pressure of getting ready to open the village, or maybe she'd been sick or was upset over Tanya.

He saw Louise Willis was also here, dressed in modern clothes, sitting off in the corner.

Great, just great, he thought. He'd get everybody upset and probably tip Dane off when he suggested to Tanya's folks that a cop should guard her room. He'd never get any privacy here to talk them into it. And how was he going to get Tanya's keys now?

"It was good of you and Kate to stay here last night," Dane said, shaking his hand. "As soon as we could after she called, Adrienne and I rushed over to comfort the Dodridges."

Jack lifted a hand to Ted and Yvonne Dodridge, whom Kate had met briefly before at their family funeral. Mr. Dodridge, a grizzle-haired man, slumped next to his weary wife, who wore a wrinkled turquoise pantsuit.

"Is Kate all right?" Dane enquired. "Where is she?"

"Resting," Jack said. "Excuse me a moment. I'd like a private word with the Dodridges."

That kept Dane where he was, but who knew for how long. Jack's next problem came from a quick hand on his sleeve.

"Hello, Mrs. Willis," he said, looking down at Louise. She plucked at his sleeve as they talked, making him even more nervous. "Who's watching the village?"

"Ben's running errands, so I guess Clint Barstow, though that's a sobering thought. I suppose we must install modern security to keep outsiders away," she told him huffily.

"I get the message."

"Oh, not you—that is, if you'd just join forces with us. Clint's best work cannot rival yours, and you know that West Family Dwelling House you own should be returned to the village."

"I'd love to debate all this, Mrs. Willis, but—"

"Kindly call me Louise or Sister Louise."

He stared down into her steady gaze. Sometimes she sounded slightly off, but she always looked rock steady. Kate thought she was smarter and more talented than most people realized. "Excuse me," he said as a sudden inspiration hit him, "but I need to offer my place to Tanya's parents in case they don't want a hotel or if Tanya's recovery gets drawn out."

"They will surely want to stay closer to her, watch her," Louise called after him. "But at least you're taking folks in as the Believers used to in that Gathering Order House you have."

"Mr. and Mrs. Dodridge," Jack said, speaking fast and trying to block out the others. Hoping his voice didn't carry, he squatted next to the short couch they shared, holding hands. The Dodridges looked close to tears. Damn, he hated places like this where parents waited to hear if their kid would make it, clinging to each other, yet ready to be torn apart. But at least it was a place that tried to help; he could accept that now.

"I'd like to get your permission," he went on, "to ask the local police to put a guard on Tanya's door, since the circumstances of her being hurt—"

"I heard," her father interrupted. He let go of his wife's hand and took his glasses off to wipe them on a handkerchief. "The flimsy barricade around the excavated well was caved in, as if there'd been a struggle. But I also heard there's some question about who was on the grounds. Besides Kate Marburn, that is. If the police pursue an investigation, that will surely implicate her. Dane Thompson didn't say exactly what, but isn't there something in her past about being suspected of foul play?''

Kate hid the sack with Tanya's notes and the Shaker records under the worktable in the distilling shed, then pulled on her work gloves. She was not going to so much as touch these special herbs of Tanya's anymore—at least, not the ones in here.

Kate realized now that however much Tanya worked with standard herbs in the sisters' shop or in her main garden outside, this was her research lab for potentially poisonous ones. Kate just hoped that didn't entail actual experimentation. Surely Tanya had not tried to prove her theories by dosing Adrienne or even Kate herself. Some of the symptoms caused by ingesting powerful herbs hit home, especially the insomnia—but Kate admitted she'd been sleepless in Toledo long before she knew Tanya. Besides, her friend had always warned her to take exact doses of valerian tea because too much could be a problem.

Kate took a small paper sack and began to clear out the supply of dried Angel's Trumpet. But she froze in mid-motion. In the small, narrow bin next to it was valerian. What if some of this deadlier herb had accidentally gotten mixed in with the valerian when Tanya mixed her tea? It must be that, for surely her friend would never intentionally harm her.

Kate cleaned out the valerian, too, dumping the dried herbs in separate sacks. Then, just to be sure no one could get at any of these curative poisons while Tanya was away—she recalled how fascinated Dane had been with them when he had stood right here—

she emptied the other herb bins and drawers into the paper bags.

Using a wooden planting flat, she lugged all the bags up to her room, then hurried back down to get the big canvas bag of Shakerabilia she'd hidden. Upstairs in her kitchen again, she got out her tin of loose valerian tea and dumped it out on a dinner plate. On a second plate, she spread out the valerian from the bin in the garden shed.

She closely compared the samples. They looked and smelled different, she reasoned, though maybe just a pinch of Angel's Trumpet couldn't be spotted in her insomniac's cure.

No more herbal tea, she vowed silently. *Ever.*

Jack tried to recover from his surprise at Mr. Dodridge's suspicions—and at his annoyance that Dane must have let something slip. Surely, Tanya's parents wouldn't expect the police to bring charges against Kate. Because she'd discovered Sarah Denbigh's body, did the local police suspect her of hurting Tanya?

His heart began to thud even harder. Now he had something else to do here besides try to get Tanya a door guard and get her keys.

"Kate Marburn was Tanya's friend, Mr. Dodridge. I can vouch for that," he insisted, keeping his voice low. "I don't have time to explain everything about the police guard on Tanya's door, but I think it's important and I hope you will request it. I certainly didn't mean to imply that Kate could have hurt Tanya."

"But Kate admitted our girl had phoned her to meet her, so Kate obviously knew Tanya was coming,'' he argued quietly, as his wife, leaning closer, nodded.

"Kate saved Tanya's life," Jack retorted, then realized he was talking too loud.

The couple exchanged glances. "Tanya thinks a lot of her," Mrs. Dodridge said, "and Kate did come to Aunt Samantha's funeral, Ted, the only one from here. Tanya spoke highly of you, too, and that herbal cabinet you were making her, Jack.''

"Mrs. Dodridge, I'm asking you to trust me, trust Kate," Jack said, speaking low and fast again. "Tanya probably had in her possession, maybe in her purse, if you have that, some sets of keys. I need those keys so Kate and I can find out if and why someone pushed your daughter—and I swear it wasn't Kate.''

"Keys to…?" Mr. Dodridge prompted, putting his glasses back on and narrowing his eyes.

Jack heard Dane's voice getting louder. He must be approaching. If he overheard this, he'd ask for the keys and probably get them.

"That's what I need to know. If you'd just—" Jack got out before Dane spoke, standing behind and above him.

"Jack, I'm going to suggest to Tanya's folks that they take a little break, you know, go down to the cafeteria, while Adrienne and I drive back to the village to check on things.''

Louise spoke up, her voice so loud Jack knew she was standing as close as Dane. Sometimes the woman seemed to glide silently rather than walk. "And I'm just going to stay right here for a while in case Tanya's condition changes," Louise said, "so I can let you all know. I'll call Ben to come pick me up later.''

When the Dodridges rose in obvious compliance to walk out with the Thompsons, Jack knew he'd failed. They would probably have the keys before he got the couple alone again.

But partway out the door, walking between Adrienne and her husband, Mrs. Dodridge turned back and motioned him over. ''Tell Kate again we are grateful for her getting the emergency squad and then calling us last night. Please give her this little note of thanks I've written....''

Blocking out the village staff, Yvonne Dodridge dug into her big purse, which Jack saw had a smaller purse within it. She pressed into his hand not a piece of paper but a ring of four keys. Squeezing them tight to keep them from clinking, he pocketed them immediately.

The mother was as sharp as Tanya, he thought. She hadn't let anyone else, even her husband, see what she'd done.

Kate called Jack's house and left a message telling him she was in her apartment. In case he was with Tanya's parents, she didn't want to interrupt him by using his cell phone number. She continued to pore over both old and new correspondence from the sealed plastic bin, some of it fascinating glimpses into the past of Shaker Run, some of it boring daily records. She read so much her eyes began to ache, so she took some of it outside.

Her roses were blooming even more today, despite the assault on them last night.

Their fragrance was starting to invade the air, and it comforted her, because she was thinking more clearly than she had for days. Kate just knew she could get to the bottom of this. But she still could not stay in this village another night. She would take Jack up on his offer to stay at his place.

She walked around the back, past the sisters' shops toward the graveyard. Not going in, she leaned on the stone fence and stared at Sister Jerusha's headstone. Though there were no dates on it, Louise had recalled that Jerusha had lived into the 1940s, the era when the last of the sisters departed—though evidently Jerusha had died here before that.

On a whim, Kate whispered, "Did you know anything about all this, Jerusha Lockhart?"

She wondered if Louise didn't lose Jerusha's diary on purpose because it revealed that the Shakers were on a special kind of Shaker high—a drugged one. Jerusha had been the rosarian, but she might have had something to do with herbs, or else she had worked closely with the Believer who was the herbalist.

Kate shook her head. She was getting as strange as Louise, hanging about this place, communing with the departed. This village as well as the entire Shaker culture was like a drug in itself, with glimpses into scenes one could only imagine.

Grateful to be alone in the village in full daylight, however low the sun was sinking, Kate forced herself to skim the papers she'd brought out. Another bunch of bills, she thought, stuffing them down under the letters. But she saw one modern bill for remodeling, attached with an old-fashioned hairpin to a handwritten bill under it for the same thing. Darn. It wasn't for an antique car; it wasn't for herbs, or Shaker furniture. Who cared?

But it snagged her gaze. It was for observation slits in the Trustees' House, each floor. Not for the Meeting House, where everyone knew observation holes existed and were even pointed out to visitors. This was for the Trustees' House, where Kate lived. The older bill had "each floor" crossed out and "each ceiling" neatly lettered in.

Kate strode back into the Trustees' Building and climbed on a chair in the staff meeting room. She skimmed the ceiling but saw nothing like the peepholes in the Meeting House. She climbed up onto the long trestle table.

There, over at the very edge, in the corner by the staircase where the ceiling met the wall, was a narrow slit. She supposed someone could have looked or listened through it in the old days. But there had been a recent bill for the repair of it, too, as if it had once been boarded over and only recently uncovered—here she dug out the top bill again—last year...just last autumn.

Kate got down and went out into the broad hall with its twin staircases. She saw no observation point on the wall beside the staircase that adjoined the meeting room. Besides, someone would have to balance on a chair on the stairs. She must be misreading the bills or just overreacting.

But the bills had said *each floor, each ceiling.* Kate ran upstairs so fast she began to feel dizzy again. That panicked her, but she was obviously just paranoid about poisons right now. She felt fine, she tried to convince herself: fine and furious.

In the spot above where the possible slit in the ceiling was located downstairs, she craned her neck to look up at her own ceiling. Yes. A crack or a slit, one she'd discounted as just a sign of an old house. But what if someone—Dane and Adrienne—had urged her to take this apartment to keep an eye on her? But why? Why? It reminded her of those one-way mirrors she'd seen on police TV dramas where detectives peered at the guilty as they were interrogated.

But that was a crazy thought, too. These were obviously historic Shaker observation slits that Dane had uncovered to show tourists; then she'd ended up living here and no one had mentioned them. If she asked, they'd say they were never used, of course. But her skin still crawled at the thought of being watched. Someone looking through the slit at this apartment level, she thought, scanning angles and distances, could probably see half of her living room and into the kitchen. At least the bedroom and bath could not be viewed from here. She scanned the rest of her rooms for slits but found no others.

But that dreadful scene of herself searching her house for hidden cameras or bugs after Mike deserted her flashed through her mind. It had been the breaking point for her. Erin had come downstairs late at night to find Kate hysterically ransacking the house for evidence to prove someone was watching, watching.... And that had sent her over the edge, sent her to the psychiatrist because she felt her sanity was slipping....

Kate pressed both hands to the sides of her head. She would not let that happen again. She would not!

She rushed out into the hall that divided the former men's and women's sides for what they called their retiring chambers. Again, she could find no entrance to a place for a watcher to stand. And the slits did not come through to this hall. Yet the words to one of the Shaker hymns, "Ye Watchers and Ye Holy Ones," taunted her.

What was keeping Jack so long? she fumed. He'd know about construction, and how things might have been built, and he could help her with this.

Kate went back downstairs to be certain she'd locked the sets of outside doors, front and back, then went up the two sets of sisters' stairs toward the attic level. There was only one narrow staircase here, as if for once the brethren and sisters could be trusted to use the same treads.

Kate climbed them cautiously and surveyed the large, bare attic. The light was good enough outside that it slanted in sharply through narrow dormer windows. She wondered why the staff didn't store things up here instead of paying for a place in town, but perhaps it was because this was a long climb and the roof banked so steeply. She'd stuck her head up here when Adrienne had originally showed her around, but she'd never returned. Still, someone else could have.

Walking the floor, Kate tried to figure out exactly what part of this ceiling was over those slits on each level below. She sneezed from the dust. Mother Ann had preached that there must be no dirt, so Louise had better send her local cleaning girls up here once in a while. She sneezed again, then saw a square trapdoor in the floor, nearly hidden because the wood grains were matched so well. It must have been built by a skilled woodworker. Its metal ring was recessed flush with the floor. Yes, this was approximately above where the slits should be.

Closer perusal showed that someone had recently dusted the door off, the only clean area of floor; it looked as if a person had sat down next to it, perhaps to scoot into the hole.

"Good," she whispered, trying to buck herself up. "At least it isn't Shaker ghosts."

Holding her breath, recalling Tanya down that dark well, Kate tugged the recessed metal ring and heaved the door up to look inside.

The orange, corrugated metal doors of Rent-a-Room Storage on the outskirts of Athens all looked the same to Jack. Aside from their location, they were only differentiated by the spray-painted numbers above each one and the random graffiti that had been crudely painted over. He had finally gotten out of the manager here, with the help of a twenty-dollar bill, that Shaker Run Village had rented E-11.

Jack knew Kate would be upset that he was checking this without her, but he was dying to know if fake Shaker furniture was stored here. Had that been the key Tanya mentioned, or was it possible Dane Thompson had more than one old car he drove? Jack had been to the Thompson house once and had just driven by again on the way here. They had a two-car garage. The sporty model Adrienne usually drove was out, and their minivan had been in the extra spot, so Dane wasn't keeping any old cars there. Besides, Zink had assured Jack that the state police were looking for the Packard, so Dane would be nuts to keep it at home.

Leaving the motor running in case he had to get away fast—afraid the manager might phone someone at the village—Jack got out and glanced up and down the maze of sheds. This entire back area was for the large units with wider doors than those out in front.

You'd think they'd put the smaller compartments back here so U-Hauls and other trucks didn't have so far to drive with heavy loads. The other poor thing about the layout was that many of these alleys, including this one, were dead ends.

In the large padlock on E-11, Jack tried each of the four keys Tanya's mother had slipped him. The fourth one opened it. His heart pounding, he bent and lifted the door. It grated up to reveal a concrete slab floor and a jammed collection of Shaker furniture with a single, narrow path down the middle.

"Bingo!" he exulted with a grin. "Expertiser's heaven."

He didn't have to check any of it, he thought. It must be wall-to-wall fakes and frauds. Dane must be the mastermind behind what was becoming an international theft and contraband scheme. Fake pieces were being produced that were clones of the authentic ones, which were then stolen and replaced with the phonies. But he couldn't resist a quick look at what pieces were here before jumping back in the car to call Kate on his cell phone.

And then he saw what Tanya meant by saying she'd found the Angel's Trumpet. A food cupboard with the tinwork metal squares stood at the back of the narrow center aisle. He hurried toward it, noting that someone had pried one of the squares loose. If Tanya had taken it, why hadn't they found it in her car or with her things?

"Because whoever threw her down the well took it." He muttered the answer to his own question, just as the door to the storage space closed with a shuddering rumble, plunging him into total darkness.

23

King Henry II had a mistress named The Fair Rosamond. Queen Eleanor poisoned her husband's mistress, disguising the deadly poison with the oil of the apothecary's rose.

—Peter Coats
Flowers in History

Kate was furious after her trip down, then up, the modern metal ladder into the narrow shaft, which measured about a yardstick square. But amazingly, she was not filthy. After getting a flashlight so she could see between floors, she had assumed the tiny space into which she'd descended would be all spiderwebs and dust, but it had been as clean as a Shaker wall. Someone who liked things clean had used it often, and recently. And no doubt to spy on her. It had taken care, cunning and a certain fastidious nature. Clint Barlow was off her list of suspects, for sure: the one watching her must have been either Adrienne or Louise.

Kate's mind raced over the numerous times she'd had private conversations with Zink or her lawyer—or Jack—from the phone here. She recalled the day Jack had come to tell her he'd found children's furniture in his storage shed and could link it to Sarah's collection. Kate had told him she'd give anything to have her struggle with Varina and Palmer over. They'd kissed and embraced, perhaps while being watched. And if someone had been spying on her then, what he or she heard that day could have endangered not only the Denbigh heirs, but Jack, too. Jack could be in just as much danger as she was. She had to reach him.

Kate closed the heavy trapdoor and headed downstairs. She supposed it was a long shot, but he could still be at the hospital. She also wanted to check up on Tanya. And then she would have to pack some things and get out of this so-called Trustees' House before it got even darker. If Jack wasn't back, she couldn't just camp out at his place, either. The car had been on that road last night. And without him, his house was just as deserted as this place.

The Shakers, she fumed, must have been crazy to live communally with the knowledge they were being watched. And Dane and Adrienne must have been crazy to think they could conveniently forget to tell her about this ladder and slits in the walls, and expect her to trust them.

Adrenaline and anger rampaged through her. For the first time in days, she was suddenly hungry. Stopping at her desk, she couldn't get Jack at either his home or cell phone number. Realizing she'd have to look up the hospital's number and that the phone book was in the kitchen, she rushed out there. She grabbed a bottle of water from the fridge and an unopened bag of taco chips from the counter as she skimmed the fine print for the hospital number, then punched it in.

"This is Kate Marburn, calling for a patient's

mother, a Mrs. Yvonne Dodridge," Kate told the receptionist. "I was told I could call to see how her
daughter, Tanya Dodridge, was doing. The patient is
in ICU after surgery, but I really need to talk to her
mother."

The phone rang and rang. Frustrated, Kate ripped
open the sack and ate a few chips; then, with the
phone wedged between her neck and shoulder, bent
to ransack the refrigerator. She yanked out bread and
jelly to make a peanut butter sandwich, then a half-
used jar of spicy salsa. After the receptionist came
back on and said she'd try the ICU line again, Kate
jammed the chips in the salsa and crunched them
down.

"Needless to say," the receptionist explained,
coming back on yet again, "if there's an emergency
in ICU, answering the phone's the last thing that gets
done."

Kate had just started to worry that an emergency
could mean Tanya was worse, when her mother came
on the line. Swallowing, Kate forced herself to inquire
first about her friend's condition.

"They tell me that both the good news and the bad
news is that her condition is unchanged," Yvonne
Dodridge explained. "They're still watching for brain
swelling, and I overheard a nurse say they're hoping
she doesn't get an epidural hematoma, so they'd have
to relieve the pressure somehow."

Relieve the pressure somehow, the woman's words
echoed in Kate's brain. "Is Jack still there?" she
asked.

"Oh, my no, long gone. And," she added, whispering now, "I gave him Tanya's keys. He said the
two of you had to check on something, and I trusted

him. I've always had good instincts about who to trust, you know.''

Kate promised to check back soon and closed the conversation, not certain of what she'd said at the end. She had once been so certain she had good instincts about people. But her former mistaken faith in Mike jabbed at her when she wanted so to trust Jack. He must have gotten Tanya's key to the Athens storage sheds and had gone there on the way back.

She tried his home phone once again; then, when the answering machine picked up, she slammed down her receiver. While she spread peanut butter on a piece of bread, one-handed, she grabbed the phone again and punched in Jack's cell phone number. Maybe he was back in his car now.

''Hey!'' Jack shouted, feeling his way out in the pitch black on the narrow path between the stacks of furniture in the storage unit. ''Someone's in here! Open the door!''

Silence, as if the door had closed itself.

He should have turned on the interior light before he stepped in, but in the rays of the setting sun he hadn't thought of it. He didn't even know where the light switch was. He couldn't get near the walls, anyway, unless he climbed up and over these massive pieces of furniture or shifted a few of them around single-handed. He shouldn't have come here without Kate, but he was relieved he had. It was bad enough that he was trapped, without her having to go through more anxiety.

Making his way back to the metal door, he banged on it. It had been lifted just a crack. He got on his knees, then sprawled on his belly to look out. Because his body lay in the aisle at a right angle to the door, he had to twist his neck.

He saw shoes, a man's, old-fashioned dressy brown ones. They lifted one at a time as the wearer got into Jack's still-idling car. Hell, in the middle of all this he was getting his car stolen, and he'd been so stupid he deserved it.

In the waning daylight, Jack watched the tires turn to take it away, slowly, strangely toward the back of this dead-end alley, not in the direction out. He fumbled for his cell phone in his jacket pocket and realized that was in his car, too. He cursed, then strained to listen. Distant footsteps. Then someone bringing his car back—a short joyride—or else pulling up in another vehicle.

It was another car, coming from the open end of the alley, a car with huge whitewall tires, polished hubcaps and a high-slung chassis, one too far off the ground for a modern car. The grillwork, like five bright silver pipes wrapping around the side to the front wheels, wasn't anything he recognized.

Jack sucked in a sharp breath as he realized the worst. Getting to his feet, he began to beat his fists on the metal door.

Kate was afraid Jack was not going to answer his cell phone. As when she called the hospital, it seemed to ring forever. She had felt energized a few moments ago, but now her stomach cramped with foreboding. Her pulse pounded, harder, harder.

Finally, he clicked on the phone.

"Jack," she cried, "it's Kate. I'm back at my apartment. Where are you?"

He didn't answer, but she could tell he was there, listening, breathing. At least, someone was.

"Jack, are you all right? Are you somewhere you can't talk?"

She was certain she heard the purr of a car engine in the background and some kind of metal pounding, as if the engine were knocking. Or could there be interference in the call somehow, and he could hear her but she couldn't hear him? Perhaps he was driving past power lines or something like that.

"Jack," she shouted, "it's Kate!"

Her voice didn't sound like her own, as if it were somehow coming from outside her body. To keep from tilting to the floor, she gripped the edge of her kitchen counter, pulling the spiral phone cord straight to reach this far from her desk. As it uncoiled, it looked like a snake—a snake in the rose garden.

She shook her head, trying to clear it. That was a stupid thought, wasn't it? Snakes weren't white, and this was thin and twisty.

But what if the snake were poisonous?

Kate pressed the phone harder to her ear, trying to hear Jack so she could know where he was. She still felt dizzy, the way she'd been before, though she'd felt better lately, hadn't she? She didn't want to be in the hospital the way Tanya was. But she was pretty sure Tanya hadn't been poisoned.

Then she heard whoever was on Jack's cell phone whisper something. It was a hiss like a snake.

Kate screamed and threw the phone down. Thank God, it slithered away from her as the snake coiled itself again.

Then, though her thoughts kept coiling up just like

that, she did know one thing for sure. She had to find out what had made that snake poisonous.

Kate dropped the bag of chips in her scramble for the herbs in the canvas sack she'd put under her sink. In the dried, molted snakeskin of their wrinkled sacks, they looked undisturbed.

"But I'm disturbed," she said aloud. She talked louder so the person on the phone could still hear. "I'm disturbed. But why?" She grabbed the jar of jelly and tipped it upside down until it all fell out. Red. Strawberries as bright as roses. She dumped the jar of salsa on the counter, bending close to examine the crimson spill. Chopped green peppers in it, onions, chilis. She was chilly, cold, then hot. But what about these pieces of dried leaves in this salsa? Parsley? Oregano, like in pizza? Pieces of pizza, pieces of furniture, pieces of herself.

Kate fought to keep her thoughts from drifting, from flying. What were those early symptoms of Angel's Trumpet? She had to call the hospital to be sure she wasn't poisoned, but what if it was in her head? She had finally come to realize her stalker was all in her head after Jack left—no, that was after Mike left. She wanted to call the hospital for help, but a long, coiled poisonous snake was still on the kitchen floor, biting the phone, and she didn't want to touch it.

"Dear God in heaven, help me," Jack whispered as he watched the same feet emerge from the black vehicle that had just pulled up, even closer to the metal door than his car had been. He'd given up pounding when he heard the engine.

He craned his neck and shoved his cheek flatter to the gritty cement, trying to catch a higher glimpse, but his angle was bad and it was getting dark in the narrow alley between the two rows of storage units. The man walked out of his line of sight; Jack couldn't see around these big pieces of furniture that formed the front of the narrow aisle. But he heard the man doing something at the corner of the storage room door.

Fortunately, he saw the feet get back into the car, so at least the man was leaving. It panicked and enraged him that the guy had probably wedged something in the door to keep him from opening it. Worse, it must be the driver who had tormented Kate. The bastard probably thought he was getting Jack out of the way so he could go after Kate again without interference.

But there was something familiar about those feet and that walk. He knew that man, didn't he? But he couldn't quite place him.

Jack heard him rev the big, old engine, but the vehicle didn't move. He didn't smell anything, but he heard it, rasping, like through a hose.

Now he knew what it was, what the man intended. He was getting him out of the way, all right. On his knees, Jack went back to shouting and beating on the metal door with all his might.

Kate was tired from so much Shaker dancing and she was pretty sure she'd lost track of time. Instead of whirling barefoot like this in such a little place— let's see, it was a kitchen—she should go outside. She could dance on holy ground, take her clothes off just like that other Shaker sister did.

But when she danced over to look out the front

window to see if it was dark out there yet, she saw a car's headlights slash the front street and then go out.

She knelt quickly by the window. "The lights died," she whispered. "Why did Sarah die? Varina, too, maybe Tanya—all dead."

Kate scrambled on her knees to turn off the lights in this place, because she knew she should be using lanterns. But she didn't want to burn things down. Leaning toward the half-opened front window, she looked out again.

A man's voice, then a woman's. She wanted it to be Jack. She wanted Jack. But it was those people who were in charge. That's right, it was Dane with Adrienne.

Kate wasn't exactly sure why, but that scared her and made her mad, very mad. For some reason, she didn't want them to come upstairs and find her. It might be because Dane would fire her for wanting roses to be beautiful, not just useful. She didn't want to cut their heads off.

Kate heard the people come in downstairs. Had she unlocked the door or had they? So much she was sure she should remember...things just out of reach. But, after all, it was their office downstairs. Then—she wasn't sure why, maybe since that white snake that held the phone hissed it to her—she knew she could just watch them and they would not see her. She knew where to peek in a window just like this open one that she'd thought about flying out of earlier.

Taking her Angel's Trumpet with her, which was really a flashlight she'd left by the door, and glad she was not really sick in the head with a swollen brain like Tanya, Kate darted out into the hall. She could hear whoever was downstairs coming up now, two people. Maybe it was Erin and Mike, because Kate was so exhausted she knew it must be time to go to bed.

Kate tiptoed partway up the stairs to the attic, then realized she was a Shaker sister on the brethren's stairs. No, there was only one set of stairs here. She heard the woman tell the man, "He said she was resting but I'm worried about her. Are you sure we have to do this now?"

"Yes, right now," he said. "If she hasn't figured it out, she's going to."

Peering around from the last steps to the attic, Kate watched them knock on her apartment door in the hall below. Dane called her name, so Kate almost went down to meet them. But when he jingled keys in his hand and opened the apartment door, she knew he shouldn't do that. What else shouldn't that man do?

Kate hurried up to the attic and lifted the door in the floor. Going down into a deep well, just like Tanya, she thought. It would be a good place to hide. She jammed her small flashlight in her cleavage, inside her bra, and descended. If she went too fast, the ladder made noise, so she slowed down. What was it that these people had done that was bad? And how had she gotten so funny-headed again?

She remembered Alice in Wonderland, falling down the rabbit's hole, falling, falling. Kate held on tighter, hugging the ladder, wishing it were Jack. Alice had eaten things that made her grow large, then small—a mushroom. Maybe, Kate tried to reason, she had eaten some kind of mushrooms, too. But there had been no mushrooms in the peanut butter, jelly, or bread or chips. But what about that spicy salsa?

"This place is a mess" Kate heard the woman say

as she stopped her descent at the top level of slits to look out. The flashlight pointing up under Kate's chin made her blink, so she held on with one hand to turn it off.

"Just look at this," the woman went on. "The phone receiver's dropped on the floor as if she'd got shocking news and just took off. Plates of dried leaves. It looks like some of Tanya's herbs, yes. Spilled chips, strawberry jelly and salsa, and a pile of papers—look, Dane, she's been going through old Shaker records, and some of your paperwork we never filed away but probably should have."

Kate squinted to watch the man—Dane—stoop to read the papers the kneeling woman handed up to him. But he tossed them back to the floor where the kitchen met the living room.

"Harmless stuff," she heard him say. "I just hope she didn't hear Tanya's taken a bad turn and go there. Maybe we'd better call the hospital. I'll just leave these photos here and talk to her about everything later, see how much she's figured out so we know exactly what to do."

Wide-eyed, Kate watched as the man pulled two pieces of paper from his shirt pocket and put them on the wooden chest in the living room. Then he picked them up and wrote something on the backs.

"Come on," he said, "we've got to find her. Let's check for her car—Tanya hid hers the other night. Maybe she's somewhere else in the village or at Kilcourse's house."

Kate started to climb back up to the attic as soon as she saw them go out and heard them close the apartment door. She was breathing much harder than she thought the climb should make her. And she was so thirsty. But she really felt like a Shaker now, keeping an eye on everyone. That woman Sister Louise would be very proud of Sister Jerusha.

Kate tiptoed back toward her apartment door and turned the knob. *Locked.* And her keys were inside. But she knew if she thought hard, very hard, she could find a way to unlock it.

Jack could only smell the tailpipe exhaust fumes—but carbon monoxide was odorless, and he knew it was flooding this nearly airtight storage unit. Since it was coming in at floor level, he could probably buy some time by climbing on top of the furniture and yelling for help from there. But how many people would be driving through a Rent-a-Room dead-end alley after dark on a Monday night?

The moment he got off the floor where the door was slightly ajar, he realized his dilemma. The only source of fresh air was the crack on the floor, so would climbing buy him more time? To avoid wearing himself out, and sucking in more fumes by shouting, Jack made himself calm down and think.

Quickly, he felt his way back to the Angel Trumpet food storage cupboard and kicked at the side of it where Tanya had evidently pulled a metal sheet loose. The one next to her hole came free in his hands, though the tin was so sharp he sliced his palm open. Ignoring that, he stuck the piece down the back of his shirt, tucking it in his belt. Its corners scraped his skin right through his shirt and T-shirt.

He felt his way back to the front of the garage and, wedging himself in the small clearance between the metal door and the outer edge of an upturned trestle table, he managed to get the table rotated so it filled the aisle. Edging along, he shoved the next piece of furniture, a corner cupboard, if he remembered correctly. Yes, his first touch confirmed that. With difficulty, he scooted it along into the space where the table had been.

He was getting so nervous and exhausted, even his palms were sweating—or was that his blood? No matter; he had no choice but to forge ahead, to fight how weak and muddled he was feeling. Concentrate. *Concentrate.*

He was now very close to the corner of the storage unit. His would-be killer had probably not reckoned on him getting to the hose to shove it out, cut it or block it with a piece of sharp metal.

If he didn't pass out first.

Kate sat at the bottom of the attic stairs for a while—she wasn't sure how long—feeling depressed and lethargic.

She had a good notion to get up and whirl and dance again, but she was exhausted. She knew she was supposed to be figuring something out, but it eluded her. The hall was dim, because the Shakers who had been here had only left a light on downstairs. Kate didn't care. Lights were starting to hurt her eyes, anyway, and she felt she could see in the dark.

Then she remembered she had a key, hidden in case she did lock herself out. Humming, twirling, then going to her tiptoes, she felt along the top of the single hall windowsill. There it was. Kate opened the door and went in to see two photos on the table. That's right. She'd seen that man leave them, and he'd written on them, too. She was better now, thinking clearly about something, like where to find keys.

She turned on a light, then shaded her eyes from it. The top photo was a yellowed black-and-white of a humped, dark car.

She knew that car! She flipped it over and read, *Shaker Run Village Buick Eight, circa 1947.*

"I've seen that before," she said, wishing her head would clear of the thick fog. "It's at Jack's sometimes."

She read the back of the next photo before she looked at the picture: *Rare photo—just found. Both are Shaker cars, brethren's Buick, sisters' Packard.*

"Two of everything!" Kate cried. "Two doors, two stairs, two cars."

She flipped to the photo side. It was a more distant shot than the other, but it had two cars in it. The car with three Shaker men standing near it was the Buick from Jack's storage shed. The other vehicle was a car she was so afraid of that it hurt her head to think about it. It was a dark car, too, with five bonneted Shaker sisters gathered around it. Each woman's name was on the photo in blue ink, with an arrow pointing to her.

Four of the names didn't mean a thing, but Kate thought she'd heard of the one named Jerusha Lockhart.

24

Ash on an old man's sleeve
Is all the ash the burnt roses leave.
Dust in the air suspended
Marks the place where the story ended.

—T.S. Eliot
Four Quartets

"Jack, are you there? I called before, but couldn't hear you. I think I'm sick. I need to go to the hospital, just like Tanya. Where are you? Can you come get me?" Kate cried into the phone.

Finally, she'd summoned the courage to pick it up from her floor. She had been afraid because part of it still looked like the snake that had gotten into her Shaker rose garden. But she'd dialed his cell phone number again. Jack didn't answer his phone, not at first.

But then he said, in a whispering, shivery voice, "I'm coming for you."

"Can't you talk?" she asked. "My head's dizzy but my voice is all right."

"Stay there," Jack whispered. "I'll be there soon."

"Talk louder. Is someone there? How's Tanya?"

It sounded as if he said, "Soon, soon." She threw

the phone with its coiled tail back on the floor. Jack better get here fast, she thought, pressing her fingertips to the sides of her head. She should be feeling better but she was feeling worse.

Jack had a roaring headache, and his legs were shaking. Worse, he was so sleepy, maybe dreaming. He knelt near the hose, he could hear the hissing now. He reached for the metal piece he'd jammed down the back of his jeans. Maybe he could shove the hose out with it, cut off its tip to make it vent outside, or jam it shut.

He tried to hold his breath but the air was bad. He thought of Kate. If he died here, she'd be alone against the man in the car, against *them.* Jack wanted to start over with Kate, with Erin, too, a new family. He hadn't let himself plan that far, and now it might be too late. Wedged in the narrow space between the furniture and metal door, he sank lower to the floor.

As he tried to block the end of the hose with the metal square, he saw Andy's face. Not Andy dying but Andy smiling…and he had wanted…to have that memory…for a very long…lost time.

"Dad, I wanted to be as strong as you," Andy said, and reached for Jack's hand to tug him toward the door to freedom and light.

Jack wished he could have been stronger, too.

When Kate heard another car outside, she turned out the light and ran to the window.

It must be Jack. She didn't see a car, but she recalled one roaring out of the darkness at her, just missing her. That car threw Tanya down a deep shaft with no ladder. It was a car filled with Shaker sisters who didn't trust men. Never ride with a man, do not use the same door or stairs. Dance in the same circles but keep away from them. Especially if the man's name is Mike or Dane.

Kate stuck her head out the window and sucked in a breath of fresh, cool air. The darkness suited her. She had looked at herself in the bathroom mirror and seen how big her eyes were—her pupils black and big like a cat's. With just her head stuck through the open window, she looked outside.

Leaning this far out, she saw the car from the photograph parked way down the street. Yes, the sisters' car, huddled, a dark shape in the nightmare. And walking away from it, coming toward the Trustees' House, was someone she recognized by his size and walk.

It was Zink, his trench coat flapping in the breeze. "Zink!" she called out, waving wildly to him. "I need to go to the hospital. I'm dizzy and sick, and Jack's not here."

He looked up at her and came closer, faster. "I'm here for you, Kate. And I know Jack's not here. What's the matter with you? Can you come down and open the door for me, or shall I break in?"

"I'll try to come down."

"I got your call about Tanya being hurt and figured I'd better come for you," he called, directly under the window now.

Kate pulled her head back in. She could not recall phoning Zink about Tanya. What about Tanya? Then a glimmer of memory teased her. Her friend was in the hospital where Kate wanted to go, where Zink would take her now.

Leaning heavily against the wall, she started slowly

downstairs to let him in. The single ceiling light at the bottom of the stairs was on. Kate recalled Louise saying that despite its antique fittings, it ruined the whole building. Use lanterns, lanterns. Use old-fashioned rose cutters, not modern ones. Kate was relieved she was remembering some things, at least.

But when she was halfway down, Zink came in. He'd used the sisters' door, but as a worldly man he didn't know any better. "Someone must have left it unlocked," he told her.

He sprinted up the stairs and put his arms around her. She leaned on him.

"Kate, that car's out there. Whose is it? I've got to call it in, but I wanted to be sure you were all right. What happened?"

"What happened?" she repeated, trying to focus on him. "I think I maybe poisoned myself with food, but someone helped. But you can work on that car if you want, since Jack's coming here. Soon, soon," she tried to assure him, nodding repeatedly.

"We're not waiting for Jack," he insisted, setting her back down on the step. "Let me just get my car and drive it up to the door to get you. You wait right here."

"But that other car—"

"I'll get its license on my way to my vehicle, then call it in while I rush you to the hospital. Stay put. I'll be right back. Whoever drives that car, we've got them now, so just relax. Trust me and don't worry."

He wrapped her fingers around the banister rungs to help her hang on. But the moment he thudded down the stairs and rushed outside, she dropped her hold on it and put her head in her hands. Her thoughts dragged, but she knew she couldn't go to sleep, couldn't just pass out. There was something about Zink she was trying to remember, something about his trench coat, something about his doing a stakeout, and then just showing up like this.

But where was he now? It was as if that black car out there devoured people. He had been gone a while, missing for as long as Jack, hadn't he?

"Midnight Cry! Midnight Cry!" someone screamed.

Kate awoke with a start. She was sprawled on the stairs just above the doors of the Trustees' House. Below her, at the threshold, with brooms sweeping madly back and forth in a ritual dance step, were a Shaker sister and a brother. Her big bonnet and his flat hat obscured their faces.

"Up, Sister Jerusha. Up, kindly up!" the woman cried in a singsong voice that was so familiar. "Tonight all sins must be examined and judgments given! The worldly men you have trespassed with have been locked away."

Kate's heart pounded, and she shook uncontrollably. Where was Zink? Did this woman mean she'd locked him away? Jack, too?

Kate half rose, half dragged herself to her feet and tried to get up the stairs. She feared they would pull her back, and was shocked when the woman came to help her. Now carrying a lantern, the man thudded up the matching brethren's staircase.

In the hall, they took her elbows to hurry her into her dark apartment. They half pulled, half shoved her in a rocking chair. As the man set the lantern down on the table, light leaped to his face, though the woman's was still hidden in the cavern of her bonnet.

Kate expected it to be Dane and Adrienne come back for her. But she knew now who it was before she saw his face.

Ben Willis.

"I should have known—it was you, but too late, too—dizzy. Louise, what are you doing here so late that—"

"*Sister* Louise. And I'm afraid you haven't had enough of a Shaker high yet," she said, her voice sharper than ever.

"You said," Ben whined to his wife, "she'd had the stuff building up for so long in that tea you doctored that she wouldn't know which end was up by now. Wouldn't know us, even if we got close this time."

"I thought she acted really out of it when I watched her just an hour ago," Louise snapped at him. "Sister Jerusha," she went on, leaning over to pull Kate's arm so hard the rocking chair tilted forward, "listen to me. Did you eat the pickle relish, mustard, the salsa or tomato juice from your refrigerator? Did you drink more of your tea?"

Kate stared into the dark depths of the woman's bonnet. Two eyes glinted. When Kate didn't answer, Louise thrust her away so Kate's head hit the back of the rocker and made it move again. Even that motion made her head spin faster, wilder.

"I put that herb in about everything in that kitchen!" Louise cried, this time to Ben instead of to Kate. "But I need to know how much of it she took."

Ben snatched the lantern and went into the kitchen. Painfully rolling her eyes to watch him, Kate recalled that he dragged his left leg slightly, though he'd certainly learned to hide that as he must have hidden so much else.

"The salsa, I'd say," he called to Louise. "It's out and spilled."

"I put a lot in there," Louise said, "but who knows how much she ate if it's spilled. It was spicy enough to hide the flavor of it."

"Valerian or Angel's Trumpet?" Kate asked. She realized too late she should not have spoken, but she felt raging fury. It was clearing her head, wasn't it?

"Too sharp, as usual—you, not the salsa spices," Louise retorted. As Ben returned with the lantern, Kate saw she looked pleased instead of angry now.

"Perhaps," Louise went on, "you'd better bring Sister Jerusha a little more un-Shaker salsa, Brother Benjamin. I wasn't the herbalist before Sister Tanya interfered, nor have I been keeping a good eye on both of you for nothing, you know," she added smugly.

Kate fought for every thought. If they forced more of that down her they must mean to kill her, unless they planned for her to remember nothing later. Yes, that's what had happened to those men at Jamestown after days of being high. But she had to make the Willises believe she was deeper into the drug than she really was. Maybe her adrenaline was an antidote, but she'd have to outsmart them. Her body felt even more lethargic than her brain, and she'd never fight them off or outrun them.

Trying to keep her head clear, Kate began to hum a Shaker song, *Keep awake, keep awake, lest ye be rent asunder.* She lifted her arms in the gathering-blessings motion Louise had taught her dancers. As Ben came in, not with the jar of salsa but the can of tomato juice, Kate managed to get to her feet and walk toward him, swaying to her own tune. She took the tomato juice can from the surprised man and held it close to her as if she would drink it of her own accord.

It was then she saw that he had a handgun of some sort stuck in the waist of his Shaker trousers. It looked like the one Zink always wore in the holster. It sometimes showed along his ribs when he stretched or when his suit coat flew open.

"Rose water, all bright and red, and I am cutting off each head," Kate sang.

She slowly, unsteadily pirouetted, letting the remains of the tomato juice dribble on the floor around her in a circle and splattered Ben's trousers and Louise's Shaker skirts like drops of blood.

"Stop her before she makes more of a mess of things, Brother Benjamin. If you can't control her, I will at last! And be sure you have the rest of the crushed herb with you. The moment she doesn't do exactly as her deaconess bids, we will see that she is thoroughly dosed again. Of course," she said, pushing Kate against the wall with her broom handle, shoving hard across her chest, "she did take the first dose willingly to be part of Mother Ann's work."

"She did, indeed, Sister Louise," Ben agreed.

The man never did have a backbone, Kate thought. But perhaps he was more dangerous following Louise's orders, especially with a gun. Although Kate had admired Louise's energy and talents, she had completely underestimated her.

"Hold her here while I fetch her proper garb," Louise commanded. "She's shockingly attired for the Midnight Cry ritual."

Louise took the lantern and went into Kate's bedroom. Kate wished she had more strength, for now was the time to shove Ben and run. Yet he held the broom harder against her than Louise had.

But the pain helped her head to clear. The old car outside... They must have been the faces behind the black glass, maybe the ones running the furniture scam. Had they murdered Sarah because she caught them stealing her furniture? They had killed Varina, too. They'd hurt Palmer and Tanya. Jack and Zink were missing. And what did she face now?

Looking quite pleased with herself, Louise emerged from the bedroom with Kate's Shaker gown, apron, breast scarf, bonnet—and a pair of panty hose.

"Brother Benjamin, turn your back, while Sister Jerusha properly clothes herself. Hurry up," she goaded, poking Kate with the broom handle when she fumbled, but then threw it down to help her don the Shaker garments.

Kate had felt momentarily better, but her whirling dance had worked against her. She felt she still spun around. Trembling at the touch of this horrid woman's hands, she managed to sway slightly as Louise tied the bonnet on for her as the finishing touch. At least, her face was hidden from them now, but Louise must have thought of that, too, because she yanked the bonnet back, nearly choking Kate before the bow came loose.

"I must tell you what happened to poor Sister Jerusha when she tried to ruin everything for the village," Louise said. She motioned Ben to bring the lantern closer. He shone it directly in Kate's dilated eyes. Even that hurt, but Kate hoped it would convince them she was deeply drugged.

"Sister Jerusha? Me?" Kate asked. At least, she didn't have to fake her fear.

"Yes, you," Louise said, studying her at such close range that her bonnet brim kept bumping Kate's brow. "She was a traitor to the cause, to the village. It was utter betrayal that a sister, whom the elders and deacons had taken in and favored, was going to go to worldly authorities with claims of drugs being forced on folks in this village."

Tanya had been right, Kate thought. But had the Willises thrown her down the well for that? Or had Tanya discovered they ran the furniture scam?

"Sister Jerusha loves roses," Kate said, hoping that sounded off-track. She had to find out about Jack and Zink, then escape to help them. If she could only grab that gun from Ben. "I do, too—love roses," Kate stammered. "Shaker roses and my Shaker furniture —Sarah's."

"You *are* Sister Jerusha," Louise insisted, so Kate nodded. "You see, the Shakers took her in and let her follow the dream of her heart to grow their roses. She became friends with Brother Benjamin when that was absolutely forbidden. He was the village herbalist."

"And my grandfather," Ben put in. "I was named for him—first name, anyway. His last name was Owens, Benjamin Owens."

The man who had written the herbal diary she'd read earlier today, Kate thought.

"After Sister Jerusha told the police the Shakers were being drugged, he had to leave this heaven on earth—they all did," Ben explained, his voice rising with anger. "Later he wed and had a family."

"Never mind all that," Louise snapped, though Kate wanted them to keep talking.

"So the Believers found out about their forbidden friendship—Brother Benjamin and Sister Jerusha's?" Kate prompted. "And made them leave before it caused a scandal?"

"Hardly. Worse than that," Ben said, his voice bitter now. "Sister Jerusha betrayed not only the entire village but Brother Benjamin, who was supposedly her friend. She told the local police that he was the one overseeing drugs for use in the village, the same ones the Shakers sold for curatives to worldly people, only, of course, in different dosages. But that got everyone in danger—deacons—"

"Deacons like we are now in Shaker Run," Louise said. "After we took you in, hoping you'd bring us your roses and Mrs. Denbigh's furniture, you put us in danger."

"Sister Jerusha ruined everything for the elders, too," Ben said. "Elders like Dane and Adrienne, who don't know a thing about our dedication and plans for the future of this village."

Then that cleared Dane and Adrienne of the furniture scam, and, Kate hoped, of everything else.

"Enough of all this," Louise interrupted. "Sister Jerusha betrayed the village. The police went to the Believers and told them they must close down or be publicly exposed—closed down in shame and sent to prison. Can you imagine, celibate brothers and sisters in prison? After being sheltered here in this paradise they had built, Sister Jerusha ruined everything. But the tables turned on her and she received justice, meted out from Mother Ann during a Midnight Cry ceremony. And you, Sister Jerusha, follow in her steps, for you, too, have brought in worldly men and tried to ruin everything. You would not accept your dark visions, but tonight you will, at last.''

Praying they would believe she didn't get the full impact of what they'd said, Kate started to hum a Shaker tune again. Her heart was thudding so hard she almost couldn't hear herself. She had to get away now, because if they wanted her to follow in Sister Jerusha's steps, that meant death.

Glancing at the photos of the two old cars Dane had left on the table, Kate was suddenly sure she knew how Jerusha Lockhart had died. The Shaker Run Believers might have used separate cars for the celibate sexes, but she'd bet her life that one of the vehicles had struck and killed Jerusha. Whether or not the original Benjamin was at the wheel, Kate could picture *this* Benjamin driving the Packard with Louise at his side, urging him on, ordering him to scare and harm—to murder—people who defied them or got in their way. Whether they were insane or criminally ingenious, Kate had to run.

She jerked free of their grasp and lunged for the gun. Yanking it from Ben's waistband, she held it with both hands, whirling to face them, pointing it, dizzy as she was.

But Louise shrieked and swung her broom to crack Kate's hands, just as the gun went off. The broom or the blast threw Kate back. Ben shoved her to the floor where she hit her head again. He pried the gun from her. Had she shot Louise?

''Praise Mother, this place is a ghost town at night,'' Louise muttered, her voice seeming to come from a great distance now. ''She's shot the wall right through a peephole, but that noise could wake our precious dead. Let's finish this. We've been watching her long enough to know how clever she is. Fetch a glass of water and give me some of those crushed leaves you're carrying.''

Before Kate could react, Louise pressed the broomstick across her, this time at her throat. Kate tried to kick and scratch. But Ben now held the broom, while Louise swished a crushed handful of leaves into the water. To avoid choking, Kate swallowed the gagging gush of water that went partly up her nose. She hacked and gasped when they sat her up; that damn woman dared to pat her on the back.

She was still sputtering as they jerked her to her feet. She tried to reason out how long it had been before she'd felt the effects of the drug in the salsa, but she only knew it had been soon, too soon.

As she gasped for breath, they bound her hands behind her back with the panty hose. They pushed her out the door, carefully locking her apartment behind them.

The only good thing, Kate thought as she stumbled down the sisters' stairs, was that she soon wouldn't even be aware of what was going to happen next. Had they given her enough of a dose to ruin reality again or to ruin her?

''What happened?''

He heard someone ask the question from far away—voices wandering down a long, gray corridor. He tried to remember where he was—remember *who* he was.

''Is he still unconscious?'' a woman asked. He wondered if it was Kate.

"His skin looks really weird—kind of bluish. Did he have a heart attack, or what?"

"I guess he got trapped in this storage shed and ran out of air. Or maybe paint thinner or something was stored in here with all this old furniture, and the fumes got him. I don't smell anything, though."

"Did you get the manager to call 911?"

"Taken care of," someone, out-of-breath, said. "How'd you see him in the first place, Andy?"

"A hand holding a piece of metal sticking out from under the door."

A boy's voice. *Andy?* Andy was here. Then he must have died and gone to heaven. He had the strangest feeling Kate should be here, too.

25

Cease your efforts to find where the last rose
lingers.

—Horace
Odes

"Stop dragging your feet," Louise ordered, as they
forced Kate downstairs and out into the night. "It will
take a few more minutes for that Angel's Trumpet to
work, so don't try anything."

"Then let's cut the lies and Shaker stuff you've
been putting over on everyone," Kate dared. "You
two are the fakes behind the other fakes—the antique
furniture, aren't you. I'll bet you've got a fortune
squirreled away from switching replicas with the real
antiques, then selling or using the originals. But that's
not what I really want to know."

Louise swung her around so hard Kate smacked
into the front of the building between the double front
doors. "You've assured your departure from here
now," Louise insisted, while Ben nervously fingered
the gun he still held. "Sister Jerusha's fate can well
be yours. If you got out of holy order—it was my
hope that you would not—that was my plan all
along."

"We can't just run over her, too," Ben blurted. As

he stepped closer to his wife, Kate noted again that he had trouble with his left leg. If she could just knock Louise down and get a start on him before he could pull out his gun...

"The furniture is not to support us but to guarantee the future of this precious place," Louise said archly. "One of our goals is to have building after building here, including Jack's property, filled with authentic furniture to honor the Shaker past and future."

"I wouldn't doubt that Dane and Adrienne are on your hit list too," Kate accused. "That way you can run everything here. But people are on to you, even foreign authorities whom Jack has already tipped off about your massive furniture scam."

Instead of the sobering effect she'd hoped for, Kate saw that Louise looked even more agitated. "On to us, hardly. It's your paramour Jack Kilcourse who's been scamming you. He's running that furniture bait-and-switch theft ring he's so zealously pretending to pursue. It's like your former husband revisited," she taunted from the depths of the bonnet. "You're wretched at picking men, aren't you? Once again, one's taken you in."

But Kate did not doubt Jack, as she would have any man a short time ago. Though she could feel the drug taking control of her again, she did not flinch or waver.

"That's not true," she insisted, as much to herself as to Louise. "I think it's Clint Barstow who's done your dirty work."

"That simpleton," Louise exploded, smacking her hands into her skirt, "is good for nothing more than taking orders."

"Exactly the way you treat Ben," Kate declared,

then nearly panicked. What, exactly had they been arguing about? Oh, yes, she remembered.

"Where's Jack?" she demanded.

"I really wouldn't know, would you, Brother Benjamin, where he is this very moment?" Louise asked, turning to frown at him.

"No—'course not," Ben said, shuffling his feet.

"And as for your suggestion that we can't just run Kate down with the sisters' Packard because that's been done before," Louise went on to him, "I'm afraid you'll have to bring that worldly pistol along so the policeman we have tied and locked in the trunk can shoot Sister Jerusha and then himself. He was arresting her at last, you see, for Sarah Denbigh's murder, and she tried to escape."

Kate wanted to argue that, but no words came. She wanted to scream at them that they couldn't keep harming people and getting away with it. But they had so far.

"Tell me what happened with Sarah Denbigh," Kate said, trying to form her words carefully so they would not think she was so affected by the drug yet. It was just the opposite of what she'd been trying earlier, because she was sinking fast. "How could you hurt her when she donated so much great furniture to this village?"

"That," Louise said, as she bent closer to study Kate, "was pure accident and sadly regrettable. But it wasn't our fault, was it, Brother Benjamin? She just came in on us, and one thing, sadly, led to another."

"We never wanted to harm her, never, nor any of the others," Ben insisted. "It's you who caused their situations. We only meant to watch you to be sure you were settling in well here and were worthy of replacing the original, defiled Sister Jerusha.''

"But," Louise interrupted him, "we saw you were keeping Sarah's death in your heart, and now we know you won't let go of Tanya's unfortunate demise.''

"Though she's not dead yet," Ben added. "If she comes out of it as Varina's brother never has, we'll have to see to her.'' He sighed heavily, and Louise nodded. Kate's eyes widened as she took in the enormity of all they were admitting—and the fact that their confession meant they intended her to die, too.

"Here, we attended Tanya's aunt's funeral—" Louise went on, becoming more impassioned, "just as we paid respects to Sarah Denbigh—and then Tanya betrays us, too. She found the furniture we had stored in town and, thinking the Thompsons were behind it, jumped to the conclusion that she could trust us to work with her, you and Jack.''

"Because you were so dedicated to the Shaker cause," Kate whispered, fighting to form her thoughts. "She believed you'd never do anything— to harm it or her. But you're out to help—only yourselves.''

"Don't shift the blame," Louise said so solemnly it sounded as if she were pronouncing final judgment. "After we killed Varina Wellesley for you and took her weak brother out of commission, you betrayed us again and again, much worse than Sister Tanya. At least, with both of you gone, there will be one other young convert we hope to trust—one especially," she said smugly, "who is about to inherit vast amounts of Sarah Denbigh's precious furniture.''

Kate's skin began to crawl, and not because she

felt the drug working—herself slipping, slipping again—but from what Louise had said last.

"Whadya mean?" Kate asked, suddenly sounding drunk to herself.

"Why, I mean someone young and pliable who is fascinated by the holy dancing and will be dedicated to this village because her mother worked here. Someone who lives nearby and will surely be willing to live at the village this summer in honor of her dear, departed stepmother, someone—"

No! Kate thought she screamed, but she must have only thought it. Though she felt she was spiraling down into a black well, Kate knew she had to make her move—and soon.

The men lifted him into a coffin on wheels and tried to close the lid. No, they were lifting him into an ambulance and kept trying to put a mask over his face.

"Breathe, breathe," one of them said. "Somehow you got carbon monoxide poisoning, so this is pure oxygen. I know you're disoriented, but just breathe, buddy. It's a miracle you're alive."

Though his limbs were weak as water, Jack tried to push the mask away.

"Feet—small feet," Jack whispered so low the other man leaned over him to try to listen. "Not Dane. A limp."

"He's worried about his extremities," that man told the other. "He probably can't feel his feet. He said 'nothing' and thinks he'll end up walking with a limp."

They pushed the mask back over his face and slid a strap behind his head to keep it in place.

Jack was so sleepy—everything was heavy in his head, his heart. Andy and Kate and Erin and that black car and the man with the small feet and the slight hitch when he walked.

"Ben. It's Ben," he said into the mask.

"Can you read his lips?" the first man asked.

"He said, 'It's been...' but he didn't finish the thought."

"It's been one hell of a night, and it's only midnight right now," a voice said, as Jack surrendered again to the dark.

"Let's forget this Midnight Cry cleansing ritual," Ben said. "We can just put her in the car and take them out on some road. You drive the Packard this time, and I'll drive the detective's car. We can't do it here."

"I'd like to do it right between the cemetery and holy ground, but she owes us a Midnight Cry first. Then she'll pay for her sins and Sister Jerusha's. I'll go get those brooms."

Though Kate's brain had started to merge with her body—light and spinning—she saw her chance when Louise walked back through the darkened door of the Trustees' House. Ben held Kate's arm, firmly but not harshly, evidently certain the drug was taking her strength again. And—it—was.

But she bumped into him to set him back, then tripped him. No chance to get his gun with her hands tied behind her back, but she'd risk his not using it. He didn't go down, but she ran toward the dark dwelling house across the street, stumbling, fighting to keep on her feet.

"Louise! Louise!" Ben cried.

Fearful of the sound of the pistol, the agony of the bullet, Kate did not look back. Her head spun, but she ran, her Shaker skirts grabbing her legs. Darkness flew at her as she danced, danced at Shaker Run.

Kate avoided the side of the house with the well and tore around the other way, past the half of the building laid out now as the infirmary. Beyond was the brethren's realm, their shops and fields. If she could just keep herself from falling, just keep the night sky from tilting...

She passed a window sash halfway up. The acrid smell of varnish or paint was strong here, like ammonia under the nose.

"Here—she went this way!" she heard Ben shout behind her.

Kate banged her knee into the corner of the root cellar. The sharp pain jolted her alert. Her mind cleared enough that she realized she should hide, not try to outrun them.

Slipping, sliding back, she mounted the slanted wooden door of the root cellar to the open windowsill. Both sitting on it and ducking her head to miss the raised sash, she rolled into the room and sprawled facedown on the floor, scraping her nose and chin.

Her eyes were already adjusted to the dark, or else they were dilating again with that drug. The corner cupboard loomed over her: if only it held a cure. Kate could imagine the Shaker sisters here, nursing those who were ill, maybe too ill from this drug that made them dance and see visions of the dead.

But Kate saw the dead in here now, too: Varina chasing her with hedge trimmers and Sarah saying, *She hates my roses, but you love them, Kate. Hide in the garden here, hide in this bed of roses.*

Kate shook her head to fight the slick slide of her thoughts. Someone was after her, and she had to hide.

"This window's open," a man's voice said, very close.

"But her hands are still tied, aren't they?" a woman asked. "That stupid Clint probably just left it open to air things out. Damn, I wish we would have tried to bribe Kilcourse into making the furniture for us, instead of that dolt. Well, go on up on that root cellar. We've got to at least look in. No, you climb in, while I look through the other outbuildings on this side of the street. Give me that lantern and be careful with that gun."

Kate saw the coffin just ahead of her, long and dark. They'd buried Sarah in one that should have been strewn with roses. She would stay here, working in this garden, until she tended the very last rose, the one that lingered after all the others were gone....

Her hands still tied behind her back, Kate got into the deep invalid's cradle and hoped it would quit rocking before everyone at the funeral saw it. Not only did it smell, but it was sticky and felt as if it could keep her glued inside forever. Back, forth—it made her even more light-headed.

The man chasing her thumped into the room, then walked slowly through it, close to her hiding place, *thud, thud.* Lying on her hands and arms, Kate held her breath. Why was she tied like this? No one tied dead people in their coffins.

"Well, is she in there?" a woman's voice called as the room became more light. "Here, take this lantern!"

"How the hell do I know, when you've got the only light?"

"She's not in the outbuildings," the woman said. "They were all locked with closed windows. Well, go let me in the front door. Never mind. Just take this lantern, and I'll climb in. I really think she's in here."

Kate lay still, very still in the dark, curled depths of the lovely last rose.

And then the sun came out blindingly bright and someone shouted her name and pulled her out.

"Is she still tied?"

"Yes. Let's get this over with, Louise! Strangers are bad enough, but Tanya and Kate, Shaker sisters—"

"They betrayed everyone just as Jerusha did. Kate Marburn *is* Jerusha Lockhart. And she owes us a Midnight Cry confession and will receive her judgment now!"

Jack woke the moment they stuck the needle in his arm. They'd done that to Andy, and he had wished he could take all the pain for his child. Though his head hurt so bad he could hardly see or talk, he said, "Get help for Kate. My house near Shaker Run. Help Kate."

"'Help Kate'? Do you know anything about this?" the doctor asked the nurse. "But he didn't get this carbon monoxide poisoning at his house, did he?"

"I know where Shaker Run is, and his address is on his driver's license."

"It's probably just the carbon monoxide talking, but have somebody check it out. After all, that village is where the police found that girl down the well."

"All right," she said. "I'll take care of it, but you're going to have to hold him down and keep that mask on him. He's got to behave or else."

* * *

They half marched, half dragged Kate toward the squat, black car. She hated it but wasn't sure why. She could hear its heartbeat; because there was a knocking, knocking from the inside of it, maybe the back part. It was almost like the knocking she'd heard on the phone when she'd called someone earlier. Had that been Erin at her door? There was something she had to remember about saving Erin.

"You will do what we say or else, Sister Jerusha," the woman told her, and yanked her to a halt before they got to the car.

They stood by her thickest, longest display of rosebushes. Kate inhaled deeply. This was much better than that terrible smell in the coffin.

"I thought you wanted to take her out to holy ground," the man argued.

"This is her holy ground, and I want her to obey me on it!" It was very dark out here, Kate thought, but darker yet inside that woman's bonnet and inside her brain.

"Untie her hands, but knock her out with that broomstick if she tries to disobey again," the Shaker woman said. "Unfortunately, we can't shoot her here."

The Shaker brother—with his hat missing—did as the woman said. When her hands were free, Kate rubbed her sore wrists, wishing she could hide herself in these roses. She recognized them, no matter how bad she felt. They were Apothecary roses, meant for curing in the old days, and she could use that now.

"Take these old shears and cut them off—one dozen," the woman said. "And I'm putting my hands on top of yours, so kindly don't try anything cute with these. No, no, we are cutting the stems off and then the rose heads separately. At least, since you brought the furniture to us here, you deserve the same roses near your grave as Sarah Denbigh and Samantha Sams had. Not on the grave, so they can be traced, but near. We regret all you have made us do. All must confess and be cleansed at the Midnight Cry.''

Kate didn't want to cut the roses this way—it hurt her, but she did it, guided by this woman's hands.

"Brother Benjamin, put the roses in your hat," the sister said.

"I—I lost it chasing her."

"No wonder Mother Ann could not abide men!" the woman said, and pulled off her own bonnet. Under it, her hair was fastened up with old-fashioned pins.

Kate knew the face and didn't like it anymore.

"Here, in here," she ordered, taking the clippers back.

Dutifully, Kate and the Shaker brother dropped in the rose heads.

"You carry the stems—I don't want any more of those thorns!" the woman insisted loudly to Kate, as if she were deaf.

They marched her the rest of the way toward the black hulk of the car. Kate pulled back. "No," she said. "No, I can't get near that, can't get in it."

The muffled knocking from the depths of the car began again. "Kate! Kate, is that you?"

She knew that voice. But before she could think of the man's name, the Shaker sister pulled open the big back door and shoved her in. It was everything she hated, everything she feared: the dark well, the huge cave, Sarah's and her own mother's caskets.

"And tie her hands again, this time to the metal

handle on the back of the front seat,'' the woman ordered.

The man produced the panty hose again and tied her hands, in front of her this time, to the door handle. He put the woman's bonnet with the rose heads in it on the floor of the car and left the thorny rose stems lying across Kate's lap.

She could feel as well as hear a man's knocking and voice now, coming from the trunk. "Who is it?'' she cried. "I can't let you out!''

The Shaker woman stuck her head in the back and acted as if she didn't even hear the man, though Kate was pretty sure now that he was a policeman.

"Get in his car and follow me in case this thing balks,'' the woman told the Shaker man. "I think I can handle this old monster for once.''

She made certain Kate was tied, slammed the door, then went around to get in the driver's seat. As the muffled roar of the engine began and the car jerked forward, Kate flew back in the seat. The ties around her wrists tensed but stretched away from the metal handle. At least, now she sat farther back from that woman behind the wheel.

The man in the trunk was still shouting something, but this engine was so loud she hardly heard him. She wished he'd stop because her head hurt so bad. Kate wanted to cry and scream. She wanted to claw her way out.

The woman turned the headlights on, and Kate could see ahead now. They bumped over the Shaker Run bridge and started toward that other house.

Jack's. It was Jack's, but it was all dark, so dark in here. And she was afraid of this car but not of this woman or the man. If this car could, it would kill her roses, cut them all off, all of their heads, right off. Her dear roses, which were like a daughter to her, all shining bright, red-haired and loving just like Erin.

Erin! These people wanted to hurt Erin and she wouldn't let them, wouldn't let them cut and kill more roses. If she could just get a little more length in this piece she was tied with, she could reach this woman's neck and cut off her head, too.

Kate scraped her arms on the thorny stems in her lap. Despite the pain, she gathered them and, yanking her wrist ties as tight as they would go, lifted the long stems over the woman's head, then scraped them down her face and across her neck.

The woman screamed and jerked the wheel. Kate saw headlights coming at them, topped by shining, blinking light-bars of red and blue and whirling white.

Their car turned, spun as if in some crazy Shaker dance, screaming like a woman. It rolled, rolled. Kate flew and bumped around inside, but her hands came free. She heard glass shattering and closed her eyes. Finally, the car—everything—lay still.

Yes, she was free now. The female driver looked broken and bloodied. As bright lights glared from every direction and men's voices came closer, on her hands and knees, Kate climbed out the side window, even though she cut herself on broken glass.

She squinted into the lights. The car following them had hit a tree, and this car was partly crushed, lying on its top. She heard shouts again, heard her name, "Kate? Kate?" They might be after her—angry, angry that Mike had taken their money and their dreams away.

Kate staggered into a nearby big building full of Shaker furniture and crumpled between some to hide.

Only the pulsing lights from the vehicles outside lit the hulking pieces, pieces of her life.

She knew where she was now, she thought, sitting up to press her painful back against the side of a cupboard. She was in Sarah's sitting room at Groveland in Toledo, waiting for her friend, who was like a mother, to come in and bring Erin, too. Or was she at Shaker Run where she'd fallen in love with Jack?

But she couldn't just stay here, hidden away. She had to face it all and not be afraid anymore, ever.

Though it took the last shred of strength and sanity she had, Kate Marburn stood as the door filled with policemen with lights and guns.

"We have to help the others," she said, holding an arm up to shade her eyes.

"They're—gone," one man said. "We'll call the medic for you."

She was pretty sure they meant they would get it for Tanya, but she nodded. And then she saw a man she knew, but he looked as banged up as she felt.

"Kate, thank God you're safe," he cried, tears in his eyes as he hurried toward her. He was all cut and bruised. "These officers say Jack and Tanya are going to make it, too."

"Make it here in time for the dancing?" she asked. She sounded silly to herself. Something was very wrong.

The floor and furniture rose up to meet her, and she was afraid Sarah would hit her head. Though she only wanted one man in the entire world to touch her, several caught her as she fell.

Kate climbed up, up from sodden sleep, fighting her way to daylight. When she opened her eyes a slit, the first thing she saw was Erin's dear face, solemn, so pale.

"How—long?" Kate whispered.

"Four days," Erin said, leaning closer to her. Kate realized the girl held her hand. "You're really bruised, but they think the fact you were drugged kept you relaxed so you didn't break any bones."

Kate tried to smile at that. She hadn't felt relaxed for years.

"But you were out of your head," Erin went on, "so they just tried to make you comfortable. You sure talked a lot—about everything. Some of it was kind of crazy, but—some of it—I understand you more now."

Kate nodded. Her throat was so dry. She tried to smile again from the sheer joy of seeing Erin safe, but her face felt so stiff she thought her skin might crack.

"They've been feeding you intravenously," Erin went on, "but I can get you ice chips. Oh, Mom, I'm so sorry," she blurted, and burst into tears. "I was so scared I would lose you, too. You are really my only parent, the one who didn't ever desert me, and I promise I'm going to take good care of you from now on!"

Erin hugged her, and Kate managed to cling, tubes and wires and all. And over Erin's shoulder, looking around the edge of the curtain by her bed, Jack's face appeared. It was the most wonderful vision she'd ever seen.

"I hope two of us can get in on that," he said, coming closer. "The taking care of you, I mean."

"Is that all?" Kate whispered as her view of them

blurred through her tears. "Don't you want to get in on the parent part, too?"

Jack leaned over the bed, embracing Kate and half hugging Erin, who was caught between them. "I'd be honored to be Erin's stepfather," he admitted, his voice cracking with emotion, "but I think I'll start making children's Shaker furniture, too."

Epilogue

Live now, believe me,
Wait not till tomorrow;
Gather the roses of life today.

—Pierre Ronsard
Sonnets pour Helen

Shaker Run Village opened the first Saturday in June, only a month later than they had planned. Dane had thought that once the bad publicity was no longer headline news the crowds would go down, but the fields that served as parking lots were packed and Kate demonstrated to group after group of visitors how she distilled the fragrant rose water.

"And the first batch was to be for Louise," she whispered to Erin, as, both dressed as Shaker sisters, they carted pecks of petals from the vibrant Apothecary bushes to the distilling shed. With each trip they made, Tanya would look across the herb garden and wave. At least, Kate thought, her bandaged skull didn't show under that deep, woven bonnet. The doctors had tried to make her promise to work half a day, but they didn't know Tanya.

But best was when Kate glanced toward the old dwelling house across the lane that housed the infirmary and woodworking shop.

Strangely, she thought of the fanatical Louise and Ben again, and of the night she had hidden from them there.

Though the Willises had told her that the authentic Shaker furniture they switched for fakes was meant for building up this village, an investigation was revealing they had sold much of it to amass a fortune for themselves. Searches of the basement and attic of their renovated farmhouse and their Rent-a-Room storage in Athens provided links to other treasure troves of real and replicated pieces waiting to be sold or switched through their extensive furniture scam. Though they had started small and locally, they had begun to branch out internationally. Kate was amazed that the Willises could function with one foot in the real world and one in their own warped minds that justified not only theft but murder.

But because both Louise and Ben had been killed in the double-car wreck just outside the village, Clint was the only one who had been arrested. Jack was overseeing things here—just for this opening week, he'd said.

"I know who you want to see," Erin whispered with a giggle, and gave Kate an elbow nudge. "Go on over and see how he's doing. I can pluck and sort these petals myself, and I'll let you salt them when I get back. I'll just answer the questions like you've been doing. Mom," she said in an exasperated voice, hands on her hips, when Kate hesitated, "I'm not a freshman in anything anymore. Go!"

"All right, but I'll be back to relieve you before Stone arrives," she said, and went tripping across the lovely scene, wishing Sarah could be here today with the other special guests who had cut the ribbon, including Governor Taft. Now, *that* was the kind of good publicity they all needed.

But halfway across the lane, a man called her name. She turned to see Zink pushing Palmer Denbigh in a wheelchair. For one moment, she froze, furious with Zink for doing this to her today and without warning. Palmer was a paraplegic since emerging from his coma, though the doctors weren't yet certain it was permanent. Kate walked toward them and extended her hand to Zink, who put a long-stemmed flower-shop rose in it. The thornless stem was stuck in a plastic water vial. Kate sniffed at the flower's aroma, but like most overbred nursery roses, it had no scent, just the lovely bloom itself.

"That rose," Zink said, "is from the big city, so you don't forget that we exist. Besides, you're too much of a modern woman to deal just with antique roses. Know what this new hybrid tea is called?" he asked, indicating his gift to her.

"My, my, Detective," she said, impressed. "You've not only become an expert of Shakerabilia but of roses. I'd say it's Honors."

"Wrong. All-American Bride," he said smugly, folding his arms across his chest. "See, Jack Kilcourse doesn't know how to keep a secret," he added, alluding to the fact Jack had asked Kate to marry him.

Jack and Zink used to do nothing *but* keep secrets, Kate thought, but she couldn't sustain this banter in front of Palmer. He was staring up at her so solemnly that she braced herself for a tirade.

"Palmer, it was good of you to come," she said, thinking his next words would be that he had come to see *his* furniture. "I was wishing Sarah could be here today, and she would be honored you came in her place.''

''Zink asked me, and I said, sure, why not.'' He shrugged his powerful shoulders, which showed that at least his upper torso was in good shape. She wondered if his partial paralysis would affect his collection of women, as well as of cars.

''I'm getting a couple of custom-built cars made so I can drive again,'' he told her, as if to answer one of her silent questions. ''I'm really anxious to take delivery now, since the new government model Zink's been issued, after those Shaker psychos crashed his other one, is not my idea of an exciting set of wheels.''

Zink laughed, but Kate was still tense as she said, ''I'm very sorry about Vari—''

''I want to ask you someth—'' he got out, before they both realized they were talking at the same time and stopped.

''Varina wasn't a happy person,'' he said, and cleared his throat. ''I—I actually think she was born that way. But our lawyer told me what you said to her when she was dying—and that you covered her up with your jacket. Anyhow, I just wanted to say that I'd appreciate it if you'd let me pick out a piece or two of my mother's Shaker furniture I've decided to sign off on. Maybe you can choose something she really liked, and the rest should be here—be yours.''

Kate clasped her hands. She could have hugged him, but biting her lower lip as her eyes filled with tears, she blurted, ''She was like a mother to me, too. I know that's hard for you to hear, and Varina didn't believe me but—''

''I believe you. I believe you now,'' he repeated

so deliberately that it was if he spoke for all those from their hometown who had once blamed her.

"Yes, of course, the furniture," she stammered. "I'll pick several of her very best, favorite pieces for you."

Palmer just nodded as if he'd said enough for one day. Zink gave Kate a hug and pushed Palmer's chair away, leaving her standing in the middle of the lane that separated the brothers' side of the street from the sisters'. Hearing Jack's strong voice the moment she crossed the lane, she hurried into the woodworking shop through the left door.

"So please feel free to look around." Jack was evidently concluding an explanation. "And don't hesitate to ask any questions," he added hastily when he saw her come in.

But he beat a path straight for her through the small crowd, leaving one of Clint's staff to demonstrate the making of Shaker boxes and two others showing the sanding and fitting. He took her elbow and moved her out the door she'd come in and around the back by the well, now returned to its historic appearance.

"But I have a question, Brother Jack," she said, trying to keep a straight face for this. Her heart was so full today, she wanted to both laugh and cry.

"Let's hear it," he said as he walked her past the well where several tourists were pitching coins into its depths. "We can't steal too much time away, not with this crowd."

"I want to know if your offer of a formal engagement of marriage is still on the table."

He almost tripped over his own feet. "It is, but a strict Shaker village hardly seems the place to talk of that forbidden state. Spiritual union, yes, but physical? I am just shocked," he said, grinning. "But since you've asked so kindly, yes, Sister Jeru—"

"Sister Kate," she corrected. "Dane didn't have time to change my name tag or the brochures, but I am Sister Kate—at least, in front of all these folks. In front of you later—we'll see."

"We will, indeed," he said, still hustling her on, away from the main crowds. "And my offer is still very much on the table, one of my handmade Shaker ones. You said you needed to talk to Erin to tell her what you were going to do. Did you?"

"Yes. I told her I'm going to marry you. She clapped and cheered and made some cornball joke about crossbreeding roses."

Jack shouted such a loud laugh that several visitors looked their way. Ignoring them—and what the long line of celibate Shakers who had once lived and toiled here would have preached—Jack pulled Kate into the small storage shed behind the furniture shop and banged the door shut behind them.

Author Note

Although the village of Shaker Run is fictional, some historically preserved Shaker settlements may still be visited today. My favorite is Pleasant Hill near Lexington, Kentucky, where visitors may spend the night in the original, beautifully restored dwelling houses and eat delicious Shaker meals.

I have completely fictionalized the idea that the Shakers used herbal hallucinogens to achieve their Shaker highs, but most of the information about this fascinating religious sect is authentic. Their furniture surely goes for such prices today that my furniture fakery ring could be valid and very lucrative. Even the archeological finds in the Shaker well are based on a *National Geographic* excavation of a well at Canterbury Shaker Village in New Hampshire. "No one wants to attack the Shakers," the author of the August 1999 article writes, "but the reality is that they were often part of mainstream America." And yet, I believe, their fascination lies in the fact that they were so very different from most Americans of their day.

Jack and Tanya's concerns with overdoses of herbal and medicinal remedies being deadly is a real, current problem. As I conclude this book in the spring of 2000, I see a recent newspaper article (in this case, from the *San Francisco Examiner*) titled "California cautions of use of herbal remedies."

Ohio University in Athens, Ohio (not to be confused with Ohio State University in Columbus, from which I also hold a degree), is my undergraduate college, and I hope I have described the lovely campus well. Thanks to Tatum Vittengl for her help and to Dean Julia Zimmerman.

Also I appreciate the expertise of the following people—if I have made mistakes in my rendering of information, the errors are mine:

Cathy Senalik and Don Love for help with legal questions;

Dick Springer for information on foreign embassies;

Craig Tiano for help in describing a Packard sedan. (If you'd like to see an online photo of this story's Packard, at the time I searched this book it was at www.voicenet.com/ctiano/packard/1947.htm);

Nancy Armstrong and Laurie Miller, RNs, for help with medical concerns;

Elizabeth Baldwin for her advice on freshman college life; my mother, expert on Toledo, and my best PR rep there; and especially our family friend, Gus Pappas, who showed me how he makes his beautiful oval Shaker boxes.

As ever to my wonderful support team, Don Harper and Meg Ruley.

Karen Harper
June 2000